PRAISE FO

"Compulsively devourable."
—Nina Laurin, bestselling author of *Girl Last Seen*

"Sarah Zettel's *The Other Sister* is as dark and twisted as they come; a compelling and sinister psychological thriller in which every character is deeply flawed, their desire for revenge understandable and relatable. With its intricate web of secrets long buried, readers won't be able to stop turning the pages!"
—Karen Dionne, internationally bestselling author of *The Marsh King's Daughter*

"An exhilarating ride full of twists and turns, this page-turner will leave you guessing until the very end!"
—Steena Holmes, *New York Times* bestselling author of *The Forgotten Ones*

"An excellent psychological thriller that's filled with dark family secrets and plenty of intrigue."
—*New York Journal of Books*

"The story of Geraldine's return to her roots is vividly told…[for] readers looking for something to follow Jeannette Walls' nonfiction *The Glass Castle*."
—*Booklist*

"An unexpected and entertaining read."
—*The Michigan Daily*

ALSO BY SARAH ZETTEL

The Other Sister

A MOTHER'S LIE

SARAH ZETTEL

GRAND CENTRAL
PUBLISHING

NEW YORK   BOSTON

Grand Central Publishing
Hachette Book Group
1290 Avenue of the Americas, New York, NY 10104
grandcentralpublishing.com
twitter.com/grandcentralpub

First edition: April 2020

Grand Central Publishing is a division of Hachette Book Group, Inc. The Grand Central Publishing name and logo is a trademark of Hachette Book Group, Inc.

The publisher is not responsible for websites (or their content) that are not owned by the publisher.

The Hachette Speakers Bureau provides a wide range of authors for speaking events. To find out more, go to www.hachettespeakersbureau.com or call (866) 376-6591.

Library of Congress Cataloging-in-Publication Data

Names: Zettel, Sarah, author.
Title: A mother's lie / Sarah Zettel.
Description: First edition. | New York : Grand Central Publishing, a division of Hachette Book Group, Inc., 2020.
Identifiers: LCCN 2019041855 | ISBN 9781538760925 (trade paperback) | ISBN 9781538760949 (ebook)
Subjects: LCSH: Mothers and daughters–Fiction. | Family secrets–Fiction. | GSAFD: Suspense fiction.
Classification: LCC PS3576.E77 M68 2020 | DDC 813/.54–dc23
LC record available at https://lccn.loc.gov/2019041855

ISBNs: 978-1-5387-6092-5 (trade paperback), 978-1-5387-6094-9 (ebook)

Printed in the United States of America

LSC-C

10 9 8 7 6 5 4 3 2 1

To Tim and Alex

*Evil is not the illegality, or the magnitude of the sin,
but the consistency of the sin.*

—M. Scott Peck, *People of the Lie*

PROLOGUE

When that first child is on the way, every woman wonders, *What kind of mother will I be?* Beth Fraser had plenty of reason to wonder, but she didn't really find out until her daughter, Dana, was four years old.

They were still living in San Francisco and had gone to Bloomingdale's, the big one on Market Street. Beth had a partners' meeting about the new fund for Lumination Ventures. There were problems with the suit she had ordered. At the time, this had seemed important.

The woman behind the counter was slower than molasses in January. Beth demanded to speak to her manager. The charge was not accepted, the alterations had not been completed as promised, and they were going to get this sorted out.

Beth had told Dana to stand right here. She promised Dana a trip to the Disney Store just as soon as they'd straightened out this one thing.

The manager came over. Beth looked down. Dana was not there.

Beth did not remember anything after that for a while.

Dana remembered a bit more. Not everything, but more.

For instance, she remembered promising she would stand *right here* so Mommy could talk to the store lady. She remembered feeling that if she could look out the big front window, maybe she could see the Disney Store. She remembered the idea that *right here* kind of included the window, because she could see the window and Mommy at the same time. She remembered not really moving. Just drifting. She was still *right here*. Mommy was arguing with the lady behind the counter. She could hear them. She was still *right here*.

"Hey there."

She remembered looking up to see a man in a gray suit and blue overcoat. His hair was slicked back in dark stripes against his pink-and-tan scalp. She remembered he had very round blue eyes and plump, pink hands.

"You lost?"

Dana shook her head.

"Where's your mommy, then?"

Dana looked around. Suddenly she wasn't sure. Mommy was by the counter. That was her dark jacket, but that wasn't her head. She didn't wear that hat. She was right here, wasn't she?

"Oh, wait," said the man. "I see her out there. Come on."

He took Dana's hand, and all at once she was walking with him. She wasn't sure how that happened.

They were going out the sliding door now, and he was right behind her, bumping into her back and kind of pushing her along. Then, they were out on the sidewalk, heading up the hill, and his big, soft hand was holding hers and he was saying, "Now, where did Mommy go? Oh! There she is. Come on!" He gave her hand a little shake and also squeezed her fingers. Dana craned her neck, trying to see what he saw. He was pulling her along too fast. His hot, damp hand hurt as he squeezed her fingers and sang, "There she is! Come on! Keep up, sweetie!"

Then the world spun, and the sidewalk slammed against her head and Dana saw stars.

She sat up, not sure how she got onto the ground. The man was on the ground too, and Mommy was there. She was screaming—bad, bad words, louder than sirens, louder than anything. A lot of people were yelling.

The man was bleeding, and Mommy was kicking him. Hard. His head was bleeding. Bright red smeared his hot, pink hands. He was crying.

Mommy kicked him again, right in the teeth. His head snapped back.

A big lady with sunglasses swept Dana into her arms.

The man with the pink hands wasn't moving anymore. Mommy turned around and walked up to the lady and to Dana.

"Give me back my daughter."

The lady handed Dana across. Mommy wrapped Dana in her arms and they sat down on the curb. Mommy held Dana on her lap. She was breathing hard. Dana could feel her chest heaving under her jacket. Her eyes were straight ahead. She was shaking all over, and tears streamed down her face.

Dana wanted to hug her. She knew she *should* hug her, but she couldn't. Not while her eyes were so blank like that. It was like she wasn't even her mother anymore.

Beth didn't know what was happening inside her daughter's mind. All she knew was that somebody had tried to take Dana away, and she stopped them. Of course, the cops were on their way now. There would be lots of cops, and eventually lawyers. There'd be questions to answer and lies to tell. So very many lies. She needed to have them all lined up and ready to go.

But Dana was safe now. That was all that really mattered. Beth could handle everything else.

She always had.

PART ONE

SHOW AND TELL

CHAPTER ONE

"Time?" called Dana. She lifted the pan full of vegetable omelet off the burner and shook it to make sure the mass of egg and zucchini was loose.

Beth held up her phone. "Thirteen minutes, forty-four seconds. You're never gonna make it!"

"Watch me!" It was down to the wire in the Fraser kitchen's morning marathon—could Dana make an edible breakfast in fifteen minutes or less?

Dana shook the pan again and eyed the distance to the ceiling.

"You're cleaning up when you miss!" Beth reminded her. The game of the fifteen-minute breakfast was their way of combining Dana's love of cooking with the morning rush that never seemed to get any easier. Beth could not stand to be late, and Dana loved to show off, so it all worked.

Dana gave the pan a swift up-down jerk. The entire golden disk of egg and vegetables launched into the air, flipped, and came down. Dana bent her knees and held out the pan and—

SPLAT!

—caught the whole thing.

"Yes!" She pumped her fist in the air. "Get the plates!"

Beth pushed the colorful Fiestaware across the breakfast bar so Dana could slide segments of omelet onto the dishes. She sprinkled feta cheese on top of each plate, along with a handful of tomato chunks, and dropped the grilled bagels next to them.

"And done!"

"Fourteen minutes, fifty-three seconds," Beth announced.

Dana threw both hands into the air. "Team Dangerface for the win!"

They both pulled their high stools up to the bar and tucked in. Dana glugged her orange juice. Beth poured a cup of coffee from the carafe. The speakers were cranked up, streaming a pulse-surging mix of Beyoncé, Adele, and Alicia Keys.

People who saw Beth and Dana together knew instantly they were mother and daughter. Beth had no idea where her ancestors had really come from. Her parents had regularly claimed to be everything from black Irish to Armenian. They had, however, gifted her and Dana with the similar oval faces, blunt noses, sandy skin, and thick brown hair. Time and determination had hardened Beth's hazel eyes, but she still smiled easily, although that smile could be a disguise as often as it was a revelation.

If Beth was an expert at hiding in plain sight, Dana was brash and loud and determined to be herself, even when she wasn't sure who that might be from day to day. Currently, she sported an uneven bob that ran down to her jawline on one side and barely covered her ear on the other. She had three piercings in one ear and four in the other. Her earrings never matched.

Dana's most striking feature, though, was her eyes. The technical term was *heterochromia iridis*, meaning her eyes were two different colors—the left one, green, the right one, brown. Dana had flirted with the idea of hiding them a couple of years ago. Since then, she'd gone the exact opposite direction to emphasize them with mascara and shadow.

"So, last day of freshman year, huh?" Beth dug into the steaming omelet.

"Halle-effing-lujah," Dana mumbled around her mouthful.

"Anything I need to know about today? And, by the way, this is really good."

"Thanks, and, um, no, I don't think so."

Beth eyed her daughter as she took another gulp of coffee. "As an experienced parent and professional lie detector, I am qualified to tell you that's a suspicious hesitation."

"I hate it when you do that."

"I know. So, what happened?"

"Nothing!" Dana tore her bagel half in two. "Except you might be getting an email about my oral presentation in English."

"Why?"

Dana huffed out a sigh. "Cuz when I was giving the report, I maybe kind of said that Holden Caulfield was a self-involved asshole and he should have jumped off that cliff he wanted to save all the kids from, like they wouldn't know it was there in the first place, and it seemed pretty obvious Salinger was full of horseshit."

"Uh-huh. And what did Mr. Kennedy have to say?"

"That I should please remember that horseshit was not a current vocabulary word, and so I said fine, Salinger was full of bullshit."

That was when the phone rang. Not Beth's cell. The landline in the kitchen.

"Do not say, 'Saved by the bell,'" said Dana as soon as Beth opened her mouth.

Beth just checked the clock. Seven thirty exactly. They both needed to be out the door in less than fifteen minutes. A well-known fact in some circles.

So, I wonder who this could possibly *be?*

Beth braced herself and picked up the receiver. "Good morning, Doug."

"Hi, Beth, it's…Oh, ha-ha," laughed Dana's father stiffly. "How did you know?"

"It's my superpower."

"Yeah, well, that's why Gutierrez pays you the big bucks, right?" Officially, Beth's title at Lumination Ventures was vice president, but unofficially, she was the chief bullshit navigator. "Anyway." Doug sighed. "I'm glad I caught you. I was afraid you might have left already."

You hoped I had left already, and that's why you called the landline. "What's going on?"

"Well, unfortunately—and this is not my fault. I really tried to get this moved, I swear, but…"

Beth stopped listening. She'd heard what she needed to. This wasn't exactly the first time Doug had called to wriggle out of a promise he'd made Dana.

"...I know this is the last second, and I should have called earlier. I know, I know..."

Exactly when did you degenerate into such a cliché, Doug?

"...I was really looking forward to this weekend..."

You were the one who always talked about living an authentic life. That really should have tipped me off right there.

"...and I just kept hoping things would work out..."

And the big ask is coming in three...two...one...

"...So, you'll tell her I'm really sorry?"

"She's right here, Doug. You can tell her yourself."

"Beth, I..."

"Dana, it's your father." Beth passed the phone to Dana.

"Yeah, I noticed," Dana said to her. Then, into the receiver she said, "What's going on, Dad?"

Dana listened and scooped up a piece of cold egg with the last of her bagel. Beth leaned back against the kitchen island and watched her daughter's face slowly closing down while Doug chattered and apologized and promised, all from a safe distance.

At least my father would lie to my face. The thought dropped into place without warning. Beth looked away, until she was sure she had her shock hidden.

"Yeah, Dad," said Dana. "It's fine. I'm sorry too. No, it's okay. I got invited to an end-of-year party at Kimi's... Yeah, so, you're right—it all worked out. Yeah. Say hi to Susan for me. Here's Mom."

Dana handed Beth the receiver and immediately dug into the last of her omelet.

"I really am sorry, Beth," said Doug. "Will you make sure Dana knows that? Please?"

Something about the particular pleading note in his voice pricked at Beth's awareness. "Are you all right, Doug? You sound"—*worse than usual*—"worried."

"What? Yeah. Fine, but, um, I don't want to keep you."

"No, of course not. Have a good day."

Beth hung up and went back to her cooling breakfast.

"Sorry, Dangerface." The nickname had come after a childhood accident. Dana tripped on the escalator and had to get five stitches in her forehead. She absolutely refused to wear a bandage, and instead ran around the house growling and shouting, "I got my danger face on!"

"It was gonna happen." Dana shrugged. "I don't know why he even bothers."

So he can tell himself he tried. But Dana already knew that.

Beth had promised herself from the start she would not get between Dana and her father, especially once they moved out to Chicago. She'd always known Doug was a hot mess and not good for much beyond romantic weekends and grandiose pronouncements. That was why she didn't marry him, even when she came up pregnant.

Especially when I came up pregnant.

Even so, she'd never expected Doug to treat his daughter first like a secret and then like an embarrassment.

"You can always say no when he starts making plans, Dana."

"Yeah. I guess." She smashed a chunk of tomato flat with her fork. "Maybe he'd like that better."

"It's just…you don't need to make things easier on him just because he's your father. That's not your job."

"I thought that was what families did."

"Families do all kinds of things."

"Yeah, well, my experience is kind of limited there."

The rebuke stung, but it was an old pain, and Beth told herself she barely noticed anymore.

Dana's phone buzzed, and she flipped it over. "Chelsea's downstairs."

Which meant all discussion was officially closed. The pair of them began the last stage of their morning routine— getting plates in the dishwasher, finding Dana's backpack and the final history paper that she'd almost forgotten, Beth's briefcase, and the extra folder out of her study that she might just need for this morning's demo session.

Beth tried not to feel relieved that there was no more time to talk. Family was a perfect storm for them. Beth had secrets, Doug had issues, and Dana had anger.

And Beth didn't know what to do about any of it. She never had.

"Phone?"

Dana opened one side of her school uniform vest to show what looked like the blank, black lining.

Every year when Dana got her new school uniforms, Beth took it to a particular tailor, a Ukrainian immigrant who made a quiet specialty of creating pockets for people who did not want security guards, or anybody else, to know just what they might be carrying.

"Mad money?"

Dana flipped open the other side.

"Text time?"

"Four thirty, on the dot," Dana recited. "Today and every day."

"Love you, Dangerface."

"Love you, Mom. Bye."

Dana kissed her on the forehead to avoid smudging her meeting-day makeup and charged out the door.

For years, Beth had walked Dana down to the lobby and waited with her until the car came. Like a lot of the parents at Pullman Preparatory Academy, Beth hired a car service to handle Dana's transportation to and from school. At least, like the parents who didn't have their own drivers.

Now, in a concession to Dana's simmering need for independence and after about a week of screaming fights, Beth waited upstairs. But she still watched, and she was not the only one.

The landline rang. Beth scooped it up off the hook. "Beth Fraser."

"Kendi at the desk, Ms. Fraser. Dana and Chelsea are in the car. Is there anything else I can do for you?"

"No, thank you, Kendi. Not today." She said good-bye and hung up. She checked out the window and saw the black Metro car pull out of the drive and into the street.

Time to get a move on. Beth grabbed her briefcase, her tote bag, her keys. She checked her phone to see that her car service was on the way. She also checked her makeup in the mirror by the door. A demonstration day always meant dressing to her personal heights—suit, stockings, and sky-high heels.

What are you looking for, Beth? She smoothed down the front of her gray Chanel jacket. *What's got you on edge?*

Because she was too anxious for a normal morning. Even Doug's phone call was perfectly normal—frustrating as all hell, but normal. Probably it was today's presentation from AllHome Healthtech. She had been trying for two weeks to impress on her boss that this particular start-up was a waste of time. Rafael wanted to let it play out, though, and he was more than just her employer. He was the one friend she'd kept from her ragged teenage years in Nowhere, Indiana. He'd pulled her out of her grandmother's trailer and presented her with the chance at a career. If Rafi wanted to waste a morning with this demonstration, they'd waste a morning. Maybe he knew something she didn't.

Her cell phone rang—an unidentified number with a San Francisco area code. Beth stuffed the phone into her red briefcase. *Let it go to voice mail.* If it was important, they'd leave a message. She was running late, and between Doug, Rafael, and her own restlessness, she had more than enough on her mental plate.

In the side pocket of her briefcase, her phone rang, and rang again, and stopped.

CHAPTER TWO

"I hate to say I told you so, Rafi…" Beth settled onto the black leather sofa in his office and kicked her shoes off under the glass-topped coffee table. "But…"

"But you told me so. Yes, yes, yes. Mea culpa." Rafael Gutierrez opened his full-size fridge and pulled out two bottles of Pellegrino sparkling water. His office was a cool, black-and-white room with a window wall that looked over Wabash Avenue toward the Sears Tower. The skyscraper had actually been renamed the Willis Tower, but nobody bothered to remember that.

Rafael was a square-built man. His family had come to the States from Mexico and Ecuador, and he'd grown up on an edge even sharper than the one Beth knew. A black unibrow made an emphatic line above his brown eyes. He wore his black hair a little long and combed straight back so that it waved around his ears and against his neck. This helped de-emphasize a tattoo that had seemed like a good idea in another place and time.

"You have to admit AllHome is a good idea." Rafi handed Beth a water bottle like a peace offering and dropped onto one of the square leather chairs. "A specialized, virtual home-health-care assistant. It's got legs."

"For somebody who knows what they're doing."

Beth's gaze flicked to the vintage chrome wall clock with its sweeping red second hand. Fifteen minutes until Dana's check-in text was due. Beth pulled her phone out and laid it facedown on the chair arm.

"When we took on TrakChange, we had to hold their hand every step of the way, and they paid off big," Rafi said.

"TrakChange overran costs by four and a half million and we came *thiiiis* close to a partner revolt." Beth pinched her fingers together. "Do we want to go through that again for this bunch?"

"We could coach them through—"

Beth's phone buzzed right then, cutting him off. She checked the screen, frowned, and put the phone back down. Rafi lifted his eyebrows at her.

"Somebody with a San Francisco area code's been calling all day. I thought it might be the BlitzCom people, but they're not leaving messages."

"So, pick up or block the number."

"Yes, Mr. Gutierrez. Right away, Mr. Gutierrez."

Rafael tossed his bottle cap at her. Beth lifted her bottle to block it. The cap pinged off its side and dropped onto the couch.

Beth sipped her water and glanced at the clock again. 4:28. Dana was due to text her at four thirty. That was their standing agreement. Four thirty, every day. No exceptions.

It was eleven years since the day at Bloomingdale's where the worst possible thing had almost happened. After that, Beth had wanted to lock all the doors of her life and never let the outside world near her daughter again. She'd wanted to kill the man, because of who he was and who he might have been.

She'd almost done it too, although that wasn't the worst part. The worst part was how very right it felt.

Since then, things had gotten better. The move to Chicago had helped. So had the fact that she'd worked out a series of necessary steps, defined them, and organized them. The daily contact was one step. It gave Dana some freedom and allowed Beth to keep breathing.

Beth pulled her mind back to the problem in front of her. "Rafi, the AllHome guys are trying to break into health care, and they haven't even started to think through the legal concerns or a real system of care for people at their lowest and most vulnerable."

Rafi eyed her over the rim of his bottle. "But you know who has?"

"HomeAssist," she answered immediately. "I've met their developers, and I've been watching their proof of concept advance for a couple of months now. I think they've got the scope and vision to actually pull this off."

Beth checked the clock again. 4:29. She laid her hand on her phone so she'd feel the buzz.

"And it just so happens that HomeAssist has a woman-led development team," Beth told him. "And their CEO is Megan Reese, who just got named one of the twenty-five Best and Brightest by *ChicagoLand Entrepreneur* magazine. They'd be perfect for the Excelsior Fund."

Excelsior was still in the planning stage, and the plans were mostly Beth's. It was a venture capital fund specifically for women from outside the traditional tech sector who wanted to get into the tech sector. Their motto: The real talent's still out there.

Rafi blew out a sigh. "How long have you had this waiting in the wings?"

"Since I got a look at the nonplans of that little huddle of Stanford tech bros who could barely get their own laptops working." She leaned forward, elbows on her knees. "Rafi, Excelsior will pay off, and HomeAssist is a perfect vehicle. It's ambitious, it's sexy, and it's timely. There is an appetite for diversity and for VC to show it's got a heart as well as a wallet."

Rafi paused, but then he nodded. "Two meetings," he said. "And two phone calls to gauge initial interest and show I'm behind the idea. After that, we'll see what bubbles up." He raised his bottle and drank another swallow.

"Done." Beth raised her own bottle in answer.

The phone buzzed. Beth snatched it up. Face ID made the screen light up and displayed the message: Dana had taken a meta-selfie of herself in the front hall mirror. In the background, her best friend, Chelsea, hoisted two cups of bubble tea. The caption read:

4:30 oclock & all swells @home w Chelsea. 😄😄

Beth put the phone down and took a very long swallow of sparkling water. Rafi drained his own bottle and pitched it into the recycle bin. "Okay, I need to get going. I've got a dinner tonight and Angela's on her tenth text. Where are we with BlitzCom? We ready for them?"

"I think so, but this one is really Zoe's baby."

"Is she ready?"

"She's completely ready. Tell Angie I said hi." Beth retrieved her shoes. He waved in acknowledgment, and Beth headed for her own office down the hall.

As soon as she had her door closed, she pumped her fist hard.

Yes!

She pulled her phone back out and hit Zoe's number.

"Zoe? Good news. Rafi's ready to move with Excelsior and HomeAssist." She yanked the phone away from her ear as Zoe let out a triumphant yelp. "Are you still in your office? Meet me down in the bar for a strategy session and celebratory cheese fries."

Zoe promised to be down in ten. Beth hung up and texted Dana.

Good news at work. Will be a little late. Save me some dinner.

Getting Rafi on board with the Excelsior Fund was an enormous success, however it happened. Beth liked her position as Lumination's BS detector. But at the same time, she itched to find out what she could do with some money of her own.

It meant putting herself in a position where she could be more publicly visible. Which was risky. Her past was still out there. As of last month, in fact, her past was sitting in a relatively nice extended-stay hotel in Perrysborough, Iowa, a little piece of nowhere near the Minnesota border. According to the last surveillance report, her past was eating a lot of pizza and ordering movies and using the ATM at the Good Neighbor's Party Store. Which meant they were doing something for money. The hotel was a cut above their usual (at least their usual recently), and the food delivery was better than peanut butter and white bread from the quickie mart. Plus, they'd been coming and going a lot.

Probably they were still hustling drinks in the bar and cheating at pool and cards. Maybe they'd found an in at the local casino where they could get to the suckers who had just won big, or lost big. But she had no direct evidence on that. Surveillance got expensive after a while.

Her past was waiting—whether they knew it or not—for her to finally decide what to do about them.

Well, they can wait a little longer. Today belongs to me.

CHAPTER THREE

"You know, my mom won't mind if you stay the night," Dana Fraser said to her best friend, Chelsea Hamilton, as they pushed out of her building's revolving door. They stood under the concrete awning to keep out of the sun. It was stupid hot. Even the breeze that funneled down the street stung her skin. "We can have a pajama party, and you can be my cupcake taster. Not like I'm doing anything else."

Dad had promised to take Dana with the rest of his family out to Warren Dunes to celebrate the end of the school year. Except, of course, now he had backed out. She'd pretty much expected it. But she'd just kinda hoped maybe this time he'd actually follow through. He'd been talking about it for a couple of weeks, which was an eternity in Dad-time. She'd even looked up a bunch of campfire cooking recipes just in case.

"Sorry," said Chelsea. "I really can't. *My* dad got home this morning, and that means Mom wants us all sitting around the supper table pretending we want to talk to each other. And, by the way, your dad sucks."

"He really sucks," admitted Dana. She looked at her phone. The app showed that the Lyft was two minutes away.

The snotty kids at Pullman Prep called Dana Fraser a freak, mostly because of her different-colored eyes. To those same snots, Chelsea Hamilton was a chunk *and* a freak. She was tall, round bodied, and round breasted. She streaked her hair white and blue and wore Hello Kitty stockings and Doc Martens with her school uniform. They sent her home for it one time, but her mom got up in the administration's face and they backed down.

Never mind that Mrs. Hamilton couldn't look at Chelsea without sarcasm pouring out of every vintage-chic pore— no bunch of schoolteachers and underpaid administrators got to criticize *her* daughter.

"At least with Dad home, Cody can't have band practice at our place," Chelsea said. "He'll be out the door as soon as Mom lets him be excused. *Gott sei Dank für kleine Gefälligkeiten*," she added. Dana remembered it meant something like "Thank God for small things."

Chelsea took German because she'd heard that the universities there offered free tuition, even to foreign students. *Four more years*, she'd said, *and I can tell them all to take their fucked-up lives and their trust fund and their codependent shitheadery and shove it up whatever orifice they got left, cuz I am outta there!*

A red Subaru with the Lyft sticker in the window pulled up the driveway. While Chelsea climbed in, Dana checked the photo of the driver on her phone against the face of the guy behind the wheel, just to be sure. Chelsea gave her the thumbs-up and flipped a wave of blue-and-white hair back over her shoulder.

Dana watched her pull away and shrugged off the loneliness that draped across her. It wasn't like she didn't have enough to do. Her internship at the Vine and Horn started next week, and she needed to get ready for that. Plus, Kimi and Keesha were having their end-of-year party tomorrow, and they'd told her to come over anytime if Dad cancelled (again). That was going to be way better than trying to keep the mosquitoes out of her nose or listening to her half siblings arguing about…something.

Who needs it, or them? I should be more like Chelsea and just peace out permanently.

"Dana Fraser?" said a woman.

Dana's head whipped around.

"It is Dana Fraser?" the woman said. "I got that right, right?"

She was bone thin with frizzy brown hair bundled into a messy bun. Her splotchy skin was tanned deep leathery brown, and the shadow line from the awning cut right down the middle of her face. Her clothes—a long-sleeved T-shirt and faded designer jeans—hung off her stick-figure body. There was a sweat stain on her chest.

Stranger danger! Dana's eyes darted this way and that, but she didn't know what she was looking for. Escape. Accomplices. Aliens, maybe? But the city went on like normal. Inside the lobby, Kendi, their doorman, leaned against the counter and turned over a tabloid page.

"No. No. I'm not going to hurt you. I just…ah, shit."

The woman didn't move even an inch closer, but Dana still took another step back.

"I'm sorry." The woman's hands dropped to her sides. "This was stupid. I never should have…of course you're scared. Jesus." The wind blew a hank of hair across her mouth, and she shoved it away. "Why wouldn't you be? I…look. I've got something for you."

The woman reached into her back pocket. Dana's whole body jerked. "I won't come any closer! I swear. Look. I just…look." The woman held up what looked like a crumpled square of folded paper. "I'll just leave it here."

Slowly, so Dana could follow every move, she laid the paper on the rim of one of the flower-filled planters that framed the door. "You can pick it up after I'm gone. Or not. Whatever. Either way, I'll be at the Starbucks on the corner tomorrow. Four o'clock." She pointed. "Nice public place." She backed up a step. "You know, you look just like your mother. You tell her I didn't scare you," the woman added suddenly, urgently. "You tell her that. Okay? I never touched you or threatened you, not once. Please. Be sure she knows that."

The woman was still backing away. *Four o'clock*, she mouthed and pointed up the street. *Starbucks*. She waved, smiled, and turned at the corner, and she was gone.

Dana's hands started shaking.

It's okay, it's okay. You're okay, she told herself, even though she wasn't sure why she should even have to. It wasn't like anything dangerous had happened. Not this time.

But she knew my name. She knows I live here. She was looking for me.

A fresh gust of hot summer wind caught the paper square and tumbled it into the planter.

Dana yanked the paper out of the dirt. It was thick, slick, and slightly sticky.

The crazy lady had left her a photograph.

Dana glanced over her shoulder. Kendi was talking to a pale, speckled lady with a snow-white bob. A black man in a gray suit with a messenger bag slung across his chest pushed out from the revolving door. A white woman in running tights with a little white dog under her arm pushed in.

All normal. No one behind her. No one looking to come grab her hand and pull her away.

Dana gritted her teeth and carefully unfolded the photo.

It was an old Polaroid, its colors faded and muddy. Ragged white lines crisscrossed the image from all the times it had been refolded.

It was taken outdoors, maybe in the desert. A woman crouched down and wrapped one arm tight around a little girl. The woman pressed her cheek against the girl's cheek and pointed toward the camera.

Look! Look! Say cheese!

The girl looked like she wanted to say *fuck you* way more than she wanted to say *cheese*. She was bone thin and tanned and frizzy haired.

This skinny, possibly crazy lady had left Dana a picture of her mother.

CHAPTER FOUR

"So this is finally for real?" Zoe asked as Beth pulled up a chair at the little marble-topped table in the lobby bar. "Rafael's on board with Excelsior?"

Beth had taken the time to load her briefcase up with all the files she was going to need for the weekend, and swapped her stockings and heels for ankle socks and white tennis shoes. This meant Zoe had beaten her down to the bar, with time to order the cheese fries, not to mention a white wine for herself and LaCroix for Beth.

Zoe Keyes was an elegant African-American woman who wore her hair natural and favored large hoop earrings and tailored suits. Her analyst skills had sped her up the ladder at Lumination. Beth had been forced to use some sharp elbow moves against three other veeps to snag Zoe for her team.

"Rafi's being careful," Beth admitted, taking a swallow of LaCroix. "But I know him. He is on board."

"Finally!" They clinked glasses.

"So, now we have to keep it up," Beth said. "Rafael was asking where we are on tomorrow's BlitzCom meeting."

"Just checking off the last few boxes." Zoe did not sound happy.

"What's going on?"

"There's something I don't like. Or maybe I just don't get it…" She shook her head. Her hoops swung and glittered. "I don't know, but there's something."

Beth nodded. Zoe had serious skills, but she was still learning to trust those nagging little "somethings" that came along with them. That could be difficult for anybody, but as usual, it was harder for women. A man's hunch might be respected as "gut instinct." For a woman, the same hunch would be laughed at, usually with a "Oh, your 'women's intuition' tell you that?" thrown in.

"Keep digging." Beth lifted her glass out of the way so the server could set down the heaping plate of cheese fries. "When you nail it down, text me or call. Even if it's four in the morning, okay?"

"Okay, but when it is four in the morning, remember you asked for it."

Beth crossed her heart a split second before her phone buzzed. She flipped it over to see the screen. San Francisco again. Her thumb hovered over the Accept button. But Zoe touched her sleeve, and Beth looked up.

Zoe was nodding toward the bar and the tanned, blond man climbing to his feet.

"What. The. Actual. Hell," murmured Beth as she got up out of her chair. "Doug!"

Doug came over and shook her hand. He was trying to beam, but it wasn't working out too well.

"Hi, Beth! I know this is a surprise, but I was on my way…"

"Camping," she said, cutting him off. "You were on your way camping with Susan and the kids."

"Yeah, well, I was. But something came up, like I said this morning."

"Oh yes. Doug, you remember Zoe Keyes?"

Zoe, who had instantly read the awkward/annoyed vibe, shut her folder before she reached out to shake hands. "Good to see you again, Doug. Sorry I can't stay. Beth, I'm just going to look into this and I'll message you later tonight."

"Thank you, Zoe."

Zoe gathered her things and strode away toward the elevator banks. Beth faced her daughter's father and tried to smile.

"Um," said Doug. "Okay if I sit down?"

Beth didn't move. "I need to get home. Dana's making dinner."

Doug looked at the cheese fries.

"Yeah, she's good like that, isn't she?" Doug sat anyway. He picked up Zoe's wineglass and looked at it like he was thinking of gulping down the remainder.

How long have you been sitting here drinking, Doug? The pinprick Beth felt when they spoke on the phone that morning returned. Doug wore his usual neat business suit, but now she could see the white shirt was rumpled. His blond hair, which she suspected he now dyed, was also in disarray, like he'd been repeatedly running his fingers through it. When he looked up at her hopefully with his bright-gray eyes, she saw the heavy bags beneath them.

She tried not to care but couldn't quite manage it.

Beth sighed, and she sat. "What's going on, Doug? You're making me nervous."

Doug fussed with Zoe's glass, using two fingers on the base to turn it around.

"I...Christ. I wish there was some way..."

"Just say it, Doug."

Instead, he ate three cheese fries. Slowly.

When he finally raised his eyes from the plate, Beth got a rush of feeling—strangled sentiment, old frustration, old affection, and the awareness of the endless, complex bond that came with facing the father of her child. "I'm in trouble, Beth."

"I'm sorry," she answered, aware that her voice was too cold. She distrusted his boozy desperation like she distrusted her own stale affection. "Is it Susan?"

"No, it's...it's money. Our money. Susan's and mine, I mean."

Beth waited for shock and surprise to form, but all she felt was the depressing realization that she should have known. She had seen this exact look before, from a hundred other men (and the occasional woman). It always came when they realized their habit of blowing past all the warning signs meant they were now driving off a cliff.

Besides, how long have you known Doug would make a perfect sucker? And don't think that's why you picked him out, because that is not true.

At least, she hoped it wasn't true, because she did not like what that would mean about her.

"Doug." Beth folded her hands on the table to keep from curling them into fists. "What did you do?"

"Nothing!" *Do you have any idea how much you sound like our fifteen-year-old when you do that?* "I took advantage of an investment opportunity and..."

"What opportunity?"

"Oh, here we go. She puts on her 'I'm the professional here' voice." But Doug saw her face harden, and she watched him abruptly remember he actually wanted something out of her. "I'm sorry, Beth. I'm just really on edge. Can we...just strike that from the record?" He tried for a smile and failed. Instead, he ate two more fries.

Something's seriously wrong here. Beth felt a thousand instincts rise to the surface as goose bumps. This was something beyond Doug and his protests of innocence. This feeling was old, like the scar on her arm that her long-sleeved blouses hid, or the sudden stabs of pain in her skull that still defied ibuprofen and talk therapy.

Calm, Beth. He's triggering a flashback. That's all.

"Okay," said Beth. "Let me guess how this 'opportunity' went. It was from somebody you knew, maybe not well, but you knew his name. He'd heard about you from mutual friends who were already investors. It was all very hot and cutting-edge. They just needed a little extra funding for regulatory paperwork, or to finalize development—something like that. Then, a few months later, they needed just a little more, and then a little more. By then you'd put in so much that a little more didn't seem to matter, because the whole project was going to turn around any day now."

"No, it was nothing like that." But the lie was plain on his face. She'd always been able to read Doug like a book. Once, that fact had given her a measure of security.

"Then what was it like?"

"Jesus, Beth, I thought you'd want to help! Whatever problems you and I have, you love Susan and the kids."

How long has it been since you let me anywhere near your wife and kids?

"I know you wouldn't want them to get hurt because I made a mistake."

What I want is to get home to my daughter. I want this feeling to get off my back. I want…

Beth realized she was losing control of her expression. She glanced quickly away, trying to remember how to breathe and be calm.

That was when she saw him—an old, lean white man with blue eyes. He wore a Cubs cap and a leather jacket, despite the heat outside. He stood directly across the lobby, and he was watching her.

No.

"I just need you to do something for me. It wouldn't take more than an hour of your time, Beth—"

You can't be here.

"This wouldn't even be a problem if we hadn't taken such a hit when—"

You're in Iowa.

Beth was on her feet.

"Beth, what…?" Doug grabbed her sleeve. She blinked, turned her head for just a second, and pulled free.

He was gone.

"Beth, are you even listening?"

The answer was no. She was racing across the lobby, forgetting to be subtle, forgetting to be anything. But the elevators had arrived, and a river of bodies spilled out—people on phones, pulling wheeled bags, walking and talking in tight knots. Delivery people going one way, suits another.

Beth stopped midstride. It was pointless. He was gone.

It wasn't him. You're just jumpy.

But her breath wouldn't calm. She closed her eyes, but the face seemed to have seared itself on her vision.

I've got to get out of here.

Doug was still sitting at the table, just as she had left him.

"Jesus, Beth. What is your problem? Are you having one of your freak-outs again?"

"Yes." Beth grabbed her briefcase and purse. "I am freaking out. That is exactly what I'm doing."

"What about...Oh shit. Beth, come on—what's the matter?"

She stopped for a split second, just long enough to process the fact that Doug was genuinely concerned.

"Contact my admin. Make an appointment," she said. "We'll talk."

She did not wait for his response, which would probably be shocked and offended. She needed all her concentration to walk calmly but quickly out of the bar and across the bright, beige marble lobby.

A yellow cab waited at the curb outside. The building concierge held the door, and Beth gave the driver her address and collapsed into the back. The driver started up the meter and cranked the wheel to wedge them into traffic as soon as he heard the door thunk shut.

Beth yanked out her phone, brought up a number, and waited while it rang.

"Good evening, Miss Fraser," said a tired, gravelly voice. "How are you?"

"Mr. Kinseki, where are the Bowens?" she demanded.

James Kinseki, private detective, fully bonded, licensed, and insured, sighed. He was a big man with gray buzz-cut hair and bulging arms that stretched the sleeves on his polo shirt. Beth had met him face-to-face exactly once. That was nine years ago, when she'd finally been able to afford someone more reliable than a greasy skip tracer.

"As far as I know, Todd and Jeannie Bowen are currently occupying room one sixteen of the YourRest Extended-Stay Hotel in Perrysborough, Iowa. Kitchenettes, weekly rates, free Wi-Fi." Kinseki's reply was calm, almost bored. Why wouldn't it be? This wasn't the first time she'd called him in a blind, baseless panic. "I had one of my guys out there just yesterday, and several of the clerks and maids have been willing to keep us updated, as I've told you in my reports."

There. Your guy is telling you. It was your imagination. You didn't see him.

But her body did not believe that. Kinseki, who had some decent instincts of his own, read her silence. "I can have my guy do a check-in if you want."

Say no. She took a deep breath. At the same time, her phone gave a low double beep.

"Wait. I've got another call coming in."

34

She checked the number. It was Doug. Beth hit Decline.

"Are you still there?" Beth asked.

"Yes, Ms. Fraser. I'm still here. Do you want me to call my guy?"

Say no. You didn't see it. You've got other problems. Doug, for instance. This is your subconscious trying to avoid what's going on with Doug.

But out loud she said, "Yes. Thanks. I'd appreciate that."

"Okay. I'll call you back as soon as I hear anything. In the meantime, if they do attempt to contact you, do not engage, okay? Get yourself a lawyer and a restraining order. As a professional, I'm telling you, if what you've said is the truth, that's your best—"

Beth hung up.

The shakes started right after that. All Beth could do was clutch the grab handle and wait for them to stop.

CHAPTER FIVE

Dana lay on her bed, with Dessa streaming from the sound system. She stared at the faded Polaroid of her mother, and…the woman.

Dana had always wanted family. She'd been jealous of the kids whose holidays overflowed with aunts and cousins, the ones who had a whole world of people to love and look out for them. She didn't even get to meet her father until after they had moved to Chicago, and that had…mixed results. Dana remembered Douglas Hoyt coming over to visit every so often. She remembered they went to the zoo and to see *Frozen*. He took her to American Girl Place for Christmas and her birthday instead of just sending gift cards.

Around the time she turned seven, Dana had asked her mom if she and Dad were divorced. That was when Mom told her they'd never been married and that he was married to somebody else now and had two other kids.

Dana had been stunned. She had a brother and a sister. Nobody told her that. Dad showed her pictures of his house and his wife and their two dogs, but he never once said he had kids.

Dana immediately asked (pestered) Mom about them. *What are their names? How old are they? Where do they go to school? Can I message them?*

But most of all, *When can I meet them?*

Patty and Marcus, I think, she'd answered. And, *Younger than you.*

And: *I don't know.*

And: *They might be too young to have their own emails.*

And: *That's up to your father, Dana.*

Without an email address, Dana reasoned she'd have to get creative. She wrote her unknown siblings letters, like they were pen pals. Neither one answered back, so she wrote again and again.

They still didn't answer. Mom caught her crying about it.

That was when Mom had called her father. Dana stayed in her room and hugged her favorite stuffed animal, Cornie Bow. Through the wall, she heard Mom talking in that firm, calm way that made you wish she'd just yell and get it over with.

After a while, Mom came in and told Dana that her father had invited her to spend the weekend at his house.

Dana convinced herself it would all be great. She'd be on her best behavior. She'd make cookies. Her brother and sister (Marcus and Patty!) would be amazing. They'd all become best friends. She'd have a whole big family, not just

Mom and the few sharp-edged stories that were all she'd ever given Dana of her grandparents.

When her father picked her up, he looked exactly like the dads in the commercials—his hair was brushed back, and he wore a red polo shirt and khaki pants. She showed him the plate of cookies she'd baked. Four kinds, she'd said proudly, because she didn't know what Patty and Marcus liked.

While he drove around the curve of Lakeshore Drive and toward the highway, she peppered him with questions. What did they look like? What were their favorite shows? Their favorite YouTubers? Did Patty play Pokémon or Mario?

He didn't answer, and the more he didn't answer, the more Dana babbled to fill the silence with guesses and possibilities. She was practically vibrating with excitement and sugar overload. She was going to meet *her* brother and *her* sister.

Her father didn't say anything until they merged into the traffic on the Skyway.

"They don't know about you, kid."

Dana remembered her jaw hanging open. She remembered she watched his mouth moving, but she didn't really hear anything for a while. Too much of her brain was occupied by trying to understand what he meant.

They don't know about you.

"It's a pretty big thing, you know, finding out you've got a sister you never, well…you're just kind of a surprise. I mean, I never thought you'd actually live close enough to visit or anything…"

"Oh. That's okay," she said. "We'll tell them together. When I get there."

"Yeah, of course. Only, not right away, okay? I mean, it's not like nobody knows about you. Susan, my wife, she knows, but my kids...I want to ease them into it, okay?"

My kids, he said. But he meant *my* real *kids*.

"So, anyway, I told Patty and Marcus you're the daughter of an old friend and you're just staying with us for the weekend, okay? I will tell them you're...well, you're related. I promise I will. But there's a lot going on right now. You know how that is, right? I just want to make this as easy as possible for everybody. You get it, right?"

She got it. He was her dad, but she wasn't his real kid. She wasn't somebody you talked about. Like Mom's parents. They were bad people. You didn't talk about the bad people in the family.

Why do you think I'm bad? What did I do?

"So, let's just...let's make a deal and not talk about how you're...you know, that I'm your dad, okay? Just for this first weekend, okay?"

Mom doesn't talk about you either.

Dana looked at her plate, the mound of cookies invisible under their layers of Saran wrap. Chocolate chip, peanut butter, "no bakes," and molasses crinkles. She'd made them all for her brother and her sister. So they'd think she was cool. So they'd be glad she was part of their family, even with her weird eyes.

"Look, Dana, I know this is...well...this is all really

complicated, okay? I didn't…I just…I need your help here, okay?"

Dana stared at the cookies. They were going to his house for the whole weekend. And he was telling her she was supposed to keep a secret that whole time.

She was supposed to *be* a secret.

I don't want to be a secret.

She looked at her father. He glanced away from traffic and smiled.

I don't want to be your secret.

Dana pushed the window button to lower the glass.

"Dana, don't!" Her father slapped his hand on his head as the wind hit his perfectly combed hair.

Dana pitched the cookies out the window. They tumbled and scattered, a long trail of crumbling comets behind the car.

She raised the window. "Okay," she said. "I won't."

Now, Dana stared at the old Polaroid picture and felt that urge again. Throw it away. Flush it. Burn it. Let these people know that whatever their problem was, it was not *her* problem, and she was not going to play their games.

But she wasn't going to do that, and she already knew it. Because she could not stop staring at the photo, at the faded background that looked like the desert, the skinny woman who looked so happy, and the little girl who looked like she wanted to kill somebody.

What's she so mad about? Dana ran her thumb down the photo's rough edge. "Dana!" The shout cut through her thoughts. "Dana! Are you here?"

It was Mom, calling from the foyer.

"Here!" Dana shoved the photo into her jeans pocket and hurried out into the front room.

Mom was beside the door, resetting the alarm. She'd dropped her briefcase and purse on the mail table and held out one arm so Dana could walk into her hug.

"You okay, Mom? Cuz you look like the car ran over a cat or something."

Mom blinked. "Long day at work," she said. But something else was under that. Dana could hear it. "I'm going to go get a shower."

"Yeah, okay," she said to Mom's back. "I'll start dinner."

"Thanks, Dangerface." Mom flashed a quick, weak smile over her shoulder and vanished down the hall.

Yeah. Okay. Dana sucked in a deep breath. *Guess we'll talk later.*

Mom was in the shower long enough for Dana to stir-fry the mini shrimp and make a sauce for them out of green curry paste, coconut milk, lime, ginger, and cilantro, and pour it all over two bowls of Thai rice noodles.

She left the picture in her jeans pocket. She could feel it there, pressed against her hip.

Well, she probably couldn't really, but she felt like she should be able to.

When Mom finally came out, she'd changed into loose sweats and a plain, blue T-shirt and had her damp hair fluffed out over her shoulders. Thankfully, she also looked a lot more relaxed.

"Here, sit." Dana pointed at the breakfast bar. She added

shredded cucumber and more cilantro to both bowls and then set one down in front of her mother, along with a pair of stainless steel chopsticks. "Eat."

Mom blinked at the food. "You shouldn't have to take care of me."

"Who's taking care of you? I'm fattening you up."

That actually got her to chuckle. "I knew taking you to *Sweeney Todd* was a mistake."

Dana sat in her usual spot with her own bowl. She put her hand in her side pocket. She took it out.

Mom saw. Of course Mom saw. Mom always saw. Dana felt the flush starting in her cheeks. *Shit.*

"How was your last day?"

"Loud AF. Hallways were crazy. You know what they did? Somebody figured out if you lick gummy bears, they'll stick to the wall. There was some seriously sick gummy graffiti going on."

"Wow. That took dedication."

Mom really started in on the curry, and all conversation ceased. When she was having a bad day, Mom ate like somebody was about to take her food away.

Dana watched her. She tried superimposing the memory of the skinny, frizzy-haired woman who might just be her grandmother onto Mom.

You tell her I didn't scare you. I never touched you or threatened you, not once. Please. Be sure she knows that.

All at once, Mom was done, and she looked up and Dana was still staring. Dana realized her fingers were digging into her pocket again. She yanked them out.

"Everything okay, Dana?"

"Yeah." *What do I say?* "But I've been thinking about my tattoo."

Mom's face went blank. Not in her scary, angry way, just in the "it's non sequitur time" way. "What tattoo?"

"The one you promised I could get when I'm sixteen. Which is in two weeks."

"And when did I make this spectacularly ill-advised promise?"

"When I was fourteen." Which was true. Dana had prepped her for the conversation with a French toast–and-bacon breakfast and specialty coffee from Haz Beanz.

Mom was giving her the side-eye. Dana countered with her own patented wide-eyed "how could you doubt me?" look.

"Oh." Mom tapped her chopsticks against the edge of the bowl a couple of times. *Tink. Tink.* "Okay. On the condition you go to Shimmerz."

"Mom! I am not letting a friend of yours do my ink! It's my tattoo! I can go where I want!"

"Until you're eighteen, you can't go anywhere without my permission, and Shimmerz knows if you get an infection or hep A or anything while he's inking your butt, I will end him."

"It's not going on my butt."

"Whatever."

"It's going on my boob."

"Shimmerz, or it is not happening."

"Okay, okay! Jeez!" Dana got to her feet and stomped down the hall.

"And it was great curry!" Mom shouted after her.

Dana kicked the door shut.

It wasn't until the slam faded and she'd flopped back on the bed again that she realized she'd just blown her best chance to ask Mom about the photo, and the woman, and what the hell was really going on.

What am I gonna do now?

But she already knew. The only question was, How?

CHAPTER SIX

Something's wrong. Beth stared down the dim hallway toward Dana's closed bedroom door. *Something's wrong, and she doesn't want to tell me.*

Maybe something happened with Chelsea. That girl's family was a mess, even by Beth's standards. Her mother was deep into denial and pills, with the one possibly feeding the other. Then there was her brother. Sorry, her *half* brother. Chelsea loudly corrected anybody who got it wrong. Half-Brother Cody was into some serious shit, and somebody, somewhere, was not leaving that girl alone. Beth recognized the look. It was in the way Chelsea hunched her shoulders and how she dressed—loose and sloppy—like she was desperate to hide her maturing body.

But that's not it. Not this time. And then, *Did I really promise her a tattoo?*

Beth tried to remember and came up empty. *Bad mommy.*

She shook her head and retrieved her briefcase from the mail table by the door.

This apartment was the first home Beth actually owned. She had determined from the get-go it would be a warm, unregimented place. No chrome, no brushed steel, no industrial chic anything.

And color, she had told the designers. *Lots of color.* She'd had enough of oatmeal-hued walls to last a lifetime.

So the living room walls were Fresh Peach, except for the one that was Burnt Gold. The kitchen was Sepia Sunrise and Blond Melon where it wasn't maple, butcher block, and art tile.

The overstuffed living room furniture all had what Dana called "maximum flop factor." The two of them found most of the pillows and afghans at thrift stores and garage sales. There were framed vacation pictures and baby pictures and every single certificate and pseudo-diploma Dana had ever earned from kindergarten graduation to eighth-grade commencement. Beth's accomplishments were there too— all her licenses and certifications and a weird collage an artist friend had made of her business cards.

Mostly, though, there were books. Beth had insisted on at least two bookcases in every room, including the kitchen. When she was a child, there were times when she spent eight or ten hours in the local library—wherever "local" was at the time—waiting until her parents were done with whatever they were doing. She also learned that nobody bothered the kid sitting quietly in the book aisles, not even in the Walmarts or Targets.

But not one of those dozens of books would help her

ask her daughter what exactly the teenage drama might be about this time. Because it was just maybe about the fact that Dana knew Beth had lied to her, yet again.

How can I tell her Doug is begging for...well, probably money? she thought toward the wall of books—paperbacks with broken spines, shiny new hardbacks, and battered treasures dug out of library sales bins. *She's got enough problems with him as it is.*

Beth had never hated Doug for ghosting her when she told him she was having the baby. He was who he was, and she'd known it when she made her decision.

But she'd never thought Doug would give in to the shame that only existed in his mind and attempt to deny that Dana was his daughter.

When Dana pressed her face against Beth's shoulder and bawled, Beth had been so ready to do murder—bloody, gleeful, public murder. The urge came back every time he broke another promise, every time he made another weasely excuse while pretending the choice that made his life easier was better for her too.

Every time, she had to watch Dana try to decide how she was going to cope with this permanently bewildered man who happened to be her father.

No. I do not have to make things worse. Not yet.

Which was probably denial and avoidance, but Beth told herself she was too tired to care.

That was when her phone buzzed.

Beth groaned. "Doug, if that's you, you are not going to like what you hear out of me."

But it wasn't Doug.

It was that same unknown caller, with the San Francisco area code. Enough of this.

Beth touched Accept. "Beth Fraser," she said.

"Beth Fraser," drawled the man on the other end. "Nice name. I like it."

A cold blizzard of memory engulfed Beth—the back seats of cars, the aisles of stores, parking lots and alleys and endless crappy motel rooms.

"Wouldn't even know it was you, Star," the man said.

Whiskey. Cigarettes. Screaming fights. The blows on her head, her butt, the backs of her legs. Crumpled bills stolen out of the register crushed tight in her hand. Praise for what a smart girl she was, what a chip off the old block.

"What…what do you want?"

The slick chill of vodka being forced down her throat. The smell of the gun smoke, the vicious kick to her shoulder.

"Now, now. Just got a quick question for you."

The iron taste of hot blood spattered against her mouth. The sound of the body falling at her feet.

"Any idea what your daughter's been up to today?"

CHAPTER SEVEN

Beth threw her phone away from her like it was burning. It banged off the wall and bounced onto the couch.

"Mom?"

Dana. She stood at the end of the hallway, her face dead white.

"What is it? What's happened?"

My nightmares. All of them. Every last one. But she couldn't say that. Not to Dana. But because she couldn't say that, she couldn't seem to say anything.

Any idea what your daughter's been up to today?

Beth pressed her knuckles against her mouth. *Calm down, Beth. Dana's here. She's okay. She's right here.*

"Is it work?"

What? For a minute Dana's words made no sense at all.

Dana ran to her and grabbed her shoulders. "Was that Rafi? Or Dad?"

"No. No. That was…something else. Dana, I need you to leave me alone for a minute."

"But, Mom…"

"Dana, please."

"No, Mom. I've got to…"

"I SAID LEAVE ME ALONE!"

Dana's face flushed red. She let go of Beth's shoulders, turned, and ran.

The bedroom door slammed.

Beth bowed her head, sick and ashamed.

Calm down. Deal with Dana in a minute. Right now, you have to think.

Any idea what your daughter's been up to today? It was her father's voice. Moreover, it was the smug, sure tone he used to talk about the money he'd won, the people he'd scammed, the loser cops, the idiot security guys in the casinos.

She'd always known that one day her parents would decide she owed them something, just like they'd decided Grammy owed them. That sense of absolute entitlement defined them both. It might be left to stew for a while, but it would never go away.

You don't know that's what's happening. You don't know where he is. He could really be in San Francisco. Anywhere. He could be bored and messing with you.

Beth stood on wobbly legs and retrieved the phone. There'd been another call. This was from a number she recognized. James Kinseki.

She hit his number. The second he picked up, she said, "Where are they?"

On the other end, Kinseki just sighed, a short, exasperated sound. "Seems I owe you an apology, Ms. Fraser."

Beth said nothing.

"It looks like the Bowens left Perrysborough maybe three weeks ago, and I've also unfortunately found out that one of my team was submitting fraudulent reports. The guy's fired, and he's losing his bond. You can press charges if you want, but I'm sending you a refund for the last three months. It just went into the mail."

Beth still said nothing.

"Is there anything I can do to make this right?"

"No. I..." Beth squeezed her eyes shut. There was a sound in her brain, a low humming noise that came from nowhere in the real world. It made it difficult to hear or think. "I need to know what changed," she said. "What set them off? Can you find that out?"

"I can try." Because Kinseki didn't want her to press those charges. Because if she did, it would be his license and his job on the line.

"Do it." Beth hung up. She rubbed her arms, trying to scrub away the goose bumps.

If her parents were close, she had to warn her daughter, to tell her...

Tell her what? That I've been lying to her for years?

Slowly, carefully, Beth walked down the hallway toward Dana's closed door.

Tell her I've had my parents watched for years? Tell her I have reports and photographs locked in a private box with the fake IDs and the cash and the gun, so she wouldn't stumble across them?

Dana had cranked her music again. An ominous bass line pounded against the walls.

"Dana!"

"What?!"

"I'm coming in!"

"Whatever!"

Beth chose to believe this meant okay.

Beth had always felt strangely proud of Dana's room. She'd been able to give her daughter a space like nothing she'd ever known. It was painted with a combination of silver and sea-foam green with black trim (Dana's choice). Posters of rappers Beth had never heard of hung alongside characters from the *Black Butler* and *Death Note* animes and, of course, *Sweeney Todd*. Cookbooks, graphic novels, and spiral-bound notebooks covered every surface that wasn't covered in clothes.

Dana was curled up in the middle of her bed hugging Cornie Bow, the stuffed unicorn with the rainbow mane that had been her best friend since she was four.

Beth hit the Off button on the speaker control. The silence was so sudden it left her ears ringing.

"I'm sorry," said Beth. "I shouldn't have yelled."

Dana looked up at Beth just long enough to make sure Beth saw her red-rimmed eyes, then deliberately turned away.

"I've just had a really bad day."

Dana shrugged.

"Was there something you wanted to ask me?" At the same time, Beth felt acutely aware of her phone in the other room. Dad might call back. Or he might put Mom on to do the dirty work.

Her phone might be ringing right now.

"Dana, listen. I want...I need you to be careful over the next couple of days."

"Why?"

The lie came too fast and far too easily.

"You were right. That call—it was a thing with work. We had to turn a guy down today, and he didn't take it well. He made some threats. So, if somebody comes up to you..." Dana had turned toward her again, and something in her bitter, surprised expression stopped Beth in midsentence. "Dana, did somebody talk to you today?"

"Lots of people, Mom." Dana laced the words with scorn and literalism. "I've got friends, you know."

"I mean a stranger. A man in a Cubs cap with a tattoo of a fan of cards on his left arm? A skinny woman, maybe in a flowery dress?"

Dana clenched her jaw, and her unicorn, and Beth knew she was right.

"What happened? Did somebody follow you?"

"What is *with* you?" Dana demanded.

"I told you. This guy is making threats!"

"Then why are you asking about some woman?" The contempt in Dana's glare sliced straight through her. "You know, Mom, if you want me to trust you, you could try telling me, like, oh, I don't know, the *truth*!"

"You could do the same for me."

Beth stared at Dana. Dana stared back, her eyes, the green one and the brown one, equally sharp and furious.

"Nothing happened," Dana said. "Nobody talked to me."

What she meant was, *If you're going to lie to me, I'm going to lie to you.*

Beth crossed the room she and Dana had created, and walked down the hallway.

You're a coward, Beth Fraser. A total fucking coward.

Behind her, Dana cranked up the music again. The bass thumped against the walls and vibrated through the floor.

Clenching her jaw until her teeth hurt, Beth rounded the kitchen half-wall and went back into the living room. Her phone was still lying on the coffee table. She flicked through the screens to display the last incoming number, the one with the San Francisco area code.

There was no conceivable way her parents were in San Francisco. They'd bought or scammed the number because they knew that since her work was funding high-tech ventures, she'd be more likely to pick up a call from Silicon Valley. They'd been checking her out. Watching her while she was watching them.

And she hadn't known. Until today, she hadn't known a damn thing.

He answered on the second ring.

"Star! I'm glad you called back. We must have gotten disconnected there."

His voice was rougher than it had been, but it still had all that laughing confidence she remembered. Dad was having a good day. She could picture him smiling and winking at her mother, who sat cross-legged on the bed, an unlit cigarette in one hand and a beer in the other.

"I'm assuming you want to meet," Beth said. "Where?"

"And that's how you talk to your old man these days?"

A MOTHER'S LIE

Her father sighed. "Well, okay, Star, if this is the way you want to play it—" He paused as if considering. "There's a little bar I found. Real old-school Chicago Irish on Eighty-Sixth off Ontario. Mike's. Who knew they still made 'em like that, huh? I can—"

"I'll find it. Noon?"

"No good. They don't open until three."

"All right. Three." Beth hung up.

That was it, then. There was no more room to hide or to kid herself. Her parents were in Chicago, probably toasting each other with cans of beer and shots of vodka. There was something they wanted, and since they were better than the rest of the slobs and losers out there, they had every right to take it.

Even if they had to take it from her.

55

CHAPTER EIGHT

When Mom shut the door, Dana flipped up the lid on her laptop. She pulled the photo out and propped it against the screen and stared at it. And started typing.

Deborah Ann Watts. That was her grandmother's name. She'd searched it a hundred times. It never did any good. The name was too common, and she had no way to narrow down the search. No birth date, nothing. Thomas Jankowski, her grandfather, had a less common name, but the search on him had never gone any better.

Not even today.

But she always kept looking. She kept her Google alerts primed and updated. She couldn't understand why she was supposed to look away. How could Mom just ignore them? Dana understood they were dangerous. Mom's parents were criminals—actual, got-arrested-but-skipped-bail criminals. They stole from gas station clerks, she said. They shoplifted and traded pills with security guards so they'd look the other way. They rigged pool games and card games and cheated the drunks in bars and lifted their wallets.

There was no "code," no red line, Mom had said. *If they needed something and they could take it off you, you were a sucker and you deserved it.*

Dana understood all that, like she understood Mom wasn't actually trying to lock Dana out of her own life. Not like Dad.

But how could she not want to *know*?

She looked at the photo again. If this was real, it was the only picture Dana had of her mother's mother. Every now and again, some teacher made the kids bring family photos to school for a multicultural day, or for a family tree project—something like that. Dana always brought pictures from her dad's family—a grandmother and grandfather she'd never met. "Aunt" Julia and "Uncle" Ron, who she'd met maybe twice. Her twin cousins Shelly and Kelly, ditto.

She hadn't even gotten them from Dad. His wife, Susan, copied and FedExed them for the first project back in first grade. Dana had been recycling them ever since.

Dana knew plenty of kids whose parents were divorced. Some of them had whole long strings of half and step siblings. Amanda Hollander's dad didn't even know she was alive.

But none of them had anything like this mess.

And then Mom came in here and just lied all over the fucking place about what was up with her. Like she'd lied when she got home. There was no guy at work.

What the hell is the matter with all of you? Dana thought

in sudden, fierce exasperation. *What the actual fuck are you all thinking?*

Didn't they get it—that all their lying and running away made things worse for her?

The woman (her grandmother? Really?) said she'd be at the Starbucks tomorrow at four o'clock.

Maybe I should go. Just talk to her. Maybe I could find out...

No. Stupid. Why do I even care? Mom was all the family that counted. Mom took care of her, and she took care of Mom. Who else had ever been there for her?

But no matter how hard she tried to smother it, Dana wanted to know more. She wanted to know *them.* She wanted to stand in front of them and see if there was anything of herself reflected inside.

I'm not a little kid. Dana bit her lip. *Not anymore.*

She rolled over and picked up her phone and started texting Chelsea. Need your help tomorrow.

I have a right to the truth about my own life.

Dana hit Send.

CHAPTER NINE

Beth could remember the first time she saw her parents. She was five.

Her name was still Star Bowen then. She lived with Grammy. From her perspective, she always had. Grammy's home was a green-and-white trailer beside the long dirt drive that ended at the gravel road. They had chickens and a vegetable garden and an apple tree. Everything was dusty in the summertime and freezing cold in winter. Their "neighbors" drove five or six miles to sit in the folding chairs Grammy set out among the weeds and the chickens. Sometimes they'd bring their kids and she'd have somebody to play with.

She was going to kindergarten in the fall. Grammy said they'd walk together down to the place the bus would stop each morning. Star would have to get up good and early, and no complaining. Star promised solemnly that she would.

Grammy didn't smile much. Grammy smelled like tobacco and Lysol. Grammy had spotty pink skin, hard hands, and a hard body. She sewed and crocheted and made do. She traded the things she made for the things the neighbors made, and they came and fixed things and she went and took care of things.

When Star asked about her mommy and daddy, Grammy told her they were traveling. Star accepted that because she was five and there were more important things to think about.

The day it all changed, Beth thought she remembered being inside. Probably she'd been watching cartoons. She thought she remembered how she heard the rattle and crunch of a car pulling up the drive, and ran to the screen door to see who it was.

She did remember (Beth was positive) being surprised when a strange dented, dust-colored station wagon with cracked wood panels on the sides bounced to a stop out front.

A man got out of the driver's side. He had a dark red-brown tan and dark hair and hairy arms. He was not happy. Star could see that right away. He looked at the trailer like he wanted to call it a bad name. She felt herself shrinking back and wondered if she should run around the back to get Grammy.

Beth sometimes thought if she had run and gotten to Grammy first, it might have been different. Grammy—hard, practical, and worn down to the bone—might have been able to save her from what came next.

But before she could make up her mind to move, a

woman climbed out of the car. She was tall and thin and tan. She wore a pretty flowery dress, and her brown hair was braided. Star thought she must be a TV lady. She looked so happy she glowed.

The woman saw Star standing behind the screen door.

"Star!" She threw both hands up in the air. "Star! It's me! It's Mommy! We're back!"

Star remembered—Beth remembered—how she'd gasped. She'd slammed the door open and run straight into the pretty woman's arms. No hiding or crying or being shy for Star Susan Bowen. The woman laughed and hugged her hard and spun her around. Beth remembered instantly liking the feel of her and the smell of her. She remembered the excitement of it. This pretty, happy lady was her very own mommy!

She didn't think at all about the hard-faced man, who pulled the cigarette out of his mouth and pitched the butt in the dirt and said nothing. She barely noticed Grammy coming around the edge of the trailer with a bucket in one hand.

"Hi, Mama," said the pretty lady to Grammy. "We're back."

The man said, "We gotta talk, Lizzy."

Grammy said nothing. She put her bucket down beside the steps where nobody would trip over it. Grammy hated it when you didn't put things away right.

"I said we gotta—"

"I heard you the first time," Grammy announced. "I don't see what there could be to talk about."

Grammy was mad. Mad rolled out of her like cold out of the fridge. Star wriggled uneasily.

"We don't have to get into it right away," Mommy said. "It's been such a long time. Can't we even say hi first?" She kissed the top of Star's head.

Grammy and the man got the same disbelieving expression on their faces. Star almost laughed, which probably would not have gone over well.

But Mommy hugged her instead. "Star, honey, why don't you show me your room?"

To Star, this was the best idea. She dragged Mommy into her bedroom at the very end of the trailer. She shoved toys and blankets into her hands, telling her all the most important things. Mommy laughed and smiled and listened. She sat cross-legged on the floor and said hello to the dolls and stuffed animals. Then, she pulled a package of Oreos out of her pocket.

"Here you go, honey," Mommy said. "A present."

Star's eyes had gone wide. "Grammy says no store cookies. She says they're a waste of money and bad for my teeth."

"Well, we won't tell her." Mommy leaned close. She smelled like summer wind. "It'll be a secret, just between you and me. Hey! I have an idea. We can have a tea party!" And Star started setting all the dolls in place while Mommy made plates and tables out of Kleenex and old alphabet blocks.

Star didn't stop to wonder about what the man and Grammy were talking about. She heard the shouts rumble through the walls, but she didn't remember being worried about them. She just remembered all the fun, and thinking that this smiling woman who sat next to her on the floor was exactly what a mommy should be.

Then Grammy opened the door.

"Say good-bye, Star. They're leaving."

"Oh, no." Mommy got to her feet. "We just got here. We haven't even had a chance to talk yet, Mama," she added softly.

Grammy's mouth went hard, and Star shrank back. That was the face that meant a spanking or a whack on the head with her high school ring.

The man appeared behind Grammy's back. "We're going."

Mommy laid her hand on Star's shoulder. "Just another minute. Please."

"We're not done with the tea party!" Star added. "It's not her fault, Grammy! She didn't know about the cookies!"

"Say good-bye to your company, Star," said Grammy.

Star didn't want to say good-bye. She cried instead— loud and screaming, just like she would if a new toy had been taken away. Grammy shouldered her way into the room and scooped Star up.

Grammy stared at Mommy, her eyes cold and dead as stones in winter. "Get out of this house."

It didn't settle in until much later that Mommy was Grammy's daughter. Grammy had stood there and ordered her own flesh and blood out of her home. All she knew that day was that Mommy left with the man, who had to be Daddy. Star stayed in her room and cried. She sulked at dinner, and Grammy sent her back to her room.

"You can just stay there until you remember how to behave."

Beth remembered being positive that this time she'd stay

in her room until she *died*. She might even have shouted that—fists balled up, whole body bent double by the force of her scream. She meant it too. She really did.

When it got dark, Star got herself changed for bed. She was mad enough that she kicked the pink princess quilt Grammy'd gotten her last Christmas onto the floor. She was hungry because she hadn't eaten dinner. She was getting scared. She wanted to understand what had happened this afternoon. What had the shouting been about? Could she say she was sorry about the cookies and promise not to do it again? Would Mommy be allowed to come back, then?

Maybe she fell asleep. She didn't remember that. She did remember the sound.

Tap, tap, tap!

Star sat up. It was dark. Moonlight filtered through the metal blinds. The sound came again.

Tap, tap, tap!

From the window. There was a shadow at the window.

"Hey," whispered a woman's voice. "Hey, Star. It's me. It's Mommy!"

Star yanked the blinds up and pushed the window open, and the screen. Mommy leaned over the aluminum sill and grinned.

"Hey, honey! Sorry about before. But it's all okay now. Come on!"

Star stared at her. Mommy held out her arms. "Come on, honey. Right out the window. Mommy's got you."

Star tried to make sense of this. Only one possibility occurred to her. "Are we going traveling?"

Mommy smiled, that same beautiful happy smile she'd

worn this afternoon, right up until the moment Grammy walked in on them. "Yes, Star. We're going traveling. Come on, now! I've got more cookies in the car."

And that was that.

Mommy wiggled her fingers, making a "come on" gesture, and Star let herself be hugged and lifted out of her bedroom window in nothing but her nightgown and slippers. She clutched her favorite teddy bear, Boo, the yellow one Grammy crocheted for her.

Mommy bundled her into the back seat of the station wagon. Mommy made Boo-Bear dance and jump up and down and squeal when he saw the fresh package of Oreos. Daddy, a silhouette in the front seat who still hadn't said a single word to her, drove them all away.

CHAPTER TEN

Beth surprised herself by sleeping late the next morning. The night had been a long one, complete with tossing and turning and getting up to make sure that the alarm really was set and that nothing had been disturbed. Which was obsessive and pointless, and she knew that, but she could not stop herself.

It was already nine thirty, and the kitchen was quiet and dark when she went in to make her coffee. Either Dana was celebrating the end of the school year in traditional teenage fashion by sleeping in extra late, or she was still sulking.

Probably it was a little of both.

I'll find a way to explain, Beth told herself as she set about grinding beans and filling the coffee maker's carafe. *I have to.*

The landline rang. Beth jumped, splashing water all over. She had to stand where she was and press one hand against the counter for a long moment before she could make herself put the carafe down gently and pick up the receiver.

"Beth Fraser."

"Ms. Fraser, this is Kendi at the front desk. I have Mr. Douglas Hoyt down here, and he is asking to come up."

Oh, this is all I need.

She heard some scuffling on the other end of the line. "Beth? It's me. I just need five minutes. That's all. I promise."

Jesus. "All right, Doug. All right."

"Thank you."

He handed the phone back to Kendi, and Beth gave Kendi her go-ahead and hung up. She poured the water into the coffee maker and watched it while it began to bubble and hiss.

She hoped Dana would decide to stay in her room a little longer. Whatever she and Doug were going to have to say to each other now, it was not a conversation she wanted Dana to be any part of.

Beth had not planned to have a child with Doug. He'd never really even been a boyfriend, never mind a potential partner. He was more like a pressure valve. They'd go clubbing and dance to bone-shaking techno and hip-hop. She fed him shot after shot of tequila, enjoying the sight of him getting insanely drunk and then getting to send him home, sometimes without his pants or to the wrong address. Then he'd call up to howl at her, and the next weekend they'd do it all over again.

He'd make grand, romantic gestures: the elaborate picnics in the park, the time he'd painted a gorgeous sunset scene on her bedroom wall to surprise her, and how he kept sneaking back in to revise this and that, never quite satisfied with what he'd done and never wanting anybody to see him doing the actual work.

That should have told her something right there. So should all those times he'd talk about how he hated San Francisco and that he wanted to live someplace *real*, to have a real job and a real life. He never talked about taking her with him.

Twenty-nine was late for this kind of craziness. But she figured she was owed an adolescence, and now was when she could afford to have it. An ongoing series of therapists told her that she was seeking out the chaos. It was comfortable to her because of her childhood.

Which was almost true, but not quite. She needed to prove that this time she could use that chaos for exactly what she wanted. *I'll handle this thing, in spite of everything you've done, in spite of everything I am. I'll make it whole and right and real and shining, and the whole world will see I'm better.*

Rafi's first fund made just enough to let him put together a second. The second did a little better and led to a third. Beth brought Doug to the party Rafi threw to announce that third fund. They popped the cork on multiple bottles of French champagne and handcrafted, locally sourced sparkling cider and toasted the future.

The next morning, she woke up sick as hell and realizing she'd lost track of her days. This was quickly followed by a trip to the drugstore for a pregnancy test kit. Then came all the gross, fumbling awkwardness of trying to pee on a stick. Then there was the sitting there with her jeans and panties around her ankles and staring at the stupid stick while the stupid little plus sign formed in the stupid little window.

Beth remembered pulling her pants up and looking at the stick again. Yes, it was still a plus sign. She flushed the toilet and went out into her bedroom. She sat on the edge of her bed.

The sun had broken through San Francisco's semipermanent cloud cover, and a beam fell on the ends of her toes. They were a mess of cracked red enamel. Doug, for reasons known only to himself, had decided he wanted to try painting her toenails, and she hadn't been able to hold still because he'd kept tickling her.

She looked around her apartment. She looked at her messed-up toes and at the sky outside her window. She exhaled.

"Okay," she said to the empty bedroom and the new clump of cells busily dividing inside her. "Okay, I guess we're doing this."

Why that choice and that time? She didn't know. She did spend a couple of nights bawling through the kind of panic attack she'd thought she'd put behind her, but she never seriously tried to change her mind.

She called Doug, and she told him, and he listened and said it was a lot to process and could he call back tomorrow? She told him yes because she figured that would be the most pain-free option.

She was right.

Three days later, she still hadn't heard back, so she called again. She got his voice mail. She checked her social media. It didn't take much looking to figure out she'd been ghosted.

And that, she figured, was the end of that.

Rafael's wife, Angela, arranged a baby shower for her and invited pretty much every venture capital woman in the valley. When her time came, Rafi drove her to the hospital, and Angela held her hand.

She sent a birth announcement to Doug. He didn't answer. She heard from a mutual friend he'd moved to Chicago and become an accounts analyst at a major insurance firm—oh, and he had met this really terrific girl he was crazy in love with.

Beth hired a nanny with excellent references who passed an ironclad background check, and then negotiated a flexible work schedule and set about trying to figure out how to be something approaching the kind of mother she wanted to be.

A year later, Rafi announced he was moving the firm's headquarters out to Chicago. He liked the business climate there better. Plus Angela was pregnant, and Silicon Valley was no place to try to put down long-term roots.

Beth had no plans to join him, until that day she almost lost Dana and suddenly nothing could make San Francisco feel safe again.

The coffee had finished. Doug was taking his time getting up here. She pictured him pacing back and forth in front of the elevator, trying to get his story straightened out. She considered opening the door to surprise him.

Instead, she poured herself a cup of coffee and added her usual four spoonfuls of sugar.

She listened for any sounds of life coming from down the bedroom hallway. Still nothing. How late had Dana stayed up last night? Beth wondered whether she should check on her.

But before she could move, a tentative knock sounded on the front door.

Finally. Beth put down her coffee and went to open it.

Doug stepped in, and Beth had to keep her jaw from dropping.

Doug was creased and crumpled and stubbled, not to mention wearing the same shirt and pants from yesterday, only the jacket and tie were gone.

"Jesus, Doug." Beth did up the door locks. "What happened?"

"Yeah, I know." He brushed at his shirt. "I look like shit. I…couldn't face going home to an empty house just now."

"Sit down." She headed toward the kitchen with Doug trailing along behind. "There's coffee."

"Thanks." He sat at the breakfast bar while she filled a second cup. She leaned back against the counter and let him drink and smooth his hair back and generally try to pull himself together.

Naturally, this was the moment when Dana shuffled out of the hall wearing her dancing-unicorn pajama bottoms and a black cami, and yawning loudly. When she registered the fact that someone besides Beth was in the kitchen, she blinked and squinted.

"Dad?"

He tried to smile. "Hi, Dana."

71

She brushed past Beth and opened the refrigerator. "What are you doing here?"

"There's some stuff your mom and I needed to talk about. Nothing big."

Dana's eyes slid from Doug to Beth and back again. She clearly noticed that her father was a mess and that he was lying just a little more stupidly than usual, and that Beth was keeping her mouth shut.

"Yeah. Okay." Dana started loading food onto a TV tray: bread, half an avocado, cream cheese, yogurt, blueberries, and a few anonymous Tupperware containers. "Mom, I'm going over to Chelsea's after breakfast, okay?"

"I'd rather she came over here today, Dana."

"What?" Dana slapped another container down on her tray. "I'm under house arrest now? Should I call Kimi and tell her she's got to bring the party to our place because my mom doesn't think I'm responsible enough to leave the house?"

So, I guess we're still mad. Beth made herself exhale before she answered. "You know that's not what I'm saying."

"Whatever."

"Hey." Doug lowered his coffee mug. "You shouldn't talk to your mother like that."

They both stared at him.

"What? She shouldn't talk to you like that."

Dana rolled her eyes, picked up her heaped tray, and retreated back into the depths of the apartment.

Doug opened his mouth.

"Doug, you say one word about parenting a teenager, and this conversation is over."

Doug closed his mouth. He also drank more coffee.

"So, listen, Beth, I'm sorry about yesterday. I'd just gotten some bad news, and I wasn't thinking straight. That's no excuse, but..."

Beth sighed. "How bad is it?"

"We could lose the house."

Beth added another spoonful of sugar to her coffee and stirred.

"What have you told Susan?"

"Nothing. I wanted to, you know, have things fixed before I did. And I just want to be really up front: I'm not asking for money."

"So what are you asking for?"

"I just...I need you to come with me to see this guy. That's all."

She looked at him again, taking in all the details of his rumpled appearance and shadowed eyes. She remembered his half-drunk desperation from yesterday when he turned up at her workplace, something he'd never done before. The way he looked at her then was the same way he looked at her now—like a little, lost boy pleading for help.

Disbelief, slow and thick, coursed through her, because all at once Beth knew what he was really asking.

"Oh my God." Beth set her coffee down before she dropped it or threw the mug at him. "You did *not* tell someone you could get Lumination to invest with them."

"No! I never said that."

"Not directly," she added for him.

"Not at all. I swear. They just...they knew you and I had a connection, and they asked if I'd talk to you. I knew you wouldn't like it, so I tried to put them off. I swear I did!"

"Shut up, Doug," said Beth softly. Thankfully, Doug did shut up. Beth drank her coffee and waited until she thought she could speak calmly.

"All right. You are going to tell me who these people are and *exactly* what you've promised them."

Doug did, and Beth listened. It was a fairly standard vaporware scheme, the kind she'd made her living helping Rafi and Lumination avoid. He showed her a business card and gave her a set of names, none of which she'd ever heard of.

"They're hounding me, Beth. They're calling, like, all the time! I can't let this go under. I've got everything tied up in this! And the returns were really good, I mean, for the first year and—"

"Yes, I'm sure they were," Beth said, cutting him off.

With an effort, she kicked her anger aside so there was room in her brain for actual thought. She'd have to call Rafi and let him know. And they had to find out whether targeting Doug was a coincidence, or if these jackasses—whoever they were—knew ahead of time they could use him to get to her.

"Okay," said Beth. "When Susan gets home, you tell her what's happened. I can put you in touch with a good lawyer who specializes in this kind of fraud complaint, and—"

"Wait, whoa. I don't need a lawyer. I just need you to come with me. You don't have to promise anything. You just have to act like you're listening for maybe fifteen minutes and then—"

"And then they start using my name and Lumination's name to recruit more suckers for their scam," Beth finished for him. "That's not happening."

"Okay, yeah, okay—I can see where that'd be a problem." Doug gripped his coffee mug. "But…then I am going to need that loan, Beth. If I can't get my investment back, I…"

"As soon as you tell Susan, we'll work something out."

"I can't tell her," he whispered. "It'll kill her."

You mean it'll kill you. "I am not going to help you lie to your family."

"You told me I could count on you. You told me if I needed you—"

Beth slammed her hand against the countertop. "I didn't tell you I'd risk my reputation and my daughter's future for you!"

"She's my daughter too!" The shout turned his face red. "This affects her."

"Yeah, it does, and I'm going to be booking her a new set of appointments with her therapist. So, thanks loads for that. Now, if you'll excuse me"—Beth headed over to the front door and started undoing the locks—"I've got somewhere I need to be."

That seemed to genuinely surprise him. "It's Saturday!"

Beth pulled the door open. "Yeah, well, as it happens, my parents are in town."

"Your…your parents?"

"Yes, and they're going to want to extort me too. So you see, I've got a lot on my plate."

Slowly, like he was trying to understand what she meant

by any of this, Doug climbed off the stool. "Beth, you can't be putting me on the same level—"

Which was all Beth could take. "No, actually, my parents are way smarter than you ever were." He started back like she'd slapped him, and Beth found she didn't really care. "Tell Susan, Doug. When you can bring her with you, I'll help."

She closed her door before he had a chance to speak and make things worse. She walked down the hallway, past the TV room. The sound of a cooking show filtered through the door. She went right on past into her study and closed the door.

I will find a way to talk to Dana. Just not now.

CHAPTER ELEVEN

As it turned out, Mike's was anything but a charming, traditional Irish pub. It was a windowless dive on a block at the very edge of the city's latest wave of gentrification. This was no surprise to Beth. She'd been in places just like it at least a hundred times before.

When she walked in, she had to pause for a minute in the doorway to let her eyes adjust. Not that there was a lot to see: a battered bar with a cluster of beery white men at the far end, and a collection of empty tables. The only brightly lit area was the pool table in the back.

Déjà vu washed over Beth, shrinking her back down to the girl she used to be: skinny, wiry, light. Eyes sharp and focused. Hunger a familiar annoyance. And she'd been so damn fast. At the high school, before it had all gone to hell, the gym teacher had actually tried to talk her into joining girls' track and field. Beth remembered staring at the woman like she'd dropped in from Mars. Who ran when no one was chasing them?

"Get you something?" the bartender called from the far end of the room. He was about the same vintage as his customers. He might even have been the owner.

"No, thanks—I'm good," she said, because she'd already spotted her father.

He was with three men—all white guys with gray beards, bulging guts, and Harley-Davidson T-shirts. They clustered around the pool table where Todd Bowen bent over the green felt, lining up his shot.

Beth took a wide circle around the room, keeping herself in shadow. Todd hadn't seen her yet, but the handful of shriveled men who weren't watching the players were all watching her. And why wouldn't they be? She was the only woman in the place not wiping down a table.

The person she did not see was her mother, and that worried her. Her parents were a dysfunctional double act. In a place like this, Jeannie Bowen would arrive on her own and install herself in a corner. She'd nurse the fanciest beer the place had to offer and wait for the suckers to come to her.

Dad pulled his arm back, pretending to keep all his attention on the shot. Beth came quietly up on his left side. The nearest, tallest Harley guy did a double take. Like he wasn't sure if he was really lucky or about to be served with papers.

"So, what'd he tell you?" Beth asked Tall Harley Guy. "That he hurt his back at the plant, and he hasn't been able to shoot straight since? Or was it the one where his girlfriend slammed his hand in her car door and broke three bones?"

The three fat, gray men looked at one another. One scratched his beard. Another looked at his hand.

Beth rolled her eyes. "Broken hand. Jesus. All this time and you couldn't even come up with a new story?"

Todd's stick thudded against the cue ball. It shot forward to click against the nine ball, which banked weakly and slow-rolled to a stop in the middle of the felt.

"You're late, Star." Todd straightened and turned, and for the first time in thirty years, Beth faced her father.

Beth always thought that someone as deceptive and violent as Todd Bowen should have the decency to look the part. But no. Todd Bowen was a medium-size man, narrow through the shoulders. His bright-blue eyes lent him an aura of openness reinforced by his square chin. The hair on his arms had always been thicker and darker than the hair on his head. It was all gray now, and his leathery skin had shrunk tight against his bones. He wore a Cubs cap and a gray T-shirt with a pocket under a green plaid work shirt. There was a big watch on his wrist and good boots on his feet. A faded tattoo decorated his left arm—a fan of cards with the king of diamonds sticking up from the other five. He looked like the neighbor who was always ready to loan out a socket wrench and knew how to fix the lawn mower.

"He used to bring me into joints like this," Beth told the Harley guys. "I'd have to wear something low cut and tight—you know, so the jerks would be watching me instead of him. Told me to quit my bitchin' because it was how we were getting our grocery money that week."

"You his girlfriend?" asked the player with the longest

beard and the biggest gut. The other two chuckled at the thought.

"I'm his daughter."

Suddenly none of them seemed to find her story so funny anymore.

"I was thirteen when he started using me to distract jackasses like you."

"And now this is you." Dad planted the butt of his pool cue on the floor. "Star Bowen, all grown up."

She'd thought she'd tell him not to call her that. She'd planned to insist her name was Elizabeth Fraser and he'd *better fucking remember that*. But hearing her old name coming out of her father's mouth was a searing reminder of who he really was and who she'd been when she was with him.

Go on, Star, just like I told you. When your grandmother answers, you give her the whole thing, just like your mother said. You understand? Remember, she's the reason we're in this mess. She's got plenty of money, and if she really loved you like she says, she'd be ready to share it with you… Go on, now. Take the phone. What're you waiting for?

"And this is you," Beth said. "Todd Bowen, who hasn't changed a bit."

"Can't say the same about you." He looked at his pool buddies. "She used to be scared of her own shadow." The admiration in his voice might even have been real.

"I used to be scared you'd beat the crap out of me."

Twenty bucks! What the hell are we supposed to do with twenty bucks? Jesus, what's the matter with you! Did you even try to convince her?

Todd sighed and tossed his cue to the nearest Harley guy. "Sorry, fellas. I'm out. Family comes first, right?"

Dad sauntered across to a scarred table in the corner. Beth slid into place opposite him. Behind her, the sounds of voices and pool balls being racked started up.

And the world goes on. Beth put her purse on the floor between her feet.

"So, Dad, what do you want bad enough to threaten my daughter? And where's Mom?"

"Now, Star." Dad shook his head slowly. "You know I never threatened your girl. I just asked after my granddaughter."

"To-may-to, to-mah-to. So, where's Mom again?"

The server, a tired-eyed white woman, came over. She looked like she could be related to the bartender. A younger sister, maybe, or even a daughter.

She pulled an order pad out of her apron. "Get you something?"

Dad looked up, and in that split second, the bar hustler was replaced by a cheerful, avuncular man. "I'll say. I am starving! What's good?"

That server met his teasing smile, and her expression thawed just a little. "The chili's not too bad."

"I'll take that. Loaded. And a Budweiser, and you are a goddess." The server smirked, letting him know he wasn't getting anywhere, but she appreciated his talk and his Paul Newman blue eyes. She looked at Beth, but Beth just shook her head. The server left, moving a little more comfortably than she had been before.

Dad could do that to you. When he wanted to.

Beth leaned her elbows on the table, taking the time to let her eyes adjust to the corner's shadows. In return, Dad considered her.

"Looks like you're doing all right, Star. All set up in the big city and raking it in from the billionaires. Your mom always said you'd go places."

Beth was in no mood to follow his lead. "Why are you here? Oh, no wait…" Beth pressed her fingertips against her forehead. "It's coming to me…Can't a man come see his own daughter once in a while? Where's the crime in that?" She lowered her hand. "Did I get it?"

The waitress brought his beer. "My angel of mercy." Dad grinned at her. She still wasn't quite buying it, but that didn't matter. She would, if Dad really wanted to sell.

He drank a solid slug of Budweiser. "You know, Star, you look like your mother now. You're getting up there, but you're holding your own. Sorry I missed seeing you in your twenties. Bet you were something else."

He was settling into his patter now, finding his rhythm and relishing the sound of his own voice.

"God, I remember the first time I saw your mother. I ever tell you that story? I was fresh outta high school and decided to bum around for a while. Worked my way across to Europe and down the coast. There's always something for a guy who knows boats, and I'd spent all those summers working for my father up in Marquette. I was in Greece and just in off a three-day run. I was hungry and horny and greasy. And there she was…" He paused, watching the sun-soaked vision form in his mind. "Sitting on the cobblestones in this faded sundress, dangling her feet over the edge of the pier, that cloud of dark hair shining in the sun. Then she turned to me and she just…smiled—Christ! That smile! It was like she already knew me. I remember thinking, *This is why people believe in past lives*."

The waitress stepped back up to the table with a massive bowl of chili, heaped with onion, shredded cheese, and tortilla chips. Somewhat to Beth's surprise, it actually smelled edible.

"Thank you, ma'am. This looks amazing." Todd favored her with yet another smile and raised the beer bottle. "And another one of these, if you would be so kind."

"Well…since you ask so nice."

Dad grinned and tucked into the chili like he hadn't eaten in a year.

"Anyway, so there I was, stinking like I'd slept in a sardine can, but I still walked right up to her, and said, 'You're with me now.' And she took my hand and said, 'I know.'" He sighed with satisfaction from the food and the beer but mostly from the story he'd spun. "Didn't even know her name. Didn't matter. We were together then and forever." He raised his bottle in a toast to the memory and drank off the last.

Beth waited until he'd set the bottle back down. "The last time you told me that story, you were in Spain. And you never lived in Marquette or anywhere else in Michigan. Your family's from Idaho, and your name isn't Todd any more than Mom's is Jeannie, so it wouldn't have mattered what you told each other."

Dad's charm, and his comfortable nostalgia for things he'd never done, cracked in two. "Where the hell did you get that?"

"Your birth name is Thomas James Jankowski," she said. "Mom is Deborah Ann Watts. You're from Boise. She's from that same patch of ground outside Springfield, Indiana, you two stole me out of. Which is most likely where you met and decided to run away together, probably to Dallas. You never actually got married."

The waitress brought over a fresh bottle of Bud and twisted off the top. "Fresh out of the fridge for you."

Dad smiled and sipped, like he was having the best afternoon of his life. "Beautiful," he said, making sure she knew he wasn't just talking about the beer. "Thank you."

She twinkled at him and left. As soon as she turned her back, Dad's smile fell away like he'd dropped it in the gutter.

"So what? All that stuff you said?" He scooped up another spoonful of chili and stuffed it into his mouth. "We're still your parents. We raised you, kept you fed…"

"Sometimes."

"Taught you right."

"Taught me how to shoplift and play lookout and distract assholes in bars and casinos."

"It wasn't all bad. We had some great times. Like when we were in Vegas and—"

"I remember you making me call Grammy so you could blackmail her. I remember picking up Mom after you beat the hell out of her…"

"Now, that you got wrong." He pointed his spoon at her. "She gave as good as she got. Those fights…that was just our way of blowin' off steam."

"Oh, don't you even *try* that bullshit on me."

Todd shrugged and swallowed another spoonful of chili. "Okay, fine, Star. Have it your way. I'm a fucking bastard. Doesn't change the fact that I'm your father, and you owe me for your bringing up."

"I don't owe you anything!"

"Oh, right," he sneered. "Because you got your fancy job with those billionaires all on your lonesome. Amazing. No school of hard knocks required for Star Bowen, thank you very much. Nobody taught you how to shovel the shit so fast there's not an asshole on the planet can keep up with you." Dad shoved his bowl away, leaned back, and folded his arms. "Just like how we never laughed together, never had a minute of good times. Never were tight as a family. Nope. Not us."

"So, you came all this way to tell me I should be grateful?"

"No. I came to tell you I need fifty thousand dollars."

Now we're getting somewhere. "What for?"

He met her gaze, his expression slowly melting from indignation into sadness. "For your mother, Star."

Beth waited.

"You been asking about her since you got in here. You want to know where she is? She's back at the motel in bed, stupid on pills with probably a fifth of vodka to help them along, because she can't deal with the pain anymore.

"Jeannie's got cancer, Star. She's dying."

CHAPTER TWELVE

When Dana asked Chelsea if she'd come to the coffee shop, her reaction was pretty one-note.

Do you have any clue how stupid this is?

It's not stupid. It's a public place. I'm bringing a friend. She could not let Chelsea know how scared she really was. *I'm just going to ask her some questions and see if she really is my grandmother.*

And if she is?

I'll figure that out later.

Will that be before or after your mom catches you? This isn't you being late for pre-calc. This is a meet-up with some random crazy lady!

Okay, so I'm about to be kidnapped and murdered. Are you going to be there to video the event or just leave me on my own?

If would serve you right if I did.

But Chelsea didn't leave her. They spent most of the

day watching videos and trying on outfits and taste-testing the cupcakes Dana had promised Kimi she was bringing to the party tonight. Chelsea left at about three thirty, looking grim.

"This is still effing stupid," she said on her way out the door. "And I shouldn't be enabling you."

Despite all that, when Dana walked into the Starbucks, Chelsea was already there—thumbing her phone in one of the square, brown armchairs right up front with her earbuds in.

Everybody's keeping promises today, thought Dana. Because the woman who had given her the photo was there too.

She sat far in the back, almost all the way to the emergency exit. Her thin hands wrapped around a small coffee, like she thought it would run away from her.

Their eyes met and the woman's face lit up, strained and hopeful. She gave a low wave, like she didn't want to call attention to herself. Dana noticed she didn't look quite as raggedy today. She wore a clean, black T-shirt, and she'd braided her hair. A few stray curls trailed against her long, crepey neck.

Dana stuffed her hand into her purse so her fingers curled around her phone.

I'm not being stupid. She threaded her way between the tables. *Nothing's going to happen. I'm not a little kid anymore. I just want to meet Mom's family. My family. That's* normal.

Maybe they'd both break down and there'd be hugs and ugly crying and babbled apologies. Or maybe Dana would end up calling the cops and finding out her grandparents were wanted in all fifty states. It didn't matter.

What mattered was that she'd know more than she did now, and this time, she'd be in the story instead of locked outside.

"Hi," the woman said when Dana reached her table. "I'm really, really glad you—"

Dana yanked out her phone and snapped a picture.

"I'm sending this to a friend of mine." She thumbed Chelsea's contact. "Also, you should know that if I don't check in every single day at exactly four thirty, my mom does an immediate and total freak-out."

The woman turned her coffee cup around a few times in her bony fingers. She had half a dozen sugar packets piled next to her on the table.

"She's just looking out for you. I get that. Especially cuz…well, cuz everything." She took a quick gulp.

Dana stared at her, trying to will some sense of recognition into being. But there was nothing—just a tired stranger who put way too much sugar in her coffee.

Which was what Mom did.

Which doesn't mean anything, Dana reminded herself.

Dana stared at the woman's hands, taking in how thin they were, how brown from the sun and spotted from age, but her nails were clean and perfectly polished. The veins ran and branched under her sagging skin, a road map to nowhere in particular. No hint of pink. No perspiration, and definitely nothing soft. Nothing like those other hands that tried to take her away.

Jesus. Relax.

But she couldn't.

"So," said the woman. "Dana Fraser."

"So…" Dana stopped. "What's your name?"

The woman gave a little, awkward laugh. "Your mom didn't even tell you that much? Christ. She must really hate us. Not that I blame her."

Dana didn't answer.

"It's okay. I'm Jeannie Bowen. You can call me Jeannie." She held out her thin, tanned hand.

Shit. Disappointment crashed down. "And we're done here." *Can't believe I fell for this!*

"What? Oh shit—wait. What's the…" The woman grabbed at Dana's arm. Panic surged and Dana struck down, knocking the hand away hard.

Heads turned. Eyes lifted from phones and laptops. Chelsea was on her feet, yanking out her earbuds.

"I'm sorry!" The woman, Jeannie, held both hands up. *See? They're empty.* "My mistake! I'm sorry!"

Dana swallowed, trying to get her breathing back under control. *Cut it out, cut it out, nothing happened.*

"Which name did she give you?" the woman asked very gently. "Cathy Hale? Teresa Sullivan? Casey Yost?" She paused. "Debbie Watts?"

Dana hesitated, and the woman nodded. "Yeah. Okay. That's my given name—Deborah Ann Watts. But I haven't gone by that since I was maybe nineteen. When you live under the radar, you have to change things up a lot, and well…anyway. Mostly I'm Jeannie Bowen now, except on your mother's birth certificate. That's still Debbie Watts."

Dana swallowed her breath. "And you're now going to pull that certificate out?"

She shook her head. "No, that's long gone. There's a

copy somewhere in Maricopa County, probably. It's true, though. I was born Deborah Watts. My mother was Elizabeth Watts, and my father was some kid who got drunk at a high school football game and wouldn't take no for an answer. We lived in a trailer outside a small town in Indiana. When I was seventeen, I met Todd Bowen and ran away from home and didn't go back until after I had your mother."

Dana glanced toward Chelsea, and Chelsea jerked her chin toward the door. Dana shook her head. Chelsea threw up both hands and dropped back into her chair, shoving her earbuds back in and thumbing her screen.

Slowly, Dana sat down at the table.

Jeannie pulled the lid off her cup. "That was really smart, bringing somebody with you." She picked up one of the six packets on the table and tore it open, pouring the long white stream of sugar into what was left of the coffee.

Dana shrugged and turned her phone over in her fingers. "Mom told me she lived with her grandmother until she was, like, five or something."

"Yeah." Jeannie held the cup in both hands like she was trying to draw some leftover warmth out of the cardboard. "Right after she was born, me and Todd—your grandfather—we were going through a bad patch, and we needed money. I thought, you know, my mother would be ready to help, because of the baby. But instead, she threatened me. Said she'd get me declared unfit if I didn't leave Todd and come home. She always was a hard-assed old bitch. Sorry. Anyway, in the end, my mother gave me a thousand dollars to go away, and I gave her your mother."

She was talking to the bottom of her cup. "I thought I needed the money more than I needed my daughter."

"But you did go back," Dana said softly, so the woman—Jeannie—wouldn't hear how her voice shook. "You took her away again."

Mom had only told her about it once. Dana was nine and having some kind of relapse. She couldn't stop crying, and she couldn't go outside without screaming. When Mom forced her to go to school, Dana hit the teacher and the nurse just so she'd get sent home again.

So Mom got her another therapist and sat curled up with her on the sofa for hours, holding her close. She helped make Dana's bed into a blanket fort so the room wouldn't feel so big when she was trying to go to sleep.

And one time, Mom took Dana's face between her hands and whispered.

It wasn't your fault, Dana. It's easy—so very, very easy—to just go with someone when they tell you to. When my parents came for me, I was barely five, and after an hour—seriously, one hour—I was ready to go away with them forever just because they gave me Oreos.

"She was my daughter," said Jeannie. "*Mine.* She belonged with me. So, yes, I went and got her. Just as soon as I could."

"But then you dumped her again."

Jeannie sighed. "Going straight for the jugular? I'd hoped maybe we could start with, How are you? Or, Was it a long drive? Or, Do you like sweet potato fries? Stuff like that." She smiled hopefully, and for some reason, Dana's temper snapped.

"Look, are we doing this or aren't we? Because I have to get home." Being angry was easier than being scared and confused. Because the story she was hearing was not the story she'd pieced together for herself. It sure as hell wasn't the one Mom told her. And whether she should or not, Dana was starting to believe it.

Plus, she really did have to watch the time. Mom kept a phone tracker on her, and if she decided to check it, she would not be happy to find Dana in the coffee shop instead of locked up safe and sound like she was supposed to be.

Dana's phone buzzed. She flipped it over. A message from Chelsea flashed onto the screen.

What's going on? You done yet? 😕

Dana shoved the phone back in her purse.

Jeannie looked out the window for a long moment, making up her mind. "Okay. We play this your way. Your mother was with us from when she was about five to when she was about fifteen, when we split up. Why? It's complicated."

"Mom said you guys were…" Dana couldn't make herself say it.

"Con artists?" Jeannie suggested. "Scammers? Criminals?"

"Serial cheats."

"Huh." Jeannie scratched her cheek with one perfectly clean, perfectly polished nail. "That's a good one. Well, she's right. We were." She paused. "Of course, she was too."

CHAPTER THIRTEEN

Jeannie's got cancer, Star.

Beth had imagined a thousand different ways her parents' demand for money would finally come down. But never this—Todd Bowen, alone, telling her Jeannie was sick.

Beth lifted her hand and pressed her thumb and forefinger together, rubbing the tips slowly back and forth.

"It's the world's smallest violin, Dad, playing just for you and Mom."

Todd sighed, tired and wounded. "Star…"

Beth shook her head. "Nuh-uh. You do not get to pull this one on me. How many times did I hear you trot out some imaginary dead relative for the suckers? How many times did you remind me that if I got caught, I should tell store security that my mother was sick and I just wanted to get her something to make her feel better?"

"Yeah, of course I forgot about all that," he said flatly.

"You think I'd pick this story if I had any choice? Like I didn't know you'd laugh in my face?" He took her hand. Beth froze. That touch was so familiar—at once so loved and so hated. "But it is true, and we need you, Star. We always have, but now...now it's all different."

Beth wanted to pull away from him, but visceral memory pinned down nerve and soul. She was in a motel room, in a diner, in the back seat of the car in the parking lot. Her father held her hand, just like this. He talked quietly to her, just like this. He told her how it was and how it was going to be. The little girl she had been listened, and she grabbed onto the certainty in her father's words—eager for it and sick of it at the same time. Not that her feelings mattered. What mattered was that she pay strict attention to every word. He was telling her what she had to be. She had to forget what she'd seen or felt or thought even just a minute before. Whatever he was saying right now, that was real, and she had to get it right.

"I know it's a lot to take in," he said, so gently. "I knew you wouldn't want to believe it, especially after all those other times. Maybe it's karma, you know? The universe is letting me know how all the suckers felt. I don't know. I just know that it's true and it's happening. I wish to God it wasn't."

A soft ache rose inside Beth, tempted by the regret and compassion in his voice, just like it always had been. Her father saw it, and he smiled.

"Hey, you still got that scar?" Todd turned her hand over and ran one finger up the inside of her forearm. "Yep. There it is." He brushed the mottled patch of pink-and-white skin right below her elbow. "God, I'm never going to forget that. The bone tore right through the skin, and all that blood. You never forget the sight of your child's blood, dripping down." Lightly, lovingly, he traced the path that blood had taken as it flowed across her skin. "I was almost sick right there. It was like it was happening to me."

Believe him, believe him! screamed the little girl inside her. *You have to.*

"You pushed me down those stairs."

"Oh, come on, Star." He squeezed her hand, gently, gently. "You know that's not how it was. You were trying to run away. I was trying to catch you. You slipped."

Believe those calm, blue eyes. That sweet voice. It doesn't matter what you really did or what he really did. This is good. Make this last as long as you can.

"You shouldn't have tried to run, Star. If you'd just stayed, nothing would have happened."

Believe because everyone will say it's your fault. You didn't leave. You didn't tell anyone. You stayed and you helped. You wanted him—them—to love you. It's your fault because you wanted your bad, bad parents to love you, even just once.

"All that blood," he whispered again. "It broke my heart to see you hurt so bad. I bawled my eyes out the whole time they were putting the cast on you."

He let her go, slowly. It took everything Beth had not to jerk her arm back.

"But that's all in the past, isn't it?" He graced her with one of his best smiles. "How about we leave it there? Time for a fresh start for the whole Bowen family. In fact, it's our last chance."

Believe him, because no one will believe you.

"How...how long has she been sick?"

Dad shrugged. "Who knows? She doesn't talk to me anymore. She barely even looks at me. It's killing me, Star. She's the only person I could ever really trust, and she's in so much pain...and I can't help her!"

Tears—real tears—shone in Todd's eyes. He scrubbed at them.

"Please, Star. You know how hard this is. If it was just me, I would have said adios and go get 'em, tiger. But this is about your mother. She needs a doctor and some decent meds so she's not screaming half the night. I need you to try—just try—to remember we are your parents. I mean, isn't that what you'd want your daughter to do, if it was you?"

Say yes. Do what he wants. It's quicker that way. Don't run. Don't try...

"Okay." Beth's throat felt thick with fear and all that ancient, calcified need. She swallowed. "Let's go."

"Go?" Dad frowned. "Where?"

Beth shrugged. "Wherever you're staying. You just told me my mother's dying of cancer. Practically bedridden, you said. I want to see her. I'll get us a Lyft." She brought out her phone. "Where are you staying again?"

Todd hesitated. Beth watched him and felt a slow, warm triumph stretch underneath all the different layers of fear. Beth tried to will her heartbeat to slow. She needed to stay in control and show only the feeling that matched her words.

"I'm not sure she's going to want to see you, Star." Dad picked up his spoon and rooted around in the depths of his chili bowl. "She's pretty messed up. You know how she hates anyone to see her when…."

"But this is different," said Beth. "If she's really sick, I need to be there. I can't just hand you some money and say go away, can I? What kind of daughter would I be if I did that?"

"Okay," Todd said finally. "I didn't think you'd want to, but okay. Can you give me that phone? I want to call, make sure she's awake and let her know you're coming back with me." He paused. "Actually, she might even be happy about that. She's missed you, you know."

Dad extended his hand for her phone. Beth hesitated. Probably the two of them had already agreed that if he called, Jeannie would hightail it back to whatever cheap motel or temporary rental dive they were staying at, so Beth would find her lying in bed, just like she was supposed to be.

The screen flashed on, displaying the alert for a new text. Beth checked the time reflexively. Only four o'clock.

Message from Chelsea.

You need to be here, it said. And there was a photo with it. Clearly taken at a Starbucks. It showed a woman sitting at a table with her hands wrapped around a coffee cup.

Anger burned, hot and dazzlingly bright, turning fear to ashes and then to hate.

"On the other hand, Dad, we don't need to bother. I know where Mom is."

"The fuck?" Todd frowned. "Star, what are you—"

Beth didn't wait for him to finish. She just grabbed her purse and ran for the door.

When she reached it, she looked back, but just like last time, Todd was already gone.

CHAPTER FOURTEEN

"How can you say Mom was a criminal?" Dana demanded. "She was *five*!"

"Four and three-quarters." Jeannie scrabbled at her empty coffee cup with her perfect nails, turning and rattling it. Dana suddenly wanted to reach across the stupid little table and snatch the cup away. "She was very clear about that, and how she was going to kindergarten as soon as we were done 'traveling.' She looked forward to that for a long time," Jeannie added softly. "Anyway. Yes, she was five, and then she grew up, and she helped her family out. A lot. She was sharp as a tack, and she could put on this totally innocent little face. Nobody who saw her believed she'd do anything wrong, at least not on purpose."

Sometimes, Dana felt like she could sense the difference in her own eyes, especially when she got mad. The brown one burned hotter. The green one saw sharper. She felt it now—a contained energy simmering inside her as she glared at this woman and all her stories.

Jeannie stared right back—calm, a little tired, but ready to be patient.

That was when Dana saw it.

She didn't guess at it or hope for it. She saw the shape of Mom's face on this other woman. She saw the stiff way Mom held herself sometimes when she was trying not to let Dana know she was mad.

She was telling the truth. This woman who called herself Jeannie Bowen was Deborah Ann Watts. Dana's grandmother.

All at once, that sickening, familiar off-balance feeling hit her, the same one she had when she'd sat all buckled into her father's car, listening to him explain how it would be too difficult to tell his kids she was their sister.

Because Mom must have known about how often and how easily Jeannie changed her name, but she never said that. She only told Dana about the one name—and it just happened to be the name that was least likely to have an internet trail.

Dana shoved her hands under the table and clamped them between her knees. She did not want Jeannie—Grandma Jeannie—to see how bad she was shaking.

But just like with Mom, it didn't do any good.

"You okay, Dana? I know this is a lot—"

Dana didn't let her finish. "So, you're saying Mom did what, exactly? She shoplifted?" She hoped she sounded blasé, but there was no way to tell.

Jeannie shrugged. "Lifted, carried, kept a lookout—

whatever we needed. She wanted to do her part for the family. And Christ, did she love it when she helped with a big score. Lit up like a Christmas tree."

Jeannie stopped again, as if she just noticed what she was saying and who she was talking to. "She was little, Dana," she said quickly. "When you're a little kid, you only know about right and wrong because of what people tell you, and her dad told her—we told her—it was all okay."

Dana looked around her. Everything was...normal. People typed on laptops and phones. The baristas called out names and orders. The air smelled like coffee and sugar. Nobody else was getting their mind blown. Nobody even noticed.

Except Chelsea, of course. Chelsea was glaring at her and seriously pissed off. Dana could tell that she was not going to hang around for much longer.

Dana looked at her phone. It was already 4:15. She needed to be done, in case Mom checked up on her or came home early. And by the time Mom did come home, Dana needed to be done feeling this—whatever the hell this weird mix of confused and scared and hopeful and sick all at once was—because Mom would see something was wrong in a hot second.

"Dana, I mean it." Jeannie ducked her head, trying to catch Dana's eye. "Nothing that happened was your mom's fault or her idea. It was just the way things were."

"You still haven't told me why you ran out on her."

Jeannie sighed. "Okay, okay. It's not...it's not pretty, all right? By the time she came along, me and Todd—your grandfather—we'd been living off the books for years.

When we were young, it was a whole big rebel-rebel thing. We wasn't gonna be no slaves to 'da man'!" She flipped both middle fingers up. "But after a while…we just didn't know how else to live. So, we hustled, whatever and however we could. And when you live like that, eventually you get into some heavy shit."

"Like what? Drugs or something?"

"Well, pills anyway. You know this whole 'opioid crisis' thing?" Jeannie made the air quotes. "It was just cranking into high gear back then. So, what Todd and I did was drive around to different clinics in different small towns, mostly down around southern Tennessee and Georgia, sometimes up as far as Kentucky or over to Pennsylvania. Anyway, when we found the right kind of clinic, we'd go in and tell them about this pain or that. They'd fill out some paperwork and hand over the pills. Then we'd take the pills and sell them to people in places where the local pharmacist maybe wasn't quite so flexible."

Dana didn't know what to say. She flashed on a memory of Chelsea's half brother and his scuzzy bandmates. They had this buddy named Ashton. He looked like he'd just walked out of a Lands' End catalogue and carried a whole backpack stuffed full of these little baggies. She remembered the band gathering around, typing in payments on their phones, or yanking wads of cash out of their jeans and practically drooling as he tossed them the pills.

One time Ashton walked up to her and dangled a baggie full of pink and yellow capsules in front of her face. *Take as many as you want.* He laughed. *Then we can all have some fun.*

He stopped laughing when Dana stuffed the whole thing into the garbage disposal. Then, he came after her. That was when they all found out Chelsea had been telling the truth about the shank she'd made from a glass nail file.

"It was a lousy way to make a living," Jeannie said. "I hated it. Hustling the losers and playing cards wasn't great, but it was better than, well, that. But Todd…you know, he pointed out it was steady money. We could finally stay put and even get a real apartment in a nice town. Abrahamsville. It had white picket fences and, like, seven different churches and all that small-town stuff. Star—Beth—your mom…she could stay in school. So, you know, I kinda stopped arguing.

"It was good for a while," Jeannie said. "For a long while, actually. But then Todd did what he does and screwed up somebody else's operation. And when Todd wouldn't pay…this guy—he threatened your mother."

Memories flashed through Dana. She remembered Mom's voice—hard and sad and bitter—but she couldn't hear the words. *Why can't I hear?* She remembered the pain in her head, and sitting up, and seeing Mom kicking the pink-hands man like she was never going to stop. None of it had anything to do with what Jeannie was telling her, but it was all there just the same.

"We didn't know what to do," Jeannie said. "It wasn't like we could tell the cops or anything. So, we sent Star back to her grandmother's and went on the run. We were going to go back and get her. I swear to God we were, but we couldn't. It just about destroyed me. I curled up into a ball and cried for hours. But this guy…if he'd found her, he would have killed her. Staying away was the only way to protect her. I thought she understood. I…"

Jeannie swallowed hard. Her eyes glistened.

A phone started ringing, loud and jagged.

Jeannie wiped at her face. "Anyway, the thing was, we'd been on the road so long we didn't know my mother was dead. So, your mom probably thought we'd just packed her off back to an empty trailer with no way to get hold of us."

That phone was still ringing. Dana realized the noise was coming from Jeannie's side of the table.

"It was all so screwed up…and…well, I told myself she'd be better off on her own." Jeannie's smile was thin and bitter. "Looks like I was right."

The phone was still ringing.

"Are you gonna get that?" Dana asked, which was way easier than thinking about anything she'd just heard.

"I know who it is." But Jeannie pulled the tiny no-brand flip phone out of her pocket anyway. "And I was right," she said, but she frowned at whatever she saw on the screen.

"Everything okay?"

"Oh, I'm just not where I'm supposed to be. Like you, I bet."

Dana didn't answer.

"I'm not blaming you or anything. I can just imagine what your mother would say if she knew…All the same, I was hoping…"

"What?"

"I really was hoping you'd talk to her for me. Tell her I'm here and—"

Dana cut her off. "Why are you here? Why now?"

"I wanted to make peace, or at least say I'm sorry."

"What about your...my..."

"Your grandfather? Yeah, well, he's still pretty angry."

"What's he got to be angry about?"

"You have to understand about Todd...Family is absolutely everything to him." The phone was ringing again, but Jeannie kept talking. "And because he cares so much, he has a tough time thinking clearly about it. The way he sees it, your Mom should have waited for us, or she should have tried to find us. When she didn't...he swore he'd never forgive her."

The ringing finally stopped. "So, is that him?" Dana nodded toward Jeannie's phone.

"Yeah. It is." Jeannie didn't even bother to check the screen. "Listen, I'm out of time. If you do figure out how to tell your mom about us, tell her that I just want to talk to her, like we're talking right now. Maybe we can...come together. As a family, I mean. And even if we can't, at least we tried, right?" Her smile was shy. She desperately wanted Dana to agree.

And Dana wanted to. She was surprised how much. She wanted just one thing about this whole conversation to be simple. But it wasn't. "I've got one question."

"Make it quick. I need..." Jeannie bit her lip. "Well, make it quick."

"Why'd you stay Jeannie Bowen? You said you mostly did. If you were in that much trouble, why not hide better?"

Jeannie's perfectly kept hands clenched into fists.

"Because," she whispered. "I wanted to be sure if your mom ever did want to find me again, she could."

Dana swallowed around all the feeling welling up in her throat. She couldn't have said anything even if she knew what she should say. She reached toward Jeannie.

But Jeannie didn't notice. She was looking over Dana's shoulder, toward the windows.

"Shit."

Dana twisted around. On the sidewalk outside, a tanned, aging man in a plaid shirt and Cubs cap squinted through the glass.

Jeannie was on her feet. "Just stay in here until we're gone, okay, Dana? And please, if you can only tell your mom just one thing, tell her...I'm trying to leave him."

Before Dana could say anything, Jeannie was pushing past the tables toward the door. Dana scrambled out of her chair, trying to follow, but Chelsea got in her way.

"What the hell?" Chelsea demanded. Over her shoulder, Dana saw Jeannie push through the door. Right away, the man in the plaid shirt started yelling. Jeannie held up both hands, answering back, trying to calm him down.

He grabbed Jeannie by the arm.

Dana dodged around Chelsea and bolted for the door.

CHAPTER FIFTEEN

Beth was still in the cab when four thirty came. She yanked her phone out of her purse.

No text from Dana. Nothing at all.

She hit the number on speed dial and pressed the phone tight against her ear. It rang, and it kept on ringing.

"Where are you, Dana?" She gripped the door handle, the cracked vinyl turning instantly damp and sticky under her palm. "Where are you?"

She desperately wished for the traffic to clear and for the cab to go faster, to *be* home. All the things Jeannie and Todd could do, would do, had done poured through her mind. Except this time, the girl trapped in those jumbled nightmares and memories was Dana.

Dana going hungry. Dana sliding shoplifted junk under her jacket. Dana pouring out tears and babbling at security guards or men in the bars while her father got away.

Dana with the shotgun in her hands while the old man stared at her, suddenly so pathetic and so very confused.

The cab swung around the corner to the shouts of a pedestrian and a blaring horn.

"This is close enough." Beth shoved two twenties into the taxi's cash slot and scrambled out into the street.

But she was too late. There was Todd. He'd beaten her here—to her block, practically her building. While she'd been running down the sidewalk frantically flagging down a cab, he'd had a car waiting. He'd known just where he needed to be.

Now he was screaming at a thin woman in front of him who cringed and put both hands up, pleading for calm.

Recognition slammed adrenaline through Beth.

That was her mother, backing away from her father.

Beth barged across the street, ignoring the traffic and the frustrated horn blasts.

Because there was Dana, ducking out of the coffee shop with Chelsea right behind her.

Stop her. Save her.

Stop Dana before they caught her. Save her from the sick, heavy storm of the past.

Beth was within earshot of her father's ranting now.

"What are you even doing here?!" Todd roared. People hurried past, but people also gathered in the Starbucks window and pulled out their phones. "You said you were too sick to move!"

"I was. But, you know, I started feeling better and…"

"And you lied to me! I'm out there practically on my knees trying to get her to believe you're sick so she'll finally give us some help, and you were lying to me the whole time!"

"Stop it!" screamed Dana.

In that same instant, Beth reached her. She grabbed Dana's shoulders and yanked her backward. Dana shrieked and spun, then saw who it was.

Beth stared into Dana's outraged eyes.

"No! I wasn't lying. I…It was just today!" cried Jeannie. Her voice shook.

Jesus, Jesus—she sounds just the same.

Dana pulled out of Beth's hands, spinning back toward her grandparents.

"She's our granddaughter!" pleaded Jeannie. "I just wanted to talk to her, and you wouldn't…what was I supposed to do? I swear I didn't ever want to lie to you, but I had to—"

Todd hit her.

It was like lightning—the blur of motion, the sick, familiar sound of fist against bone and a sudden scream. In an eyeblink, Jeannie was on her back. Her skull cracked hard against the sidewalk.

Dana screamed and dropped to her knees beside her grandmother. More people on the sidewalk stopped. More phones came out—people held them up to record the event, or held them to their ears to call 911.

Todd saw the phones, and his face went dead white. He looked across his wife's body at Beth. "Swear to God, Star. I had no idea what she was doing. Everything I said to you was the truth."

"Fuck you!" screamed Dana. Todd stared at her, disgusted, exhausted.

Jeannie struggled to push herself upright. A thin thread of blood trickled down the side of her face. Dana wrapped her arms around Jeannie's shoulders, trying to support her or maybe hold her in place. Beth couldn't tell.

"Get up," Todd said to Jeannie. "We're outta here."

But it was Dana who moved. She rose slowly from her crouch. Green and brown eyes both glittered. There was no more time. Beth needed to move now. Because Dana didn't know how these two had staged public fights before. They used them the same way they used the stories of illness, poverty, and death. Because Beth had no time to explain that now.

Because Dana's expression promised there'd be no forgiveness if Beth didn't intervene.

Todd sighed, exasperated. He grabbed Jeannie's arm. Jeannie shrieked as he yanked her to her feet. All the phone people gasped.

"Stop it!" Beth barged forward, getting right up into Todd's face. "Let her go! Right now!"

Beth pulled Jeannie back and away so that now she was between her parents. Inside, the little girl she used to be screamed, *Stop it! Stop it now!*

"Cops are on their way!" shouted somebody.

"You gonna wait for them?" Beth asked Todd. "Maybe hit me too?"

Dana moved past Beth to stand right beside Jeannie. Beth felt what was left of her heart crumble into dust.

"You leave her alone," Dana croaked at Todd.

Chelsea loomed at Dana's back. She had her hand in her pocket, gripping something. Dana grabbed hold of her friend's wrist, reassuring and warning.

Todd took in the gaggle of women trying to stand up to him, the crowds and the phones, all bearing witness to what he did next. Witness that could most definitely be used against him.

All at once, he grinned—sly and knowing.

"Okay, I get it, Star." He nodded. "This is your idea of payback for all that aw-poor-baby stuff when you were a kid. You think"—he snickered—"you really think you're going to take my wife away from me."

"I'm not taking her anywhere," said Beth. "But I'm not letting you beat on her while I'm watching. Not again." She glanced at Jeannie. "If you want to go with him, Mom, fine. That's your choice."

"Don't do it!" shouted someone from the crowd.

Jeannie's hand strayed to the blood trickling down her cheek. She turned her shadowed, exhausted gaze toward her husband. "I can't do this anymore."

Todd threw up both hands. "This is what I get!" he said to the crowd, to God in heaven, and to anybody else who might be listening. "When all I've ever done is take care of you! What happened to 'till death do us part'?"

Jeannie looked at her husband. She looked at Beth, Dana, and Chelsea.

"I'm not telling you again. We're *going*."

Jeannie shook her head.

"Fuck yeah!" a woman shouted. "Get the fuck outta here, douchebag! You're done!"

Todd ignored her. He stalked forward until he was so close Beth could feel his breath against her face, and then he leaned even closer. "I know what you're up to."

She could get both hands around his neck right now. She could strangle him. She could dig her nails into his lower lip, or his ear, or the loose flesh under his chin and yank and twist. She could make him scream. Make him beg.

It was this understanding that allowed Beth to keep still while he leaned over her, blowing his stale breath into her face. He smelled like chili, beer, sweat, and metallic anger. She remembered this smell and the feel of his heat against her skin. She remembered all the times as a little girl she had sobbed because he'd hit her too. And then she'd sob again because her mother would tell her she should not disrespect her father. *What did you do to make him so angry?* she'd ask. Her father loved her so much. He just got angry sometimes because that was how he showed he cared.

What's changed? Beth wondered. But she knew. Nothing had. Nothing could.

"You've been waiting for your chance this whole time, haven't you?" Todd whispered. "What did you promise her so she'd help you pull off this little scene? Money? Pills? A widdle home all cozy and bwight fow just us girls?" He made a kissy face.

"You. Will. Back. Off," said Beth. "Right now."

Todd held up both his hands, showing everyone they were empty.

"Nothing changes," he said as he walked calmly

backward. "We are still flesh and blood." He stabbed his finger past her shoulder, right at Jeannie. "All of us."

Todd turned and deliberately banged into one of the bystanders behind him. The guy reeled back. Todd walked away, vanishing around the corner.

Nobody followed.

PART TWO

TRUTH OR DARE

CHAPTER SIXTEEN

What just happened?

Dana had her arm around her grandmother's shoulders. Somebody was shaking. Dana couldn't tell if it was her or Jeannie. But she stared at Chelsea over Jeannie's head and knew her friend was thinking the exact same thing.

What the actual *fuck just happened?*

This bony, frightened woman was her grandmother—not the shadow Mom hid her from, but a real flesh-and-blood person.

*Flesh-and-*bleeding *person.* Dana jerked into motion. She dug into her purse and found a pack of Kleenex. She handed one to Jeannie.

"Thanks," Jeannie breathed and blotted at the cut. A bright-red blotch spread across her temple from where he'd hit her.

Mom was talking to the cops, or at least, she was talking to one cop. Another cop was surrounded by people who were all shoving phones at him so he could see the photos and videos they'd taken. The rest of the crowd drained away, most of them tweeting and texting as they went.

The cops had questioned Dana, of course. They asked how things started and what she'd seen. They also asked why she was at this particular coffee shop at this particular time, with this particular woman.

She had to tell them, with Mom listening to every word.

Mom took a card from one of the cops and tucked it into her purse. The cop said something into his shoulder radio and went over to join his partner with the crowd of wannabe court witnesses.

Finally, Mom walked back to stand with Dana and Chelsea. And Jeannie.

"Please don't be mad at her." Jeannie gripped Dana's hand. "She's a good kid. None of this is her fault."

"She just wanted to talk, Mom," said Dana. "I swear— that's all that was happening. She didn't…"

But Mom had already turned away. "Chelsea, please take Dana home." She pointed down the half-block to their building's entrance, as if Chelsea needed a reminder.

Chelsea didn't budge. "She's telling the truth, Ms. Fraser. I know I sent you the picture and everything—"

"You did *what*?!" shouted Dana. Chelsea ignored her.

"—but they were just talking. I was there the whole time. Look." Chelsea held up her phone. The grainy, off-kilter video showed Dana and Jeannie sitting at the table. It was too far away for the mic to have picked up their voices.

"Wait!" Dana grabbed her friend's wrist. "You *really* recorded us?!"

A MOTHER'S LIE

"What the hell was I supposed to do?" Chelsea jerked away and stuffed her phone in her jeans pocket. "We might have needed evidence!"

"I'm sorry," whispered Jeannie. She was shaking again. She hadn't been able to get all the blood off her face, and there were dark-red streaks smeared across her cheek and jawline.

"Let's get inside." Mom took Jeannie's hand out of Dana's and walked her across the street.

Dana faced Chelsea. Her friend shifted from foot to foot and thumbed her phone screen without really looking at it.

"I should probably go home," Chelsea said.

"Yeah," agreed Dana, but Chelsea didn't actually move.

"Do you want me to try to stay?"

Dana glanced over her shoulder. From here, she could see Mom was letting Jeannie push through the revolving door, but she was watching them. Even from here, Dana could feel the pressure of that look. "No. Go home. I'll be okay."

"Text me, Dana. Real soon. Let me know what's…"

"Yeah. I will." She had to move. Mom was waiting for her. "Don't tell anybody, okay? I don't know what—"

"Dana?" Mom called. "Let's go!"

Chelsea flashed Mom a thumbs-up.

"Do yourself a favor, Dana," she said quickly. "Do not try to fix this."

"What do you mean? It's my mom and my grand-mother!" *I've got a grandmother. She's real—she's there. Finally. I did that too. I…I'm found.*

119

"Yeah, she's your grandma. And that's all you know, and look how bad it is already. You want to kick over rocks to see what crawls out—that's one thing. You try and catch the things and put them back—that's going to make it way worse."

Chelsea was wrong, but there wasn't any time to argue.

"Hey!" Chelsea shook Dana's shoulder. "Are you gonna be okay? Cuz you do realize this is seriously fucked up. I mean, even by my standards."

Dana felt her mouth twist up tight and sour. "Yeah, thanks. I figured that out. Be careful, Chelsea," she said. "My...that guy might be hanging around." *Maybe watching. Maybe stalking.* Fear grabbed hold and squeezed.

But Chelsea grinned and pulled out the glass nail file she kept in her pocket. She'd spent weeks honing down the edge and the tip, following all the directions from the how-to on YouTube. It could get past a metal detector and was hard to see on an X-ray. Perfect for the girl on the go who might need to stab somebody. She'd even made Dana one just like it for her internship, in case any of the guys on the line decided to get grabby.

"Oh, I hope he's hanging around," Chelsea whispered. "I really, really hope."

She tossed her hair over her shoulder and headed back for the Starbucks. Dana was left to turn and walk toward her mother, her grandmother, and whatever was coming next.

CHAPTER SEVENTEEN

Beth followed her mother and her daughter across the building lobby. She watched Jeannie watch Dana swipe her card for the elevator. She watched both of them taking little glances over their shoulders at her, waiting to see what she'd do.

A vague memory flickered through her. It was a picture of a little man in a jail cell—from a comic book, maybe? A shadowy crowd of thugs loomed over the little man, chuckling about how he was now trapped with them.

You don't get it, the little man said. *I'm not locked in here with you. You're locked in here with me.*

Beth walked down the hallway to her own door (and watched Jeannie take note of the apartment number). Beth opened it before Dana could fish out her keys, and stood back to let them both walk inside.

She shoved the door shut. She wished it would slam, but

this was a high-end building and noises that might distress the neighbors were not permitted. She worked the locks, set the chain and the alarm. She knew without looking that Jeannie and Dana stood shoulder to shoulder behind her, waiting. Beth turned. She was right.

Jeannie rested her thin hand on Dana's shoulder.

The room went red.

You do not get to touch her. Beth curled her fist against her thigh. *You do not get to pretend you love her.*

"This isn't Jeannie's fault," Dana was saying. "This was me. I decided to go meet her."

Beth ignored this. There was no way Dana had decided anything, not without a lot of help. "Will you go to your room, please, Dana? I need to talk to...my mother privately."

Dana didn't move. "I've got a right to hear."

Beth's hold on her patience slipped. "No, actually, you don't."

Which, of course, gave Jeannie a perfect opportunity to play the victim. "This was a mistake. I should go. She's a good kid, St—Beth. Don't be too hard on her, okay?" She started for the door.

"No!" Dana put a hand on Jeannie's arm. "You're not going! Mom, you can't! She's hurt!"

From memory, Beth saw Grammy standing in her bedroom doorway, back in the rusted trailer—hard-eyed, exhausted, and hating the pretty lady who smiled so easily and hugged little Star so tightly.

That's me now. She's set the whole scenario up all over again.

And why shouldn't she? It had worked so very well then.

Beth sighed. "All right. All right. Why don't we just sit down?"

"Here, Grandma." Dana hurried to adjust the throw pillow on the chair-and-a-half. The invitation and the "Grandma" were her warning shots. Dana was already choosing sides. While "Grandma" settled back with a sigh of relief in Dana's favorite chair, Dana perched on the arm.

A united front. You already think I ought to forgive her for the things that happened before you were born. You're thinking, "Here's this hurt, sad, starving woman asking for nothing but a safe space to exist."

Jeannie pulled a Juul e-cigarette out of her pocket and took a hit.

"This isn't how I wanted things, Star. Beth," Jeannie amended. "I didn't plan on any of this." It was an old line, simple and highly polished from frequent use. "I thought I'd just meet my granddaughter, just once." Her voice grew thick with the threat of tears.

Beth took a deep breath. "Todd said you've got cancer."

"*What?!*" Dana shrieked. Jeannie just took another hit off the Juul.

"I do. Stomach cancer. Funny, I always thought it would be lungs."

And of course it's pure coincidence you got the kind that took out Grammy instead. After all, these things do run in families.

"Todd says you stay in bed with pain pills and vodka."

"This is one of my good days. I get them." She smiled, quick and tentative, not at Beth, but at Dana. Which only made sense. Dana was the one Jeannie had to make sure she won over.

"Why didn't you come straight to me?"

"Would you have believed me? Would you have even listened? Of course you wouldn't," Jeannie answered for her. "And I don't blame you." She fiddled with her Juul, turning it over in her fingers, sucking on it quickly, turning it over again. Dana watched her grandmother, openly worried and fascinated. From where she stood, Beth could only see Dana's brown eye. The light in it was soft, hopeful, and frightened all at once as she strained to understand what it meant that this woman was really here.

"I didn't even know he was planning on finding you," Jeannie continued. "He knew I'd try to stop him."

"So, what did he tell you?" Beth asked. She could not sound angry. Not even a little. Tired was okay. Bewildered was fine. But not angry.

"He said he was working on somebody who could get me into a clinic. A good one." She sucked on the Juul again, and for the first time, Beth saw the old, calcified bitterness shine in her bruised eye. "But that turned out to be another one of his lies."

Dana hugged her and held on tight. Beth had to look away.

When Dana finally let her go, Jeannie sniffed. Dana immediately pulled a Kleenex out of the box on the coffee table so her grandmother could wipe her nose and her eyes.

"J— Mom. Do you really want to leave Todd?" Beth knew she should not sound so incredulous. It was the wrong emotion to be showing her daughter now.

"Of course she does!" snapped Dana. "You were there! You saw what he did!"

How did Beth remind her that was nothing new? Todd had knocked his "wife" around for years, but Jeannie Bowen always stood by her man. She engineered the setups for his scams, ran interference with the clerks, or played the suckers who could be distracted by a pretty smile and a discreet brush of boob. Then, when he accused her of enjoying herself too much and decided she had to be reminded who was boss, she sat and took it.

The answer, of course, was that Beth couldn't. Love and pain bore down on her heart.

"You don't have to let me stay here. I won't ask that," Jeannie said. "But I don't want to...I don't want to die while he's out hustling another poker game or trying to walk out with the tip jar."

As a performance, it was Oscarworthy. It also gave Beth her opening.

Beth made herself lean back. She sighed. She let her eyes roam around the room, taking in the comfortable, eclectic details of the home she and Dana had made together. She counted to ten.

"Mom, if you're sick, if you're...trying to change, of course we'll help." Dana straightened and her eyes lit up. "But we have to be smart about this. Dad's already making threats, and he knows where you are. The first thing we have to do is start contacting the women's shelters and see which one's got room."

Jeannie stared at her. So did Dana.

"I know it's scary, but it's the best thing. We've got to

keep you safe." Beth walked over and crouched down so that her gaze was level with Jeannie's. This close, she could clearly see how the red smear around Jeannie's right eye was already darkening. It'd be a black bruise by morning. "First thing Monday, I'll get my lawyer to work on a restraining order. And once that's in place…well, we can figure out what's next."

She looked directly into Jeannie's eyes and made herself smile, just a little. *Check it out, Jeannie. This is what calling a bluff looks like.*

"But, Mom, you know, we've got the guest room," said Dana. "And building security…"

"Yeah, I know, Dana. I also know how good Todd is at talking his way past people. Mom needs someplace where she can stay anonymous until we get that restraining order." She steeled herself and covered her mother's hand with her own. "At a shelter, they'll be ready for his kind of act, and they'll be able to get you into counseling and help sign you up for insurance and disability and all that. You're going to need it all to get on your feet."

Sorry, Mom. Beth lifted her hand and tentatively touched the bruise. Jeannie winced. So did Dana. *This is as far into my home as you get.*

Jeannie raised her Juul to her mouth but did not take the hit. She just ran the corner of it along her chin, slow and thoughtful. Her eyes traveled up and down, taking in Beth's posture, her gaze, the color in her cheeks, the light in her eyes. She was looking for the tells, searching for the cracks and the fear.

Beth let her look.

It was too much for Dana. "But she can stay tonight," she prompted.

"Dana…" Beth began.

"Mom! She just got here! You can't! I want to…at least let me make dinner!"

"Dana." Jeannie spoke her name hard enough that Dana stopped, startled. "It's okay," she went on, more gently now. "Your mom's right. It's better if I go."

"Mom?" breathed Dana.

She could not let Jeannie sink back into the role of tragic victim being abandoned by her hard-hearted daughter. Beth hesitated, searching desperately for a reason that would work quickly and found none.

Instead, she stood up and made her voice turn brusque. "All right. It's probably for the best anyway. We'll need tonight to get things in motion. So. I'm going to call security and let them know about Todd. Dana, how about you get going on that dinner?"

"Um, sure, yeah." Dana slid off the chair arm. "Do you have any allergies, Jeannie? Are you vegetarian or anything?"

"No." Jeannie's smile was tolerant and might even have been real. "Nothing like that."

"Great. Because we've got, like, this whole ton of bacon."

"I love bacon."

Dana grinned and followed Beth into the kitchen. Beth put her hand on the landline but paused.

"So what were you and Chelsea talking about downstairs?"

"Oh." Dana pulled the fridge door open and ducked her

head and shoulders inside, very obviously trying to hide. "Um, nothing…"

The phone rang under Beth's hand. She frowned and picked up.

"Fraser residence," she said.

"Beth? Are you okay?" It was Rafael, his voice filled with deliberate calm. "You got some bad video going on the internet."

CHAPTER EIGHTEEN

"Apparently there's this video up on YouTube of you and…" Rafael paused. Computer keys clicked. "Are those your parents?"

"Yes." Beth retreated through the living room and out the balcony doors. The signal from the wireless handset would just about reach, and the traffic noise would help cover her voice. She did not want Jeannie or Dana hearing this. She should go into her study. But she couldn't make herself let Dana entirely out of her sight.

"Christ, Beth, why didn't you tell me they were back?" Rafael knew more about Beth's parents than anyone else. That had not been entirely her choice. There had been times back in their teenage years when she needed his help, and Rafael did not help anyone without knowing exactly what he was getting into.

"There was no time," she told him. Which was mostly true. "I just found out last night and then…this happened and…well, my mother is here now. She says she's sick and she wants to leave my father."

"Do you believe her?"

Beth could smell bacon and toast. Back inside the apartment, Jeannie had moved over to the breakfast bar and perched on one of the stools. Dana sliced a hunk of cheese off the brick she was grating and held it out.

"You need to eat," she said.

"I think that's supposed to be me who says that." Jeannie took the cheese and nibbled.

"Role reversal," Dana said solemnly. "All the cool kids are doing it."

"Beth, you there?" said Rafael into her ear.

"Yes. I'm here."

"I asked, Do you believe her? Your mother?"

"I don't know yet."

"Is Dana okay?"

"Mostly. I think so. I…" Beth clenched her fingers around the balcony rail. "Rafi, there's something else you need to know. Doug came to see me today too."

"It never rains, but it pours. What did he want?"

"He's made a stupid investment in some kind of vaporware, and…he promised them that he could get Lumination interested."

Rafi muttered a few well-honed Spanish curses. "I knew I never liked that guy."

"I'm going to need time to clear all this shit out."

"Yeah. I can see that. Do you think Zoe's ready to fill in for you?"

"She'll be amazing," Beth answered immediately.

"Okay. I'm going to have to get with the emergency communications team about this video and find out about Doug. I want us to have a strategy ready in case this thing blows up. What's the name of Doug's guys?"

She told him.

"Okay. I'll have our people see if we can find out who's behind this one. Be a good job for Zoe, actually."

"Thank you. I'm...I'm sorry, Rafi."

"This is not your fault. You just take care of you and Dana."

"I will."

"Are you going to be okay?"

"I'm going to have to be."

Beth hung up. From where she stood, she could see her mother's profile. She watched Jeannie's hands playing restlessly with the Juul, watched her eyes dart here and there to take in the details of the apartment—that is, when she wasn't staring at Dana like she wanted to swallow her whole.

Beth hit the speed dial for building security.

Fortunately, Mr. Verdes was still in his office. He listened to Beth's description of her father and of the danger he represented. She heard the keys clicking and the pencil scratching as he made his lists and notes. There would be an alert issued. He recommended she change her security code. He would issue new swipe cards to her and Dana, just in case. Someone would be bringing those up in just a few minutes.

Was there anything else he could do?

Unfortunately, there was not. Beth thanked him and hung

SARAH ZETTEL

up the phone. She went to the door and worked the keys on the alarm, deleting the old PIN and setting the new one.

You're locked in here with me.

"Dinner!" Dana called out behind her. Beth inhaled the rich scents of bacon, butter, and cheese and tried to feel something other than sick.

Then, she bent her mouth into a smile and went to the table.

Dinner was exhausting.

Dana went all in on the comfort food: grilled bacon, cheese, and tomato sandwiches with spiced sweet potato wedges she'd pulled out of the freezer. There was salad on the side so they could pretend they were being a little healthy, at least until they dug into the ice cream with caramel sauce for dessert.

Jeannie was absolutely in her element. She cracked wry little jokes and asked comfortable questions to draw Dana out. It all began as soon as the exclamations over how fantastic the food looked ended.

"So, tell me about you," Jeannie said around a bite of sandwich.

"Nothing to tell."

"Come on—humor me. We've got fifteen years to catch up on. Tell me...oh, I don't know. You got a boyfriend? Or a girlfriend? That one you were with at the coffee shop— she was cute, you know, in a tough-girl kinda way."

Dana laughed. "Listen to you, being all inclusive."

"Never too late to learn, right? So, come on—spill the tea."

So Dana talked. It started with the usual bare outline she trotted out for nosey grown-ups—how she wanted to be a chef, she was in the business program at school, and she had an internship lined up for the summer at the Vine and Horn. But under Jeannie's careful encouragement, Dana picked up steam until it was like she couldn't stop. She talked about Chelsea and her dysfunctional family, and all about school and what she hated and what she loved, and how boys were all pathetic and she really wanted to open her own restaurant one day, just like Gabrielle Hamilton did with Prune in New York, and how she was going to have her own Netflix show and travel around the world and eat and cook and see everything and…and…and…and…

…and Jeannie listened. She ate too—huge bites of sandwich halves and salad and sweet potato. But before each smiling bite, Jeannie steeled herself, just a little, like she wasn't sure she was going to be able to get this hot, rich food to stay down.

Dana didn't notice, but Beth did, even though she didn't want to. She did not want to have to entertain the possibility that Jeannie might really be sick. She wanted this woman strong and whole and playing all her old games (*because she is*). She did not want to have to challenge any old assumptions (*not assumptions, facts*).

Beth thought about the "go-bag" she kept underneath her bed. She thought about the car keys she kept in the kitchen junk drawer along with the paper clips, Scotch tape, and the old ball of kite string. She imagined waiting until her mother went to sleep. She would go to the private garage and reclaim the little Honda Fit she kept there, registered under a name that was not hers. She'd bring the fake IDs and birth certificates and cash she kept in her safe-deposit box. She'd wake Dana up, and they'd both just drive away. They could go to New York, or Dallas, or L.A. Disappear into the urban maze and start over.

Or, she could give bag, car, cash, and IDs to Jeannie and tell her to leave, now, before Beth went to the police.

In the morning, Beth could tell Dana her grandmother vanished. She would be able to honestly say she had no idea where Jeannie had gone, or if she'd ever be back. Dana would grieve, but she'd heal. Eventually.

Sometimes you had to hurt children to do what was best for them.

Finally, everybody had scooped the last dollop of caramel sauce out of their bowls and drained at least one mug of their preferred hot beverage. Beth started piling up the dishes to take to the sink.

"Lemme get this," said Jeannie.

"Nope. You're the guest."

"At least let me help."

Beth put the plates down and faced her. "You know what? You must be exhausted. How about I show you the guest room? There are spare pajamas and stuff."

Jeannie opened her mouth but saw the light in Beth's eyes and changed her mind.

"Thanks. I am kind of worn out."

Beth took her into the guest room. It was as colorful as the rest of the apartment and stocked with books and quilts and throws.

"Bathroom's through there," Beth said as she breezed over to the dresser and opened the middle drawer. "Pajamas and robe, here. I'm pretty sure there's a toothbrush." She went into the bathroom and pulled open the top drawer of the vanity. "Yep. Here we go."

Mostly, Beth kept the room ready in case Chelsea needed a place to stay on short notice, but there had been other people who'd needed it—friends fleeing bad relationships or needing a place to crash because a gig fell through. She'd never once imagined she'd be sheltering her mother here.

Beth handed her the toothbrush. She also took a moment to make sure Jeannie was looking right at her.

"You'll probably want to go straight to bed."

"Yeah, I probably will." No one could accuse Jeannie Bowen of being slow on the uptake. "I'm really tired."

"Sleep tight."

"You too."

Beth left her there. She closed the door and turned, and almost ran into Dana, standing in the hall and fidgeting.

Dana took a deep breath. Clearly, she'd been getting a speech ready, and she was going to get it out. Beth touched her hand to interrupt her and led her back into the front room.

"Okay." Beth faced her daughter. "Now."

Dana took another deep breath.

"Mom, I know this is hard for you. I know…I know there's all kinds of bad stuff between you. I do. I listened when you told me. Every time. And I do know, really, that she might…leave or go back to him or, you know, something shitty like that. But at least we can say we tried, right? And at least I, you know, got to meet her."

All Beth's words evaporated. All she could do was raise her arms, just a fraction of an inch. It was enough. Dana fell forward and Beth caught her.

"I love you," Beth whispered in her daughter's ear. "No matter what happens next, no matter what anyone tells you. I will always, always love you."

They stood like that, leaning together, holding onto each other tightly, not speaking, just feeling the strength and the nearness of each other.

For that one moment, that was enough too.

CHAPTER NINETEEN

Beth and Dana stayed beside each other the rest of the evening, mostly sharing the couch, mostly with Dana on her phone and Beth on her laptop. Dana had to fill Kimi in on why she wasn't at the year-end party, then talk to just about everybody who was there (or so it seemed). Beth had to start contacting women's shelters and lawyers.

It was almost eleven when Dana finally kissed her cheek.

"Love you too, Mom," she said. "No matter what."

Beth looked at her daughter, and she said it, the one universal lie every parent told. "Everything's going to be okay, Dangerface. I promise."

As soon as Dana retreated to her room, Beth closed her laptop. She thought about how her life had grown so tangled with people and relationships, and how all that might have to come undone now.

She felt sick. She tried to ignore it.

She didn't even consider going to bed. It would have

been pointless. She was not going to sleep. Instead, she went to her study and fired up her laptop again. There were accounts that had to be checked into, money that had to be ready to go, in case the worst happened.

It was almost midnight when Beth lit up her cell and called Zoe. Zoe picked up anyway.

"I wondered when you were going to get around to calling."

"Yeah, I was wondering about that too," Beth admitted.

"So." Cloth rustled. Beth pictured Zoe settling back for a long story. "What the hell was that video?"

"Goddamn YouTube," muttered Beth. "And 'that' was my dysfunctional family out in public."

There was a clicking noise, probably Zoe's fingernails drumming against a tabletop. "Well. Now I guess I know why you never talk about them. Does Rafael know about this?"

"Yeah, and he's going to be talking to you about that, and...some other stuff. Zoe, I'm going to be gone for a while. I need...I need you to watch Lumination for me."

"Watch how?"

"Do the real job. Keep them from stepping in the shit, whether they want to hear you or not. Make sure...make sure there's something for me to come back to." *If I'm coming back.*

"Beth, what's going on? This isn't just some family BS."

"That's exactly what it is," she answered. "And that's why it's this bad."

Zoe was silent for a long time. "Okay," she said. "Thanks for the heads-up." Zoe was not happy, but she understood you had to know the worst up front so you could figure the angles. If you waited, you'd get caught under the landslide. That was why Beth called her.

"And there's something else."

"Why am I not surprised?"

"I need your...special computer friends to get a look at my ex's bank accounts."

Beth had never told Rafi exactly why she wanted Zoe on her team so badly. It was because she recognized the look in Zoe's eyes. She was someone trying to claw out of the hole they'd been pounded into. She would not ever let appearances blind her. No pretty story would sway her when it wasn't backed by hard numbers and plenty of verifiable cash.

But she also knew about Zoe's connections in the "black hat" software community and maybe a few stories that Zoe herself hadn't gotten around to telling Rafi yet. That was okay. Everybody benefited from keeping a few secrets.

Maybe. Sometimes.

"I'd do it myself, but it's...super time critical, and I've got the distinct feeling he's doing something really, really stupid."

"That's nothing new from what you've said about him."

"Yeah, but this time, he wants me to bail him out. Me and Lumination."

"Ah. Okay. I think I know who to ask."

Beth gave her what details she had. "Be sure to kill your exes when you're done with them," she added.

"Why do you think there's a dirt floor in my basement?"

Beth felt a smile flicker across her face. "I am sorry

SARAH ZETTEL

about all this, Zoe. So, thank you for everything, and no matter what, you are going to be a rock star." She paused, very aware that what she was about to say amounted to good-bye. "Take care of Excelsior for me."

"Take care of yourself, Beth."

"Do my best."

They said good-bye and hung up. Beth planted her elbows on her desk and leaned her forehead on her hands. She hated bringing Zoe into this, but if something was going on—beyond Doug being an idiot and some random pyramid scheme floggers sensing an opportunity—she didn't want Zoe blindsided.

She told herself fixing up all her loose ends wasn't betraying Rafi. This was watching out for him. Which was exactly why he'd hired her in the first place.

When Rafi left Indiana, Beth never thought she'd see him again, and for four years she was right. Beth got her degree and a pile of student debt from the community college and was trying to figure out what in the hell she was actually going to do next, because it was turning out every even semidecent job required a background check.

Star Bowen had become Elizabeth Fraser by then, and Beth Fraser had no background, at least not one she could let anybody actually see.

Then, out of the blue, Rafi called.

Get your ass out here, Beth.

Where are you, even?

Silicon Valley, sister, and you an' me—we're gonna take this place over.

She didn't believe him, but she didn't have any other

plans. Plus, he paid for the plane ticket. He met her at the airport with a rental car, and he took her straight to a good diner and told her to order anything she wanted.

While she wolfed down a bacon burger and loaded Tater Tots that for some unfathomable reason had avocado on top of the melted cheese (so did the burger, for that matter), Rafi drank coffee with extra sugar and talked.

"We're going into venture capital, Beth—you and me."

"Do you even know what that is?"

"It's when very rich people give you money to spend on making businesses work, so they can make more money, so they can give you more money to make more money." She remembered how he spread his hands and grinned. "It's the circle of life."

"And just how are you going to get them to give you the money?"

"I'm gonna hire you."

She slurped her Coke at him.

"I'm serious, Beth. The people out here are nowhere near as smart as they're telling themselves. I need somebody who can figure out which ones are actually worth getting in with and which ones are just blowing smoke out their ass."

"Oh, is that all?"

"That's all, Beth. Come on, sister—you can't leave me alone out here."

The possibility scared the hell out of her. She'd wanted to leave the scams and the lies and the showboating behind. They led to nothing except blood and secrets and abandoning the people you were supposed to take care of.

But what else was she going to do?

She was never sure what got her to say yes. Maybe it was just looking at Rafi in his decent clothes. Maybe she was stoned on grease and avocado, or the realization she didn't even have enough money left for a bus ticket to L.A., never mind back to Indiana.

Maybe it was because what he really offered was a way to take charge of what had been done to her.

So, Beth let him introduce her to a friend with a couch she could sleep on, and they got to work. There was so much *money*, and so many people looking to give it away. The men with their thousand-dollar suits liked Rafi. They liked Beth, his steely eyed "assistant." They liked Lumination and the story behind it, most of which Beth had made up. It was every beer-fueled, pie-in-the-sky vision of stupid rich guys her father had ever trotted out.

That whole high-flying, high-pressure beauty of Northern California and its tightly cocooned money world brought her everything she'd ever been promised, and a little bit more.

Everything that she might now have to leave behind.

A door creaked.

Beth sat up a little straighter. She heard the soft whisper of feet against carpet and caught movement through the crack where her door was open just a little.

She stayed very still until it passed. She waited for the sound of the bathroom door, for running water or the flushing toilet. Nothing.

Beth got up and softly followed her mother out into the front room.

CHAPTER TWENTY

Jeannie didn't turn the lights on. She just trailed her fingers along the breakfast bar and paused to spin one stool. The streetlights filtered through the curtains, but it did nothing to soften the sharp angles of her silhouette.

Beth stood at the hallway junction, waiting for her mother to turn and see her.

Jeannie wore the plain, quilted bathrobe from the guest room dresser. Her feet were bare. She twirled something restlessly between her fingers. It took Beth a second to realize it was an unlit cigarette.

Beth tensed as her mother drifted to the front door and examined the alarm, the deadbolt, and the chain. But Jeannie didn't touch anything. She just stuck the cigarette between her lips and moved on to the living area. The cigarette bobbed up and down as she leaned closer to read the spines of the books on their shelves.

She was still looking at the bookcases, shaking her head

as she pulled something, probably a lighter, out of her pocket. But then she paused, her head up, as if listening. Beth shrank back instinctively. But Jeannie didn't turn— she just headed for the balcony. Maybe she realized there were no ashtrays, or that Beth (or Dana) might not like her smoking in the house. She found the lock and the security bar and pulled the door open, letting in a rush of warm city air and traffic noise.

All at once, Jeannie froze. She dropped into a crouch. The cigarette fell.

Beth ran forward before she could think. She grabbed Jeannie and pulled her backward and upright at the same time.

"He's here!" Jeannie twisted like she was trying to escape Beth's hold and beat her palm frantically against Beth's shoulder. "He's here!"

Beth peered past her mother to try to see between the bars of the balcony railing. She could just see the car parked across the street, right under the streetlight. A thin, familiar shadow leaned against the driver's side door, not even trying to hide. Smoke rose in pale spirals from the cigarette in his fingers.

Beth lunged past her mother and yanked her phone out of her pocket at the same time.

"No! Beth!"

Beth did not listen. She pressed herself right up against the balcony railing.

Across the street, her father lifted his head.

Beth held up the phone and flashed a picture. And another.

Dad pushed himself away from the car. He pitched his cigarette aside. Slowly, without any sign of concern, he raised his index finger and traced a wavering line down through the air in front of him. An answering shudder ran down the inside of Beth's arm, starting at the scar, reminding her how he'd touched her. Reminding her how easily he could make her bleed.

Todd climbed casually into the car and started the engine.

Beth flashed another picture as it drove away. She meant to check it right away, to see if she got the license plate, but she became aware of a low moaning behind her.

Jeannie huddled on the couch, her face pressed against her hands.

"He'll be back," Jeannie wailed. "He's not gonna stop." She lifted her face, and Beth saw her tears shining against her ashy skin. "He won't ever stop. Not until somebody's dead."

Beth stared at her, caught between simple, sour anger and a stirring of new feeling she did not want.

"I've screwed everything up," Jeannie whispered. "I should have never...He's gonna be so mad, Star. Beth. So mad. He'll come after you. Even if I go back now, he will, because he knows you helped me."

Beth stared down at her, trying desperately to pull herself back from the fragile sympathy unfurling inside.

Because it's a trap, same as always.

"I have to get out of here. I can't stay. I can't...he'll kill you. He'll kill Dana."

Jeannie teetered to her feet and stumbled to the door. She scrabbled at the chain and the lock.

It's not real, Beth told herself, even as she moved to her mother's side.

"Stop, Mom." Beth laid her hand on her mother's and felt how cold it was.

"I can't. He won't. Not until somebody's dead."

"I know."

Slowly, with stiff, jerking movements, Beth wrapped her arms around her mother's shoulders. She felt Jeannie's shoulder blades press against the pulse points on her wrists.

I remember.

She remembered wanting this and missing this—this press of this sinewy body, this scent, the prickle of Jeannie's wiry hair against her cheek—everything that came with the simple act of holding someone and being held. She was five. She was eight. She was ten. She was thirteen and fourteen, and she knew everything this woman was and knew a single moment changed nothing. But she still wanted her mother's embrace.

She'd told herself this need was a sickness, like an addiction. It was brainwashing and Stockholm syndrome and a dozen other mental pathologies. It was anything and everything, except love. It could not ever be love.

"It'll be okay, Mom," Beth whispered. "First thing to-morrow, we're getting you out of here. The Haven House shelter has room and—"

Jeannie stiffened. "I can't go there."

"You'll be safe. I know these people. A friend of mine does their fundraising. I was able to—"

"No. I can't." Jeannie was shaking, patting her pockets,

rummaging for a cigarette. "They'll shut me up and tell me all the things I can't do. Probably won't even let me smoke." She looked at her fingers, where the cigarette had been.

Beth refused to take the hint.

"They'll get you help. If you want to get away from Todd, you're going to have to start thinking about how you'll survive." She let those words sit. Jeannie stuffed her hand back into her pocket, and Beth watched her fist flex and curl.

"You're really going to hand me over to a bunch of strangers?" whispered Jeannie. "You owe me!"

Here we go. Beth felt the strange urge to smile. This was the woman she understood. Not the sad, broken creature she'd glimpsed a moment ago. This woman—she knew how to fight.

"I owe you?"

"Who do you think kept him away from you and your daughter for so long? Huh? That was me!" Jeannie beat her chest with her open palm. "Did you even once stop to think about that?"

"Honestly?" said Beth. "No."

Jeannie snorted, as if to say she'd known it all along. "You have no idea what it was like after you left us."

"I left you? Is that what we're calling it now?"

Jeannie ignored her.

"Everything went to hell," she croaked. "We were ripping off quickie marts. Stealing cartons of cigarettes and selling them as loosies. We got arrested twice." She swallowed. "I was whoring, Star." Her whisper was little more than a breath of air. "He'd bring me suckers he met in the bars, and I…" She shook her head. "He wouldn't even talk about things getting better anymore. None of those stories about how we were going to find a big score, no more saying it'll be better in the next town. Just…drifting.

"Every now and again he'd get a bug up his butt about you, and how we should find you and make you pay up. But I talked him down. Every time. I'd convince him you'd have fancy lawyers now, and how it was so much easier for cops to talk to each other with the internet and everything—you could just call them and maybe you wouldn't even care if we said…stuff about you, because you would have been able to pay to get it all fixed up."

She lifted her face, her eyes glittering. "Beth, I worked every day to keep him away from you and your daughter. For *years*, all so you'd have some kind of chance."

Do not believe her. You cannot believe her. She is lying to guilt-trip you. She is trying the story out on you before she tries it out on Dana.

There was a problem, though, because Beth really had wondered what kept them away for so long. The more money she made, the better her life became, the more often she wondered when they would come for her. They'd barely left Grammy alone for a minute, and she'd had nothing to give.

"So what changed, Mom?"

"Shit." Jeannie dropped onto the couch and yanked the lighter out, along with a whole pack of cigarettes. She didn't even bother looking at Beth. She just shoved one between her lips, lit it, and inhaled hard. She blew the smoke out at the ceiling. "The women—that's what changed."

"What?"

"He came home one night—well, came back. We were living out of the car. He had this wad of cash, and he told me to find a motel room and said he'd be back in a couple of days. So, I did, and he was back a week later, with more cash.

"I was worried he'd gotten into something heavy again, but he told me...he told me he met this woman in a bar. Called her Stacey. Said her boyfriend had just dumped her and she was really upset about it. She was pretty drunk. He helped her get home safe.

"I thought maybe he stole her purse or something. He said he'd planned to, but then he got a better idea. He tucked her up in bed and went out and got them breakfast and basically sweet-talked her. You know, like he does."

"Yeah, I know."

"Well, it worked. Eventually, he told her his car was impounded for a busted taillight and asked for a loan, and she was all ready to give it to him. He told me he had her on the hook hard, and he wanted to see where it would go. But, he said, she was looking for a boyfriend, so he was going to have to play the part."

"How is this new? Dad's always sweet-talking some-body."

She got abruptly to her feet and strode into the kitchen. "Yeah, well, he never *lived* with them before." Finally, the wounded, frightened facade had cracked. Finally, there was spite, and there was anger, and finally, it was real.

Jeannie took a long drag on her cigarette and then tapped ash into the sink. "He never fixed their cars or their houses or let them buy him clothes and stuff. None of them ever…had real money. Not like these bimbos."

"These?"

"Stacey was just the first. It became a regular thing." She ground out the cigarette in the sink and pulled the pack out again. "They'd get bored, or he would, or they'd catch on, or…whatever. And he'd just leave and find another one. He joked about the endless supply and what a gold mine the dating sites are. He even roped me into the act. He'd tell them I'm his *sister* and how he needs money for 'his sister's' chemo because he got laid off from his job because of his bad back." She waved a fresh cigarette vaguely in Beth's direction. "No, seriously—he said that."

Never change a game that works.

"So who are these women? What are their names?"

Jeannie shook her head and lit the new cigarette. She took another drag and exhaled more smoke. This time, her shakes eased, and so did some of the strain in her voice. "I only remember some of them. Stacey Walsh— she was the first, I told you." Her eyes narrowed. "There was a Felicity Brandt. Oh, and get this—Amanda Pace Martin. He loved saying that name. He thought it was just soooo classy."

"Sounds like it was a good racket," Beth said bluntly. "What was the problem?"

"He kept *talking* about them!" she shouted. "How pretty this one was, or how smart that one was. He'd go on and on about all the stuff they'd done with their lives. What had I done? Huh? We hooked up when I was seventeen! Seventeen! What have I done but stand by him and take care of him my entire goddamn life! And now that I was sick, and old and ugly...he was going to leave me." She stared at the cigarette and ground it out hard in the bottom of the sink. "I knew sooner or later he was going to leave me for one of *them*! So, I decided to leave him first."

Beth waited.

"Only I didn't have anywhere to go."

"So you came here."

"I tried to warn you. You were getting phone calls yesterday, right? At least two of those were me. But you didn't pick up, and Todd caught me with his phone and started asking questions. That's when I decided to wait outside your building."

"How'd you even know who Dana was?"

"She looks just like you." Jeannie paused, fidgeting. It was starting to sink in she might have showed Beth too much of the truth.

"I think maybe I ate too much," Jeannie said suddenly. "She's a really good cook, your girl."

Beth sighed. "I'll get you some Tums."

"Thanks." Jeanne climbed up onto one of the breakfast bar stools. Beth found the tablets in the medicine cabinet and brought them back. Jeannie popped an entire handful and chewed.

"Jesus, Mom."

"Yeah, well." She was rubbing her stomach again. "I told you. I'm sick. That's why I can't go..."

"No," said Beth firmly. "You are not staying here. Not while Dad is out there. I can't keep you and Dana safe!"

"But you've got security! You've got people! You…" She winced and pressed her hands against her stomach. "You've got everything, Star."

A choking noise tore at her throat. All at once, Jeannie doubled over. Beth thought she was starting to cry again, but that wasn't it.

"I hurt. Jesus. It hurts."

Looking for sympathy…doesn't want me to throw her out. Planning something. Beth stared, unable and unwilling to believe as her mother screwed her face up.

"I can't…I can't…it's hurting."

Jeannie all but toppled off the stool and stumbled to the sink. Without thinking, Beth ran to her side and shoved her hair back while she vomited up a stream of bile and filth.

I remember this too. Christ, I remember all of this…

Standing beside Jeannie in the hotel rooms, while she was on her knees over the toilet, or bent over the sink. Standing beside her in the alley or behind a dumpster in the parking lot. The days when there'd been too much booze, too much pain, too much…just too much.

Mom had not been back twenty-four hours yet, and here she was again.

Eventually, there was nothing left inside Jeannie but dry heaves. But she stayed bent over the sink, shuddering and gagging. When Jeannie did look up, she was white as death and snow. She looked confused, like she didn't know where she was anymore. But that was only for a single frantic heartbeat before she crumpled in on herself and fell.

Beth heard a gasp and a whimper. Her head jerked up. There was Dana, both hands pressed against her mouth, staring down at her grandmother, unconscious on her kitchen floor.

CHAPTER TWENTY-ONE

"Grandma?" Dana wrapped her hands around the gurney rail. "Grandma, we're here."

Jeannie didn't move.

It had taken forever to get in here. They couldn't ride in the ambulance and had to take a cab. When they finally got to the hospital, they had to wait in line at the desk to find out if Jeannie had arrived yet. Then they had to be checked in as visitors. Then, they had to wait to be walked back to the emergency room.

The emergency room was white-and-steel beds in alcoves framed by curtains. There was a babble of voices, and the sounds of confusion and pain, people in scrubs moving with purpose.

It smelled—lots of disinfectant and humans and all their problems. Jeannie was in bed 20, in the back corner. Somebody had dressed her in a hospital gown, tied in the front to allow access to her frail body. Dana could clearly see her sagging breasts and the incongruous, rounded lump of her stomach. The veins on her legs were thread-thin nests of black and blue. The branching veins on the backs of her hands ran up her arms to meet brown bruises that peeked out from under the gown's short, loose sleeves.

"Grandma?" said Dana again. Jeannie still didn't move.

Mom muttered something and grabbed a thin white blanket that had been left on one of the cabinets. She shook it out and Dana grabbed one side. Together, they covered Jeannie up, carefully moving her hand to try not to disturb the IV.

Eventually, people started bringing paperwork and questions. Mom filled out a crap ton of forms. And then everybody went away for a while. Then, a man came and introduced himself as Dr. Yasim and took Mom out past the curtains to talk.

When Mom came back, she stood by the bed railing and stared down at Jeannie.

"What are they saying?"

"Nothing." Mom bit the word off. "They're just asking questions right now. Oh, but she is showing signs of malnutrition. And...there are some signs consistent with a cancer diagnosis."

Mom pretty much stopped talking after that.

Don't die, Grandma. Dana twisted her hands. She couldn't keep them still. She needed to do something—watch something, or thumb or make or chop something. She couldn't just sit here.

Except that was all she could do, because there were signs on every wall about how you had to keep your phone turned off. So, all Dana had to do was listen to the ebb and flow of voices on the other side of the curtains and stare at Jeannie and think, *Don't die, don't die—please don't die.*

Either that or, *Do something. Do something, do something, do something.*

Finally, a white woman in scrubs with rainbow-colored hearts all over them pulled the curtain back and told them they had a room ready on the twenty-fifth floor.

That woman and an African-American man came and fussed with the gurney bed and the IV and rolled Jeannie away. Which left Dana and Mom nothing to do but gather up their stuff and try to navigate corridors and elevator banks up to the room.

When they finally got to the right hallway, Mom put a hand on her shoulder.

"You go on ahead. I need to talk to the nurse at the desk."

So Dana went on ahead, but when she found the room, she looked back over her shoulder. Mom stood at the reception desk, talking with a young, brown-skinned woman in dark-blue scrubs.

Mom was crying. Not ugly crying or anything, but she had a Kleenex clutched in her hand and dabbed at her eyes and her nose.

Dana watched numbly. *I don't get it.* Mom never cried.

The nurse took Mom's hand and said something. They stood like that for a minute, and then Mom walked briskly down the wide hallway.

The tears had stopped like she'd thrown a switch.

"What was that?" asked Dana.

"Getting the room phone hooked up." Mom brushed

past her. "And I wanted to try to make sure somebody's going to let me know if Todd makes a surprise visit."

The hospital room was quiet, dim, beige, and private. There was an abstract print on the wall, and a whiteboard with the date and the nurse and the doctor on duty written in blue marker. There was a tall cupboard, a vinyl recliner, and a window onto the sprawling network of parking lots. Dana could see the Skyway in the distance.

They had Jeannie on her back in the bed, wired up to…everything. The monitor beeped. She was frowning in her sleep, her face all clenched up tight.

Mom set the plastic bag with Jeannie's stuff down beside the narrow cupboard that was the room's closet. Then she turned away and dug into her purse. "Listen, Dangerface, did you see that café we passed in the lobby? Why don't you go get some breakfast? And I think the gift shop is open, or it should be soon. Can you go get y—your grandmother some things? Toothbrush, soap. Socks are good. Your feet are always cold in the hospital. Maybe they'll have some pajamas or something comfortable she can wear until we can get home and pack a proper bag for her."

"But I want to be here when she wakes up."

"I'm not going anywhere," said Mom. "I'm going to be right here." Why did that suddenly sound like a threat? Mom handed Dana some bills. "That should be enough."

"Can we have our phones on here? You'll text me if she wakes up, right?"

"Right away. Promise."

Dana took the money reluctantly. *I don't want to leave. I want to…I want to…*

What did she want? What did she think was actually going to happen if she left Mom and Grandma alone right now?

But Dana didn't know, and that was the problem.

When Dana stepped out of the elevator, the first thing she did was switch her phone back on. The signs said cell phone use was allowed in the lobby. There were a couple of messages. Kimi and Keesha sent pictures from the party she had missed, trying to share the fun. It was like she was looking at another life.

She shoved her phone in her pocket. She didn't want to think, and she definitely did not want to feel. She had a job to do. Jeannie needed stuff.

In the gift shop, Dana grabbed a handbasket and immediately found the aisle of travel-size soaps and toothpastes. Jeannie would probably like a brush better than a comb. There was a whole rack of socks. She picked two pairs: one with puppies and one with kittens. There were nightshirts. She got a pink one that said PRINCESS IN TRAINING. It looked happy and goofy.

She stopped in front of the rack of balloons. Maybe just one? She wanted to bring Jeannie something to eat, but the doctors might be putting her on a restricted diet or something, and if there were…stomach problems, she should probably wait and…

"Dana?"

"The fuck!" Dana jumped and spun.

It was Dad. Right behind her.

CHAPTER TWENTY-TWO

As soon as the door closed behind Dana, Beth collapsed into the room's vinyl recliner and squeezed her burning eyes shut. *I wish I weren't so tired. I wish I could think. I wish…*

If wishes were fishes, we'd all cast nets. That was Grammy, stomping across the dirt yard, with little Star trailing after her. Before this all started, before, before, before…

Stay awake, Beth. Beth blinked hard and knuckled her eyes. *You've got things to do before Dana gets back.*

She thought about her daughter downstairs, shopping for little things to make this woman comfortable. Fear was automatic. What if something happened? She shoved it aside. She needed Dana gone. She would be all right for fifteen minutes in a hospital lobby.

Beth made herself get out her phone and switch it back on. There were missed calls from Doug, all of which she ignored. Nothing from Rafi, or Zoe, or her father.

She pulled up James Kinseki's number. While it rang, she crossed to the doorway, so it would be at least a little less likely the sound of her voice would wake Jeannie up.

"What?"

"It's Beth Fraser, Mr. Kinseki."

"Yeah." She heard rustling and pictured him sitting up in bed. It was only eight thirty on a Sunday morning. They had been in the hospital since two a.m. "What can I do for you?"

"I need you to track down some names."

Kinseki sighed. "Yeah, okay. Hang on…" There was more rustling and then shuffling and a sound that might have been a drawer dragging open. "Okay. Shoot."

Beth dug down hard into her tired memory. "Amanda Pace Martin is probably the most recent. Felicia…no, Felicity. Felicity Brandt. And Stacey Walsh."

"You got anything to help me on this? A bunch of names isn't really enough to work with if I'm trying to find somebody."

"They all would live within a few hours of places my parents were staying over the past year, maybe two. And they are all women my father scammed."

"Well, that's new." Kinseki finally sounded like he was waking up.

"Yeah. And it might not be true. But I need to know, and I need to know right now."

"I'll see if I can turn up anything. No promises, and we are back on the meter."

"I understand."

Kinseki hung up and Beth hung up.

What now? What should I be doing?

She knew there was something. There had to be. But in the fog of her own exhaustion, all she could do was stare at the frail woman in the bed.

A cancer diagnosis would be consistent with some of the symptoms we're seeing. The doctor's words rose softly out of Beth's sleep-deprived brain.

It doesn't matter if it's true, she tried to tell herself. *It doesn't change anything. She is what she is. What she always has been.*

So why did Beth feel so suddenly, deeply sick? She curled her knees up to her chest. She should have been dancing in the streets. One of them would finally be dead and gone, and she didn't have to lift a finger. How long had she wanted this?

But not this way. And that was the clawing feeling that made no sense. She did not want to watch her mother really, finally failing. She did not want the awareness that Jeannie was weak and dependent and that there was no one left in her world, except Beth. Beth and Dana.

And Todd. Oh yes, Todd, always and forever.

He's not gonna stop. The memory of Jeannie's sobs rippled through her. *Not until somebody's dead.*

Something bothered Beth. Something about those sobs and the darkness and what she'd seen while her mother wandered around her home.

She stared out the window over the parking lot. She made herself see Jeannie's silhouette, with the cigarette bobbing in her mouth as she leaned forward to look at the books. See her reach into her pocket and pull out the lighter and hold it up and...

And did she hesitate? Like she heard something?

Did she know I was there?

Then Jeannie went to the balcony and saw Dad, and she dropped like she'd been shot. Or had she hesitated then too? Was that what bothered her?

Something…something…something…

Beth's phone beeped. It was Dana, texting to say she was getting breakfast in the café and did Beth want anything? She texted back a no.

She levered herself out of the chair and went over to the plastic bag of Jeannie's possessions. Moving carefully, Beth pulled the clothes out. She went through the bathrobe and sweatpants pockets and found the lighter, the cigarettes, an unmarked amber plastic bottle half-full of bicolored capsules. *Should tell the doctors.* She laid those aside.

She also found the flip phone.

It could just about fit in the palm of her hand. Beth tried to imagine how it would look in the dark.

In the dark it might—*maybe*—be mistaken for a cigarette lighter. In the dark, her mother could hide it in her bathrobe pocket and head out to the balcony, not to get a smoke, but to talk to Todd, who was waiting across the street.

The memory fit into the ragged places in her mind. But was it real? Or just what she wanted?

Beth heard rustling behind her. She slid the phone into her jeans pocket and turned.

Jeannie had opened her eyes. They were bloodshot and darted back and forth wildly.

"Shit," she mumbled. "Where the hell…"

"West Chicago County Hospital." Beth stepped into her

line of sight. "You passed out in my apartment. Do you remember?"

Jeannie frowned at her for a couple of seconds. Then, she started shoving back the blanket. "I've got to get out of here," she snapped, or at least she tried to. Her words were slurring.

"No, Mom." Beth grabbed the blanket and held it, and Jeannie, in place. "You need to stay. In fact, it's what we all need."

Jeannie glowered at her, but she did stop fighting with the blanket. "What are you talking about?"

Beth picked up the remote control that was cabled to the bedside.

"You wanted to leave Todd, right?" She pushed one of the buttons to raise the bed's head. "And you didn't want to go to the shelter. Well, this is not the shelter, *and* Todd's not going to be able to get at you."

"What are you talking about? He's my husband. They'll let him in the second he shows up!" Jeannie coughed, and coughed again.

There was a skinny tray table on wheels and some cups wrapped in plastic like in a motel. Beth ripped one open and filled it from the sink. She held the cup to Jeannie's mouth. Jeannie gave her another hard glare, but she took a swallow. And another.

"The rules have changed." Beth set the cup on the table. "They won't let him in unless you put his name on your visitors' list. They can't even tell him you're here, and he can't ask for you if he doesn't know what name you're checked in under."

"You got me in here as Debbie Watts?" Jeannie snapped. "Jesus! Why the hell…?"

"You told me you had cancer," Beth answered. "Of *course* I told the doctors your given name. They have to be able to get your full records. So you see?" Beth spread her hands. "As long as you don't invite him in, you're practically in witness protection. You'll be fine. Dana's bringing you some stuff from the gift shop. Then I'm going to take her home so—"

"No!" Sudden panic filled Jeannie's voice. "Don't leave me alone. I hate this! I'm not staying! I'm not!"

"You have to," said Beth. "You're sick, remember? You're dying of cancer and you wanted to get help." She leaned in closer. "Unless there's something you want to tell me before I hear it from the doctors?"

Jeannie grabbed her hand. She squeezed, or she tried to. Her fingers felt too light around Beth's.

That was when the nurse knocked on the door. Jeannie froze like she'd been caught in the act.

"Come in." Beth yanked her hand free and backed away, wrapping her arms tightly around her chest, like she was afraid something was going to break free. Beth stood by the window, trying to keep out of the way while the nurse checked the IV and the machines and asked all the questions. Jeannie answered, very clearly both annoyed and bored. She also watched Beth the whole time.

This is your fault, her expression said. *You're why I have to put up with this shit.*

When the nurse left, Jeannie rolled over on her side and pretended to go to sleep. Beth sat back down in the recliner and let her. She got out her own phone and texted Dana.

You okay?

She waited while the message flashed from Delivered to Read. She waited while the three little dots appeared.

Jeannie's breathing deepened. The beep from the monitor slowed.

Yeah, Dana's text came back. Back soon.

Beth laid her phone on the chair arm.

Jeannie still wasn't moving. Her breathing was deep and easy.

Beth brought out the other phone and flipped it open. She found the most recent number called. There was that San Francisco area code. There was the time.

Saturday, 8:15 p.m.

When Mom was in the guest room, full of Dana's comfort food, swearing she was leaving him.

Beth closed her eyes briefly. *Oh, Dana. I'm sorry. There is no way you are ever going to believe that. But I am.*

Beth touched the number and waited while it rang.

"Where the fuck have you been!" shouted Todd on the other end. "Do you have any idea how long I've been stuck out here with this j—"

"It's me, Dad," Beth said, and when the stunned silence fell, she added. "I think we better talk."

CHAPTER TWENTY-THREE

"Sorry!" Dad reached toward Dana, not quite touching her. "I didn't…Are you okay?"

Except you just about gave me a heart attack! Dana swallowed and started checking to see if she'd dropped anything out of her shopping basket when she jumped. "I, uh, what are you even doing here?"

"I was at your place. I needed to talk to your mom, but the guy at the desk told me she'd left, and that there'd been an ambulance and— They wouldn't tell me anything here…" He waved toward the reception desk. "Are you guys okay?"

Now that Dana had a chance to really look at him, she could see he was kind of a wreck. He wore his usual polo shirt and khakis—standard-issue white-guy uniform, Chelsea called it. But everything was creased, like he'd just pulled it out of the package. His hair was all messed up too. She could see his scalp shining through the thin patches.

Dad liked to look perfect, sophisticated, ready for

anything. Right now he just looked confused. It hit Dana that if Dad was here, he must have been coming to see them at, like, seven a.m. On a Sunday.

"Is your mom...okay?" he asked.

"Oh, um, yeah. It's not her. It's her mom."

"*Her* mom?" he repeated. "Her mom is here?"

"Yeah, she's...she was...visiting." Which sounded lame, but what else was she going to call it?

"Wow." He looked back over his shoulder at the lobby, like he thought Mom was going to sneak up on him. "Uh. I didn't think she'd...you know, she's never wanted anything to do with her folks."

Dana shrugged. "It's kind of complicated. You want to come up and see her?"

"Huh? Uh, no, no—I don't want to bother her now. It's...it's not a good time." Dad was looking over his shoulder again.

"Is something wrong, Dad?"

"No, no. Uh...look, there's a coffee shop on the other side of the lobby. Let's talk there."

Dana hesitated. Her last coffee shop meeting had gone badly really fast. But she was starving, and Mom did say she should get breakfast.

"Okay, but I gotta pay for this stuff."

"I'll go get a table." Dad practically ran for the door.

Dana stared for a second, trying to understand what could possibly be going on. Nothing came. So, she just paid for the stuff. As an afterthought, she texted Mom.

Getting breakfast @ coffee shop. Want anything?

The answer was short and to the point. No. Dana stuffed her phone in her pocket and gritted her teeth.

Just get this over with. Whatever it is.

The lobby café made an effort to be cute and casual, but nobody at the tables looked casual. They looked sad, exhausted, and stunned. Except for the guy by the window who was thumbing his phone and grinning. There was a security guard talking to the barista, or whatever you would call her in here. Dana felt her shoulders relax just a little. Which was stupid. Her father was about as danger-ous as spilled milk. Half the time they were together, she was taking care of him. Some days she even liked getting to play the grown-up.

Today was not one of those days.

She ordered a giant blueberry muffin and a large coffee and joined Dad at the table. He watched her take a slurp of (the surprisingly not too bad) coffee.

"Should you be drinking that?"

"Less caffeine than a Diet Coke," she said as she peeled the paper off the muffin and pulled off the top. "And no chemical sweetener."

"Oh. Uh. Okay."

"So, like, why are you even here?"

He was taking too long to answer. She hated his silences. They usually meant he was trying to figure out how to spin-meister some kind of bad news.

"Dana, I need you to talk to your mom for me." He said it really fast, like he was afraid he was going to lose his nerve in the middle of the sentence.

"Why?"

"Well, it's complicated, but there've been some mistakes, and there's some stuff I need to talk to her about. Money stuff. But she won't talk to me. I think she's mad about this weekend and…well, everything."

Wow. This is some serious bullshit. "You can call her."

"She won't pick up. Dana, I'm so sorry to have to drag you into this. I don't want to, but…you're smart. You've always understood how things are. I have to take care of Susan and my k—Marcus and Patty. You've always had your mom. They've got nobody but me. I can't let them down. You understand that, right?"

He wasn't looking at her while he talked. He kept looking across the lobby, toward the reception desk, or toward the door, or over at the security guy. Or at the happy guy who was taking selfies and thumbing his phone.

"I did not want to tell you this, I really didn't, but…I don't have a choice anymore." He swallowed. "Your mother…she's committing fraud, Dana."

"The *fuck*?"

"Watch your mouth!" he snapped.

"Like you have *ever* cared!" she snapped back.

"Listen to me! I am here to warn her, and you! She's running a scam, and she's maybe stealing from her boss—"

"She would never—"

"Dana!" Now he did touch her. In fact, he grabbed her wrist and held on. "Your mom has always had secrets. I knew that when we were together. That's why I never…why we never got married. I couldn't trust her. She's done some stuff, some really, really bad stuff that she can't let the cops or anybody know about…"

"What are you even talking about?" Dana yanked her hand back, twisting hard to break his grip. She knew what he was doing. He wanted her to take all his hints and put them together so she could get the bad news without him having to do something hard, like actually explain it to her. Except this time he wasn't just hinting about blowing off another weekend.

Dad rubbed his hands together, like he was the one who felt hurt. "She's always been really weird about money. Really controlling and secretive. I thought it was because of how her parents raised her, but now, it's looking like it might be something else."

"I am not going to listen to this." Dana scrabbled for her bags.

"Dana! Please! Just tell her what I told you, and tell her I have to talk to her, or this is only going to get worse." He reached for her again, but she stopped him with one hard glare. "I know you think I'm never around, but that is not my fault. She wanted to keep me away from you so I wouldn't ever tell you what she's really like. But you're not a kid anymore. She's got no right to keep secrets from you. Dana…"

You do not get to talk this kind of horseshit! Dana opened her mouth.

"Dana, she killed a man."

CHAPTER TWENTY-FOUR

Suddenly, Dana was looking at a stranger. She did not know this man. She did not understand what he was saying. Except that he was lying.

"She never hurt anybody!" The pink-hands man huddled on the sidewalk—that didn't count. "She was saving me!"

"No, not that," Dad said quickly. "There was another time, in a place called Abrahamsville, before you were born."

"What has this got to do with anything? You start telling me you got some money thing going down, and then you...you..."

"Your mother is stealing from me, Dana," he said. "And from other people too, and if I don't do something, I'm going to get in trouble for it. I don't want you—"

Dana planted both hands on the table and leaned forward, getting right up in his face.

"I do not know what is going on with you," she spoke carefully. She did not want him to miss a single word. "But

I do know you have never done anything but cover your own ass. You do not get to pretend you care so much about me now!"

His jaw hardened. His eyes flickered toward the lobby again. Dana whirled around, but all she saw were anonymous people coming and going—carrying flowers or balloons or pushing people in wheelchairs or stopping at the desk.

"I'm going upstairs," she announced.

"Dana, your mother has got to take responsibility for what she's done before it hurts you. You *have* to make her understand how she has got to listen to me."

"Whatever!" Dana sneered, rage turning her deliberately, intensely bratty. She marched away and did not look back.

Back in the room, she was about to tell everybody what just happened, but then she saw that Mom was curled up in the recliner, her head pillowed on her arm, sound asleep. All her plans fell out of her, like she'd torn a seam open.

Jeannie, on the other hand, was awake, lying on her back and blinking at the ceiling. The TV was on—some Sunday-morning talk show with perfectly groomed hosts sitting with ferns and politicians. There wasn't any sound. Jeannie put a finger to her lips and pointed at Mom asleep in the recliner.

"I guess she was a little tired," Jeannie said softly.

"Yeah." Dana set her bags down carefully on the bed. *What do I do? Do I wake her up? I can't, but I…Jesus. What do I do?*

Dad was messed up. She'd known it pretty much since day one. But this was a whole new level. And it couldn't be true.

"Something wrong?" whispered Jeannie. "I mean, something new?"

"I...uh...no. Not really." She reached into the bags, trying not to let the plastic crinkle too much. "I got you some stuff. Socks and...this." She shook out the nightshirt. Jeannie smiled. "I hope it'll fit okay, and I thought maybe you'd want a nail kit...I'll just put it all in there." She carried the bags over to the cupboard. "Um. Unless you want to change now or anything?"

"No, no. I don't want to disturb your mom."

Dana nodded. She saw a blanket on the cupboard shelf and pulled it down. She laid it over Mom. Mom muttered something and shrank down underneath it. Dana stared at her, trying not to feel so lonely.

"I know we don't know each other," said Jeannie softly. "And I know you don't...but, well, if you want to talk, I'm listening."

Jeannie waited. She did not look good. Her cheeks were all pasty and sunken in. But Dana had to tell somebody, or her head was going to explode.

Dana folded her arms. "My father is a hyperprivileged jerkwad who wants to blame everybody else for his screwups."

"That happens."

"He wants to pretend he lives on some kind of *Leave It to Beaver* island where nobody's ever had an outside kid. *And* he blames Mom for having me. He's said so."

"God, I wish I wasn't in this bed. I'd make that fucker pay." They were talking in stage whispers, but somehow that just made Jeannie's threat sound more intense. Curiosity lifted above Dana's anger for a second.

"Like, what would you do?"

Jeannie grinned. "Nothing too much. Just strip him to his shorts."

"You could do that?"

"Have you been listening to one single thing your mother's said? Yes, I could do it. Once. Probably. It'd depend on how stupid your father actually is."

"He ghosted my mom right after she found out she was pregnant."

"That's pretty stupid."

"Like, what would you have to do?" Dana didn't mean it. Not really. It was just something to talk about and a way to cover the memory of Dad's stupid lies. *She killed a man.*

She was not afraid of her mother. Mom loved her. She could not be afraid.

Jeannie shifted onto her side and crooked the arm that wasn't hooked up to the IV under her head. "If you're going to try to hook somebody for more than a quick score— you know, if you want to keep milking them—you need two lies. You need the little lie and the big lie. The little lie gets them to trust you. Once they trust you, then they're ready to believe the big lie.

"If I wanted to get your father to trust me, I'd be telling him things like how I was so sorry for him, and how everybody was treating him so unfair, and that none of this was his fault. I'd keep saying I wished I could help. Little lie. Then, I'd make him think I could get him something he wanted, only he'd have to give me something first. Big lie." She stopped and squinted at Dana. "Dana, do not go getting ideas. Your mother's got enough problems. I'm just a bored, old, sick woman talking because I've got nothing better to do."

I know that. I do. Dana pulled out her phone. No new messages. She put it back. Mom was still sleeping. Jeannie was still watching her.

"Dad said…he said Mom did some…really bad stuff back when she was with you. Like stuff the police maybe shouldn't know about."

Jeannie reached over to touch Dana, but the IV tube wouldn't stretch far enough, so she just curled her fingers around the bed railing. "Do not let him get into your head, honey. Your mom did what she needed to survive. Just like the rest of us."

"Yeah, but was there something…you know, big? I'm only asking because Dad's getting angry and, you know, he said some stuff…" She stopped. "You said something about Abrahamsville before and how you were…you know…" *Crap. I sound just like Dad!*

Jeannie rolled flat on her back. "No, that was nothing," she said, but she was talking to the ceiling, not to Dana. "That was where things finally went bad and we split up, like I told you."

"You're lying." Dana hadn't meant to say it out loud, but there was already too much inside her to hold back one more thing. "Just like everybody else."

"No, honey…"

"Which is it, huh? Is this the big lie or the little lie?"

But she'd been too loud, and Mom shifted and blinked. She shoved the blanket down, trying to stand up before she was even all the way awake.

"Dana?" Mom knuckled her eyes. "Everything okay?"

"Fine," said Dana, doing her best to sound all sweetness and light. "Just talking to Grandma."

Dana waited for Jeannie to say something, to tell Mom she was the one lying now.

But Jeannie just lay on her back and smiled.

CHAPTER TWENTY-FIVE

Beth opened her mouth to ask more questions. It was impossible to trust her mother when she smiled. But an orderly came in with a breakfast tray, and a nurse came in with meds, which Jeannie acted like she was dutifully swallowing, although with her you never knew. Then the doctor came in—not Dr. Yasim from the emergency room, but a gray-haired Taiwanese woman who introduced herself as Dr. Chen—and Beth had to give her the pills she'd found in her mother's things. Then they all had to listen to Jeannie try to lie about them being "prescription." The doctor did not believe her any more than Beth did and began a solemn lecture about how she wasn't here to make any judgment calls—she just wanted to provide Jeannie with the care she needed and she couldn't do that if Jeannie wasn't open with her.

That was when Beth's phone buzzed. It was an email

from Kinseki, with the subject line "Amanda Pace Martin." There was an address in Schaumburg, a telephone number, and a photo.

"…I know, I know," Jeannie was saying. "But the pain…it's so bad. I had to do something."

"And how is your pain now?"

Jeannie squeezed her eyes shut and shook her head. The doctor made a note on her clipboard.

Dana circled the bed and came to stand beside Beth. "What's going on?" she whispered.

"Rafi." Beth blanked the phone. "Checking in. Wants to know if there's anything he can do. You okay?"

Dana shook her head, and Beth put her arm around her daughter's shoulders. "Me neither," she whispered.

The silver lining of all this was that Dana barely protested when Beth said they should go and let Jeannie eat and rest. Also, thankfully, Jeannie did not kick up any more fuss about being left alone. Probably it had something to do with the doctor promising she'd be put on an "enhanced pain-management schedule."

She also didn't seem to notice that Beth had taken her little flip phone. But she would.

They caught a cab back home. As soon as they pulled away from the curb, Dana laid her head on Beth's shoulder. By the time they'd gone a block and a half, she was snoring.

Beth smiled and looped one arm over her daughter's shoulders. Moving carefully, she pulled her own phone out with her free hand and thumbed it until she brought up Kinseki's email and the photo he'd sent with it.

It was a screenshot captured off Facebook, and it showed a selfie of a slender white woman. She'd had her face done at least once, and her hair was dyed ash blonde. Beth was pretty sure both her scarf and her bag were Hermès, which meant she had plenty of money to spare.

And there, behind her, was a blur in the shadows, but a blur Beth recognized. It was Todd, grinning, with his eyes fixed on Ms. Pace Martin.

Beth shut off her phone and leaned her cheek against the top of Dana's head. *Oh, Dangerface. What do we do now?*

Beth supported, guided, and cajoled her half-awake daughter into the apartment and her bedroom. Dana toppled face-first onto her bed, the picture of teenage drama in exhaustion. Beth smiled at the fierce love that rose in her.

Dana grabbed the corner of her bedspread and rolled herself up in it.

Beth turned off the light and went into her study and closed the door.

I should wait. She flipped open her laptop and brought up Kinseki's email. Her nap in Jeannie's hospital room had done very little to clear the fog out of her mind. *Sleep, shower, food…get my head together first.*

But she did not have time. Everything was shifting around her, and she didn't know enough to make a new plan yet.

One thing she did know for certain: Wherever Todd was, he was not just sitting around waiting for her call. Hers or Jeannie's.

And there was still Doug, and all those calls, lurking in the background. She did not have time to get her head together.

Beth squinted at the number Kinseki sent in the email. She punched it into her phone and tried to think through a message for the voice mail she was sure she was about to get forwarded to.

So she was caught by surprise when a woman picked up on the third ring.

"Hello?"

"Um, yes," Beth stammered in her professional voice. "I'm trying to…trying to reach Amanda Pace Martin. My name is"—*Which one?*—"Star…"

"*Star?*" cried Amanda Pace Martin. "Oh my gosh, *hi*! I'm so glad to finally get to talk to you! How's your dad doing?"

Beth was suddenly and absurdly glad this was not a video call. She in no way wanted this woman to see the expression on her face.

She swallowed hard and fought to think up something generic. And fast. "Um, yeah, he's good. Really good."

"Oh, good." Amanda Pace Martin sighed happily. "I miss him so much, but I'm only out here in London one more week, and then I'm home for six months! He's been so sweet and supportive about it too. He calls me every day and sends flowers. Oh gosh, I still have to thank him for the roses! It's just so…oh, I don't know, like, old-school romantic!"

"Yes, he's always been like that."

This was surreal. She literally could not think about

what she was hearing. All she could do was react. *The truth. Jeannie had been telling the truth.*

"I'm just so glad he finally felt like he could tell you about us being together. He said losing your mother hit you really hard."

"Uh, yeah. Yeah. I still can't believe she's gone."

"You must know your father is so proud of you. He talks about you all the time. My daughter, Star, speaker to billionaires! How's the weather out in San Francisco?"

"Uh, a little uncertain today." Beth looked out the window toward Lake Michigan. "We might be in for a storm." *I have to steer this...somehow.* "Um, listen, Ms. Martin..."

"Oh, for heaven's sake! Amanda, Star, Amanda!"

"Yeah. Right. Sorry. Amanda. I just, this might be a little awkward..."

"Oh, go ahead—you can say anything." Beth pictured Amanda crossing her legs and leaning into the phone, getting ready for new confidences. "Now that we're talking, I want us to be completely open with each other!"

"Yeah, me too." Beth hurried to the study door and locked it. Now was not the time for Dana to come peeking in. "Has Dad ever mentioned a woman named Stacey Walsh? Or Felicity Brandt?"

"Oh God, that bitch!" Beth heard her slap her hand over her mouth. "Oh, I'm sorry, Star!"

"No, no, that's okay. I just..."

"She hasn't been harassing you, has she? Your dad was afraid she might."

"No, not yet anyway. But I'm just"—*What?*—"worried. Dad hasn't said much—you know how he is..."

SARAH ZETTEL

"Oh, I do know. He's so protective. It's one of the things I love about him. But listen, you cannot believe anything that woman says. She's been hounding your father for money. I keep telling him he needs to cut her off, but he feels so responsible...He won't even think about talking to my lawyer. But maybe if you and I can double-team him. Especially if she's been in touch...Has she been in touch?"

"Nothing to worry about yet. I can take care of her. I just wanted to know for sure."

"Well, I'm so glad you called. And like I told you, I'm home next week. We *have to* get together right after that, okay?"

"Yeah, sure, that sounds great." Finally a couple of pieces managed to fit together inside Beth's confusion. "Um, you said you're out of the country..."

"Yes, yes. Business. Everybody trying to figure out what's going on with Brexit. *You* know how that is."

"Yeah. Well, the truth of the matter is Dad's been talking about you so much, and I was planning on a trip out to Chicago anyway...but it was going to be Thursday, so maybe..."

"Oh! Oh perfect! No, seriously. You can stay at the house with your dad until I get home."

"Dad's at your place?"

"Yes. He's house-sitting for me. He must have told you!"

"Oh yeah, right, right. Slipped my mind for a second there. And thank you, but I don't want to impose..."

"Oh, it's no imposition! We're practically family already, right? Oh, I can't *wait* to meet you, Star. I wish I was there now."

"Yeah, me too. Thanks for talking to me, Amanda. How about you, uh, text me your itinerary and stuff and...maybe I can come with Dad and meet you at the airport?"

"Oh perfect! This number?"

"Uh-huh. Yes. Um, you take care now!"

There were about six iterations of good-bye after that, but finally Amanda let her hang up. All Beth could do was sit where she was and stare at the wall. She'd always watched her father flirt and charm and sweet-talk, but there'd never been anything like this.

That you knew of.

Beth bit her lip.

He never lived with them before! Jeannie had said.

Her parents had always disappeared at random intervals. One or both of them could be gone for days. When they came back, they'd either have money, or it would be time to pick up and go again.

Her parents had always used people too. They always said if someone was stupid enough to trust them, they deserved what they got.

I was whoring. Jeannie said that. She didn't say if that was the first time.

What they did then doesn't matter. What matters is now.

And now she had an answer to one question that had been nagging her since she saw her parents pretending to fight on the sidewalk. Jeannie and Todd had definitely been in the area much longer than they'd admitted. They'd had plenty of time to get settled, to find her and follow her. Beth closed her eyes against the phantom pain in her skull.

Plenty of time to find out everything they needed to know about Dana.

Beth's eyes flew open.

And Doug.

CHAPTER TWENTY-SIX

"It's one o'clock in the afternoon on what has to be classed as one of the worst days ever," Dana muttered to herself. "Here is Dana Fraser, and what is she doing?"

Dana shook the water droplets off her fingers and watched them skitter and dance across the hot griddle. "She's making pancakes. Fucking pathetic."

She took the pat of butter she had wrapped in a paper towel and rubbed it on the griddle. It hissed and steamed. She inhaled the warm scent. Usually it made her happy. Today, nothing.

Her few hours of sleep hadn't straightened her head out at all. Everything was still one great, huge, honking mess. The grandmother she'd just met was in the hospital and was probably dying of cancer. Her stupid "estranged" father had accused her mother of murder.

Oh, yeah, and her grandfather was out there somewhere, probably stalking all of them.

She stirred her batter one more time and drizzled several ladlesful onto the griddle, watching it spread across the hot surface.

Gradually, the bubbles started rising to the surface of the batter. They popped open soundlessly, leaving holes behind that wouldn't close.

Pretty much how I feel. Dana flipped over the first pancake and watched it puff up.

She heard Mom before she saw her.

"Hey, Dangerface."

Mom had showered and changed. She had her wet hair pulled back in a ponytail. She looked normal, like none of the past two days had happened.

She's committing fraud.

"Those smell fantastic." Mom slid past her, heading straight for the coffee maker. "Thanks for making them."

She's stealing from me.

"Don't thank me yet," Dana told her. "I'm half-asleep, and I'm not sure what all I put in here."

"Well, I'm starved, so I'm not sure I'm gonna care."

She killed a man.

Dana shoveled the finished pancakes onto the plate she had waiting and ladled on the fresh batter while Mom ground her batch of beans. Dana wanted to face her. She wanted to say, all casual, *Hey, you'll never guess who was at the hospital. Dad! He wasn't looking so good. What do you think's up with that?*

But all she did was grit her teeth and watch her batter turn into pancakes. She checked and flipped and watched some more, and did not say anything while the bitter smell of brewing coffee rose up to join the scent of hot sugar and butter.

Mom pulled the carafe out and poured a cup and added milk from the jug Dana had left out. She leaned her butt back against the counter.

"There's something I have to tell you, Dangerface."

"Something new?" Dana flipped the last pancake over.

"Yeah. And the timing is terrible. I meant to tell you before, but everything got crazy." She swallowed more coffee, made a face, and poured more milk into the mug. "Your father's in trouble."

It was what had been filling Dana's head, but it was still a shock to hear Mom come out and say it. "What kind of trouble?"

"I'm still trying to figure that out. It looks like he got caught in some kind of vaporware investment. He's...he's probably lost a lot of money."

She's committing fraud. She's stealing from me.

Dana did not believe that. She could not believe that, because her father was always so full of it. She knew that. She'd always known that. So, why couldn't she stop hearing it?

Do not let him get into your head, Grandma had warned. But he was already there.

Dana turned off the burner under the griddle. The last three pancakes needed to come off, but she stood there with the spatula up, like she couldn't remember what to do next. "How come you know about it?"

"Because he came to find me on Friday, to ask me to use Lumination's name to...well, help this company, whatever it turns out to be, raise more money."

"Oh." *I should have known it was something like that. I never should have believed him, not even for a second.* "So, like, when you told me that thing, about the guy who'd got upset at you cuz you turned him down…"

"That was your father. I'm sorry. Honestly, I was hoping I wouldn't have to tell you, at least, not until I knew more."

Motion returned. Dana shoveled up the pancakes and dumped them onto the stack. "Food," she said.

Mom got out plates. Dana put the platter on the breakfast bar and retrieved the butter and the maple syrup.

"Do you know more now?" Dana asked as she climbed up on the high stool.

"Not really."

Dana focused on drizzling sharp zigzags of syrup over her pancakes. In an actual restaurant, you were supposed to be able to do this in the same pattern, every single time. "What are you going to do?"

She heard Mom's fork *tink* against the plate.

"I don't know yet. But what I *do* know is you're going to have to go away for a while."

Dana's head jerked up and her hand wobbled, turning her neat zig into a squiggle. "What? Why!"

"It's just until I've cleared things up with your father, and Todd and Jeannie." Mom mumbled the names through a mouthful of pancakes. "I am not going to be able to do all that and look after you."

"Who says you have to look after me?" *You can't!* she screamed inside. *I'll never find out what's going on!* Then: *You don't want me to find out what's going on.* Because that was what her mother did. She told the truth in bits and pieces, when she was damn good and ready, or when she had no choice. It was what she had done Dana's whole life. "You're still only fifteen," Mom said. *Of course.* Because she was still a mom.

"For two more weeks," Dana reminded her. "I can take care of myself."

"Normally, yes, but Todd...he's already turning violent. He might come after me. Or Jeannie. Or you."

Dana didn't want to talk about that. Or think about it. Instead, she ate. More like wolfed. She was starving. Mom didn't even bother to tell her to slow down. Not like she was exactly holding back either. Despite everything, that made Dana feel better. She could still do something right, and Mom was still acting at least a little bit normal.

"So what are you going to do?" said Dana finally. "Hire a bodyguard and send me to a cabin in the woods?"

"Kind of." Mom speared another pancake off the pile. "There is an enrichment camp out in Connecticut. It's for kids whose parents...are better off but might be having legal problems and the kids need to be somewhere else while they get sorted out."

"There's a summer camp for the kids of bad billionaires? No, wait." Dana waved her full fork at Mom to cut her off. "Of course there is. Cuz this is America. Jesus."

"I know, right?"

"How do you even know this one percenters camp will take me?"

That got her a tired smile. "We are one percenters, Dana, and they're holding a slot for you."

Did you set this up in case you had to run? Dana sawed her pancake into perfect little squares, trimming off the curved parts and eating them first. *In case the police came after you? And you never told me. I'm the one this is happening to, and you never—*

Don't think like that! Don't!

"What if nothing happens?" she asked out loud. "What if everything is okay?"

"We can't count on that. I'm sorry. This is happening. You are leaving Wednesday."

"But my internship. They only take two high school students a year!"

"This is not your decision, Dana." Mom's voice was flat and hard, and very final. "And they know emergencies happen. This is an emergency."

"It's not an emergency. Not a real one. It's not like anybody's died!" Dana knew she was whining, and she sounded pathetic, but she couldn't stop. This was important. Mom knew it was the most important thing so far in her life, and she was acting like she didn't care.

"I'm supposed to go fill out my paperwork tomorrow!"

"Dana, this is not your decision."

Dana tossed her fork down and folded her arms. This was it. Everything was now officially destroyed. She had been looking forward to this for months. The second she had toured the kitchen at the Vine and Horn, she had been able to see herself standing there with all those focused, frantic, laughing, swearing people making all that gorgeous food. She had known instantly that this was when her life was really going to get started.

And now Mom was telling her she had to give it up like it was no big deal. Just because Mom was afraid of her grandparents and her pathetic father.

Because she doesn't want me to know what's really happening with my own family. Again!

The leftover pancake-and-syrup flavor suddenly felt too thick on Dana's tongue. She reached for her juice, but Mom touched her hand to stop her.

"I did not want any of this for you," Mom said. "I do know what this summer meant to you…"

Meant—note the use of the past tense.

"But I cannot leave you where Todd or your father can get to you if they decide you might be useful to them."

Anger poured through her—thick, putrid, blinding. All she wanted was for her mother to feel it, all the way down in her veins. Dana had nowhere to hide—her mother shouldn't either.

"If you're really that worried about what Todd's gonna do, can't you just call the police?" she heard herself saying.

But Mom was already shaking her head. "I wish I could, but what would I tell them? I can say he hit Jeannie, but nothing's going to happen unless she presses charges, and maybe not even then. And I can tell you for a fact she is not going to press charges."

"Well, you could at least get them to open a file! They do that, right? We could—"

"We can't, Dana!" shouted Mom, but then she tried to take it back. "At least, we can't yet. Maybe later."

"Later? This is not a trip to the zoo!" Dana shouted back. "You do not get to hide from me! You do not get to make another secret out of me, or them, or anything! This is my life! Anybody would think you were scared of the cops!"

Mom's face went hard, and the raw, hot resentment that was so awful and familiar shone in her eyes. For a moment, it felt like victory.

"What's going on, Dana? What do you want from me?"

I want you to know you can't keep this from me anymore. "I want to know if you ever killed somebody."

CHAPTER TWENTY-SEVEN

"What?" Beth heard herself say.

She was not stunned. She was not hurt. Dana's words rocketed her past either of those things into a numb state of being where thought and breath were equally inaccessible.

"I want to know…"

Dana's condescending singsong snapped Beth back into herself. "Where did that even come from?" Beth didn't wait for her answer. "This is Jeannie. She told you."

"No."

"Then who?!"

"Does it matter?"

"Yes, Dana! It really does!"

"Then it's true! That's why you won't go to the police! You're afraid they'll find out!"

Slowly, Beth got up and walked over to the balcony doors. She told herself she was looking for her father, or her mother, or Doug. That was irrational but more acceptable than being afraid of her own child.

Beth tried to imagine what her daughter must be going through. Her secrets were more than burdens. They were vicious, living things with claws and fangs. She tried to imagine what it would be like the first time they came bursting out of the dark.

Every old instinct in her screamed at her to lie. To feed the monsters so they would go back to sleep.

No, I never actually killed anybody. I did come close once.

Beth licked her lips. She tasted copper and iron and gunpowder.

Dana wasn't going to let her go. She marched right up to the balcony doors to stand in front of Beth, defiant and frightened like the child she still was.

"What happened? Tell me!"

It was after your grandparents left me. I was trying to steal his car...

She looked at her daughter. Took in her defiant, amazing self. Beth curled her fingers around the pull handle on the door, like she was thinking of escape.

"It's true, Dana," she said. "His name was Robert MacNamera Early."

Beth waited for the flashback, for the shakes and violent tears that used to leave her crouching on the floor of her therapist's office. Or maybe there would be some sense of relief. Confession was supposed to be good for you, wasn't it? But Beth just felt...gray.

"He'd held me hostage for three days," she said. "He was waiting for my parents to come back so he could kill them."

"Oh," breathed Dana. Beth didn't let her get any further.

"It had been a pretty good time for us, as things went, before…that," she said. "We'd been able to stick around this one town for…it was at least a year. Maybe a little longer. We had an actual apartment. Top floor of a house out by the freeway. It was pretty crappy, but it was better than a lot of places we'd stayed. Mom had a job as a delivery driver. At least, that's what she told me she was doing."

Dana looked away. *So.* She already knew that "deliveries" weren't what Jeannie was doing. Beth sighed. She'd have to find out just what Jeannie had said.

One more thing for the to-do list.

"So, anyway, we had money. Which meant Dad was in a good mood most of the time. I was actually in school. I hated it. I was pretty sure all the kids and teachers hated me, but you know, it was better than other stuff, so I went. What happened…It started on a Saturday morning. I was home, watching TV."

She could still see the room. It had a pea green carpet, with three cigarette holes and a grungy path worn down the middle leading from the couch to the kitchen area, which was marked out by curling, speckled linoleum tile. The TV sat on a cart that had only three wheels. Somebody had shoved a wad of tinfoil under the spot where the fourth one should have been, to make the cart sit sort of level.

There was one other room where her parents slept. Star—she was still Star then—slept on the beige striped fold-out couch, which also had three cigarette holes, just like the carpet.

Mom had said they were looking for a better place. Mom said it'd be soon.

"My parents told me they were going out for groceries. They told me to lock the door and stay inside. I didn't think anything of it. They did that a lot, especially when we were staying in the crap motels. I pretty much ignored them."

Beth shrugged. Dana shook her head. *Right. What's this got to do with anything?*

"But that time, I did stay in. Did some homework. Read. Watched more TV. It got dark. They didn't come back. I wasn't worried. Well. Okay. I was worried, because I thought it meant they'd gotten into trouble and we were going to have to hit the road again.

"When they weren't back in the morning, I got a little more worried. I figured I'd better be ready to go. So I went out to the gas station and I bought some Slim Jims and peanuts and stuff so there'd be something to eat in case we had to drive all night."

Beth was vaguely aware she didn't have to tell Dana all this. It was enough for her daughter to know the bad thing had happened, and why it did. But she kept going, despite the look on her daughter's face, despite the pain squeezing her ribs.

Who am I punishing? Me or her?

Both of us. All of us.

"And when I went back…there was this guy in the living room."

A skinny, little, bald white man with gray stubble on his cheeks and the edges of his scalp. He wore dark pants and a white shirt over a white T-shirt.

He had a gun pointed right at her. Not a handgun. A double-barreled shotgun.

Two blank, black holes leveled right at her face.

Close the door, he said.

"He was sitting on one of the kitchen chairs, facing the door." *Plastic-and-chrome chairs, with beige seats. The one was cracked down the middle. Dad had fixed it up with duct tape.* "He had a shotgun. I was lucky he didn't shoot right away."

"Jesus," breathed Dana. "Who was he?"

"I didn't actually find out until I read about him in the paper. But that was later." *Years later, when I finally had the nerve to look up the archives online.*

The article about his death said his friends called him Bobbie Mac. It said he was a respected local pharmacist and businessman. It said his wife and children had no idea he'd been having financial troubles related to his business.

It also said they had no idea he'd been filing fraudulent workers' compensation claims that allowed the patients who came to his pain clinic to receive large amounts of prescription opioids.

"He wanted…he wanted to know where my parents were. I told him I didn't know. He didn't believe me. He said we'd wait for them to come back."

He told me to get on my knees, and he put the gun to my head. I can touch the exact spot. When I get a headache, it always starts there.

Where the fuck are they? he shouted. *I'll shoot you if you don't tell me where the fuck they are!*

I don't know, I don't know, I don't know!

She felt the screams burning in her throat. She smelled her own piss. Saw the bags of junk food scattered on the linoleum.

Well, we'll just wait for them, he said. *You and me.*

Saw the cigarette burns in the carpet. Tried to think what she could say to make this all go away.

They might not come back. They've been gone since yesterday.

Don't lie to me! What kind of parents would do that to their own kid?

My kind.

She'd meant to say that, but the words dissolved in a flood of acid certainty.

Her parents had known this was coming—this guy and his shotgun. That was why they'd left. Maybe they thought he wouldn't shoot a kid. But maybe not. Maybe they wanted to use her as a decoy. While he was busy shooting her, they could get a few miles farther away.

But all that really mattered right then was that this guy was ready to shoot her dead, and she knew that nobody was coming to save her.

Beth said, "He kept the phone near him, and I didn't have a cell or anything like that, so I couldn't call nine-one-one. At first, I thought I'd just wait until he fell asleep and run away. But my parents had a couple fifths of vodka in the cupboard, and he made me drink it with these pills he had. Oxycontin or something, I guess. So, I was out cold for a lot of the time, and when I was awake, I was sick and shaky."

They lived off the peanuts and Slim Jims and peanut butter sandwiches. He ordered pizza once.

"By the third day, he was getting crazier. He kept talking about getting into his car with me and driving until he found them and...and about all the things he was going to do when he did. He was always making calls to somebody...asking about the cops and other people, and...by then, I had figured...I was puking up pretty much everything as soon as I could get into the bathroom and get my finger down my throat, so I was kind of straight.

"Anyway, I...eventually I pretended to pass out. He went to the toilet, and that was when I got up."

The couch springs creaked. My heart stopped beating. I stopped breathing. I wasn't in my body. I was floating along that worn-down carpet path.

"I snuck over and I opened the bathroom door."

And he was sitting there with his pants around his ankles and his penis shoved down between his legs. His eyes wide, his mouth open. Couldn't believe I'd broke in on him while he was dumping his load.

"And I grabbed the gun off the floor and I shot him."

I pointed the gun right at his chest and I pulled the trigger and the thing kicked back like it hated me and probably cracked a rib. And the inside of Robert MacNamera Early exploded all over the wall and the sink and the mirror and the toilet, and me.

And he fell over and he died.

Dana pressed her hand against her mouth. For a moment Beth thought she was going to run away, be sick, or fall down screaming. But Dana was stronger than that. She was not going to run until she had heard the whole truth.

"This is the part where I should probably say I didn't

mean to do it," Beth told her, "that it was an accident and the gun just went off in my hands. But it wasn't an accident, and I did mean to."

I scrubbed off in the kitchen sink and threw the bag of bloody clothes in a McDonald's dumpster, then gave a blow job to the kid who saw me so he'd keep his damn mouth shut if the cops came and asked.

"I went back to my grandmother's, because I didn't know where else to go. And I met Rafael and…" She waved vaguely toward that pile of memories. "I became Beth Fraser, and little Star Bowen vanished off the face of the earth."

CHAPTER TWENTY-EIGHT

If this were a movie, Dana knew what would happen now.

She'd take the three steps over to Mom and hug her close. Mom would dissolve into tears, and they'd cry together. The music would rise. The camera would pan out to some significant and panoramic scene. Then it would all fade to black and the commercial break, or the credits. Whatever.

Dana realized that on some level, she was actually waiting for that fade-out. It didn't come. Everything stayed exactly where it was—the apartment, her, Mom, the whole world. The world that had always had this thing in it. She just hadn't known.

"Why didn't you tell me?" Dana whispered, and she knew it was a stupid question the second she asked it, because Mom had so clearly hit her limit.

"When, Dana?" she demanded. "When should I have

told you? When you were six? Eight? Nine and having your relapse? Or twelve and getting your period and flunking junior high at the same time?" Mom's voice rose, the shout turning into a scream. "I know it'll come as a big surprise, but the parenting books do not discuss the appropriate age for telling your teenager you're a murderer!"

"I know, I'm sorry, and I mean...well, I mean, it was self-defense, right?" she said, because she had to say something. There had to be a way to make this new knowledge fit. She couldn't leave it as it was, just this...this big, heavy *thing* falling through the air toward her.

A mind's-eye flash—a bright, sick blur of memory and fantasy blinded her. She was there on the sidewalk. Her head hurt. Her hands hurt. She saw Mom...she saw Mom...felt her eyes burn as she tried to black it all out.

But she did see. She saw Mom with a shotgun, blowing the pink-hands man away.

Her knees were buckling. She was sliding down the balcony door to sit on the floor. She didn't know why, but she didn't stop herself. "You didn't know if anybody was coming to help you. You didn't know, you couldn't know, and you were out of your head, and he was going to kill you, and I mean, what the fuck were you *supposed* to do!"

Slowly, Mom slid down to sit next to her. "I could have just run out the door. He wouldn't have known until he got out of the bathroom. But I didn't. I went in there after him instead."

Dana leaned her head against Mom's shoulder. Mom rested her hand on Dana's head and kissed her. They stayed like that for a while, until Dana started to feel—well, normal was the wrong word—but at least like she might eventually be able to get back to normal one day.

She sat up, and Mom let her.

"What are you going to do?"

Mom let out a long breath. "Well, first, I'm planning to go see Todd tonight, and I'm going to try to make him go away."

Jesus. Dana pushed her hands through her hair. This should have been the big news. But now it seemed kind of…an anticlimax or something. "Are you going to, like, pay him off?"

"Hopefully it won't come to that, but maybe. I'm going to at least get a better line on what he's really after. But I don't want you here on your own while I'm gone. Can you ask Chelsea if she can come over?"

"Yeah. I guess."

"But nobody else. I mean nobody."

"Yeah, okay. But what about…Grandma?"

Mom pushed herself up off the floor. "Nothing's changed there, Dana. I promise. But there's the other piece of this." She paused, searching for the right words, or any words. "I'm telling Kendi and Mr. Verdes that Doug isn't allowed past the lobby anymore. I don't know what's going on with him."

"Mom…" Dana tried to brace herself to get up off the floor. She felt like a baby just sitting here. But she couldn't move yet.

"What?" Mom asked. She looked beyond exhausted. She looked like she'd been completely hollowed out.

Dana flashed on Jeannie lying on the gurney in the

emergency room, looking more dead than alive. She remembered wondering if she would ever wake up.

"I'm worried," Dana said. "I mean, Todd—what if he hurts you?"

"I'm not Jeannie, Dangerface. If he tries that on me, he's going to find himself with more than he can handle."

"I love you, Mom."

And then Dana did stand up, and they did hug, just like they were supposed to. But Dana didn't hear music rise inside her mind or see the camera pan or any of that. Instead, she saw her father in the hospital coffee shop with his desperate eyes and his whiny voice. *Your mother has got to take responsibility for what she's done before it hurts you!*

But he didn't give a shit about her. He just wanted to turn her against Mom, make her afraid. He wanted to use her. For what, even? It didn't matter.

He did not get to do that, and she was going to make sure he never tried it again.

CHAPTER TWENTY-NINE

When Todd walked into Beth's office, it was very clear he'd made an effort to live up to his surroundings. He was freshly shaved and had on a dry-cleaned, button-down shirt and linen slacks. He'd changed his boots for dress shoes.

Amanda Pace Martin clearly took good care of her man. She hadn't seen her father so well dressed since she was a little girl, back when they still sometimes tried to make a play in Vegas or Atlantic City.

Beth had never told Dana about the high times when they were in the money, living in plush hotels. Or how she and Mom would go on shopping sprees that would make a Kardashian blush. Beth wanted to shield her from the glamour, because those luxury sprints always ended in another midnight drive, with her huddled in the back seat and her parents screaming at each other in the front. Then, in a few days, there'd be another call to Grammy and more tears for more money, and it would all begin again.

Todd strolled around the edges of her office, whistling. He opened the fridge and pulled out a bottle of Pellegrino.

"What is this shit? You got all this"—he waved the bottle at the rest of her office—"and all you keep around is green juice and fancy water."

Beth shrugged. "Alcohol makes you stupid."

"Can't argue with that. So." He dropped onto her couch and spread his arms across the back. "I'm here. What have you got to say?"

"Seventy-five thousand dollars."

Todd raised his eyebrows.

Beth reached into her top drawer and pulled out a stack of paper.

"What's that?" he asked.

"It's a corporation," said Beth. "Or it will be as soon as the last of the paperwork goes through." She spent hours on the phone with her lawyer, Noah Beresford, finalizing the details. "S and J, Inc., LLC. Capitalized to the tune of seventy-five thousand dollars, all of which is yours as soon as you sign."

For a long moment, Todd didn't move. He just looked at her and the papers. He was recalibrating. The world had taken a left turn, and he had to adjust his plan to match.

His plan had depended on a helpless, desperate, worried little Star who was still trying to hide all the worst from her daughter.

Finally, Todd heaved himself to his feet and strolled over to the desk. Beth folded her hands on the shiny, empty surface. She'd cleared everything off and locked it all away before he'd gotten here. *Can't be too careful.* The desktop computer remained, of course, humming quietly to itself.

Smile for the camera, Dad.

"You're giving me seventy-five thousand?" Dad said.

She let out a long, theatrical sigh. "You're trying to take care of my dear mother who is dying of cancer. See, that's where I got the corporation idea. You'll be able to buy her health insurance more easily. And as a bonus, you'll be able to tell any of your girlfriends that you're a businessman and entrepreneur."

His condescension evaporated, replaced by a fresh wariness. "What are you talking about, girlfriends?"

"Stacey, Felicity, and Amanda. And all the rest of them."

Dad rolled his eyes. "Christ. You've been talking to your mother."

"Yes," Beth admitted.

"So, you do know where she is?" he asked, just a little too casually. "Cuz she ain't at your place no more."

Are you fishing here, or do you really not know? It was possible he didn't know. She'd talked to the hospital switchboard earlier. Given them the sob story about her father the abuser. They'd told her there were no calls recorded from Jeannie's room.

"Yes, as a matter of fact, I do know where she is."

Dad folded his arms and looked down his nose at her. "Are you going to tell me?"

Beth mimicked his pose, leaning back in her chair and crossing her legs at the knee for good measure. "We haven't come to an understanding yet. I will give you this money,

SARAH ZETTEL

only on the condition that you take Mom with you and you both get the hell out of my life."

I'm sorry, Dana. I am. But the thought was distant and without real urgency. She was ninety percent certain Todd and Jeannie were running some kind of scam on Doug. But with Todd gone, that plan, whatever it was, would collapse, or at least it would be put on hold and buy Beth some time. And because Beth had no way to know how far Jeannie was in on the plan, there was no way she could leave her near Dana. No matter what else might be happening, Jeannie had to go.

Todd caught Beth's gaze and held it while he picked up the papers. His lips moved as he skimmed, trying to keep up with the legal language.

Beth tried to stay focused on him and not let her eyes flick to the clock or her mind wander to whether Dana was okay and what she was telling Chelsea and what Chelsea was telling her.

Todd dropped the whole pile back down on the desk. "I don't need your money. You are going to tell me where you've got my wife, Star, because otherwise she's on your hands for the rest of her life, and we both know you really don't want that."

"Besides, you don't need her now that you've got Amanda on the hook," Beth added for him. "But, you know, that might change."

"I really hope you're not threatening me." His voice was soft and low and full of warning. "I don't want to hurt you—you know that. But you do not get to disrespect me."

She raised both eyebrows. "Would I disrespect you, Dad?"

"Maybe not before, but I'm pretty sure that's what's going on here. I think you might be getting me to sign some pile of papers to entrap me and shit like that."

"No." She spoke the word without blinking. "This is all completely legit. I am paying you to take your wife and go away. I do not want to have to do anything like call Amanda back and tell her you're a fraud who's scammed her out of heaven knows how much, or that civil proceedings are a genuine possibility for her, and I know several excellent lawyers." She paused. "Plus, there are these YouTube videos of you hitting a defenseless woman outside a Starbucks that she might need to have a look at."

Being who he was, it did not take Todd long to focus in on the important point in her little speech.

"You said call Amanda *back*?"

Beth pushed the phone toward him. "Call if you want. I'm sure she'll be glad to tell you what a great conversation we had."

Todd didn't even reach for the phone. He kept his eyes on Beth, and he waited.

"This is a really straightforward proposition. You want money and you want Mom. I'm happy to hand over both. All you have to do is leave."

"What if I told you I don't want your mother anymore? What if I've just..." He shrugged. "What if her running out on me was the last fucking straw?"

Then why are you still asking where she is?

SARAH ZETTEL

"What happens to Jeannie after you get her out of Chicago is totally up to you."

To her surprise, Todd laughed—his best warmhearted belly laugh.

"Wow! Being around all these rich fuckers has really made you into a hard-ass, hasn't it, Star? Here, lemme use that phone." He made a come-here gesture with two fingers.

Beth pushed nine for the outside line and handed him the receiver. She watched him dial a number and wait while it rang.

"Hey, Amanda, honey. How are you?" All Todd's carefully cultivated charm came flooding out of him. He smiled and twinkled, and leaned back, fully relaxed and in the moment. Beth felt something clench up under her ribs. "Yeah, yeah, I know. I'm sorry it's so early. I just...I really needed to hear your voice, and I forgot all about the time change...Forgive me?...Yeah. I know, I know. I miss you too. Listen, I was talking to my girl...Oh, uh-huh?...Yeah. Wow. Well, good."

All at once, Beth remembered Jeannie unconscious in the hospital bed, her stick-thin legs and bony wrists lying limp against the white sheets. She remembered standing by the sink while her mother heaved her guts out. She remembered the bitter anger and accusations, all of which were turning out to be real.

And all the years with their bruises and blood, and all the times she had to apologize for making her father mad.

And now she got to sit and listen to him spread all his charms for a stranger. Beth had not believed there was room for more hatred inside her. She'd been so very wrong.

"...I really am glad," he was saying. "And I'm sorry I kept putting off introducing you...Yeah, yeah, well...Sounds like it's all worked out for the best. Yeah...Oh, everything's fine. Yeah...She said that?" Dad cocked an eyebrow at Beth. "Jesus. That bitch Stacey...Sorry, Amanda. I just get so mad."

Note to self, thought Beth sourly. *Contact Stacey next and find out what happened.*

"No, no, I'll make sure she knows all about it. Don't worry." Dad was flipping the legal papers with his thumb while he talked, riffling them like cards. "Yeah, I know. I do. Listen, you go back to sleep. Dream of me. Ha-ha...Oh yeah. Just wait till you get home, naughty girl...Yeah. Love you too. Bye."

Dad hung up. He didn't say anything for a minute, just watched her, considering.

"Did I mention there's a signing bonus?" Beth asked. "A check for three thousand dollars." She pulled the cashier's check out of the drawer and pushed it across the desk.

But Dad ignored the check, or pretended to. Instead, he picked up the papers again and flipped through them, but he wasn't reading. He was inside his own head, playing out different scenarios, trying to see all the ways he could look like he was taking the deal and still come back for more. And even more after that.

He won't ever stop. Not until somebody's dead—Mom's words echoed back through her mind. And she was right. All Beth was doing with her stack of papers was buying a little time, but that time was all she needed.

Come on, Dad. It's everything you wanted. You'll have the money and you'll have ways to keep me on the hook for the rest of your life, just like what you did to Grammy.

"Okay," he said. "I'm in."

Beth concentrated on getting out her fountain pen, the one she saved for special occasions, and pulling off its cap. She needed that minute to make sure she could speak without any relief, or triumph, in her voice.

"As soon as this is endorsed," she said as she signed the check, "you can go to any branch of this bank"—she pushed the check and a business card across the desk— "and cash it. Once you've done that, you call *this* guy." She brought out another business card. "He's your lawyer now. He can answer any questions and take care of any problems. He also understands that if I ever see you again, the whole thing's over and done."

Todd was sizing her up again, trying to make sure he still had the upper hand. He had to have caught the loophole. *If I ever see you again.* That didn't rule out calls, emails— anything like that. He could still harass her and hurt her, mostly by making sure she knew he'd won, despite all her precautions. That was important.

"Gimme that pen."

Beth did, and she flipped the papers back to the first little sticky tab that marked where he needed to sign.

Todd bent over the paper and scrawled his signature.

"I didn't mean what I said before, you know, about not wanting Jeannie anymore. That was just to see what you'd do," he told her. "I love Jeannie, and I will never, ever leave her alone. I'm going to be right there, no matter what happens. But a man's got to provide somehow, and I am just not as fast as I used to be." He flipped through the papers, signing and initialing just where she showed him. "And do you know, Star, there is an endless supply of the dumbest possible bitches out there? And all of them rich and lining up for the ol' silver fox." He smoothed his gray hair back. "And desperate! My God, you would not believe how effin' desperate! Amanda? She bellows like a goddamned cow. Unbelievable." He chuckled. "You were smart not to marry that guy of yours—Dave, Doug, who-ever the fuck. Just keep yourself a string running, and you can have all the money you need. Now"—Todd shoved all the papers toward her—"where is my wife?"

CHAPTER THIRTY

"What's wrong with your mom?" Chelsea dropped her duffle bag on Dana's bedroom floor and kicked the door shut. "Fuck me. What's wrong with you?"

Dana was curled up on her bed with Cornie Bow. She'd been in pretty much this position the whole afternoon. Most of the time, she just felt numb, but then these waves of anger would come over her—anger at Mom and at her grandparents and her dad and at the dead man and pink-hands man, and she'd break down crying into the pillows so Mom wouldn't hear.

And then she'd be numb again, until the next wave hit.

There was a plate of the cupcakes that never got taken to the party she never went to beside her. Chelsea yanked off her boots, sat cross-legged on the bed, grabbed a cake, and peeled off the paper. She broke it in half and held one half out to Dana. Dana curled farther in on herself.

Chelsea shrugged and ate both halves. "Come on, Dana, what's going on?"

Dana opened her laptop and turned the screen toward Chelsea so she could see the enormous headline standing out against the gray, flyspecked page.

LOCAL MAN FOUND DEAD, FAMILY DISAPPEARS

It was an article from the Abrahamsville *County Register*, from the eighties. It had taken all of one phone call to the local library and one breathless story about a school project to get the librarian to go find the microfilm page, print it out, scan it, and send it to her.

Dana wasn't sure why she did it. Maybe she didn't want to think about why. Maybe she was afraid that as bad as the story Mom told her was, reality might be worse.

Which was also something she did not want to think about.

Chelsea read.

"...was found shot to death in the upper-floor apartment that had been leased to Thomas J. Jankowski and his wife, Deborah. The couple lived there with their daughter, Star, 15, a sophomore at...was apparently shot once at close range with the double-barreled shotgun found at the scene. Police refused to rule out suicide...whereabouts of the Jankowski family are currently unknown, but they are wanted for questioning..."

Chelsea pressed her hand over her mouth and stared. Dana nodded and turned the laptop back around.

"Holy shit!" breathed Chelsea. "Are these your *grand-parents*?"

"And my mom. The guy was holding her hostage for three days, and she killed him and ran."

There was a picture of a body. It was old and grainy, and black and white, but you could still see the mess that had been made of him and the black splatter of blood, like someone had tossed a whole gallon of paint straight at his chest.

"Wow. I knew your mom was a badass, but this is... next-level...and—" Chelsea stopped, clearly because she'd gotten a look at Dana's face. "Okay, what am I missing?"

Dana took a deep breath. She wanted to tell Chelsea everything, but somehow, the words did not want to string themselves together. "I saw my dad. He came to the hospital yesterday, and he...he was hinting around that Mom had done some...really bad stuff."

"Seriously? Usually he only hints around that he wants to blow you off again."

"Yeah. Something's changed. He's in trouble. I don't know what exactly. Mom says it's money, and she always knows when it's money. Anyway. He tried to tell me she killed somebody. He tried...he wanted to get me scared of her. He...he's gone off the fucking rails this time."

A wave of anger swelled again, hot and unnerving. She could feel herself trying to let it go already, to just...accept that Dad did and said shit like this, and it didn't matter.

This time, it matters. It really, seriously matters.

"I am sick of him jerking me around," she said. Each word dropped harder than the last. "And he's gonna hear it from *me*. Me! Not Mom!"

"Just as soon as you stop crying," remarked Chelsea.

"Oh, *fuck*!" Dana slapped the nearest pillow up against her face and bawled. And because Chelsea understood and Chelsea was her BFF, Chelsea grabbed a Kleenex and shoved it under the pillow.

"Rag for the ugly cry," she said. Dana laughed and cried and dropped the pillow and took the Kleenex and honked when she blew her nose.

Chelsea handed a cupcake to Dana and took one for herself.

"What are you gonna do?"

"I'm going to find out exactly what the hell my dad's talking about. Then I'm going to tell him he doesn't get to hide me, then use me. Fuck that."

"Yeah, fuck that fucker into the middle of next fucking week!" Chelsea raised her cupcake like she wanted to make a toast. Dana bumped what was left of her cake up against Chelsea's.

"But…thing is, I need your help."

Chelsea glared at her, which would have been way more intimidating without the blob of frosting on her cheek. "I am not helping you do any more stupid stuff. Look what happened last time."

"Come on—it's not going to be any big deal. I just need you to cover for me with my mom—that's all."

"Yeah." Chelsea scrunched the cupcake wrapper tight in her fist. "Cuz when everything's fine and it's no big deal, that's always when you need somebody to cover for you!"

"All I'm doing is telling my dad I know he's full of it, and he should fuck off and never come back."

"So call him! Phone's right there!" She stabbed a finger at Dana's cell, which was next to her laptop.

"I have to do this to his face. It's the only way I can be sure he's listening, and I've only got two days!"

That stopped Chelsea in her tracks. "Why two days?"

Dana swallowed. "Cuz Mom's making me go away to this stupid 'enrichment camp' for rich kids whose parents need to get them out of the way while they're investigated by the special counsel or something." Telling Chelsea made it way more real. Her whole summer, her internship—everything—was all done before it even got started. She was being shoved aside. So she'd be safe and out of the picture. "I'm supposed to leave Wednesday."

Suddenly, Chelsea got up off the bed and stalked over to the window.

"Fuck!" she said to the city outside. "Just...fuck! Dana! Why'd you have to go screwing around with this?! Huh? I told you it'd just mess everything up! Why couldn't you *listen*?!"

"What the hell, Chelsea? What's going on?!"

But it was like Chelsea didn't even hear her. "You...you don't *think*—that's what's going on! You get all tied up in knots and your own little world and you don't even see what you're doing to everybody else!"

"Chelsea!" Dana jumped off the bed and grabbed her friend's shoulders. "What's wrong?"

To Dana's utter shock, Chelsea was crying.

"Jesus, Chelsea, what..."

"All the shit at home...it's gotten worse. It's..."

Dana went cold. "Oh, Christ. Did Cody...did he..."

"No, not that. But you remember that douche Ashton? With the pills? Well, he's gone and got the whole goddamn band in on it with him. They've been getting all these frat party gigs and stuff, but it's only because they're bringing the drugs. And they're around, like, all the time now. And it's summer and I haven't got anywhere to go and I know it's gonna get worse. Cody got arrested last month, and Dad got it all hushed up and stuff, and Mom hasn't left her room for, like, *days*...I think he's giving her pills too. I don't know if Dad knows..." The words trailed away. "I was going to ask if I could stay with you guys for, you know, a while, but..." She wiped at her eyes. "If you're leaving...there's nowhere to go."

"Oh. Oh no. Oh shit. Chelsea, I'm so sorry. But it won't happen. Mom won't leave you there. I swear she won't."

"Yeah, like what's she going to do now, when you're not even going to be here?"

"Maybe I won't have to go. There's still a couple of days. Maybe..."

But even while she said it, she knew she was just bullshitting herself, and if she hadn't known it, the look on Chelsea's face would have absolutely clued her in.

"At least promise me you'll stay away from your dad."

"Jesus, Chels. I know shit's bad and stuff, but we're talking about my *dad*. He can't put a Band-Aid on a cut by himself."

"You've...you've never really seen how desperate rich people get when somebody's about to take their money away."

"And you have?"

"Shit, yeah. You know how my mom talks about that 'little separation' she and Dad had when we were kids?"

"Yeah?"

"He was in prison for tax fraud. And beating up his accountant."

"Fuck. I thought your mom was the crazy one."

"Oh, in the Hamilton family, we are all about the equal-opportunity dysfunction." She picked up another cupcake and started peeling off the wrapper.

Dana made up her mind, all at once, about a whole bunch of things.

"And don't worry, we'll figure out how to talk Mom into letting you stay for the summer."

"But you're going to bad-billionaire camp."

"So, I'll guilt her into letting you come with me."

Chelsea grinned. "We will be running the place inside a week." She held up her hand, and Dana slapped it in a high five, hard.

"Everything's going to be okay, Chelsea." Dana laced her fingers through Chelsea's and held on. *I will fix this.* "It will. I promise."

CHAPTER THIRTY-ONE

Dana was going to be devastated when she found out her grandmother had vanished.

I'm sorry, Dangerface. I'm so, so sorry. The words unspooled themselves inside Beth's head. *I don't know how he got to her.*

When the office door closed behind her father, Beth stayed exactly where she was and counted to ten. She wanted to be sure she could move without shaking. She also wanted to be sure that Todd wasn't going to decide it would be really funny to come back and have the last-last word.

The door remained closed.

Beth worked the keyboard on her desktop computer, shutting down the video-conference program that had been running during the entire meeting.

Dana was right. It was time to be done with secrets.

Except the one.

Jeannie must have called him, and…and I just don't know what happened. I'm sorry.

She saved the file of her conversation with Todd, first to the computer hard drive, and then to her private Dropbox account.

You tried to help. You really tried. She just…wasn't ready to accept it. That's all.

Beth opened her desk drawer and pulled out the recorder.

It was an old-fashioned one, with an actual microcassette in it. She quickly extracted the cassette and sealed it into an envelope, which she'd already addressed to her lawyer.

Todd Bowen had very few blind spots, but one of them was that he would assume that if the sucker paid out, that was the beginning and the end of that sucker's plan.

Once Todd had Jeannie out of state and once Beth had settled whatever the hell was up with Doug, she could talk with Amanda Martin and any others that Kinseki tracked down. She could play them the recordings, tell them the truth, "help" them decide what to do about it.

Lumination's emergency communications team would help with any media attention that might arise. And it wouldn't be the first time Beth had needed to finesse her own story for public consumption.

Beth started collecting her things. She needed to get home. She had left Dana alone too long as it was. She lit up her phone and texted:

Heading home. All okay there?

👍

She looked at the emoji for a while, seeking reassurance. There was still this nagging whisper in her head that it had gone too well. That maybe she'd misjudged her father or overplayed her hand.

But she couldn't do anything more about her parents until tomorrow at the very earliest. Right now, she had to focus on the other half of this fine mess.

She had to find out if Dad really was behind Doug's money troubles, or if her ex coming to her for help now was just a coincidence. Not that Doug would ever voluntarily admit anything. And of course, neither would Todd.

So, she would just have to go around them.

CHAPTER THIRTY-TWO

"Dana?" Mom knocked on her bedroom door. "Dana, I've got some news."

Shit. Now what?

Worry stabbed at her. Last night, Mom had come home grim but hopeful from meeting Todd. She hadn't wanted to go into details, but that just made it easier for Dana to put the plan she'd worked out into action.

Step One—explain very calmly and rationally why she should be allowed to go to the Vine and Horn on her own to explain why she was pulling out of the internship at the last minute.

"I still might have a chance to work there," she'd pointed out. "I can't go in with my mom following me around like I'm just some irresponsible kid."

She'd expected hours of wrangling and maybe even having to throw a full-bore tantrum. But Mom had agreed almost right away. In fact, she'd maybe even looked a little relieved.

Except maybe this morning, she'd changed her mind.

"Come in!" Dana called.

The door opened and Dana's heart sank. Mom really looked like she was having second thoughts. *No, no, you can't. I have to do this...*

"I just got a call from the hospital." Mom cut through her rising panic. "Jeannie's labs came back this morning."

"What do they say?"

Mom shook her head. "They can't talk about it over the phone. Privacy regulations. But after I drop you off at the restaurant, I'm going to talk with the doctors, okay?"

"Can I come meet you after I'm done? I want to see Jeannie."

Mom hesitated. "I don't know how long this will take. But text me as soon as you're done. I'll come get you, and we'll head straight back, okay?"

"I can get a Lyft..." But Dana knew that was a nonstarter before she finished the sentence.

"Humor me," said Mom. "I'm having a tough enough time letting you out of my sight today as it is."

"Yeah, sure, okay." Even as she said it, though, Dana felt there was something...off. She couldn't put her finger on it, but it was there. But it wasn't like she could argue. She had to take whatever breathing room Mom was willing to give her.

Mom was already hesitating. "And swear you'll stay put until I come get you. You won't go anywhere with anybody?"

"Swear." Dana crossed her heart. "Stranger danger. Three steps back and run like the wind. And it's not like the place is going to be empty," she added as she pulled on her school blazer. "There's going to be, like, a zillion people around with knives and fire."

That actually got Mom to smile. "Phone?" she said.

Dana flipped open one side of the blazer to show her the lining and the hidden pocket.

"Mad money?"

Dana flipped open the other side.

"Text time? Because you're humoring me," she added when she saw Dana's eye roll.

"Four thirty, on the dot," Dana recited. "Today and every day."

"Love you, Dangerface."

"Love you, Mom."

Dana turned away. *Time for Step Two.*

"Well, we'll be sorry not to have you with us, Dana." Ramona Lee, the manager of Vine and Horn, closed the manila folder in front of her. "But we all understand family has to come first. Hopefully, you'll be able to reapply next summer."

Next summer. Dana repeated the words to herself. *Next summer. First we deal with the shit storm.*

Dana smiled and said thanks and sure and good-bye and all the other polite stuff she should. She picked up her purse and let herself be steered out of the cramped office, through the busy kitchen, and into the empty dining room. It was Monday, and the restaurant was closed, although you'd never know it from the amount of frantic prep work underway.

"Um, sorry, Ms. Lee," said Dana. "Is it okay if I make a call?"

"Of course, but I have to get back to the kitchen. Just make sure the door shuts all the way behind you when you leave."

Dana promised and waited until Ms. Lee pushed back through the swinging doors. She swallowed the lump in her throat and reached into one of her inside jacket pockets.

This morning, Mom had clearly been glad to see her wearing one of her "special" blazers. She would have been less thrilled to know that Dana had loaded one of her pockets with her backup phone—the one she'd bought with her own cash so Mom didn't have to know about it. There were times she just plain did not want to deal with Mom and her tracking apps.

Dana touched her father's number and waited.

"H-hello?" He sounded sleepy. *Or hungover. Dad? No. He'd never. Would he?*

"It's me, Dad."

"Dana! Hi. I'm, uh, it's good to hear from you. Did you talk to your mom?"

"Not yet, but, um, I need to talk to you—like, now."

"Yeah, yeah, okay. You'll have to come to my hotel. I'm waiting on this call, but…"

"Hotel? Why are you at a hotel?"

"I'm, uh, it's just temporary. We're having some work done on the house while Susan and the kids are camping, and—"

"I thought that was just the weekend?" Dana cut him off. She did not have time for him to start rambling.

"Yeah, well, it…" She heard him getting ready to lie. But then, it seemed, he changed his mind. "Dana, I…She's left me."

"*What?*" Dana barely remembered she should keep her voice down.

"This thing with your mother and the money—it was too much for her. It's why I've been so crazy. I'm just trying to fix this so I can get her back."

Un-effing-believable. Dana squeezed her eyes shut. Nothing could ever be simple with her father. Nothing could ever get better. It just had to keep falling further apart.

But what was she going to do? She had to find out everything she could from him before she told him to get the hell out of her life forever. She had to know if he was telling the truth about the fraud. She wouldn't have believed him, never in a thousand years, except he'd told the truth about the…the other thing.

If Mom was in that much trouble, if she was lying about something that huge, Dana had to know. She didn't believe it. It couldn't be true. Except the other thing was. She had to know.

"Dana? Are you still there?"

"Uh, yeah. Okay. Where are you?"

He gave her the name of an extended-stay place and said it was out by the highway. She was going to have to call a ride, but she had her debit card to cover it.

Dana told him she'd be there in maybe fifteen minutes,

A MOTHER'S LIE

and she hung up. *Step Three.* She bit her lip, hard, and then she messaged Chelsea.

Going to see Dad. She added the hotel name and his room number. DO NOT FREAK!!! 🙏🙏🙏 Will message every 10 minutes from backup phone. If I miss one, you can freak.

She hit Send and dropped the phone back into her pocket. It clinked against the "special" nail file Chelsea had given her, in case of other kinds of emergencies. Not that she'd need it. Dad was pathetic, not crazy.

Dana looked toward the kitchen door, and then she laid her other phone—the one Mom tracked—down on the chair and walked out the front door.

CHAPTER THIRTY-THREE

"Susan." Beth smiled as the other woman sat down at the café's sidewalk table. "Thank you for agreeing to see me."

"You're welcome, Beth." Susan Hoyt appeared as collected and perfectly put together as she had the few other times Beth had met her. Doug's wife looked like she'd been called in from central casting to play a suburban homemaker. Her pale skin was enhanced with sunblock, moisturizer, and facials rather than nips and tucks. She was thin but not too skinny. Her wide blue eyes tended to make her look a little anxious. But there was an extra air of distance and caution in the mix today.

Not that I blame her. Beth flipped her phone over. The phone-tracker app was up and running. It showed Dana's location as a green circle on the map and stayed steady.

Dana's fine. I need to focus.

Beth needed to find the right way to ask this woman

she barely knew about the current state of her family finances, and if she knew who her husband had been giving money to.

The server came over with water and to take drink orders. Beth ordered a cold brew coffee. Susan, despite the already warm day, ordered herbal tea.

Beth asked about Patty and Marcus. Susan asked about Dana.

Beth asked about the house and the rose garden that was always Susan's special pride. Susan asked about work.

Beth couldn't help noticing how good Susan was at small talk. Really, professional grade. She never let the silence stretch a second too long before she had another question ready. But then, this was exactly why Doug gravitated to this woman. Susan took "detail oriented" to new heights. For her, problem solving for anyone in her near orbit was a personal triumph, and she had always seemed to believe she could discover the exact combination of love, kindness, and competence that would get Doug to leave his personal Neverland and finally grow up.

Their drinks came, and while Beth shoveled sugar into her coffee, Susan dunked her mint tea bag into her cup exactly ten times, before pulling it out and settling it on the saucer. Then, she lifted the cup, wiped the bottom with her napkin, and set the saucer aside.

Beth decided to take that as her signal to get down to business.

"I'm sure you're wondering why I called…"

"I actually expected to hear from you sooner." Susan lifted her cup in both hands. "I imagine you have a great deal of gloating to do, and that sort of thing is always so much more satisfying in person."

The cold declaration hit Beth with physical force. "What are you talking about?"

The corner of Susan's mouth twitched. "Please. You've never been anything but jealous of me and my children."

"Is that what Doug told you?" *And you believed him?*

"Of course he told me. That's why you've always tried to shove your daughter into our family, so you could use her to spy on us. I love Doug," Susan continued with surprising ferocity. "I have always, *always* tried to be what he needed. You can sneer all you want, but that's the truth."

It took all Beth's years of personal discipline to keep from blurting out her response. She knew next to nothing about Doug's wife. Since she and Dana moved to Chicago, Beth had met Susan only three or four times. They would make small talk about the kids and the city. Susan would talk fondly about Doug and all his problems and all her solutions. Somewhere during the conversation, Susan would explain how some failure of Doug to live up to some promise was actually her fault. And Beth had always been able to picture Doug standing behind her, smiling and relieved and oh so grateful.

Beth had seen it was a mask, but it was a very good one. Maybe she could have gotten under it, but that would have taken time and effort, and she hadn't believed it would accomplish much of anything.

Except maybe get me ready for this. Beth took another swallow of coffee and pushed the cup aside. Whatever she said next, she would have to choose her words very, very carefully.

She met Susan's proud, worried gaze. *She's scared of me.*

"I have never once sneered at you, Susan," she said. "As far as I'm concerned, you and your family are the one thing Doug actually has going for him. I called you because you need to know he's gotten himself into some kind of pyramid scheme."

Susan stared at her, plainly unable to believe what she was hearing, but Beth kept on going. "I've got people tracking it down. We should be able to identify the source before too long, but until then, you need to keep an eye on your money, just in case. None of this is Doug's fault," she added quickly. "These people are very smooth operators and—"

"These people! What people?" Susan demanded.

But Beth just said, "Susan, what's happened?"

Susan turned her face away. She watched the traffic easing by in the street. Watched the people and the pigeons, watched everything except Beth while she brought herself back under control.

Oh, Susan, I've screwed up so badly. I should have gotten to know you. I should have taken the time. But she'd been so glad somebody else was managing Doug that she'd been more than willing to just leave Susan to it. She'd never thought about what kind of stories he might be spinning, or that it might ever matter.

After all, Doug was harmless.

I knew everything he'd done to me and to Dana, and I still kept telling myself he was harmless. How the hell did I let that happen?

"All I ever wanted was a home," Susan said at last, keeping her face turned toward the city. "And someone who needed me. *Me*." She patted her chest. "I told him, right up front when we first started getting serious, that the one thing I would not tolerate was him keeping secrets. I swore I was done with that." Memory took her gaze even farther away.

Beth burned to ask what lay behind that distant look, but now was not the time. Maybe that time would never come.

My fault. Again.

"The money's gone," said Susan. "At least, his is."

"His?"

This, evidently, was something her pride could stand to talk about, and Susan turned toward Beth again. "When we got married, I told him I was going to keep my own investment accounts, just in case something happened. I wanted to be able to provide for myself and any children during any…transition period. He didn't like talking about dying, of course, but in the end, he came around to it.

"That was actually my first hint that there was trouble. Recently, he started pressing to get his name on my accounts, in case something happened, he said."

And you turned him down, and that brought him to me.

"Susan, I don't know what Doug has been telling you about me, but I might be able to help recover at least some of the money."

Her mouth twitched. "Which is ironic in the extreme, since Doug said you were the one who stole it."

Ah. Beth sat back, disappointed but not terribly surprised.

Damn, Doug. I've really made it easy for you to turn me into your scapegoat, haven't I?

"Do you believe him?"

Susan took a swallow of her tea and made a face. She retrieved the tea bag and dropped it back into the water. "I don't know," she said. "Maybe."

"Can you answer me one more question? Have you ever seen Doug with this man?"

Beth pulled a photograph out of her purse and slid it across the table. She'd pulled the picture from one of her Kinseki reports. It was Todd in three-quarter profile, laughing at some joke.

"Where did you get this?" asked Susan.

"Do you know him?" Beth countered.

"That's Rafael Gutierrez. He and his wife came to dinner with us three weeks ago." She pressed her hand over her mouth. "She's the reason I wouldn't let Doug near my money."

CHAPTER THIRTY-FOUR

The MaxRest America Extended-Stay Hotel was about as generic as you could ask for. Dad had a ground-floor room on the same side as the (empty) outdoor swimming pool. The clerk barely glanced at Dana as she headed across the lobby and down the hall.

Dana stopped in front of the room and messaged Chelsea.

Still OK 👍

She tucked her phone into her side pocket and banged on the door. There was some shuffling from inside and then the sound of the deadbolt and the chain being worked.

"Hi, Dana," said Dad. "Come on in."

"Yeah, thanks," she sneered and walked inside.

It was a hotel suite, all shades of beige. There was an oversize TV in the living area and a kitchenette with a full-size fridge and a separate bedroom. The door was closed.

"You want to sit down?" Dad asked nervously. Of course he was nervous. He was trying to mess with her head and maybe he was already getting the idea it wasn't working. "Something to drink?"

"You know what I want, Dad?" Dana snapped. "I want you to tell me the truth!"

She'd meant to go slow. She'd meant to try to sweet-talk him. But coming straight from the wreck of all her plans for the summer and seeing him like this—she just didn't have enough left in her to play the good cop.

Her father spread his hand, giving her the "calm down" wave, which had never calmed anybody down, ever. Her anger flared up fresh just seeing it. But she also saw he was all rumpled again, and stubbled, and red eyed.

Good. Everything sucks. Everything should suck for you!

"Dana, I know you're mad, and you've got reason to be. But you need to sit down and try to listen to what we've got to tell you. It's important."

"No! I am done listening to you! I…" She stopped, and she was pretty sure she did a double take. "Wait. *We?*"

"Yeah." Dad rubbed his hands together. "You see…"

That was when the bedroom door opened, and the lean, gray man stepped out.

It was Todd.

CHAPTER THIRTY-FIVE

"Doug told you this man"—Beth tapped the photograph—
"was Rafael Gutierrez? Head of Lumination?"

Susan nodded. "They said Doug was helping do the risk
assessment on a new fund. I didn't think it sounded…I
don't know what I thought it sounded like. I knew he was
your boss, and I knew you'd never go along with Doug
working on any project you were involved with…"

Well, finally we're both on the same page about something.
Beth tried to stop her head from spinning. She tried to
focus on hearing what Susan was actually saying.

"I meant to start asking questions. I did, but then—" She
swallowed. "Then, his wife…We were in the restroom,
and she told me that there was an investigation going on
at Lumination, and Doug was in over his head. She told
me I should keep an eye on our money for the time being,
and not let Doug take out too much. She said she wasn't
supposed to be telling me, because it might interfere with

the inquiries, but she…she was a mother too, she said, and she knew I had nothing to do with it, and she didn't want our kids to get hurt."

And of course you couldn't ask any questions after that. You were too busy trying to save yourself and your kids. Beth pulled a second photo out of her purse. "Was this his wife?" She laid Jeannie's picture down on the table. "Yes. Angela. What—" The sound of Beth's phone ringing cut her off.

It was Chelsea. Beth forgot all about Susan and Doug.

"Hello? Chelsea?" She pressed her free ear closer to hear better. "What's happening?"

"Uh, hi, um, Ms. Fraser, I…"

Shit. "Deep breath, Chelsea. I'm listening."

"It's Dana. She's in trouble."

CHAPTER THIRTY-SIX

"Hello, Dana." Todd Bowen smiled and spread his hands. Unlike her father, he was perfectly combed, and his shirt was crisp and clean. In fact, it was like they'd swapped places or something. "I know this has got to be a surprise, but..."

Dana recovered her voice. "A *surprise*!" she shouted. "Dad! What is this guy even doing here?! Do you know who this is?"

Dad seemed to deflate. He crossed the room and collapsed onto the couch like he didn't have the strength to keep standing. Then, to Dana's complete shock, Todd walked over and patted Dad's shoulder.

"The FBI is investigating your mother, Dana." Dad said it to the wall. He rubbed his hands together, like he was trying to get them warm.

"What?!"

"Her and Lumination, and they're probably coming after me."

"Oh, for f— Why?!"

But it was Todd who answered. "Because your mother has been hiding client money in fake accounts and using your father's name to do it." He sighed heavily. "And mine, for that matter. And your grandmother's."

What he was saying made no sense. There was no possible alternate universe in which Dad could be slouched there with this utter loser saying Mom had stolen from her clients.

"I know you probably don't know much about your mother's business," said Todd softly. "I mean, why would you? She's never been…really careful about where her money comes from. But she is very careful about what she does with it, and, well, careful's not always the same as legal, is it? Anyway, the feds are finally going to catch up with her."

"How do you even know this?"

"I told you. Some of the accounts are under my name," said Todd. "That's the real reason why me and Jeannie were in Chicago. We were answering questions. At least, we were supposed to. We couldn't actually tell them much."

"Oh, this is so much bullshit."

"I know what it sounds like, Dana," said Todd sadly. "But I just need you to hear me out, okay? That's all."

"Why should I?"

"Because none of us want you to get hurt," said Dad.

"Us!" She couldn't stop shouting. She couldn't think straight. It was like she'd suddenly walked into some kind of bizarro mirror world where everything was backward.

"Your father's told me the kind of things your mom

has said about us," said Todd. "About us being criminals. About us running drugs and kidnapping her from her grandmother. All that."

"Well, it's true!"

"No, Dana. It isn't. None of it."

"Yeah, and I suppose it's not true that you hit your wife right in front of me!"

Todd winced. "Yeah, okay, that was bad. I admit that. I…I have a temper, and…I'd been sitting in a room answering questions for three days, or trying to. I thought I was going to jail—I really did. And then I found out that Jeannie was planning on *warning* your mother about the investigation…I just lost it. I just lost it." He looked out the French doors to the pool and the parking lot. "I just hope one day Jeannie will be able to forgive me, because I'm never going to be able to forgive myself."

"You're a liar!" Dana shouted at Todd. "He's a liar!" she shouted at her father.

Dad just looked at her with his sad, shadowed eyes and said nothing at all.

Dana shoved both hands into her hair as if she were trying to keep her head from flying off. She had to get out of here, right this second. Because something terrifying was happening in her. Something was twisting in her mind, trying to lay what Todd was saying over top of what she knew was the truth. Memory and reality were both shifting, right inside her.

"Dana, please!" Dad started halfway to his feet but didn't make it and just dropped back down. "I'm trying to help you. Your mom—she's got problems."

"We tried to help her, but we didn't have the money," Todd said. "She's kept you away from us all this time because she didn't want you to know how badly she's been lying her whole life."

Dad nodded, way too fast.

"We realized something was wrong when she was little," Todd said. "Even then, she was always lashing out. She'd lie and argue about every little thing. None of the teachers could control her. We couldn't keep her in school. We were constantly driving around to all these appointments, one specialist after another, to try to figure out what was wrong. And they just kept putting her on all these pills...I mean, it felt like dozens some days. She wouldn't take them, and I almost couldn't blame her," he added in a whisper. "Anyway, nothing helped, and in the end...she just ran away." His hands fell to his sides. "We looked for her for years. But every time we got close, she'd disappear again. Finally, we just stopped trying.

"We tried to keep an eye out, you know, a little, online and stuff. But we were scared in case she got mad...She could be so violent. We didn't want to set her off."

Red. Red and stars and the hard sidewalk and more red on Mommy's hands and her feet and her face and...

No. No. Don't listen. This is not true!

"But then, the feds found us, and they were asking questions about her. We couldn't tell them much, but...we were worried, and we thought maybe, because of you, we should tell your dad, so he could get you away before...well, before it all came crashing down."

Dad jumped in. "And that's when we found out about

the money stuff, and we started putting two and two together."

"That's what's going on, Dana," said Todd. "That's the truth."

Do not let this guy use his spin on you. None of this is the truth, and you know it!

Dana folded her arms. "Then how come Jeannie wants to leave you, huh? How come she's in the hospital dying of cancer and saying—"

"I know where she is," said Todd softly. "I heard from her just this morning."

"You...she called you?"

"Yeah. Jeannie's terrified. Your mom was threatening her. I'm...I'm surprised she even let her get as far out of sight as the hospital."

Dad was trying to smile, but he just looked as sick as she felt. "Dana, I know what a shock this is, but there's no need to panic. There's a way out for everybody. That's what we want to talk to you about. We just need you to do one thing."

Dana scowled. "What?"

Dad rubbed his hands together again, and he glanced at Todd, like he was asking permission. Dana threw her hands up and let them drop—*slap*—against her sides.

"We told you—your mother has a bunch of accounts with the money she's hidden," Dad said. "They're all password-protected and stuff. All you have to do is find the account numbers and passwords, and give them to me. I'll give them to the investigators when they show up. Then they'll know I had nothing to do with any of this."

You think this is about you! For a minute, Dana thought she was going to be sick. Then she thought she might laugh. Finally, something was exactly like normal. Her father was in the middle of an enormous disaster and worrying about what would happen to him.

And she had no idea how she was going to pull him out of it.

Except maybe one.

Dana faced Todd and put her back to her father. She couldn't stand to see him sitting there, all hunched over and rubbing his hands. "You say you're telling me the truth? How about this truth? Who's Thomas Jankowski? Deborah Ann Watts?" She paused to make sure she had his full attention. She so did. "How about Robert MacNamera Early?"

Todd's whole body stiffened, and for a split second, she thought she saw fear behind his eyes.

"Dana, what are you talking about?" demanded Dad.

"I'll tell you." Dana took her father's wrist. "But not in front of this guy. Come on." She tugged his arm.

Why do I even care what Dad does? But she did care. Todd Bowen—or Thomas Jankowski or whoever the hell—was playing some kind of con game, and Dad was already in trouble. If she didn't get him out of here, it'd just get worse, and then it'd be her fault. She had to try.

But Dad didn't move. "Dana, you have to help me," he pleaded. "If you don't do this, I'm going to go to prison!"

Todd turned his back, like he couldn't stand to witness any more.

"I cannot believe you're actually buying this shit! Jesus, Dad, I knew you were stupid, but—"

Todd looked back over his shoulder. "You see how she's taught your daughter to talk to you? You see what she is?"

"If I can just get the accounts, then I'm in the clear. I can tell Susan I'm cooperating, and we'll be okay, and you can come stay with us until..."

"Until you can figure out how to unload me on somebody else!" screamed Dana. "It's a lie, Dad! It's all a great, big lie!" *And a bunch of little lies, all wrapped up together so you won't think about them too hard.* "I cannot believe I even came here! That I even ever tried..."

Tears blinded her. Her throat burned. Dana whipped around and headed for the door.

"You come back here!" Dad shouted. "I am not going to jail over something she did!"

He was on her before Dana knew what was happening. He grabbed her by her shoulders, and he dragged her backward into the kitchenette and shoved her against the counter. The edge bit into her back and she shrieked. But he didn't let go.

You've never really seen how desperate... Chelsea's voice sounded in her brain. In front of her, Dad's face was red and swollen and blurred. He was shaking her, jarring her back against the counter edge.

"Stop it!" she screamed.

"You will listen to me!"

Dana didn't even know how her hand moved, but it did and it dived into her pocket and it came up with the nail file.

Dad saw the flash, and some instinct took over and he let go.

Dana gasped. Her head hurt, and her back hurt where it had banged against the counter. Stars. She saw stars, and red…

And Todd Bowen.

Todd hadn't moved. He hadn't come to help either one of them. He'd just stood there and watched.

Dana wiped her mouth with her free hand. Her face was covered in her own spit. "Dad, I don't know what this douche has told you, but he is not some kind of good guy! And I am walking out of here right now."

"Dana," her father croaked. He held up his hands again—surrender, calm down, help me. "Stop being ridiculous and put that down. Listen to me…"

"No! What is your fucking issue, *Dad*? Look this guy up on the internet, why don't you? There's a whole video with him hitting his wife and Mom getting in the way! Now he's mad that she got Jeannie away from him! She's *leaving* the asshole, and I. Am. Leaving. You!"

Dana turned. She meant to run out the door, but Todd was there, even faster than Dad had been. He grabbed her wrist.

"Hey!" Dad shouted.

Dana twisted and yanked down, breaking his hold. She kicked out, but her sneakers didn't have much impact, and Dad hauled her back at the same time.

"No, wait. Look…" Dad let her go to step between them, but Todd shoved him back into Dana, and she screamed and heaved him sideways with everything she had. He stumbled and slid, and his head came down—*smack!*—against the counter.

And Dad crumpled onto the kitchen floor.

"Dad!" Dana dropped down next to him. He looked at her vaguely. There was a straight line on his forehead, and it blossomed red.

"Oh Jesus," Dana gasped. "Dad, get up!" She tried to get her arm under his shoulders. "Dad, come on—help me! We have to get…"

"You are not leaving." Todd loomed over them. "You are going to obey your father."

"You shut up!" Dana screamed. She still had the nail file in her hand, and she pointed it right at Todd. "And back off!"

She did not like the way Todd was looking at her, did not like the calculations running in those blue eyes. She brandished the nail file at him and tugged on Dad's sleeve at the same time. "Dad, Dad, please. Get up. We gotta go now."

"Oh Jesus," Dad gasped and tried to lever himself up off the floor. He looked confused. He pressed his fingers against his head and saw the blood on his hand and looked up at Todd like he'd never seen the man before. "We were just gonna scare her!"

"*WHAT?!*" The force of her scream pulled Dana to her feet.

"I'm sorry," Dad said from the floor. "I'm sorry. This was a mistake. It was stupid. You're right. We'll…we'll go. Really."

"No," said Todd grimly. "You really won't. Not until we get this settled."

"Dana!"

Someone was banging on a door. It sounded like it was coming from the…bedroom?

"Dana! I'm here!"

"*Jeannie?*" How…?

It didn't matter. Dana lunged for the door, but Todd grabbed her around the waist and spun her. Dana got the file up, but Todd pulled her past him, and she fell sprawling across her father's chest.

Dad shrieked and sat up, and Dana rolled off him and scrambled to sit up. She groped across the tile floor for the nail file, but she couldn't find it.

Where is it?

"Dana!" screamed her grandmother.

Dad was clawing at his stomach. Dark red stained his shirt, where the nail file stuck out between the buttons, a stupid little white nubbin.

It had gone all the way in. Almost.

Dad stared, confused. Then, he yanked it out. Blood fountained, gushed, and smacked her in the face. Dana screamed. She tasted hot iron and salt and gagged hard.

"Oh fuck!" screamed Jeannie from…somewhere.

Then, all at once, she was right there. She grabbed Dana's shoulders, dragging her backward, hauling her to her feet. Turning her away. Dad choked. Now Dana screamed. Now she fought, but Jeannie held her tightly.

"No, honey—no, don't look."

"Oh, sweet Jesus, what's happening? What do we do…?"

Jeannie's bony hand cupped the back of Dana's skull and pressed Dana's face to her shoulder. "Come on, hon-bun. We gotta go now. Come on."

Some shred of sense, or fear, made Dana try to push away. "I can't. We...I can't...I didn't mean to..."

"We're going!" snapped Jeannie.

There was noise from outside, and she was jostled sideways. Grandma just pushed Dana's face down against her shoulder again. Someone was grunting. There was a tearing noise.

Grandma wouldn't let her lift her head up. "Oh, honey, I'm sorry, I'm sorry, but we gotta keep going."

Still holding her tight, Jeannie shoved her forward.

Fear robbed Dana of any ability to think. She couldn't even see straight. She was being pushed and shoved into the dark away from everything...away from everybody...

This was wrong, this was wrong, this was all wrong.

Memory boiled over and sloshed hard into the real world. Sweating hands held and pushed her. Someone was right behind her, pushing her too fast, bumping right up against her, shoving her. She wanted to stop, she couldn't stop, they wouldn't let her stop.

Where did Mommy go? Oh! There she is. Come on!

She wanted Mommy, but she couldn't see Mommy, and the person was pushing her, hurting her, moving her farther away from Mommy, from help, from everything.

And this time Mommy wasn't coming to save her.

Dana lurched into the present long enough to be aware of being shoved into a car's back seat. Grandma climbed in behind her, slammed the door. Clicked the lock.

"Did he hurt you? Come on, honey. Let me see!" Grandma's twig-like fingers grabbed her chin, twisting her head this way and that. She grabbed Dana's hands, checking her arms. "Okay, okay," Grandma was muttering. "You're okay, hon. You're okay."

I need to get out of here. Something was missing, something was wrong, but she couldn't think what it was.

"Shit."

The car's front door was yanked open. A man threw himself into the driver's seat.

"Go! Go!" screamed Grandma. The driver gunned the engine, and the force of the acceleration shoved Dana backward.

I gotta get out of here. She knew the car was moving, but she reached for the door handle anyway.

"Jesus! No, no, you gotta get down—get down."

Dana was pressed down onto the floor. She was shaking. She was cold. Except for her palms and her legs. The places where the blood smeared across her skin. Those burned.

Something was missing. Lost. Gone.

Me. I'm gone. I'm lost.

Tires squealed, and the car slowed. She tried to sit up, but Grandma pushed her down again.

"Stay down, honey. Here, I'm going to cover you up, okay? You just stay down and keep breathing."

Something—a blanket—was pulled over her. Dana huddled under it, crouched on the floor of the back seat. Crumbs and gravel dug into her knees and shins and palms. Every bump rattled her teeth. Her chin banged against the wheel well, and she bit her tongue. More blood. She smelled gasoline and mildew and old coffee and maybe piss.

She couldn't stop shaking. She'd never stop shaking.

It was too much. She couldn't stand it. She wanted it to all go away. It had to go away. It couldn't be real. It had to be gone.

And for a while, it was.

CHAPTER THIRTY-SEVEN

Beth was out of the town car before it stopped moving.

The ride had been a nightmare. The college-kid driver had done everything he could—run every stop sign and light. Clipped fenders. Took corners like a lunatic. And it still took too long. She was still sick and filled with stark, blazing panic.

Get inside. She stumbled across the parking lot. *Find the lobby, find the desk. Tell them...tell them...*

But movement caught her eye. One of the ground-level rooms had its glass door wide open. Curtains flapped in the breeze.

Shit! Beth bolted past the pool enclosure and straight for the open door.

She shoved her way through the stiff fabric and into the room.

A thick cloud of stink rose up around her. She recognized it instantly. Iron. Copper. Fear. The smell jammed itself into her throat and tore open the membrane between her and all her nightmares. Beth's hands curled and released reflexively, dropping the gun she'd dropped years ago. Her ears rang from the shot. Her shoulder hurt from the kick of the gun. The blood stung her eyes and her skin.

Robert MacNamera Early lay in the kitchenette, a limp and untidy bundle like a broken doll all covered in fresh red paint.

Except it wasn't Bob Early on the floor this time. It was Doug.

People said the dead look surprised. They were wrong. With their open eyes and slack jaws, the dead look terrified and confused. Doug looked like he wanted so desperately to ask why all this had happened. Because whatever it was, it was not his fault.

This life. This death. This hotel room, this bed, this floor, and all this blood. There was blood on the cabinets and the fridge too, and on the door to the hallway. It oozed black and putrid from the tear in his shirt and pooled red in the gaping slash across his throat.

Dana was not here. Not now. But she had been. She'd been brought here or sent here or coaxed here.

To watch her father die.

Outside, an engine gunned, tires squealed. Beth tried to move, but she stumbled, and by the time she got to the window, all she saw were taillights. The town car was gone. She was on her own.

She stood there, fists curling and releasing, dropping that shotgun in that other room. Dropping it, and dropping it again, and again.

Stop it! Stop it! You are not there! You are here! You are here and now, and where's Dana?!

Where is your daughter?!

Beth forced herself to turn back toward the room and the stench. Now she saw a flash of white in the blood beside his head.

Knife?

No. A nail file. A glass nail file. Dana had told her Chelsea carried a nail file like that. It had a wicked-sharp tip and could get past metal detectors, Chelsea said. You could sharpen the edge too, she said, if you had the time.

There was a phone on the floor with the nail file. A small, thick iPhone, several generations old, probably reconditioned. Its screen was smashed, like somebody had stomped on it.

The backup phone. Chelsea said Dana kept a backup phone. Because sometimes she didn't want Beth to be able to track her.

Sirens cut the air—high, painful wails and sharp air-horn bursts. Through the flapping curtains, she saw lights flash red and blue. Police. At least two carloads of them roared into the parking lot.

Beth grabbed the phone and the nail file. She ran to the bathroom and dropped them both into the toilet.

Doors slammed. Voices bellowed.

She flushed, but the trash didn't go down. She flushed again.

There was the static of radios and more shouting, and she was here, trying to flush away the evidence.

Boots drummed against concrete. She needed to run too. Again. But this time there was nowhere she could go.

"Police!"

Beth sank slowly to her knees and raised her hands.

PART THREE

HIDE-AND-SEEK

CHAPTER THIRTY-EIGHT

Maybe she slept. Maybe she just passed out. Dana had no way to know. The next thing that penetrated her mind was Jeannie shaking her shoulder.

"We're here, honey. Here. Put this on."

The blanket peeled back. Hands urged her upright. Her palms and face felt scraped raw. Her neck hurt. Her head hurt.

Somebody dragged a sweatshirt down over her and yanked the hood over her face as far as it would go.

What's happening? She tried to look up, but somebody shoved her head quickly down and pushed her out of the car.

It was dark.

That someone (Jeannie?) wrapped an arm around her shoulders and steered her, stumbling, up some steps toward a dark doorway and down a dark hall.

There were more stairs. She stubbed her toes on the first one and again at the top.

She hurt so bad. Back, neck, head, throat, hands.

Another dark hallway. Another dark door. A light snapped on. A door slammed behind them, and a lock turned. She saw burgundy carpet through the tunnel of the sweatshirt hood, and the corner of a table.

"There. It's okay now. You can come out."

Dana pushed the hood back. She blinked in the track lighting.

They were in a bedroom. It was all pale oranges and brick reds. A Navajo blanket hung on one wall. Gauzy curtains looked out onto a patio, a green lawn, and big trees. The place smelled like laundry, or air freshener.

Dana started to shake. She wrapped her arms around herself.

Jeannie stepped into her line of sight. She brushed the hair back from Dana's forehead. "Oh, honey. Just look at you."

"I am," growled a man behind her. "We have got to get her cleaned up. Now."

Dana whipped around. Todd had changed clothes and was now wearing a green T-shirt and jeans.

The change made her aware of how she looked—her shirt rumpled and stretched, her hair everywhere, her skin itching in a hundred places because she was covered in dried blood.

Dad's blood.

A flash flood of shame roared through her, and Dana thought she was going to drown. She tried to push herself above it, but she couldn't.

"How...how..."

"It's okay, Dana." Jeannie pulled Dana close and rubbed her arms, trying to smooth away the goose bumps. "Todd, take it easy. She's been through a lot, okay? Come on, hon. He's right—let's get you cleaned up."

Todd waved a gesture of dismissal and headed back out into the hall. Jeannie tried to turn her toward the bedroom doorway, but Dana stayed rooted to the spot. She listened while Todd clumped down the stairs.

"What's happening?!"

"I'm sorry, hon. I am. I'll explain everything. But we really, really have to get you cleaned up."

She'd stabbed her father. It was an accident—an *accident*. But her hand still felt the little homemade knife slide into him. She still saw his look of surprise as he stared at her.

Footsteps were coming back up the stairs. Todd was coming for her.

"What is he...why's he..."

"Shh, honey," breathed Jeannie, but it was too late. Todd had already opened the door, and he'd heard.

"Why's he here?" Todd drawled. "Gosh. Where else should I be but with my own family?"

"I...want to go home," Dana whispered. Like a baby. She hated herself for it, but she couldn't stop it, like she couldn't stop the shakes or the tears that trickled out of the corners of her eyes.

"Yeah, well, that's not an option," snapped Todd.

"Please." Fear filled Dana to overflowing. She wanted this not to be happening. She wanted it to have never happened.

She wanted her mother.

"Listen to me." Todd stalked forward. Jeannie pulled Dana back, but not far enough. He loomed over her. She saw his stubbled jawline tighten. "You killed a man. You killed *your father.* You do not go back from that."

No. No. He's not dead. He can't be dead. I didn't. I couldn't. "That's not…that's not what…" *I was trying to help him! I was trying to get him away from you!*

"That's exactly 'what,'" said Todd. "And that's what the cops are going to see, and what your mother is going to see, and what the rest of the world is going to see the second this ends up in the news."

"But only because you were there! You were trying to…to…"

"I was not the one who brought a fucking shank! I was not the one who started screaming and shoving." He leaned in close. "You don't have a mommy and you don't have a home. You don't have anything at all anymore, except her." He jerked his chin toward Jeannie. Then, something seemed to occur to him, because a wide, open, entirely cheerful grin spread across his sharp face. "Her and me."

CHAPTER THIRTY-NINE

"Elizabeth Jean Fraser," the detective said as she sat down on the other side of the table from Beth. "I'm Detective Nalini Patel." Beth had already been in custody for hours, and she'd been passed along to a lot of different people. They'd photographed her face and hands. They scanned her fingerprints. They scraped under her nails. They took her clothes and bagged them up and gave her a receipt to sign. They brought her here to this interview room, where she sat wearing some outsize sweats and paper hospital slippers.

Nalini Patel was a woman about her own height. Her skin was a warm, earthy brown, and she wore her black hair in a herringbone braid. She had a small diamond stud in her nose and another above her eyebrow. She favored thick slashes of rosy eye shadow. She wore a gray jacket and a blue blouse and black slacks. Her accent told Beth this person came from a family that had lived, worked, and died in the Windy City for generations.

"Are you okay, Ms. Fraser?" The detective dropped the stack of stuff she'd carried in onto the table. There were manila folders and a zippered envelope and, of course, a lot of forms. "You want anything?"

I want my daughter. I want my parents so I can choke the life out of them. I want Doug to be alive so I can send him home for Susan to clean up and for his other children to pity.

I want to never have been born. I want to have never believed I could have a child.

"I am exercising my right to remain silent," Beth croaked. "I want to have my lawyer present for any questioning."

Detective Patel did not seem particularly perturbed by this declaration.

"You are not currently under arrest."

Detective Patel opened the top file and started flicking through papers. Her demeanor remained cool and tired. She was another member of the system—chronically over-worked and surviving on habit and some remaining belief that she was making a difference.

It was hot and stale in the room. There was the one-way mirror, just like on all the cop shows. Beth wondered if there was someone back there now.

Probably.

There was no clock or window or any other way to tell how much time had passed since the patrol had hauled her out of the hotel room and away from Doug's body.

"I've been told your lawyer is on his way, or is that your boss's lawyer?" Detective Patel raised the eyebrow with the diamond stud.

Beth did not answer. The police had taken away Beth's

cell phone. Since then, she had been given the obligatory phone call on the station's landline. She'd used it to wake up her lawyer.

I have to get out of here.

"What were you doing in room one twenty-one of the MaxRest America Extended-Stay Hotel?" Detective Patel asked.

Dana, what were you doing there? How did they get you there? What have they done to you?

"Did you arrange for Mr. Hoyt to meet you there?"

Saying nothing was easier than Beth had thought it would be, especially as tired and strung out as she was. Although, if she stopped to think about it, she had a lot of practice saying nothing to the cops. She could do it for a little longer. She just had to remember the feel of that improvised knife in her hand and all the blood. And Dana's phone, smashed on the floor beside her murdered father.

I have to get to her.

Patel didn't seem to mind Beth's actual silence any more than she had her declaration that she intended to keep quiet.

"I understand you and Mr. Hoyt have a long history. He is your daughter's father, I think?" She paused, waiting for Beth to confirm this. "We've been talking to Mrs. Hoyt. She says he might have been having some money trouble."

Poor Susan. All that time trying to keep Doug's life together. Trying to make everything just perfect for him so he'd finally, finally be happy.

"Had he said anything to you about needing money?" Patel flicked through another few pages. Her nails were

265

neatly filed and polished navy blue. The color of a Chicago cop's uniform, Beth realized. Detective Patel had a sense of humor.

"I have a report here that he came to your workplace last Friday. Was that usual for him to meet you there?"

Detective Patel did not wear a wedding ring. There was no hint that she ever had. She also, evidently, had exhausted the store of information in her printed pages. She set them down and folded her hands on top of them.

"Look, Ms. Fraser," said Detective Patel. "If there's an explanation for this, I want to hear it. Maybe he was bugging you for money and you wanted to arrange for a nice, quiet place to talk the situation over. He was your daughter's father. You wanted to spare him embarrassment if you could. But he was upset, and he got pushy. Maybe even desperate. Maybe he grabbed you and you defended yourself."

Don't look at her. Don't fall in with all that fake sympathy.

"You're better off talking to me."

No. I'm not.

"Because it's not the first time you've done this, is it?"

Beth's head snapped up.

To her credit, Detective Patel did not smile. "You have a previous conviction for aggravated assault in San Francisco. You only almost killed the guy that time."

"He took my daughter." The words were out before Beth could think, before her mind replayed the detective's words: *You only* almost *killed the guy* that *time.*

Detective Patel nodded. "Is that what happened? Did Doug threaten to try to get custody of his daughter if you wouldn't help him out? Or was he going to tell her something out of your past that maybe you wanted kept hidden?" She paused. "By the way, Ms. Fraser, where is Dana? Do you want me to call her and let her know you're okay? And you're going to need to make arrangements for someone she can stay with. I hate to tell you this, but you're probably going to be here awhile."

Beth's mouth went dry. Her ears were ringing again.

Detective Patel reached into the zippered pouch and pulled out two evidence bags. One held the smashed cell phone. The other held the neatly honed nail file, stained dark red along its entire length.

She laid these out on the blank space of tabletop between them and folded her hands.

"Do you even know where your daughter is right now?"

CHAPTER FORTY

Dana wanted to be sick. Violently, immediately. She wanted to vomit up everything that had happened in the last twenty-four hours. The last forty-eight.

Her whole life.

"Oh great, Todd, that's really helping." Jeannie propelled Dana past him and out into the hallway. It was white and polished wood. "Why don't you do something useful like get us something to eat? The poor kid's starving. Come on, hon—let's get you cleaned up."

Jeannie shut the door on the moss green tiled bathroom and locked it. She turned on the water in the sunken tub.

"Get those clothes off."

Dana didn't move.

"You need to get cleaned up, hon. I've got some things you can borrow."

Dana still didn't move. "What's he..." she choked. "You said—"

"Shh! Shh!" Jeannie pressed her hand against Dana's mouth. "Honey, I am so sorry," she said softly. "Believe me. It wasn't supposed to be like this. He got suspicious, Dana. He was going to make trouble. He was going to tell your mom you'd been planning something with me, so when he came and got me, I had to go with him." She lifted her hand away. "I thought I could keep him away from you."

"How'd he even find you?!"

"I told you he would. I told you both," she added bitterly. "Look, it's all going to be okay. We've just got to lie low for a little while."

"But…"

Jeannie took hold of both of Dana's shoulders. "You listen to me now. We are so far up shit's creek there's no way back. You *have* to trust me or it's going to get even worse."

Dana couldn't speak. She was practically standing on Jeannie's toes right now. Dana could smell cigarettes and lily of the valley perfume and beer. The steam was rising from the hot water in the tub, and that was only making it worse.

As if it could be worse.

Dana didn't know what to do. She did know she had to get the blood off her—off her hands and her face and her throat. All of it. Right now. So she stripped down and climbed into the tub as quickly as she could. But she couldn't make herself stand up to turn on the shower. Instead, she huddled in the middle, her arms wrapped around her knees.

"Okay, okay, that's good." Jeannie worked the drain so the water started to rise over Dana's toes.

Her toes didn't have any blood on them. She could look at her toes.

"Where are we?" she asked.

"Some place Todd found." Jeannie was pulling toiletries off the vanity. Shampoo, conditioner, and shower gel in Easter egg colors. "They're going to be watching all the roads, and with the cameras and stuff, we have to hang tight for a while." Jeannie knelt by the tub's edge and covered Dana's hand. "I know this sucks, hon—believe me, I do know. But we have to stay put. Just a few days. Just until the cops take their eye off the ball." She cupped her hand around Dana's cheek. Like Mom did. "You are not going to jail, Dana. I am getting you out of this, even if I have to tell them I killed your father myself. But while we're here, we've got to keep Todd sweet, okay? So, you're going to hear me say some things and do some things that are…not what I've been telling you, all right? But whatever you see, you just say to yourself, 'She's keeping him sweet until we can split.' Go on. Say that."

"She's keeping him sweet until we can split," whispered Dana.

"That's it. And as soon as we do split, we'll get a message to your mom and tell her what happened and make sure she knows you're okay. That's the plan. You just have to hang onto that."

Dana couldn't make herself answer, so she just nodded. She didn't really agree, and she knew something wasn't right, but she couldn't come up with the questions she needed. She was too exhausted and way too sick.

When she closed her eyes, she saw her father and that

last, confused look. She wanted so badly to explain to him what was really happening.

"Okay." Jeannie smiled and held out the bottles of toiletries. "Here you go. You'll probably end up smelling like…I don't know what…but it's what we got."

Dana stared at the things. She knew what they all were, but somehow, she couldn't remember what she was supposed to do with them.

Jeannie sighed. "Okay, let me help you. Dunk your head."

Dana dunked and came up gasping. Jeannie poured out some shampoo, making a stream of extra coldness down Dana's head. Her hard fingers massaged Dana's scalp, and Dana dunked again. She was handed a washcloth so she could wipe off the blood.

It flaked off her skin and stained her nails. All the blood that had sprayed out of Dad's chest and dripped down the front of his shirt. He was so confused. He was so angry. He'd grabbed her—he'd grabbed her and she'd screamed, and he'd thrown her backward and she'd…she'd…

"Dana, stay with me now, hon," said Jeannie.

But Jeannie was a world away. Dana was with her father. She felt the homemade knife in her hand, felt how it had pushed right through him and how hot the blood had been as it came out of him. She tasted iron and copper, and he'd looked so surprised…

"Dana!" Grandma had her by the shoulders and shook her once, hard. "Dana! It's over! It's all over."

But it wasn't over, and she was shaking and crying and naked and freezing in filthy water that was turning sick pink from the blood running off her.

SARAH ZETTEL

"I want to go home," she cried. "Please! I just want to go home!"

Jeannie took Dana's face in both hands and wrenched it toward her.

"Dana, you've got to promise you'll stick with me, okay? Please." Her hands were ice-cold as she stroked Dana's cheek. "We will get out of this, honey. Together. I promise. You've just got to give it some time. That's all."

"We've got to call Mom. She's…she's…We've got to. She needs to know. She freaks out if she doesn't hear from me every day! She needs to know!"

Grandma sat back on her knees, her eyes bright with worry and tears.

"Look, honey, this is something else you've got to know. Your mom showed up right after we pulled you out of there. I don't know how she found you, but she did, and she…"

"What?" Dana gripped the edge of the tub. "What happened?"

"They arrested her."

CHAPTER FORTY-ONE

When Beth's lawyer finally puffed into the interview room, Beth had only one thing to say. "Noah, get me out of here."

Noah Beresford was a big man. He'd gotten through Loyola on a football scholarship. After school, the bulk had turned into fat without a fight. Now, he was leaving middle age behind. He flushed red when he moved, and his wedding ring had dug deep into the flesh of his left hand. His custom suits and shirts fit immaculately, and if his mind moved as deliberately as his body, it was also extremely resistant to shock.

"I need you to be patient, Beth." Noah set his briefcase on the table and lowered himself carefully into the chair beside her.

"I need to be out of here."

"And we're working on that. But it would help if you

told me what you were doing in that hotel room, and why you booked it in the first place."

It was those last words that actually snagged Beth's attention.

"Wh-what?"

"The room was booked through an online service in your name."

Of course it was. Beth ran her hands through her hair and tried to suppress the sick laugh welling up in her. *I really should have seen that one coming.*

"You have to tell me what's going on, Beth," said Noah.

How long had they been setting her up? At least three weeks from what Susan told her, but they could have been hanging around for months. Driving back and forth from Perrysborough—picking those times when Kinseki's gullible idiot was on shift, figuring out which members of the staff were on his payroll—building their possibilities, mapping out her life, waiting for their chance.

"Noah, all you need to know is that I have to get out of here. If they're not charging me, they can't hold me, right? You tell them whatever you need to, but you get me out of here. Now."

She did not have a whole lot of time. Patel would already be at work. She'd talk to Susan. She'd talk to Rafi and Angela. Rafi knew Beth's given name, and he knew more about her parents than anyone else did.

Rafi won't say anything. I can trust him.

Then again, Rafi's silence would just let Detective Patel know that he had information. It would be easy for her to find out that Beth and Rafi had been friends back in the bad old days. Those old details could lead to old names. If the detective was patient, and she felt to Beth like a very patient person.

Once Patel had Beth's given name and even a partial list of her parents' aliases, she'd have no problem finding Beth's first victim.

Beth had to be gone before that happened.

CHAPTER FORTY-TWO

"It's everywhere!" roared Todd as Dana and Jeannie came into the kitchen. "It's all over the fucking news!"

This was a nice house, and it had a nice kitchen—polished wood cabinets and soapstone counters. And Todd was in the middle of it, microwaving burritos. There was a party-size bag of Doritos on the dining table. And a plate of taquitos on the pass-through.

The whole meal is going to rhyme, thought Dana, dazed. She collapsed into the nearest chair. Except for the booze. Because there was also a full bottle of vodka and a six-pack of beer.

Dana was wearing too-long yoga pants and a pink sweatshirt with cutouts on the shoulders. She didn't want to think about how she was hiding in somebody else's house and probably wearing their clothes. It made her sick on a whole different level. That was probably stupid, but it was true.

"What's on the news?" Jeannie grabbed the taquitos off the counter and brought them to the table. "Here you go, hon-bun." She put one on Dana's plate.

Dana couldn't even make herself look at the "food." She stared straight ahead of her. There were French doors off the dining area, and she could see that the house had a nice back deck and stairs going down to a nice patio and a nice spread of lawn. There was a nice privacy fence and nice old trees. She couldn't see any other houses, but they'd probably be just as nice.

There is no way we are still in Chicago, she thought.

"Your goddamned fuckup!" roared Todd. "It's all *over* the fucking news!"

Jeannie pointed at Dana's taquito. "Now, you eat that, hon." As if to demonstrate how this worked, she ate one of her own in two bites, and, still chewing, she tore open the bag of Doritos.

The smell of the fake cheese hit Dana hard, and to her shock, her mouth watered.

"Come on." Jeannie shoved the bag toward her. "You'll feel better. I promise."

"Oh yeah, listen to her and all her promises." Todd cracked the seal on the bottle of vodka. "Just look where they've gotten you so far."

"Did they say anything about Mom?" she asked.

Todd stared at her, like he'd forgotten she could talk. "Yeah, they did. They said you better be praying she doesn't decide to throw you under the bus for killing your father."

"Todd! What are you doing? Don't listen to him, Dana. Your mother would never do anything to hurt you."

Dana nibbled a chip. And suddenly she was devouring taquitos. And about half the chips. Todd finished microwaving the burritos, and she wolfed one of those down too. At some point, Jeannie got some LaCroix out of the fridge, and Dana drank three, one right after the other.

This was not okay. This was not right. Her body should not be working. She should not be up and walking around. The whole world had fucking ended. How could she be eating Doritos? Postapocalyptic fake cheese.

A laugh tried to leak out of her. *Oh crap.*

Todd stood by the patio doors and drank the vodka, watching them. Finally, he screwed the cap back on the bottle.

"Now, I am going to explain how this is gonna go, and you geniuses are going to listen and do exactly what I say. You got it?"

"Okay, Todd, okay." Jeannie waved a chip at him. "You don't have to be such a bastard. We're listening, right, Dana?"

Dana nodded and made herself swallow her mouthful of Doritos.

"Everybody's gonna get some sleep. In the morning, I'm going to go…see people. We're going to need a new car and some cash to get started with. You will stay here. You don't go anywhere. You don't do anything. You hear me?"

"Yeah, yeah, we hear you." Jeannie took Dana's hand and gave it a little shake. "We'll be good girls, right, Dana?"

Dana nodded. Her mouth suddenly filled with a sour

taste that had nothing to do with all the bad food she'd just forced down.

"You better be," muttered Todd darkly. "Come on—let's go to bed."

He sounded hollow.

Something's wrong.

As soon as she thought that, Dana wanted to laugh. Because everything was wrong. Mom was arrested. Dad was dead. She was…she was…

"It'll be okay, hon-bun." Jeannie suddenly hugged Dana. "Let's get some sleep. You'll feel better."

Jeannie took Dana's arm and steered her up the stairs to the room with the Navajo rug.

"Here, you can use this." Jeannie handed her an over-size T-shirt that read LIVE YOUR DREAM EVERY DAY! "And remember what I told you before," she said. "All we've got to do is keep him sweet. Just for now, okay?" She patted Dana's hands and headed back out into the hallway, closing the door behind her.

The T-shirt fell halfway down Dana's shins and was too tight across her shoulders and boobs. Dana climbed into the bed. The unfamiliar mattress shifted under her. The blankets smelled like fake lavender. It was utterly quiet— no traffic noise, no train whistles or sirens. Not even distant ones.

To her shock, Dana fell asleep as soon as her head hit the pillow.

Sometime that night, she woke up. Her hand reached out, trying to find her phone so she could check the time, check messages, know she was still hooked into the outside world.

But her phone was gone. She had been unplugged. Wiped out. Disappeared.

When the morning came, Chelsea and Kimi and Keesha would all wake up and they'd look at their own phones full of pictures, words, music, and links. And what they'd hear was the story that Dana's mom had been arrested for killing Dana's father.

They'd try to text and call. They'd check her feeds and streams, and they'd post and demand to know what was happening and did she know she was famous and what the fuck, Dana?

And she wouldn't answer. The Dana Fraser that shared their world was being replaced by something else. An image in the news. A blurry picture they'd flash on CNN.

Dana squeezed her eyes shut hard so she wouldn't start crying again, but that was no good, because the red under her eyelids just turned into blood, and she felt it stinging her skin again, stinging her eyes, cracking on her lips like paint, filling her mouth with that sick taste.

And she saw Dad, perfectly clear. Right there. Dead on the floor. His eyes stared at her, blank, wet, gone.

Ghosted. Wiped out. Finished. Done.

Dead.

She should be dead. After what she'd done. Dead and gone. Then they could just blame her and let Mom go.

Then she thought, *Mom's going to hate me.* Dana looked toward the bedroom door. *Like she hates them.*

Because not only had she screwed up everything, Dana

was all set to just vanish, like Todd and Jeannie had just vanished when Mom was a teenager. And Mom would never know why Dana had left her either.

Mom would never know she'd just wanted to help.

Tears spilled down her cheeks and dropped onto the fat down pillows. She shoved her hand over her mouth to keep the sobs inside.

CHAPTER FORTY-THREE

The instant the car pulled up to her building, Beth scrambled out and pushed through the revolving door. Thankfully, Noah did not try to follow.

She had (so far) escaped being charged, but that was not for lack of trying on Detective Patel's part. Noah said it was a series of little things that saved her—like that there was no definitive proof that she had deliberately attempted to tamper with a crime scene. The car service couldn't find the college kid who had driven her to the hotel, but they had the call and the destination logged. The camera in her building lobby showed her coming and going.

But that same camera showed her going out with Dana and how Dana hadn't come home. The manager at Vine and Horn showed them Dana's completed paperwork.

They found Dana's cell phone in the restaurant, right where she'd left it to fool Beth into thinking she'd kept her promise.

"Let us help you, Ms. Fraser," Detective Patel had said as

the desk sergeant handed Beth back the few things of hers that weren't thought to be useful as evidence. "We all want Dana to get home safe."

"In this case, Beth," Noah had said when they climbed into the town car he'd called for them, "helping the police find Dana is highly advisable."

Beth had not answered either one of them. She didn't know how to, because she didn't know what was happening, and that fact was burning a hole through her.

She shoved her way into the lobby. The TV was on over the faux fireplace. A bleached-blonde reporter was speaking with that particularly grave enthusiasm reserved for death and other tragedies.

"...and in Chicagoland, at the top of the hour we have an update on the gruesome and shocking murder of Douglas Hoyt..."

Movement jerked Beth's attention away from the screen before they could flash whatever photo they had from the scene. A man struggled to his feet from the couch, rumpled and disheveled.

Rafael.

His face was grim as he took in Beth's appearance. Noah had been allowed to bring her a change of clothes, but there was no disguising the fact that she'd been awake all night or seen the end of the world lying bloody on the floor in front of her.

"Ms. Fraser?"

Beth turned to the desk. It was Kendi who spoke. She'd walked right past him without seeing him. He was hanging up the phone.

"Is there anything we can do, Ms. Fraser?"

Beth shook her head. She could not trust her voice. Not yet. Fortunately Kendi seemed to understand that and did not press the issue.

"We are praying for Dana," he said.

"Thank you," Rafael said for her, which allowed Beth to continue to the elevators. Rafael followed.

The doors opened, and they both filed inside. The doors closed, and they stood there, watching the red numbers flicker and hearing the beeps that indicated the passing floors.

"Beth?" said Rafi finally. He was trying to be gentle. He was trying to be patient. They were friends, and something very bad had just happened. "Beth, where's Dana?"

Beth said nothing.

Inside the apartment, Beth closed the door. She checked the locks. She checked the alarm. Nothing had been disturbed. She turned and brushed past Rafael, wading into the stale silence that filled her home.

"I've been trying to get hold of you all night," Rafi told her. "I started calling the second I heard what happened to Doug."

Which she would have known if she had been able to use her phone. She jammed the charger into the dead phone so hard that for a moment she was afraid she'd bent it.

Beth stared at the icon of the battery with the flashing red line indicating it was out of charge. She pressed her hand over the warm screen, willing that red line to turn to green so the phone would start working again.

Because maybe Dana had called. Maybe the worst hadn't

happened. Maybe she was somewhere Beth could get to her. But most importantly, maybe she was still alone. Maybe she got away. That could still be true.

Finally the screen lit up.

Dozens of messages from Zoe's number, from Chelsea's, and from Rafi's, of course.

None from her father.

None from her mother.

None at all from Dana, or from any unknown number that might be Dana.

Rafi came around the counter to stand beside her. They did not hug. That was never something they did. He just took hold of her hand, and they stayed like that until she was able to lift her head again.

"Dana…" she began.

And of course, that was when the landline rang.

Beth jumped. It was Rafi who picked up.

"Fraser residence," he said, and he listened, and then he covered the receiver with his hand. "It's Susan."

Of course it was. Of course the police, led by the patient Detective Patel, had already been to see Doug's family.

Beth kept one hand pressed against her cell as she took the landline handset.

"I'm here, Susan."

"What did you do to my husband?!" screamed the other woman.

"Please, Susan, I'm so sorry. I—"

"The police were just here! He's dead! They kept asking about you and your child and…and…I believed you!"

Beth said nothing. What could she say?

"I believed you when you told me you had nothing to do with Doug losing his money! I tried to make peace with you! Now you…you…I'm telling them EVERYTHING!"

"Susan…" Beth tried again, but Susan hung up and left Beth staring at the phone.

I'm telling them EVERYTHING! Susan's scream rang in her ears. She tried to tell herself the woman had just had the worst possible shock. Of course she was shattered. Of course she would take it out on Beth. Who else was there?

Beth pressed her back against the counter and dropped her face into her hands. Her cell wasn't ringing. Dana hadn't called. Susan was telling all Doug's stories to the police, and Dana hadn't called.

Rafi touched her shoulder. "Beth, you're going to need help. You're coming home with me and—"

"No." She made herself look up. "There's too much I need to do."

"Come on, sister," he breathed. "You can't leave me alone out here."

Beth tried to estimate how much time she'd spent with this man. She knew him better than any lover she'd ever been in bed with. They shared so many late nights, plotting world domination over balance sheets, websites, books, and junk food. Together, they'd worked the angles, judged the men, and sometimes the women. They put together their plans and targeted the money. They'd built businesses, changed lives and worlds.

Rafi was the only one who'd ever been able to see beneath her surface, because only Rafi knew what Beth was really hiding from. And he had always understood that there were times when the only answer that would keep everything together was a hard, cold one.

"Rafi, you cannot be here. You need to go home and take care of Angela and the kids and Lumination. This thing…It's going to hit Lumination like a ton of bricks."

"You're telling me to throw you under the bus?"

"I'm telling you to do whatever it takes to keep your family and Lumination together," she said. "Dana's going to need all of you when this is all over."

Rafi pulled back. His face showed no panic, no shock. Just that deep comprehension she had always counted on.

"Keep Zoe in the loop. Hand to God, you can trust her with everything."

Rafi still said nothing.

"Promise me," she said, because what she needed was beyond anything even Rafi's silence could convey. "Promise me you will take care of Dana. I need to know she'll be with people who love her."

He nodded once. "I promise. You…take care of yourself, Beth."

She hoped he did not expect any kind of reply to that. But he did wait for a moment, just in case. When she did not say anything else, he turned and walked away. Beth shut her eyes so she wouldn't have to see him leave. She didn't open them again until she heard the door close.

Beth headed for her bedroom.

As the screen in the lobby so helpfully informed her, the "gruesome and shocking" murder of Douglas Hoyt was already news. Very soon, the media machine, with all its fast-moving, multilayered efficiency, would find out who that hotel room had been registered to. If they didn't know already.

She had to be gone before they got here.

Beth kept her go-bag under her bed. It was an anonymous blue duffle she bought at Target she didn't even remember how long ago. She went through it every so often, making sure the clothes still fit reasonably well and updating the consumables.

There was a box of Clif bars and a couple of bottles of water. There was an extra flip phone and a portable charger. A little bit of cash. There were scans of important documents: the passports and birth certificates and credit cards, all in her own name or Dana's.

Not one of those was of any use to her now. She dropped them onto the dresser and slung the bag over her shoulder.

The keys to the padlock on the garage and the car inside the garage were in the junk drawer in the kitchen, along with all the other keys to locks that had been forgotten about over the years. She dug them out and stuffed them into her pocket.

She'd go to the safe-deposit box first. She'd need the other IDs that were in there, the cards, and the much more substantial amount of cash.

And she'd need the gun.

The landline rang again. The knock on the door came as she was diving to grab the handset.

That was when she knew what was happening. She ignored the knocking and the ringing and ran back to her bedroom. She grabbed the document scans off the dresser, crammed them back into the bag, and kicked it all under the bed.

The ringing stopped. The knocking started up again, harder this time.

Beth smoothed her hair down and went to open the door for the cops and Detective Patel, who had a warrant to search her premises.

CHAPTER FORTY-FOUR

The room had no clock. All Dana knew when she woke up was that the sun was slanting through her window and her bladder was about ready to give way.

She sprinted for the bathroom.

When she'd finished and flushed, she stood there for a while, hugging herself and listening. She didn't hear any noises. She opened the door a crack and peeked out. The hallway was empty.

What do I do? She bit her lip. *What can I do?*

Moving quietly, she hurried back to her room. She went through the dresser, but whoever owned this house wasn't as good at planning as Mom, and the drawers were all empty, except for some spare sheets and stuff. But the clean clothes from last night were still there. Dana dressed again and pulled her socks and shoes on. Her purse was on the dresser. So was her jacket.

She grabbed them both. She peeked into the hallway again. Still nothing.

I'll be quick.

She didn't let herself think. She just tiptoed down the stairs. The wood was polished smooth, and it didn't creak at all.

I'll be quick. Just see where I am.

The stairs went straight down to the flagstone foyer and the front door. There was a brass umbrella stand with umbrellas, and a whole row of coat hooks with women's coats on all of them except the last one, which had Todd's old leather jacket hanging on it.

They'll never know I'm gone.

She worked the deadbolt and the knob lock.

"Far enough, Granddaughter."

Dana jumped out of her skin. Her jacket and purse flew out of her hands, and she screamed. She couldn't help it.

"Oh Jesus. Fuck," muttered Todd.

He was standing at the top of the stairs, wearing nothing but baggy plaid boxers and a sleeveless T-shirt. Dana backed up against the wall and doubled over, trying to get her heart to slow down.

"I'm sorry," she croaked. "I wasn't going anywhere. Not really. I'm sorry."

Todd sighed and thudded down the stairs. He closed the deadbolt and squinted out the stained-glass sidelights before he grabbed her by the elbow and took her into the kitchen and stationed her right beside the big butcher-block-topped island.

"Stay." He pointed his index finger at her. "I'm gonna go get decent."

Dana sat down at the kitchen island and put her jacket on the counter, and her arms on her jacket, and her head on her arms. She tried not to cry, or think, or do anything.

When Todd came back, he had on new jeans and a Black Sabbath T-shirt and clean tube socks. Thick, gray stubble covered his chin, and what was left of his hair stood up in spikes.

He pulled out a stool and sat down next to her.

"You doing all right?" he asked abruptly.

Dana straightened up. "Seriously?"

He shrugged. Dana shrugged back.

"Sleep okay?"

Dana didn't bother to answer.

"Where did you think you were going?"

She licked her lips. "I thought…I wanted to find out where we are."

He narrowed his eyes at her, and Dana fought the need to squirm. Then he shrugged again. "Fair enough, but I'm telling you right now: It doesn't matter where we are, because we are not staying."

"Where's Jeannie?" she blurted out.

"Still conked out." Todd scratched at his stubble. "Don't think this is gonna be one of her good days. So, you and me, we need to talk."

Dana tensed. Todd must have noticed because he sighed and leaned forward, pressing his palms together between his knees. His eyes were very blue, Dana noticed, and he looked directly at her.

"Look. Given what all's happened, I don't really expect you to believe what I'm gonna say here. But I am sorry we've all landed in this, and I am going to do what I can to get us out of it, you included."

"What about Mom?"

Todd shook his head. "Yeah, Jeannie told me. That's hard. Case of being too smart for her own damn good. But she didn't do anything, and she's got some amazing goddamn lawyers, so my guess is she'll be out before too much longer."

"And then I can go home?"

Todd didn't answer.

"And then I can go home?" Dana repeated.

"Dana, you're a smart girl. You can see this for what it is. You *killed* your father. Okay, it was an accident, but you know, with all the history between you and him and your mom, are the cops really going to believe that?"

Dana shoved past that. She couldn't get stuck there. She'd go under again. "Why were you even *there*?" she demanded.

"Well, me and your Dad ran into each other down in your lobby, you know? And he recognized me from the YouTube thing, and we got to talking. Once he calmed down, anyhow. He wanted my help. Said if I helped him get some money from your mom, he'd make sure I got some more money for your grandmother's treatment."

"That's not what you said before."

This time Todd's sigh was sharp and more than a little exasperated. "I guess I'm just going to have to keep apologizing, aren't I? All that stuff back there—that was not my idea. Doug told me he was going to try to scare you into helping him"—he put up his hands—"and I said no way. We don't mess with the kid, I said, *and* I said he should be telling you the truth. You guys were flesh and blood, I said. You're a good kid. You wouldn't leave him out in the cold."

Dana felt her mind turning over hard. She didn't want this to be true, none of it. It *shouldn't* be.

But it could be. Or it could be all lies. Big lies and little lies, and how would she even know?

"But, you know, he had this idea about you being your mother's daughter and all..." He shook his head. "Now, I admit I went along with his plan in the end partly because I was mad. Jeannie's *dying*, and your mom won't even help her."

"That's not true!" shouted Dana. "She was taking care of everything!"

"Is that what she told you?" Todd scratched at his chin again. "Yeah. Okay. I'm sorry to have to tell you different, Dana. Because your mom—she was offering me money to take your grandma away."

"You're a liar!"

"Yeah, but not this time."

He reached into the T-shirt pocket and pulled out a folded piece of paper. He smoothed it out on the counter so Dana could read it.

It was a check for three thousand dollars, and there was Mom's signature at the bottom.

"This was just the down payment," Todd said. "Your mom offered me seventy-five thousand dollars if I'd take your grandma and get outta town." He folded the check back up and tucked it away in his pocket. "Told me what hospital Jeannie was in, what name she was under, everything."

"She wouldn't do that," Dana breathed.

But Mom hated both of them. Because of all the stuff that had happened. And Mom did go see him Sunday night, and she did say she was going to pay him to go away...

Him though. Not Jeannie. Jeannie was sick and hurt and trying to leave. Mom wouldn't just give her back to this guy. No matter how much she hated her. She wouldn't do that.

Would she?

"I couldn't believe it either," Todd said. "She thinks I care more about money than about Jeannie's *life*. So, here comes this guy—the guy she loved enough to have a baby with—and he's telling me she won't help him either? So, I'm not proud of it, but I got mad, and I went along."

Dana bit her lip.

"I know this is a lot to lay on you all at once, but there are times when you have got to face things head-on. Your mom is under suspicion for what you did to your father. That's a fact. Now, what are the cops gonna find out? They're gonna find out your dad was giving her grief and then he started pestering you. What do you think the cops are gonna make out of that? Then there's that thing back in Abrahamsville. It kind of starts to add up," he went on with surprising gentleness. "I mean, you see that, right? She is in a whole lot of trouble on her own, even without you there to have to look out for."

Dana said nothing. She didn't trust her voice, or the thoughts whirling through her head. This guy was a

SARAH ZETTEL

dealer. He was a cheat and a liar. He'd beat on her
grandmother, her mother, and he'd tried to put one over
on her dad...

He's lying. He's got to be.

The problem was his story made sense, mostly, and he
had that check with Mom's signature. Dana swallowed
against the bile that rose up in her throat. Todd's words
twisted around her brain while what really happened in
the hotel room squirmed and tried to get away.

Todd leaned forward so he was exactly eye level with
her. His breath smelled like Listerine.

"I know you're confused," he said softly. "I know you
know I'm a regular rat-bastard. It's too late for me to
change that now. But you see what a mess we're in, me and
your grandmother both? When we pulled you outta there,
we became accessories to Doug's murder. So, you know,
you can't really blame me for raising my voice a little last
night. Because it's our necks on the chopping block too
now, you see?"

"Yes," Dana whispered. Todd smiled, like he understood.

"Now, I also know you love your mother. That's good.
That's right. What kind of daughter would you be to
turn on her, no matter what she's done? But she loves you
too, more than anyone in the whole world. So, what's she
gonna do if you try to go back now? Let you go to prison?
She's never gonna let that happen. She'll confess first. You
know she will, Dana, and she'll do it to save you."

He was looking right into her eyes.

"So, I'm asking you, for your mother's sake, and your
grandmother's, to help us. Let us get you—and us—outta

296

here. That way, your mom can concentrate on taking care of herself."

"Why are you doing this?" The question fell out of Dana's mouth before she had a chance to think about it. She wasn't even sure what she was really asking.

"Because, Dana." Todd lifted his hand and ran his index finger down her cheek, like he was tracing a tear. "We're family."

CHAPTER FORTY-FIVE

It took the police two hours to search her home.

Beth spent most of it out on the balcony. She stood above her familiar street, with all the traffic and the pedestrians going about their business beneath her. They had no idea that the world had ended, that a child had gone missing, and that a carefully constructed life had been smashed to pieces.

She leaned on the railing with her phone in her hands. She couldn't make herself put it down, in case Dana called. In case her parents did.

They must have spotted Doug in the lobby the day he'd first come to beg for her help. She'd seen Todd then. She'd seen him and she'd known him, but she hadn't trusted herself enough to believe it. So, they'd gotten to Doug and inside of thirty seconds they saw that they could use him against her, and against Dana.

And Beth had let it happen. She'd sat there, feeling so

smug with her plans and her precautions, and she let them take her daughter.

So, what would they do next?

On one level she knew, of course. They'd start demanding money. They'd promise to keep Dana safe from the police or whoever else, as long as Beth paid. Then, when that stopped working, they'd promise to give Dana back, just as long as the money kept coming. When that stopped working, they'd think of something else. And something else after that.

Because they never had enough, and they never kept what they had. Because they would scrounge and scam and steal whatever they wanted, and keep right on telling themselves the same old stories to justify what they were doing.

"You might want to come inside, Ms. Fraser."

Beth was too worn out even to jump. She just looked back over her shoulder and raised an eyebrow at Detective Patel. The detective pointed through the railing, down to where a news van was trying to negotiate a tight parking spot.

"Yeah." Beth shoved her phone into her back pocket. Patel's warrant didn't cover her cell. At least, not yet. That might come later. Depending. Dana's phone—the one she'd left at the restaurant—had already vanished into evidence somewhere. Now they were taking the rest of her daughter's life to join it. The dining table was covered with bagged and tagged objects: Dana's computers, her hairbrushes, shoes, and even her notebooks. Uniformed cops labeled more bags and boxes. They snapped pictures with their phones and made notes in little black books.

"Sorry about the mess," said Detective Patel.

Beth shrugged.

"You must be exhausted. Is there somebody we can call for you?"

"No. Nobody."

"You sure? You really shouldn't be alone now."

"I'll be fine."

Patel sighed impatiently. "How can that possibly be true, Beth?"

Beth looked at her. Patel was good. Gentle. Compassionate. She sounded like she really cared, even though she had to be at least as tired as Beth. Even though she had to know that Beth was consciously, deliberately withholding huge piles of information.

"It's true because it has to be," Beth answered. "Is there anything else, Detective?"

Patel didn't blink, but her jaw hardened. *Okay*, that jawline said. *I tried. It's game on.*

Game on, agreed Beth, and she knew Patel understood.

That was when her phone buzzed. Beth jumped, hard.

Patel waited for two more buzzes. "Are you going to answer?"

"They'll call back," Beth said.

Patel held her gaze for another buzz. Then she sighed and threw up her hands, signaling that she had given up on Beth Fraser once and for all.

One of the uniforms handed Beth a written receipt for all the things they were taking. Patel left another card, just in case Beth had lost the first one. She also warned Beth she would be calling with more questions.

Beth's phone finally stopped buzzing.

Beth let them out of the apartment. She watched them all leave. She shut the door and locked it.

Only then did her knees give out. She fell against the wall, gasping, and grabbed her phone out of her pocket. She didn't recognize the number, but it was a local area code.

Oh.

There was no message. Beth stabbed the number to call it back.

Oh, please.

She staggered into the living room, vaguely aware she should not be near the door when the person on the other end answered. Just in case Patel had decided to wait outside, just to see what she could hear.

Please, please, please. Be Dana. Be my daughter. Please, please.

The ring cut off.

"Beth?"

Beth fell onto the couch, strength gone, breath gone.

It was Jeannie.

CHAPTER FORTY-SIX

"I've got Dana," Jeannie said. "She's okay. She's here with us."

Beth's heart had stopped. Now, it stuttered into a frantic motion that nearly choked her. She swallowed, and swallowed again to try to clear her throat so she could speak.

"Where are you?"

"Some big house in the suburbs. I don't know exactly."

Suburbs. Beth's mind raced back to her conversation with Amanda. "Could it be Schaumburg?" Amanda had said Dad was house-sitting for her. Beth slapped her hand across her mouth. How perfect would that be? Nice house, nice neighborhood, nice big lots with privacy fences…

He'd been setting her up for a long, long time.

"Maybe. I don't know," Mom was saying. "I haven't been outside. Listen, Beth, we're not staying here for long. Todd…he says we're going to Detroit, and then down to Cincinnati. I think he wants to head for Miami eventually.

When he's got the money. He's actually talking about maybe going to Cuba. Cuba, can you believe it?" Mom paused, like she actually expected Beth to laugh along with her.

Beth ignored this. "Is Dana okay? Can I talk to her?"

"She's still asleep, poor kid. I don't want to wake her."

You're lying! She clenched her phone until she thought it would shatter in her hand. *Let me talk to my daughter! You have to let me talk to her!*

Beth squeezed her eyes shut. "But she's okay? Nobody hurt her?"

"She's fine. Completely fine. I checked."

"Okay. Okay. Uh...where is Dad now?"

"Coming to you. Because...well...you know..."

"Yeah, yeah, I know. How long has he been gone?"

"I don't know. I...I didn't have a good morning. Maybe fifteen minutes? Maybe more."

"Okay. Okay." Her mind was racing as fast as her heart now. "Look, Mom. I think I know where you are."

"You...*know?*"

"Yes. You're in one of Dad's girlfriends' houses. She told me he was watching it for her. Get Dana ready to go, and get out. Go...There's got to be a coffee shop or something. A gas station. Library. Strip mall. Anything. I'll leave right now. I can be there in an hour."

"I can't, Beth."

"Why not?!"

"This place...it's one of these really fancy houses with security cameras and alarms in all the rooms and shit. Your dad has it all hooked up to his phone so he'll get an alert as soon as anybody undoes one of the locks."

Of course. It was all planned. Every detail. He'd had weeks.

Except it might not be true. She only had Jeannie's word.

"Okay. Then call the cops," she said. "I've got the number right here for you. I'll pay for all the lawyers. I'll pay for everything. Whatever you need. Just—"

"Dana killed him, Beth."

Beth's mouth closed.

"I know you don't want to believe that, but I was standing right there. It was an accident, but it was her." Jeannie paused to make sure that had time to sink in. "And Todd's already told her that he'll tell the cops on her the second she tries to step outside the door. Do you still want me to call them?"

Say yes. Call the bluff. Do it. But the words would not come. Because she could not turn her daughter in.

"No," she whispered. "No, don't."

"I don't want to do any of this. I just want to get us underground. Jesus, if anybody can hide her, I can, but…you know your dad's not going to go for that, don't you?"

"Yes." Beth leaned back, tired beyond endurance. Why were they even bothering?

"Beth, you're going to have to kill him."

Beth said nothing.

"There's no other choice. He's not going to just let her go hide out. He's not going to let *any* of us go. He's going to use what she did to keep yanking money out of you."

"I know," said Beth.

"I'm keeping her as safe as I can, but I don't know how long that's going to work. He's already suspicious. That's why this stuff with the cameras."

Beth's thoughts felt frozen. She beat the heel of her hand against her forehead, hard, like that would break them loose.

"Beth, there's something I need to know," she said. "He told me…he told me you paid him to get me out of the way. He showed me that cashier's check, and…is that true, Beth? Did you do that to me?"

Beth's hand fell, useless, numb.

"No," she said. "No, of course not. I was just trying to get him to go away." She squeezed her eyes shut. "I don't know how he found you." She didn't give Jeannie time to think about that. "What happened, after he got you out of the hospital?"

"He took me out to the hotel, and he put me in the bedroom, and then Doug showed up and…and then it all went to hell." She gulped. "Beth, I'm so sorry. I never meant for it to be like this."

Despair was deep, thick, gray, and filthy as slush in the winter streets. It filled Beth's lungs and her veins. "Will you at least take care of Dana?" she whispered. "Please. That's all I'm asking."

"I'm doing my best, Star."

At the sound of her old name, Beth's thoughts shifted. Slowly, painfully they broke through the filthy slush, and she was able to understand them.

Jeannie will take care of her because Dana's the hostage. Without her, what has she got to keep me on the hook? This is the ransom call. Jeannie's ransom.

"Beth, you have to hurry. He's really frightened. I don't know what he'll do next."

"Yeah. Yeah. I hear you." *I hear you. And I know what you want.* "Mom...tell Dana I love her, okay?"

"I will. And I'll call back as soon as I can."

Jeannie hung up, and Beth was alone again, except for the echoes of Jeannie's words left inside her.

Dana killed him, Beth...It was an accident, but it was her.

That could not be true, but it didn't matter what Beth believed. If it became necessary, Todd would lie and condemn his granddaughter to save himself.

He would not stop until he was dead.

And if he was dead, Beth would have only her mother left to worry about.

CHAPTER FORTY-SEVEN

For a long time after Todd left, Dana just sat in the kitchen, her mind blank. Eventually, she got up and went and opened the fridge. Maybe if she could cook something, or at least chop something, her mind would start to settle down.

There was a carton of egg substitute, a pack of soy cheese, some silken tofu that had gone fuzzy, and a carton of oat milk with a dubious gray crust around the spout.

Three deflated oranges huddled together in the fruit drawer.

She tried the freezer. It was a whole different world in there. Piles of burritos and frozen dinners and minute steak. Boxes of toaster waffles and bags of French fries.

Dana closed the door. She walked back to her stool and picked up her jacket and hugged it like it was Cornie Bow. She didn't know why. But it was hers and she wanted to hold on to it. She felt in the pockets and came up with a Kleenex and a tube of mascara.

She checked the hidden pockets. One was empty. The other had a twenty. *Mad money.* In case shit went wrong and she needed to get herself home. Shit had gone very wrong. And she couldn't go home. Smoothing the jacket over her arm, she went out to the foyer. The stairway was empty—so was what she could see of the upstairs hall. She looked out through the sidelights at the empty street again.

I have to do something.

There was nothing keeping her here. She could just walk out that door.

I cannot just sit here and wait for...him to come back.

Even if she could figure out where to go to catch a bus or the train without being seen and stopped, where would she go? She couldn't go home. And she didn't have enough money to go anyplace else.

She stared at the door.

Why would Jeannie even believe he would help? Why didn't she...find somebody else? Like Mom?

Fresh goose bumps crawled across her arms, because she realized that was a really good question. Why *didn't* Jeannie call Mom when she knew things were going bad? She had Mom's number. And sure, Mom would be mad. But she was still better than Todd.

Jeannie said she was trying to protect Dana and keep her safe.

But...but...

But there was something else too. Something trying to dig itself out from the back of Dana's brain but that hadn't quite made it yet.

Where is Jeannie?

Todd had said, *Don't think this is gonna be one of her good days.*

She shook her head. *Don't think about that either. Think about what you're going to do. There has to be something. There has to be.*

And there was.

Chelsea.

Dana could call Chelsea right now. There was a phone in the kitchen. Nobody would be watching Chelsea, would they? Dana could let her know she was okay but that she had to say good-bye.

Chelsea could tell Mom Dana loved her. And that she was sorry for everything. That she wasn't vanishing. Just...leaving.

"Hey, hon-bun." Jeannie's voice cut through her thoughts. Dana spun around to see her grandmother walking silently down the stairs. "What's going on?"

CHAPTER FORTY-EIGHT

Beth dashed back into her bedroom, or at least she tried to. She was tired. She hadn't eaten, hadn't slept. Her brain felt thick, and her body ached. But she couldn't stop. Not yet.

She changed into jeans and a green T-shirt. She found a floppy beach hat in the back of the closet and jammed it over her hair.

The cops had searched through her go-bag, but they hadn't taken anything. They'd taken Dana's away, sealed in plastic, carefully tagged and photographed.

Beth slung her bag over her shoulder along with her purse.

The question was how to get out of the building without being seen. A quick glance out the balcony doors showed that the media were downstairs in force. Mr. Verdes would at least try to keep them cleared out of the lobby, but there wouldn't be a thing he could do about the crowd on the sidewalk.

It was entirely possible Patel had left somebody in with the crowd to keep an eye out for her.

Beth drummed her fingers for a minute on her purse's shoulder strap. Then she picked up the landline and dialed.

"Desk," Kendi answered. Voices buzzed and muttered in the background. The media were definitely there—with or without a cop hidden in the pack.

"Kendi," said Beth. "I need to get out. I'm going down the service stairs."

"Yes, ma'am," he answered calmly. "That has been taken care of." He paused. "Yes, Mr. Verdes will have that ready for you." He added, "Garage, yes."

"Thank you, Kendi."

"Yes, ma'am," he replied, and hung up.

Beth headed out the door. She didn't check the locks or reset the alarm. If she and Dana came home, she'd deal with anything that happened then.

If they didn't...then what did it matter?

Most people looking for a luxury home wanted the highest possible floor. Upper floors were quieter, with better views and more sunlight.

Beth had deliberately chosen a lower floor, because she knew there might be a day when she'd need to get away down the stairs. She pounded down the chipped, gray steps and pushed through the fireproof door labeled PARKING.

As Kendi had promised, Mr. Verdes was waiting for her. He stood between the tiny office and the white maintenance van. Verdes had removed his uniform blazer for the occasion and donned a baseball cap with the building logo instead.

"I thought the back…" he said. "It won't be comfortable…"

"Thank you, Mr. Verdes." Beth tossed her bag into the van's cargo hold and hoisted herself in after it. "I can't tell you how much I appreciate this."

Mr. Verdes waved her words away. His face spoke volumes about what he thought of the people up front disturbing his building's peace and quiet.

Beth climbed into the back and waited for him to close the doors. But he hesitated.

"There is something you should know, Ms. Fraser. Kendi says there was an old man here a few days ago. He tried chatting up Kendi about you, and then Carla on the night desk. Kendi says he thinks he saw him back today."

Beth sat down, far more abruptly than she meant to.

"When?"

Mr. Verdes shook his head. "I don't know, but recently."

She gathered her knees under herself. Could he be here already? Maybe. Jeannie said she didn't know exactly when he left…

"Okay," she said. "Thank you, and thank Kendi." *Again.*

"Let's get you out of here."

Mr. Verdes slammed the doors shut, leaving Beth sitting alone in the dark.

The crowd in front of Beth's building parted grudgingly for the van as it eased up the parking ramp. Cameras swung in their direction and reporters craned their necks hopefully. Others held their phones up over the heads of those who were just gawking.

Mr. Verdes leaned on the horn and muttered some Spanish curses. Beth clutched her go-bag with one hand and the rack bolted to the side of the van with the other.

Mr. Verdes kept making hard use of both the horn and the curses as he negotiated the street traffic trying to thread between the news vans. At last, he got them around the corner and hit the gas. Beth jerked backward and banged her head against the roll of hose hanging behind her.

At the end of the next block, he stopped and nodded to her over his shoulder.

"Thank you." Beth grabbed her things and ducked out the cargo doors.

"We are praying for Dana," he said, and Beth found herself wondering what she had done to earn that very human mercy.

She would have to try to understand that later.

Her initial plan had been to head straight to her safe-deposit box. But that had to change now. As soon as Mr. Verdes's van was out of sight, Beth swung around and started back toward her block and her building. If Dad was out in that mob, she had to know.

If Dad was in the mob…

She sprinted down the sidewalk but slowed as soon as she got to the corner. She could not call attention to herself. She had to see him first.

It took all of two seconds.

Todd Bowen leaned against a WGN news van. He'd dressed for this occasion too—that same button-down shirt he'd worn to her office, but this time he had a nylon messenger bag slung over his shoulder. He looked like he could be working for a newspaper. He looked like he could be anybody at all.

Todd was busy cracking jokes with a burly man in black jeans and a T-shirt. She was too far away to hear what he was saying, but the WGN guy laughed and jerked his chin at the chaos across the street. Dad laughed too and shook his head. He was doing what he did best—making friends. Getting all the latest news about the ruin of her life. About what was happening to her while he held on to her daughter.

All she wanted to do was throw him to the ground, kick him bloody, hear him scream, hear him beg for his life for what he had done.

They'll be on me in a hot minute. Arrest me. Leave Dana with them.

This thought cleared the red haze inside Beth. Not much, but enough to let her think. Dad wanted her money and her fear. He wanted to be in control of her again.

Do you know Jeannie's finally had enough? she wondered. *Do you know Jeannie is helping you hold on to Dana so I'll kill you first?*

Probably not. Because he had his blind spots, just like everybody did. And if the other person was paying out, well, they couldn't possibly have a plan of their own, could they?

Beth gripped her purse strap and stepped out into the street.

Come on, Dad. Over here. Look over here.

Todd talked, and Todd laughed. Seconds ticked by, and Beth felt every fiber in her body clench. *Over here.*

Todd slapped the other man's arm, and his gaze drifted for just a moment. Just far enough.

Their eyes locked.

Beth pressed her hand over her mouth, all surprise and fear. She whisked around and jogged away.

Okay, Dad—it's you and me now, she thought as she rushed straight down the middle of the sidewalk. *Follow the leader.*

CHAPTER FORTY-NINE

"You weren't thinking of running, hon-bun, were you?"

Todd had been right. Jeannie did not look good. Her tanned face was taut and pale. The bruise around her right eye was a tattered ring of black and velvet red. Looking at it, Dana felt an answering pain in her own face.

"I'm sorry," Dana breathed.

Jeannie put her hand on the jacket Dana had looped over her arm and squeezed. "Dana, I know you're scared, and I know you're confused, but you *cannot* just walk out of here. Never mind that every cop in the state is looking for you, when Todd catches you, he's going to be madder than a wet hen, and you've seen how he gets. One of us will end up beaten to a pulp."

"I said I'm sorry!"

"Yes, you're sorry. Now you have to be smart! If you make too much trouble, he can always just call the cops. He can turn you in any minute, Dana, and he will!"

It was too much. "Why are you still here?" demanded Dana.

"I'm trying to keep you safe, honey."

"What is safe about *this*?" She threw her arms out to encompass the whole huge, empty house. "With him in it!"

"We've got to keep you hidden," Jeannie told her. "We've just got to stay…"

Dana did not want to hear it. She didn't believe it. She didn't understand it. Fear and confusion overwhelmed all the other memories. "You said they arrested my mom!"

"I know they did, but you can't—"

"She's taking the blame for what I did!" *We did.*

"Not for long, honey. Her lawyers will get her off. I'm positive."

"How can you be so sure? What if…what if she confesses to protect me?" Guilt pressed down, smothering her. One more thing and she'd be crushed for good.

Jeannie took Dana's face in both her hands. "Your mom is really smart. You have to let her play this out her way. She can't be worrying about you right now."

Don't you understand anything?! "Worry about me? She's going to be fucking *hating* me! She's going to think I'm dead, Jeannie! Or worse! And he's just going to keep…Shit, how do you even live with it?!"

Jeannie pulled back and stared at her. Then she turned and stalked away into the kitchen. Dana trailed after her and found her staring at the inside of the freezer.

"Jesus." Jeannie grabbed a box of toaster waffles and ripped the flaps open. She yanked out a plastic pack and struggled to tear it. Finally, she gave up and threw it down on the counter and just stared at it.

"How do I live with myself?" Jeannie demanded of the counter and the waffles and Dana, and maybe God. "Because I want to keep living. That's how. I do what I have to do. Just like Todd does, and like your mother does, and like you will start doing if you've got a brain in your head!"

"But he's gone! We can just walk out of here."

"And get picked up by the cops ten minutes later?"

"Maybe that wouldn't be so bad," whispered Dana.

Jeannie pulled a knife out of the block on the counter and stabbed it into the waffle pack. "Dana. Honey." The words sounded like curses as she slit the bag, fast, right down the middle. "You don't know what you're talking about, okay?" She tossed the knife down and spread the plastic open like wings. Like skin. "You don't know what the cops'll do once they get hold of you. They're already calling you names on the news and—"

"So we tell them Todd did it," said Dana.

The words hung echoing in the air while Jeannie stared at her, her eyes wide and that one ragged bruise making her look all lopsided. Dana felt like she was looking in a weird horror-show mirror, finally seeing somebody else who had two different eyes.

But even as she stared at her wounded grandmother, Dana's own words filled her with a slow warmth.

We can fix this! We can do it. Two birds with one fucking stone!

"We get our story together and we tell—whoever—that Todd killed Dad." Dana was babbling now and she knew it, and she didn't stop. "It wouldn't be much of a stretch. I mean, he was right there." She was missing something. She knew that too, but she ignored it. If she stopped talking, she might lose her nerve. "And so were you, and you can say you saw him. We've got that video proving how he beats you, and we know he was threatening Mom for money and all that. I can tell them how Dad came and found me and got me to go to that hotel and…" *And blame Dad for getting killed.* Dana felt suddenly sick, but she told herself it didn't matter. He was dead. He couldn't care.

The nausea did not go away.

Jeannie was looking at Dana like she had stopped speaking English. It wasn't just confusion—it was disbelief and something more that Dana couldn't put a name to.

But Dana didn't let that stop her. "Then they arrest Todd, and we get bail or whatever, and…" *And we go home. And Mom doesn't have to take the blame to try to save me.* "And he's locked up, and if we still have to run away or anything, we do that. Mom's had all that set up for fucking *years.*"

Because she was always afraid of you and what you might do when you came back.

"Dana," said Jeannie slowly. "I keep trying to tell you. This isn't some game. This is real life."

"I know that!" Dana shouted. "Jesus! Where do you think I've *been* the past couple of days? You keep saying you want to leave, but…"

"We just need…"

"We need to get out of here, but you won't *go*! That door is effing open! We don't even have to leave! All we have to do is call the cops!"

"He'll kill me!" Jeannie screamed.

"He'll be in *jail*!"

Jeannie threw up one hand, shielding herself from Dana's shout, and Dana immediately shrank backward, her resolve and her insides crumpling. Jeannie shook and blinked hard.

"Please, Grandma," Dana said more gently this time. "Please. We can do this."

But Jeannie was already turning away. She pressed her face into her hands and shook her head. Her whole body trembled.

"It won't work," she sobbed. "Nothing will stop him! Not until he's dead."

Dana laid a hand on Jeannie's shoulders. She could feel every last one of her grandmother's bones as they shifted beneath her shirt and her skin. "I know you're scared. I do. But you're not alone anymore. You've got me. You've got Mom." *Even now. Really. That thing Todd said—it wasn't true. Mom wouldn't…she couldn't…*

"You?" sneered Jeannie, and the contempt in that single word snatched what was left of Dana's breath right out of her throat.

Jeannie lifted her head and let Dana see the tears streaming down her sunken cheeks. "I've got *you*? The only reason I'm in this fucking mess was because I wanted to help you! I could have gotten away on my own, but I wasn't going to leave you with him. I just wanted to help keep my granddaughter safe…And now *you're* gonna get me ki—"

Her words choked off and she doubled over, all her breath leaving her in a sharp hiss. "Oh shit."

"Grandma?"

Jeannie shook her head and pressed her hands against her stomach. Her legs shook and buckled, and Jeannie sank to her knees.

"Oh, Jesus Christ, it hurts. It hurts!"

Grandma's perfect fingernails dragged against the floorboards.

It was a seizure, a fit. It was the cancer or…whatever. Dana didn't move. She just stood there and watched and felt how her mind turned so very cold as Jeannie panted and whimpered.

"I'm sorry," breathed Jeannie to the floorboards. "I'm sorry. I tried. I didn't want to hurt you too. I just…" She squeezed her eyes shut, and her body shuddered. "I just wanted to help."

Dana felt strangely, starkly aware of each movement as she went to kneel beside her grandmother and took her by the shoulders.

"Come on," Dana said harshly. "I'll get you to bed."

She held on to Jeannie's shoulders and supported her up the stairs to the master bedroom. It was sunny and modern, and there were framed positive affirmations on all four walls. The bed was king-size, piled with pillows and a red striped duvet. Dana helped her grandmother climb in and covered her up.

Jeannie knotted her fingers into the pillow. "Pills," she whispered. "I need my pills."

There were three unlabeled amber bottles on the nightstand beside the clock. Dana went into the attached bathroom and filled a water glass.

She came back into the bedroom.

"Which one?" she asked.

"Doesn't matter," croaked Jeannie. "All the same."

Dana shook out one pill into her hand.

"Three," breathed Jeannie. "It's too bad. I need three. Please, honey. It hurts."

Dana added two more, just like she was told. "It hurts, but it's not cancer, is it?"

"It's cancer and pills and booze and fifty goddamn years of not being able to stop. I just want to stop," she cried.

Jeannie lifted her head, and Dana held the glass to her lips so she could wash down the pills.

Jeannie fell back onto the pillow. Dana took the glass back to the bathroom.

"Dana?"

Dana, surprised at her own reluctance, returned to the bed's side. Jeannie had stretched one hand out from under the cheerful duvet for Dana to take. "I'm sorry. I wish there was another way. I do," Jeannie said.

"You rest, Grandma," Dana said. "He's going to be back soon."

"Thank you, hon-bun. I do love you." She looked up at Dana for a long time, and Dana wondered what she was seeing.

At last, Jeannie's eyelids fluttered closed. Dana stayed there until she was sure her grandmother was really asleep.

Dana walked back down the stairs. On reflex, she went back into that nice kitchen. She stared at the waffles lying naked on the black counter. She looked out the windows into the perfectly groomed backyard. There was a squirrel sitting on top of the privacy fence.

I could just leave. Let the cops do whatever they'd do. Let the whole world know what I am. Let Chelsea and Kimi and everybody at Vine and Horn and Mom and the whole rest of the world know...

Let Todd come back and find Jeannie all alone.

He'd beat on Jeannie for letting Dana go. He might even kill her.

She could still go. Now.

And let him.

CHAPTER FIFTY

Twice Beth thought she'd lost Todd.

The first time was when she had ducked across the street and around the corner. She gave herself a count of three and checked the reflection in the brewpub window but didn't see him. She made herself keep breathing and keep watching. Finally, the light changed and the red delivery truck moved, and she spotted him again, standing across the street.

She took off before he could notice she was waiting for him.

The second time, she was afraid she'd gotten a little too clever. She cut through a corner Walgreens so it would look like she really was doing her best to throw him off. She lingered in the feminine hygiene aisle. When he didn't appear, she assumed he was waiting outside. She bought a pack of gum and walked casually out the door, and he was gone.

Panic drove itself knife sharp through her exhausted brain. Beth looked wildly up and down the street, forgetting subtlety, forgetting everything. But she spotted him again. This time, he stood in the bus shelter, pretending to read the ads.

Beth bolted across the street, jaywalking to a chorus of horns.

Of course he saw. Of course he followed.

Thank God.

One reason for living right downtown despite the cost was that there was so much within walking distance. This included McKeirnan's Secure Deposit Company.

Beth tapped her door code on McKeirnan's PIN pad and waited for its light to blink green. The outer door buzzed and clicked. She ducked through, then pushed open the inner door. She immediately slid sideways to the corner of the lobby where she wouldn't be easily seen.

Come on, Dad. You saw me go in here. You couldn't miss me.

He didn't. Through the glass doors, Beth watched Todd stroll up casually and try the handle. He looked up at the sign. He cupped his hand around his eyes and peered into the empty white-tiled lobby.

Beth held her breath and walked calmly but quickly across the lobby to the stairs that led down to the basement and her box.

Right across Todd's line of sight.

Now, you just wait there a second, Dad.

McKeirnan's lower level was a series of aisles tiled in the same speckled white as its lobby. Beth's box was in aisle 4, a stark, silent corridor lined with identical metal doors, each about a foot square.

There were bigger doors on other levels for those who had more to hide.

Like the front door, the safe-deposit box had a keypad, this one with white buttons like tiny pills. She entered her combination and tugged the handle to slide the box open.

She pulled out the fake IDs she kept for Dana and stashed them in her purse. She removed her own cards from her wallet, dropped those into the box, and replaced them with the driver's license, credit cards, and passport that had been made up in the name of Gretchen Murkowski.

She stowed the Glock and its box of ammunition in her go-bag, along with two unmarked envelopes, each of which held five thousand dollars.

Beth zipped the bag up and closed the box. Then she grabbed her phone and Detective Patel's card.

There were only so many ways she could deal with the fact that her father was following her now. She could confront him. She could plead with him. She could try to lose him.

Or she could do the one thing he'd never expect.

The detective answered on the fourth ring. "Patel."

"This is Beth Fraser," Beth whispered. Just in case she'd missed the sound of footsteps on the stairs. Just in case there was somebody waiting around the corner she couldn't hear.

"How can I help you, Ms. Fraser?"

Beth slid to the end of the hall and stared around her, looking for shadows on the floor or the walls. Nothing.

"I'm at McKeirnan's Secure Deposit Company." She added the street address. "There's a man out front." *Please let him be out front.* She tiptoed to the other end of the aisle. "About seventy years old, thin, wearing a white button-down shirt and jeans and carrying a black messenger bag."

On the other end of the line, a pencil scraped and stabbed against a paper. "Yes?"

"He's my father."

Patel's breath hissed sharply between her teeth. "You didn't mention you had family in town."

Beth ignored that. "His real name is Thomas James Jankowski. He uses the alias Todd Bowen."

"That's a surprise, Ms. Fraser." Something was tapping on a desktop, nails or that pencil—Beth wasn't sure which. "Neither of those names is listed with your information."

"I know. But he was one of the people in Doug Hoyt's hotel room last night, and he knows where Dana is." She paused. "There's security footage from Lumination's building of him entering my office Sunday and audio of him making threats to me."

"And you didn't mention any of this before?"

"No."

"But you're sure he knows something about your daughter's whereabouts?"

"Yes."

Patel was silent for a long moment. "All right. We'll call this a tip, and I can have some men come down and pick him up on suspicion. But, Ms. Fraser, this will all go a lot faster if you'd talk—"

Beth hung up, shut her phone down, and stuffed it back in her purse.

Mom wanted Dad dead. Well, she'd have to settle for arrested. Unless the cops wanted to do the dirty work for her.

While Dad was dealing with that, she'd head out to Schaumburg and get Dana back.

There was one other stairway out of the basement. It came up into an interior hallway instead of the lobby. There was a door to the pedestrian alley at one end. At the other was a door to another stairway and more vaults and offices and whatever the hell else McKeirnan's kept for its people.

Beth had the hall to herself. No one needed anything this afternoon. No one but her.

Exactly halfway down the hall, a pair of old-school steel doors with square windows and push bars led to the lobby and the front doors.

Beth walked up to the seam between the nearest door and the wall. She clutched her bag and held her breath. She angled herself and craned her neck until she could just see out the window, across the lobby, and through the front doors to the sidewalk.

Until she could see Todd pacing back and forth out front with his phone pressed to his ear.

Relief burned as badly as hope. He moved out of her line of sight, then back in. Just another guy, talking to…whoever. It didn't matter. He probably wasn't talking to anybody. It was just an excuse to be standing there, in case anybody glanced his way.

What mattered was he was still there, waiting for her to come out.

She saw herself walking past him and leading him away down the pedestrian walk and into an alley. She saw herself offering him the ten thousand she had with her, if he'd just give her Dana back. Or she could just pull the gun. He'd never believe she'd shoot. She'd aim for the center of his body. Leave him bleeding his life out on the concrete for Detective Patel to find.

Beth moved quickly down the hall. The smaller door to the alley was unlocked from the inside at least. She pushed through into the sunshine.

She hoped Patel's people were on their way. She hoped Dad gave them a fight. She needed time to get to Dana, and then more time after that to find out what really happened in that hotel room. She needed to know what she had to do next. If it was Dana who...

If it was Dana...

It wasn't Dana. I will not let it be Dana.

"Jesus, Star. Why do you keep making things so hard on everybody?"

CHAPTER FIFTY-ONE

Todd stood right at the building's corner, all clean and casual. Just another midlevel businessman on the streets of Chicago.

I should have known, thought Beth.

Of course he'd spotted the side door. She'd given him plenty of time. If she'd thought about it, she would have realized the reason he was walking back and forth while making his fake phone call was so he could keep an eye on both exits.

"Hello, Dad," she said, because she couldn't think of anything else to say. Because she had to keep him calm.

She had to keep him *here*.

"Don't you 'hello, Dad' me, young lady," he said with a mocking frown. "Especially not when you're getting ready to skip out on me. Damn." He shook his head. "Your girl is going to be really disappointed."

Beth's ability to playact evaporated. "How is she? Is she okay?"

"As if you actually care. Leading me all over town like this instead of sitting down and working things out."

Beth bit back her immediate answer. She was so tired. She was standing in the June sunlight, and her hands were still cold as ice. But all she could really feel was how very much she wanted this man dead.

He won't stop. He won't stop until he's dead.

"What was I supposed to do?" she asked. "Sit home and wait for the phone to ring? I got cops looking for an excuse to arrest me."

"Yeah, about that." His quick, sly smile slid into place. "You do know your little girl did the deed, right?"

I don't believe that. Not with that sick look in those eyes right in front of me.

But she did know there was exactly one way she could get him to stay and listen.

Beth made herself start shaking. It wasn't hard. She was at the end of her strength. She just had to let go a little before her hands began to tremble, her knees, her voice. Her heart.

"Take me to her," she begged. "Please, Dad. Let me see my daughter."

He didn't answer right away. Of course he wouldn't. He wanted to savor the moment, here with his ungrateful daughter shaking and begging. "Now, why would I do that?"

She held up the gym bag. "Because I've got ten thousand dollars right here for you."

This time the pause felt different. This time he was surprised. She thought. She hoped.

"Chicken feed," he announced finally.

"Just the beginning. That seventy-five K I promised you? We can still get to it, if we're a little careful, and there's more where that came from."

Todd dipped his chin and arched both eyebrows.

"The Bowens, together again, Dad." Beth moved forward one step. She tried to force enough bravado into her voice to smooth out the raw edge of her desperation. "I've got to get out of here, and so do you and Jeannie. So does Dana. We might as well just go together. You can have everything I've got. I don't care. We'll need it all anyway. I've been getting ready to cut and run for *years*. You would not believe what I've got stashed away, starting with a car, all gassed up and ready to go. You know, you were right." She gave him a painful, tentative smile. "You did teach me everything I know. I just…scaled it up a little."

He wanted to believe this was true. His shoulders were hunching, his eyes narrowing just a little. It was one of his few tells. Beth was shocked to find herself remembering it.

"How could I ever be sure you'd behave?"

"Same way you knew I'd pay up. Because you could turn my daughter in anytime. Well, now you'll have two of us." She spread her hands, showing him they were empty.

Believe it, Dad. Believe me.

His pinpoint attention crawled across her face, looking for the crack in the story. Beth had no choice but to hold still and let it happen. She didn't dare move until he was good and ready.

He was almost there. She could see it. He knew in his blood and bones that in the end, she belonged to him.

And this was the end. The bitter, final, for-real end. He stared at her, and in that moment, Beth realized she'd never really seen her father. She'd maybe caught a glimpse, here and there. But this naked, impersonal calculation had remained hidden under his alternating masks of rage and cheerful affection.

"Let's see what's really in that bag," said Todd.

"Okay."

She did not want him to know she was carrying, but there was nothing she could do now, and she could not let him see her hesitate. She tossed the bag to him.

Theoretically, he could just grab it and run. But he wouldn't. Because she had more than what was in there. Dad never took half the pot.

He glanced over his shoulder. Her eyes fastened on his throat. Her ears rang. She smelled smoke.

No one was looking; no one was coming. Not that he could see. Or hear.

She smelled iron and tasted copper and salt.

Dad moved into the shadow by the wall and unzipped the bag. He shook it and lifted his eyebrows at her.

He'd seen the gun. She shrugged. "World's a dangerous place, Dad," she whispered. "And you're going to want to make your mind up really soon."

"Why?"

"Because I called the cops."

He tucked his chin so he could look down his nose at her. "And why would you go and do a damn fool thing like that?"

"Because you might have said no."

He pulled the Glock out, thumbed the safety. Beth felt her body seize up.

Then he grinned his best, most open grin and tucked the gun in his jacket pocket.

"Okay, Daughter," he said. "Let's go get that car."

Todd bowed and gestured for her to go first. Beth led her father calmly away down the alley, to the timeless city serenade of police sirens.

CHAPTER FIFTY-TWO

Schaumburg was a place of well-spaced single-family homes and sloping lawns and old trees. Little strip-mall districts were allowed at decorous intervals, and even the gas stations looked like they cared about appearances.

Dad was obviously very familiar with the route. He had no problem directing her through the exits and turns and roundabouts into the depths of a quiet, shady neighborhood and onto one particular driveway on one particular street.

"Hey, get a load o' this, Star. I love this." He pointed his phone at the garage door, and it rose gracefully. "Like magic!"

Beth drove in and parked. Dad hit a button on his phone, and the door closed behind them, shutting them both into the dark.

Dad patted her arm and climbed out of the car. Beth got out more slowly behind him. She didn't know what to hope for. She wanted to see Dana like she wanted to keep breathing. But part of her wanted Dana to have escaped. She wanted her daughter to have not believed their lies and to be out there somewhere, looking for a way back home. Todd fished out his key and opened the door to the house.

"We're back!" he bellowed.

Beth was vaguely aware they'd come out of the dark into a sunny mudroom and that there was one step up into an even sunnier kitchen. The only thing she really saw was the person who came to stand in the doorway, a fork in one hand.

Dana.

Dana whole and alive and standing in front of her. Dana wide-eyed and jaw-dropped and unable to believe what was happening.

Dana. My daughter. Dangerface. Dana.

Dana rushed forward. The fork clattered to the floor. Beth wrapped her arms around her and pulled her daughter against her. She held her, unable to think, unable to move, just breathing in her scent, feeling the trembling reality of her body. Beth hugged her like her life depended on it. It did. The ability of her heart to keep beating depended on Dana's warmth seeping into her body.

She was crying. "I'm sorry, Mom. I'm so sorry. I just...I didn't..."

"Shh. Shh." Beth kissed the top of her head. "It's not your fault. It's not your fault."

"I did it." Dana pressed her face hard against Beth's shoulder. Her tears soaked through the thin T-shirt. "I did it. I..."

"Dana, Dana—look at me." Taking her face between her hands, feeling the familiar shape against her palms. Inhaling the scent of her, feeling the strength of her. Seeing Dana staring up at her with her beautiful, beautiful eyes filled with fear and questions.

"It is not your fault." Beth poured every ounce of meaning she could into the words. "None of it."

"Are we going home?" asked Dana.

She sounded so small, so lost. Beth wrapped her arms around her daughter again and looked over her head at her parents.

Todd stood grinning, positively radiating triumph. Why wouldn't he? He had everything he wanted. Here was his entire family, all in one room and all absolutely dependent on him.

Jeannie, though—Jeannie looked wary. Blinking hard, probably coming down off something.

You did this, Beth thought at them. *You did this and you brought me here and I will make you sorry.*

Jeannie turned a little pale. Todd just clapped his hands together, hard.

"Okay, enough waterworks," he announced. "Everybody, get your stuff. We're hitting the road."

That startled Jeannie. "You said we were staying for a couple more days."

"Change of plans."

Dana pulled back, just far enough to look right into Beth's eyes. Beth kept her arms around Dana's shoulders, trying to will silent reassurance into her daughter's body.

"Our girl thought ahead enough to have a car ready to

go," Dad was saying. "And then she went and called the cops on me." He shook his head in disbelief at this bit of mischief. "We are outta here. Get your stuff, Jeannie. You too, Granddaughter."

"But, Mom... what...?"

"Shh. It's going to be okay."

Dana squeezed her arm. It hurt, but not as bad as the pressure in her heart and her head at the sight of her daughter's bewildered distress. "We're not going with them! You're not! We're going home!"

"No, Dana. Not yet. It's okay. Everything's going to be fine. It's just for a little while."

"You're talking like them."

The love and excitement bled out of Dana's eyes, replaced by confusion and betrayal. Beth gripped her shoulders. *Look at me, Dana. See me. Please, please—you have to.*

But Dana didn't want to see. She slowly drew herself away. She picked up her purse and slung it over her shoulder and wrapped her arms around herself.

"Jeannie?" Todd put a note of warning into the name. "Let's go."

"Yeah, Todd. Sure." Jeannie finally moved into the other room. Beth heard her rummaging around.

Dad didn't put the duffle bag down once.

Beth gathered Dana close again, kissing the top of her head. "He's got a gun, Dana," she breathed. Dana's head jerked up. "We go along for now."

She held her daughter's gaze. Something hardened inside, a determination that she had rarely felt. Dana was already changed, already broken by everything that had happened to her. Her kind girl, the fixer, the cheerful and irreverent foodie, was already damaged.

My fault. My fault.

She could not sink into that blame. To do so would be to drag Dana with her.

Jeannie came back into the room, dragging a wheeled suitcase with her. Beth wondered how much stuff Amanda Pace Martin was going to be missing when she finally got home.

"So, here's what's going on," announced Todd. "We're going to head for Detroit. If we push, we can make it by tonight. I still know a couple of guys who can help us out with some fresh IDs. Then we're headed down to Miami. No more winters! Sun and fun on the beach for everybody!"

"Sounds great, Todd," said Jeannie.

"Whaddya say, Dana?"

Dana just tightened her jaw.

"Okay, we got the sulks. You'll feel better when you've had a chance to get used to the idea. Besides, we're gonna have fun. This is a family trip. All the Bowens together for the first time!"

Beth kept her hands on Dana's shoulders. "No fuss, Dana, okay?"

Hear me. Hear what I'm really saying. Look at me. Look at me. You know me. We know each other.

This time Dana did look, and Dana saw.

But she wasn't the only one who did. Beth turned and found both parents watching her. Todd was confident and brimming with happiness.

And then there was Jeannie. For a split second, Beth saw the rage burning on Jeannie's face. One single instant when the calculations had all broken and revealed the woman underneath.

The woman who at that moment wanted them all dead.

CHAPTER FIFTY-THREE

Beth drove.

The ragged ruins between Chicago and Gary slowly gave way to fields of beans and corn. Trucks and SUVs rumbled past. The sun setting behind them. The awareness of her father beside her, her mother behind her.

As often as she could, Beth glanced into the rearview mirror, trying to see Dana. Dana didn't look back. She curled up in the corner of the seat as tightly as the belt allowed and watched the flat country and the traffic roll past.

It was Jeannie's gaze she kept catching.

Dad talked the whole time. Having a captive audience always did make him expansive. Now, he spun pictures of all the bright lights and fun they were going to have in Miami. He didn't expect answers or input. He just talked, and Beth just drove.

But with every word, every second, and each mile post

Beth felt her life recede. Nothing she had accomplished mattered now—not her escape from Bob Early, not finding Rafi, not Lumination. Not the long years when she begged, borrowed, stole, and ultimately built a life from the ruins that had been gifted to her by her parents. None of it. She was right back where she'd started, only worse.

Because before, she didn't have any choice. This time...it was because she'd failed. Failed herself and failed Dana.

"Indiana state line," said Dad cheerfully. "Everybody breathe."

Beth's head jerked up. *Shit.* She'd almost fallen asleep. "Rest stop," she croaked. "Um, okay, Dad?"

"Yeah!" Dana announced abruptly from the back seat. "I gotta pee!"

"Hey, I know what!" Jeannie leaned forward and draped her arms over Todd's seat. "I remember there's this outlet mall in Michigan City. Remember that, Todd? We should stop there."

"Shopping?" said Dana, appalled.

"Actually, it's not a bad idea." Beth tried to catch Dana's eye in the mirror. "We're all going to need clothes and stuff. It's a long way to Miami."

"Women." Dad rolled his eyes. "Okay, pull in here." He pointed to the rest-stop sign, like Beth couldn't read. "Quick pee and then I guess we're going to the mall."

Jeannie squealed like a little girl and bounced up and down in her seat. Dana looked out the window, tired and disgusted.

Beth turned the wheel.

Once she'd pulled into the empty parking lot and turned

off the engine, Dad shifted in his seat so he could talk to the whole family at once.

"Now, I want you all to know we're on the buddy system from here on out. Safety first, right?" He grinned and tapped the side of his nose. "Dana, you and me go while your mom stays here with your grandma. When we get back, you two can go, okay? Okay." He unbuckled himself. "Come on, Granddaughter."

Dana stared at Beth, her eyes wide, silently urging her to do something. But there was nothing she could do. Not yet.

"Go on, Dana."

Her daughter's disappointment cut deep, but Beth hugged that pain close. It woke her up better than any hit of caffeine could. This was what was real. This was why she had to keep swimming.

Todd climbed out of the car, and so did Dana. Beth watched her father put his hand on Dana's shoulder. She gripped the steering wheel until she thought it would break. She watched him walk Dana away. The windows were up. She could not hear what he was saying, but she saw Dana's shoulders slump.

That was when Jeannie shouted.

"What in God's name do you think you're doing? You were going to kill him! I *told* you! You *said*—"

"I know what I said." Beth cut her off. Jeannie was panicky. That was not good. "I've got to pick my moment, Mom." Jeannie at least paused at that. "The cops already think I killed Doug. Who would they be looking for if Todd turned up dead too? I had to get him out of state first, and then…if there's going to be any chance of a life after this for Dana, whatever I do has got to look like self-defense."

"You actually think you can go back after this?"

Beth twisted her hands on the wheel, trying to wring it out like a rag. "Dana has to be able to."

"Well, then you're a goddamn fool, Star Bowen. Whatever you had, he's already taken it all away from you *and* her, and you'd both better hurry up and get used to it."

"Careful, Mom," said Beth softly. "You brought me here because you can't make yourself kill him—"

"He knows me too well. He'd see it!"

"You don't want me thinking about two birds with one stone, do you?"

Beth felt a sick surge of satisfaction at the flicker of fear that crossed her mother's bruised face. "Yes, yes, of course you have to think about Dana. But you can't wait too long, Beth. He's got plans. He's going to get you to sign over your money. He's not going to leave you with anything."

Jeannie was babbling, acquiescing, reassessing. She was trying to find some argument that would both soothe and frighten her daughter. But her eyes remained hard and watchful.

Fear sent a surge of adrenaline through Beth. Because Jeannie was the dangerous one. She always had been, and Beth could not forget that for a single second.

Because Jeannie had something she wanted Beth to do, and if she started thinking that Beth might not get it done, she might also decide there was no point in dragging her along anymore.

CHAPTER FIFTY-FOUR

This was surreal.

Barely a full day after killing her father, Dana was walking into a mall. The happiest, blandest, most normal place in America, surrounded by outlet stores and crammed with people. Michigan City (which was still in Indiana—what was up with that?) clearly did not have a whole lot else going on.

Oh, and she was on the run. Literally. This was what on the run was. This feeling like she'd been lit up from the inside and everybody could see there was something wrong. Like she still had all the blood all over her face and down her shirt. Any second now, someone would turn and see it. She was on the run with her crazy grandparents.

And her mom.

When Mom had walked into that house, Dana had fallen into her arms. She'd been warm and safe. Saved. For about two seconds. Then it all came crashing down.

And there was the unbelievable car ride. The whole time, Jeannie kept trying to hold her hand and mouthed little things at her. Dana had to stop looking at her. It made her sick—like, carsick but worse. She didn't know what to do. She'd thought maybe something would happen at the rest stop. Like Mom would find a way to smuggle them both out in one of the semis parked on the far side. Something. Anything.

But all that happened was everybody peed and they all got back in the car. And came here, where they were just one more family in the crowd.

And Jeannie and Todd were up ahead, and for this little pocket of a moment, they were not being watched.

Dana twined her fingers into her mother's. "Now?" she said as quietly as she could. "He's not gonna shoot up a mall." *He's not that kind of crazy. He can't be. He can't.*

Mom squeezed her fingers. "Not yet," she breathed. "Soon."

Disappointment tasted just like bile.

All of a sudden, Jeannie squealed. "Ooo, look—a Ruby Tuesday!" She grabbed Todd's arm. "I'm starving! Let's get something. Can we please?" She laid her head on his shoulder and blinked at him.

Todd laughed and put an arm around her. "Sure. Why not? Keep up, girls!"

Un-effing-believable.

But in another couple of minutes, there they were—sitting at the table, all ordering burgers and fries. Todd flirted with the pretty waitress, and Jeannie didn't even seem to mind. *Where the fuck is your #MeToo mojo?*

346

And Todd was *still* talking. Now it was all about how great this trip was going to be. "Hey, what about Disney World? Have you ever been? No? We'll go. Man, I remember this one time—"

"You, at Disney?" Mom gave him the side-eye.

"Oh, hell yeah. You never know who you're going to run into. Lemme tell you…"

And he launched into this long, complicated story about a buddy of his who got him in and how they ran around the place at night with all the guys who spent their days in the costumes. ("They make them live in these dormitories. Practically lock 'em in, but they all get out anyway. Magic Kingdom, my lily-white ass! Anyway, one night, me and this guy, we…")

Dana found herself listening without really meaning to. Then she found herself laughing. Her burger came, and it was juicy and tasted way better than it should have. She finished it and all her fries. Then she stole some of Mom's. Mom drank cup after cup of coffee. Jeannie begged for dessert like a little kid, so they got a blondie sundae to split. Todd argued over shares and made this huge production of dividing it into exactly equal pieces, and then he started telling another story about working at a Dairy Queen in BFE Indiana and…and…

"Okay." Mom wiped her mouth. "Bathroom. Dana?"

Dana didn't get a chance to answer.

"She's fine." Todd's hand came down on her wrist. "We'll wait for you here."

Just like that, the illusion exploded. It was everything Dana could do not to heave up her whole meal right there.

She wanted to scream and turn the table over because she was so suddenly sick and very frightened.

Because for a minute, it was like nothing else had ever happened. They were a real family, on a real road trip. She'd actually, *literally*, forgotten how she got here and what these two had done, what she had done, what Mom had let happen.

How the hell was that even possible?

"Okay." Mom left and headed for the restroom. Todd called the waitress for the check.

Jeannie beamed at Dana. But there was something hard behind her eyes. *Keep going*, it said. *Whatever you're thinking now, just keep going.* "You know, I saw the cutest pair of jeans when we passed that Forever 21. I know they'd be just perfect for you, Dana…"

But it was gone. Fake. Had never been. They were on the run again, and when Mom came back, Dana caught her eye, silently pleading for help.

Wait for it, said her mother's eyes.

Keep going, said her grandmother's.

And what else could she do?

CHAPTER FIFTY-FIVE

They finally wound up at a Holiday Inn Express by the Detroit airport. It was sometime past midnight. Beth had drained her third truck stop coffee since leaving the outlet mall. Her whole body was taut and vibrating from caffeine and adrenaline. Each time they stopped, Dad kept Dana in the car with him, making Jeannie be Beth's keeper.

"We'll get our chance," Beth murmured to her mother. "Don't worry. I just need to get him clear of Dana. She cannot see this."

And she just had to keep praying Jeannie kept believing.

The clerk behind the Holiday Inn desk was a small, brisk, black-haired woman who registered no surprise when a rumpled and slightly dazed family with shopping bags and duffles walked into her lobby. She ran Beth's false credit card through the system without a second thought.

"One room or two?" she asked.

"Two rooms, I think, this time, Dad," Beth said and grinned at the clerk. "Girl needs her bathroom space."

"Adjoining if you got 'em?" added Todd with a grin of his own. Beth tried not to be disappointed. She did try to catch Dana's eye, but Dana was looking over her shoulder like she was measuring the distance to the lobby door.

She hadn't had a chance to talk to her daughter alone since that brief moment back in Schaumburg. She had no idea what Dana really believed about what was happening. All she could do was hope, and right now, her hope was running on fumes.

Jeannie noticed where Dana's attention had wandered as well. She put her arm around Dana's shoulders.

"It's okay, hon." Jeannie gave her a gentle shake and smiled at the clerk. "We'll all be able to get some sleep real soon."

The clerk clicked her mouse and found two adjoining rooms on the third floor. She handed over the little cardboard folder with four keys. Beth reached for it, but Dad beat her to it. He slid the keys into the same pocket where he'd put the gun.

In the narrow elevator, Beth crowded into the back, next to Dana for the first time in hours. She hooked her fingers into her daughter's. After a heartbreaking moment, she felt Dana squeeze her fingers in answer, and Beth found she had a little hope left after all.

She tried not to see how Jeannie held Dana's other hand.

Dad opened the first of the rooms and stood back while they herded themselves inside. He opened the other room, then went to the connecting door and knocked. "Lemme in!" he called cheerfully.

"Jesus, Todd," muttered Jeannie as she undid the door. "Keep it down, would you? We don't need anybody calling the management over your big mouth!"

Beth wrapped her arm around Dana's cold shoulders and rubbed. Dana tolerated her, but nothing more. Beth wanted to tell her it would be okay, that there was a plan, that she would get them both out of here, just as soon... just as soon...

"Okay, a few more house rules, and we can all get comfy," Todd announced. "The connecting door does not close." He took a washcloth off the rack and wedged it in place. "Family does not lock each other out. Clear? Okay. Now, I gotta go find my guys. Lemme have your IDs." He made the gimme gesture. "Not you, Star. I know you're set. Jeannie, yours, and Dana, what you got?"

Dana scowled but dug her wallet out of her purse and handed over her student ID.

"You sure? No learner's permit?"

"Yeah, like I really want to learn to drive now," she muttered.

Todd took two steps forward. Beth clenched her fists, but Jeannie just threaded her arm through his.

"Easy, babe. She's just tired. We all are."

Todd deflated, at least a little. "Yeah, yeah, well, you two better get some sleep, then. Star, you're coming with me."

For a minute, Beth wanted to protest. Actually, she wanted to whine and stomp her feet. *I'm too tired! I can't drive anymore. I can't leave my daughter again! I'm not going!*

Jeannie gave Beth a big smile and a quick hug. "Don't worry, Beth. Dana and I will be fine until you get back."

But her hard eyes had an entirely different message.

Now's your chance, they said.

In answer, Beth gave her the smallest possible nod. Then, she turned away and let her father usher her out of the room.

CHAPTER FIFTY-SIX

Detroit at night was a strange place. It had been a long time since Beth had been on a city street that was so deserted, but it was the scale that really got to her. Woodward Avenue was four broad lanes, all of them completely empty. They didn't even pass any parked cars. Eventually, the downtown's grand Gilded Age skyscrapers gave way to stretches of single-story brick buildings, where at least some signs for bars and party stores were lit. But that was only for a couple of blocks. After that came block after block of brick and clapboard houses, all of them boarded up or burned out or both. A blanked-out brick apartment building stood alone in the middle of a field of weeds.

It was a whole city of nobody home, and it got under Beth's skin. She clenched the steering wheel hard and kept her eyes on the crumbling road.

Todd frowned at the derelict houses and dented street

signs. *Do you really know where we're going?* she wondered, and her hands tightened on the wheel again.

Finally, the abandoned houses gave way to another highway overpass, and then a gas station, and then a liquor store and another block of brick buildings with their doors gated and their windows barred.

"Here," Dad said, pointing. Beth turned into the potholed driveway and the tiny, weedy parking lot in back.

She shut off the engine. Silence settled, broken only by the distant rush of the trucks on I-75. There were no streetlights here, just the glow from yet another party store's sign leaking over the flat roof.

Beth could feel her father watching her in the dark.

She moved to unbuckle her seat belt, but Todd grabbed her arm.

"Let's you and me take a minute, Star."

Beth made herself sag back into the seat. *Let him talk. You need to know what he's thinking.*

"Now, you're going to tell me just exactly what kind of lies you've been feeding Jeannie." He said it casually, like he was still spinning bullshit stories about sneaking into Disney World.

With the engine and the air conditioner off, the night's warmth seeped straight into the car. Sweat prickled Beth's arms and the back of her neck. "It's nothing, Dad. I just need Mom to help keep Dana calm. She's really confused about what's going on and…"

Dad reached his free hand into his jacket pocket. He pulled Beth's gun out and rested it on his thigh.

Pain stabbed like a spike into a single point of Beth's

skull. There'd never been a gun between them before. She was intimately familiar with his fists, his shouts, his hands closed around her arms and, once, her throat. She was ready for all those again. But there'd never been a gun. A gun was the apartment and Robert Early and knowing no one would save her. A gun was days of sickness and crazy and desperation.

She had not for a minute forgotten he had it. It had been the implicit threat since he'd taken it off her. But seeing how casually and comfortably he held it renewed Beth's awareness of how helpless she really was. Even if someone out in this strange, silent city night noticed when that thing went off, no one would come see what happened. She'd vanish for good this time, and Dana would never know why.

"Dad, will you listen to me?" Beth hated how her voice shook, hated the bitter fear that rose up in her and the way her heart hammered. "Please, just…"

There was just enough light to show her when Todd's hand tightened on the grip.

"Dad, please. There is something I have to tell you, and I couldn't before, and…"

"What you have to tell me, Star Bowen, is that you are never, ever going to try to break up my family again." His voice caressed each word, like this was something he'd been wanting to say for a long time. "You think that girl is yours anymore? She is mine. Just like you and Jeannie have always been mine." He spoke patiently. He understood she was slow and that she needed precise instructions. "I want you to say you're mine, Star. Right now." His thumb moved to rest on the safety.

"We're yours, Dad." The words tasted like iron and copper. They smelled like smoke. "All of us."

"Good girl." He patted her hand. "Smart girl. And you know it's the truth, don't you? You know it's the truth for now and forever." His thumb did not move off the safety. His gun hand did not stir at all. Beth stared at it, unable to lift her eyes.

"Yes, Dad. I know it."

"There." He took his free hand and caressed her chin, lifting her face until she had to look at his gentle smile. "Now, you had something that you wanted to say to me?"

Her mouth had gone entirely dry. She had to swallow before she could speak again. "Nothing. Never mind."

"No, no, come on." He cupped her cheek. "You can talk to me. I'm your father."

Think, think. You have to find a way to get this back on track. But her mind was as frozen as the rest of her, and all she could do was tell him the truth. "I'm afraid what you're going to do to me."

His brows arched. "I'm not going to do anything, as long as you tell me the truth. Promise. Here. Look." He set the gun on the dashboard, halfway between their seats. "There. That's how much I trust you. What is it you want to tell me?"

Beth felt suspended in midair. She kept her eyes on the gun. The butt was tilted toward Todd. The barrel toward her. Dad would see her the second she moved.

Jeannie was waiting for Beth to kill this man, like she'd killed Bob Early. Her mother wanted him dead because she'd had enough and wanted out.

Grab it. Her mouth that had been so dry had begun to water like she was hungry. *Do it!*

"Jeannie's not happy," Beth heard herself say.

"Yeah." Todd sighed. "I had to do some stuff a few months back. She got jealous. You know how she is." He smiled, inviting her to acknowledge their shared memories.

Grab it. You're still fast. You can do it.

"Yeah. Well, she's a little more than just jealous this time." Beth rubbed her sweating palms against her jeans. "I think it's the cancer. I think it's got her, you know. I think it's like she doesn't care anymore."

"I'll make it up to her. That's why we're going to Miami. She'll cheer up as soon as we get down there. You know how she loves the heat."

Do it. End this. All of this. He deserves it.

"You know, now that things are opening up, we might even be able to go to Cuba. Wouldn't that just be the best?"

Do it for Dana. You can handle Jeannie once he's gone.

"I mean, think about it. Rum and sun, and nobody gives a shit what you do as long as you're not…"

For Dana.

"She wants me to kill you, Dad."

He stopped.

Beth still could not look away from the gun. Her fingers curled around the belt across her chest. "She called me before I met up with you back at McKeirnan's and told me the only way I was going to get Dana back was to kill you."

Silence dropped. Even the sound of the trucks had vanished. There was nothing left but the harsh sound of breath rattling in a tight throat. Beth couldn't tell if it was his or hers.

"Jeannie would never do that to me." Todd breathed the words out like cigarette smoke. "This is you. You're trying to get your kid out of here."

You got that right. Beth did not allow herself to hesitate. "Jeannie was the one who went and found Dana. Jeannie set her up and pulled her into all this mess. She ruined my life, Dad, and my daughter's life. But she's trying to end yours." Beth stopped there and made sure he was looking directly into her eyes.

See him. You know what he wants. He's already told you what it is a thousand times. That's where you hit, and you do it now.

"I know that none of this was your idea," she said. "You just wanted to take care of Jeannie, like you always took care of us. But she was getting jealous of your girlfriends." Her mouth curled into a smile, but she did not know why. "You know, you can kind of see it. Some of them must have made some serious plays. I mean, how could they not?"

"That's what I told her! *I* was the one fighting *them* off! I never, ever did *anything*!"

The lie was so familiar and expected that Beth's confusion shattered. She found herself back on stable ground, able to look Todd in the face and remember that he was not the only one who had come here with a plan.

"I know that, Dad! And so should Mom, especially after everything you've been through together." Beth let her voice drop. "But instead of trusting you, she just goes ahead on her own and drags you into her trouble."

She shifted, turning her torso so she faced him fully.

Look at me, Dad. See me. You taught me everything I know. Trust this monster you've made.

"Mom was the one who actually killed Doug, wasn't she? She set this whole goddamn thing up, and she killed him so Dana would be too scared to run away before she could bring me back here."

Beth laid her warm hand over her father's cold one. She felt all the branches of his veins lying beneath his soft, old-man skin.

"Jeannie took my daughter hostage and then told me I'd have to kill you to get her back. That is what I'm supposed to be doing right now."

"You're talking shit." Todd yanked his hand out from under hers. "Jeannie's just mad. She'll get over it."

Beth shrugged and sighed. "Okay, Dad. You know best. Are we going to go see these guys or what?" She reached for her seat belt buckle again.

"Wait. Now, you listen to me, Star—"

There was no reason to hear the rest. "I'm done, Dad. I don't care anymore. My life is pretty much over, so why should I? But Mom does not get to play me again."

"Star…"

Now she did it. She grabbed the Glock off the dashboard. She held it high, finger off the trigger but on the safety.

Dad's eyes bulged, and his jaw dropped. A sweet, almost sexual warmth flooded Beth at the sight of her father's blatant fear.

Beth turned the gun around in her hand and held it out to him, butt first.

"I'm not lying."

Beth waited. Todd lifted a steady hand and took the gun from her. Neither one of them looked away from the other. Neither one of them blinked.

"I haven't done anything worth dying for," she said. "But I'm telling you, Jeannie has."

CHAPTER FIFTY-SEVEN

When the door closed behind Mom and Todd, all Dana wanted to do was to run after her.

Don't leave me here.

Jeannie let out a long, slow breath. "Whew! Okay. We made it."

I thought we were going to get out of here.

"Hey, I'm hungry. Lunch was a long time ago. Are you hungry? Want to get a pizza or something?"

Dana wasn't really listening. It hit her that if she did run out the door, there was no way Jeannie could stop her. She could be out the emergency exit before the older woman could even start to catch up.

Then what? She didn't have a phone. She didn't have any money except the bills in her jacket's hidden pocket. She didn't even have her dorky school ID anymore. But here they were, sitting in the middle of a whole strip of hotels and diners and gas stations with quickie marts. Maybe she had enough to buy a cheap phone. She could call Chelsea. Chelsea would help her figure out something.

But what about Mom? What would Mom do if Dana wasn't here when she got back? And what would Todd do to her?

"Oh, hon-bun," said Jeannie. And that was when Dana realized she hadn't moved an inch. "You are not thinking about doing something stupid again, are you?"

But she was.

Run, run, run—the word drummed against the inside of her skull. *Do it now. Don't give Jeannie time to talk you out of it again. Mom will be okay. She can handle them. She's done it before. Run.*

Jeannie put down the pizza flyer she was reading and came over to take both of Dana's hands.

This time, Dana pulled away immediately. Jeannie looked hurt and folded her arms, tucking her hands tight under her armpits.

"Dana, listen to me. I couldn't tell you this before, but I can now. Your mother and me, we got a plan."

Don't listen. She's lying again. "When could you—"

"Why do you think she's even here? I *called* her, honey. I told her where we were!"

Dana's resolve to not listen died. "You called her?"

"What did you think? That I was just going to let her believe…" She stopped and stared. "Oh, Dana," she breathed. "Oh Jesus. I've screwed all this up. I'm really sorry. I've been dying to tell you this whole time. We got it all figured out, and she's just been waiting for her chance, you see?" Jeannie's face lit up, like a little kid with a secret. "Todd doesn't know it, but he's just screwed up big-time by making her go with him. He might not even be coming back at all."

The memory of blood sent fresh prickles across Dana's skin. Was that ever going away? "What're you...what are you saying?"

Jeannie read her mind, and her eyes went wide. Her bruise stretched tight. "Oh no. Honey! Nothing like that! She's not going to hurt him! Not permanently anyway. She's going to find a way to ditch him, see? She wanted to at the mall, but he was watching everything too close. Now, though—now is the perfect time."

"I don't believe you," whispered Dana. Something was wrong. Memory was getting mixed up with emotion again, and the words were pouring in and shaking it all to bits.

"I know, I know," said Jeannie. "And you're right to be angry, but if you don't believe me, believe your mom. Do you honestly think she would walk in here without a plan?"

Mom had said that. She'd *said* she had a plan. Back at the house. Dana was sure.

"She's just been waiting for her chance, and *this* is her chance." Jeannie squeezed Dana's hand again, and this time Dana did not pull back. "Think about it. They're probably going to a bar, right? That's where all this kind of stuff happens. She'll get Todd drinking, get him talking. Let me tell you, once he starts in on either one of those, he does not stop. So, she pours him into the car and dumps him out by the side of the road someplace and comes right back to us. Piece of cake.

"All you and me have to do is sit tight and be ready to go as soon as she gets back."

She's just trying to keep me sweet. The cold thought trickled into Dana's mind. *She'll say anything so I don't leave.*

"I know you don't want to be here, Dana, and I know you're sick of waiting for something to happen. But you have to keep it together just a little bit longer. You need us, Dana. I don't want to upset you, swear to God I don't, but you do not know how to live on the run. The cops will catch up with you within a couple of days. But you cannot ever forget that if they catch you, no matter how bad things get for you, it's your mother who's really going to suffer for it. You still killed your father. Whatever we've done, you were the one who did that."

It was an accident! But it didn't matter how loud she screamed that inside her own head. It didn't wipe out the heat of her father's blood, literally on her hands. Suddenly, she just needed to get out of that room.

"I want a shower," she announced.

Jeannie smiled and squeezed her hands one more time. "Oh, me too. Jeez, I could strip off my own skin it's so filthy." She let go and instead went to pick up the flyers on the desk. "And what about that pizza? You want Domino's? Or Little Caesar's?"

"They're both shit," said Dana.

"Yeah, but they deliver." Jeannie picked up the hotel phone. "You get your shower, and I'll order. I think they've got Netflix on the cable here too. We can get a movie."

"Whatever," said Dana, not caring which one she was saying yes to. She snatched the shopping bag off the desk chair and headed into the bathroom.

Dana closed the door and locked it for good measure. She

turned the hot water on full. She stripped down, climbed into the tub, tilted her face up to the shower, and closed her eyes. She held her breath as long as she could, praying the water would boil her clean. She needed the heat to get all the way inside and obliterate the memories of all the blood and her father's lost eyes. She didn't want it—any of it. She wanted to step through the thick cloud of steam and find herself at home. She wanted to hear Mom singing off-key to the *Mamma Mia!* soundtrack. She wanted to be planning breakfast for them both and to know that tomorrow she'd be putting on her black pants and the white jacket with the Vine and Horn logo.

She wanted to go back to having a future in front of her, not this dead, gray blank.

She stayed under the water until she actually felt like she might be starting to burn.

Finally, she shut the water off and dried herself and put on clean black jeans and a black T-shirt. She brushed her teeth and looked at herself in the mirror.

Her reflection didn't show any hints about what she should do, so she walked back out into the room.

"There you are! I was starting to think you'd drowned."

Jeannie was on the bed with the remote. The pizza guy must have shown up while Dana was in the shower, because Jeannie had the box open beside her and was halfway through a slice of pepperoni and sausage.

"What do you want to watch?"

Dana sat down on the other half of the bed, one leg dangling over the edge. "Nothing. You pick."

"Come on, honey. We gotta keep it together for just a

SARAH ZETTEL

little bit longer, okay? Get some coffee. Eat something." Jeannie elbowed the box toward her. "Your mom will be back as soon as she can."

Dana looked at her for a long time. She couldn't trust this woman she'd waited her whole life to know. But she could trust Mom. Mom would know what to do about Jeannie.

It wasn't a future, but it was better than nothing.

Dana picked up a slice and bit into the tip.

"That's really bad."

"Yeah, but it's hot. Come on. Show me how to work this thing." She held the remote toward Dana.

Dana sighed and worked the controls to bring up Netflix.

It's just until Mom gets back, she told herself. *Then we are outta here.*

On impulse, she chose the *Great British Baking Show*. While the hosts joked about biscuits and the narrator extolled the skills of the new set of bakers, Dana got up to pour herself a cup of coffee from the little pot on the dresser. She plopped back down on the bed and reclaimed her piece of pizza. It was greasy and it sagged under the weight of its toppings, but she bit into it anyway, because apparently there was some kind of physical law that you couldn't leave a slice uneaten, no matter how bad it was. So she ate. She drank. The coffee was as bad as the pizza, but she finished both of them anyway. The first episode ended and segued straight into the second. She ate more bad pizza and tried to decide what she would do if she were a contestant. Maybe it could still happen. Maybe one day. After Mom got back.

Dana Fraser, will you please bring that spectacular *biscuit tower up to the gingham altar?*

…And what flavor are these?

Those are the cardamom and chocolate, and those are the greasy pizza cheese and blood…

Dana shook her head. *Jesus, I'm falling asleep in my pizza.* She tried to focus on the screen, but she kept slowly sagging back against the headboard.

"It's okay, hon." Grandma lifted the paper coffee cup from her fingers. "Close your eyes. I'll wake you up as soon as your mom gets back."

"Yeah, but I want…I want…"

"I know. Here. Lean on me." Jeannie wrapped her arm around Dana's shoulders and pulled her close.

Dana couldn't resist. She just leaned her head against her grandmother's shoulder. She didn't want to sit like this. She didn't like the feeling of her grandmother's bony shoulder digging into her ear. But she didn't pull away. It didn't seem worth the effort. She wanted to turn her face toward the screen too. The male judge—Paul Hollywood—was giving somebody shit about their biscuits lacking snap. But she couldn't manage even that much motion. All she could do was blink at the little amber bottle on the nightstand. She hadn't noticed it before. Why hadn't she noticed it before?

Grandma was stroking her hair. "It'll be okay, honey. I promise. Hey, watch. The guy with the…"

Dana never heard. The world had gone away.

CHAPTER FIFTY-EIGHT

Buying the new IDs had been remarkably straightforward. The apartment was raggedy but no worse than other places Beth had been in. The two unshaven white guys had beer guts and blank eyes. They looked at the real IDs, pulled some fresh cards out of a file cabinet, and made sure the names on each set matched. They took Todd's money, they handed the new cards over, and that was that.

Dad was unusually quiet on the drive back, but she could feel him watching her the entire way. The gun stayed in his pocket now, its threat veiled but not gone. Beth glanced at him once and was surprised to see how old and tired he looked in the flickering headlights beside her.

It was getting light by the time Beth pulled back into the hotel parking lot. Her head and her throat ached from lack of sleep, from what she'd said and what she hadn't. She shut the engine off. Dad held out his hand. She understood and dropped the keys into his palm.

"I'm not forgetting what you told me," he said. His eyes were cold, but she couldn't read what waited under that ice.

"Good," she said, but at the same time, a fresh shiver ran up from the scar on her arm.

Dad used his key card to let them in a side door and made sure she walked ahead of him to the room. He was on edge. Beth tried to tell herself that was a good thing. It meant he believed her.

She hoped.

Todd slid the card into the slot on the door and stood back so Beth could open it. The smell of warm pizza wafted out.

The room was completely dark.

"Shh! The kid's asleep," Jeannie stage-whispered from the shadows.

Beth blinked hard to help her aching eyes adjust. She saw Jeannie curled up in the armchair beside the bed. Dana was tucked in under the blankets, lying on her side, dead to the world.

Then Todd walked in, and Jeannie sat up straight.

"Hey, babe." Todd walked over and kissed her cheek. "Happy to see me?"

He stayed bent over the chair, waiting for her answering kiss. Jeannie stared at Beth. No one had closed the blackout curtains, and there was enough light for Beth to see her blank face and wide eyes.

Todd took Jeannie's chin and turned her face toward him. "I asked, Are you happy to see me?"

"Of course, babe!" Jeannie threw her arms around him,

and the enthusiastic gesture almost pulled him right down into her lap, but Dad caught himself on the chair arm.

Beth watched her parents kiss, long and deep and loud, too tired to feel anything but cold.

Todd finally broke the kiss. He touched the corner of her bruised eye, and all at once, he pinched her there, hard. Jeannie squealed sharply from the pain.

Dana didn't even move.

"Good," Todd murmured. He straightened up and pulled out his wallet.

Behind him, Jeannie touched her bruise and looked at Beth, like Beth was the one who'd hurt her.

She probably believes that.

Todd fished a couple of the new cards out of his wallet and handed them to Jeannie. "Get those in your purse. I'll keep Dana's. Jesus, I'm tired." He wandered over to the open pizza box on the desk beside the TV and grabbed a slice. He gestured with it to Jeannie. She got out of the chair so he could sit down, and moved to sit on the bed beside Dana.

Dana still didn't even roll over. Something tightened around Beth's ribs. Beth hurried to the bedside and leaned over Dana.

"Dana? Dana, honey?" She laid a soft hand on her shoulder. "Wake up. We're back."

"Oh, come on. Leave her," whispered Jeannie. "It's been a really rough—"

"Dana?" Beth shook her daughter gently. "Dana?"

Dana twitched. Her eyelids fluttered. She looked up at Beth, but Beth couldn't tell if her daughter registered her face. Dana's eyes closed again.

Beth straightened up and she turned.

"What did you do to her?" The words rasped like splinters in her throat.

"Nothing!"

Beth knew what real anger felt like. She knew all its nuances and all the ways it could burn a person from the inside out. She knew what it was to want to kill somebody with her bare hands.

But it was not like this. It was never like this. This was a special kind of hyperawareness. Beth could see every edge of every piece of furniture. She seemed to feel instinctively how every object around her might be grabbed up, broken, and used. The whole *world* was a weapon waiting for her.

Except for Jeannie. Jeannie was a paper doll. Her, Beth could tear in two.

Beth grabbed her mother's shoulders and pulled her up off the bed. Her fingers dug down to the curves of Jeannie's bones. She could crush those bones. It would hurt when they shattered. It would hurt a lot.

"WHAT DID YOU DO TO MY DAUGHTER?!" Beth screamed.

"Nothing!" Jeannie struggled to get her hands up between them. "She was so antsy, Star! She was scared for you, and she couldn't sleep! She *asked*, Star. She asked me for something to calm her down! I gave her half a pill. Less. I didn't want to, but she was so scared and she needed to sleep so bad. That's all it was! I've been checking on her the whole time. She's fine!"

Beth shoved Jeannie backward. She didn't even feel the motion. One minute Jeannie was in her hands, the next there was a slam, and her mother had collapsed against the wall, crouching and cowering.

A hand clamped onto the back of Beth's neck. "That's enough, Star. I'll take care of this."

Todd. Beth had forgotten he was still here.

"Please, please!" Jeannie sobbed. "I just wanted to help her! That's all—I promise!"

Beth didn't move.

Todd yanked her sideways. Beth stumbled and banged against the bed, sitting down abruptly. Todd grabbed Jeannie and hauled her to her feet. She sagged against him, trembling and tearful. Beth watched and hated her. Hated them.

"I'm sorry, babe. I didn't mean anything. I was just afraid the girl was going to do something stupid. That's all!"

"Yeah, yeah, I know." He patted the back of her head, rocking them both back and forth a little. "But that was not a good move, huh? Getting our Star all worried like that."

Beth turned back to Dana. She laid a palm against her forehead. How many times had she done this for her daughter, this thing that every parent did? They checked for fever, listened to their breathing in the dark. She'd snuck into her room at night to do this when she was little. She did it first thing in the morning when little Dana came to the table tired and cranky. Dana's skin was warm to her touch but not too warm. No sweat, no clammy feeling. Dana breathed deeply, easily, normally. Slowly, Beth settled back into herself. Slowly, she was able to think and to breathe again, and to remember where she was and why, and everything she needed to be doing.

Todd was watching her.

"Okay?" said Todd to Beth.

Beth rubbed her palms against her jeans. She nodded.

"Okay?" he said to Jeannie. Jeannie peered at Beth from around Todd's shoulder. Sheltering behind the man she wanted Beth to kill for her.

She nodded too.

"Good." Todd pushed Jeannie away from him gently. "I gotta take a leak," he said, and then pointed a finger at Beth. "Play nice."

Beth folded her arms. Todd rolled his eyes and headed for the bathroom.

As soon as the door shut, Jeannie grabbed Beth and dragged her to the other side of the room.

"What is the matter with you?" she demanded, her tears and trembling both gone like she'd thrown a switch. "Why didn't you take care of him?"

Beth took Jeannie's hand and lifted it off her arm. "You really, really do not want to be talking to me right now."

"She's *fine*, Beth! It was half a pill, and she asked for it! What is the matter with you? We had a plan!" The toilet flushed. Jeannie took a step back, her eyes cold and assessing. Jeannie pressed a hand against her stomach. "You cannot leave me hanging, Star."

Water ran in the bathroom sink.

Beth looked at her. She felt her thoughts ticking off what she saw. There was no more remembering she wanted to be called Beth. Like Todd, Jeannie wanted Star back. Star took care of her. Little Star had comforted her, and was frightened for her, and kept trying to make things better.

Todd came out of the bathroom. "Well, I was gonna get us back on the road, but I guess we're staying here." He picked up a slice of cold pizza and took a healthy bite. "Everybody might as well get some sleep." He looked his wife up and down. "You should clean up, Jean. You're a fucking wreck."

"Yeah, okay." Jeannie paused as she passed Todd to press a kiss against his cheek. "You keep an eye on our girls."

She disappeared into the adjoining room. Beth heard the bathroom door close. Dad shoved the last of his partly eaten crust into his mouth.

"You're not going to start giving me trouble now, are you, Star?" he mumbled as he chewed.

Beth looked at Dana lying so still on the bed. She pulled the blankets up around her shoulders. *She's okay.* She smoothed Dana's hair back, feeling one more time how her skin was warm and dry. How her breath came steady and normal. *She's okay.*

She was able to straighten up and face her father. She could make her voice low and pleading.

"Can I...can I sleep in here? Please. Just in case she gets sick or something. She's had a bad reaction to sleeping pills before." Which was a total lie, but Todd would not stop to think how a normal mother might not drug a child into unconsciousness.

Todd grabbed another slice out of the box and bit into it. He took his time chewing and swallowing.

"Yeah, sure." He sucked pizza grease off his thumb. "Why not? After all, we're one big, happy family, right?"

"Right, Dad."

He picked up the pizza box and carried it into the other room and sat down on the other bed, in full view of the open connecting door. Beth saw him pick up the remote and turn on the TV. ESPN was talking about the Tigers.

Beth found her shopping bags and dug out the plain gray nightshirt she'd bought. Numb, she went into the empty bathroom and changed out of her clothes.

The water shut off in the other bathroom.

Out in the bedroom, Beth folded her clothes up out of habit. She was so tired, but when you lived in small spaces, you had to be tidy. There was no room for extra mess.

Through the open connecting door, Beth saw her mother come out of the other bathroom. She went straight into the other room and threw herself on the bed, snuggling up next to Todd. He put an arm around her and she opened her mouth like a baby bird, and he started feeding pizza into it.

Beth watched her mother playing the little girl, feeding his ego, eating the food from his hand.

And Todd smiled down at his wife, as if she were the most beautiful thing in the world.

That was when Beth knew how badly she had miscalculated.

Because more than anything, Todd believed in Jeannie's absolute dependency on him.

In his mind, she not only loved him, but she needed his support and his approval to live. He had made sure that she belonged to him solely and wholly. He would defend that belief to the death.

And Jeannie knew it. She played on that need to stay

alive, and if Beth did not do as she said, Jeannie would make Dad go off, as surely as if she'd pulled the trigger on his gun.

Beth turned away, sick in her head and in her heart. She curled up beside her daughter. She slid her arm around Dana's ribs. She didn't close her eyes. She just lay there, feeling the rise and fall of Dana's chest. At the same time she listened to Jeannie's soft laughter and the sound of cable sports.

Beth thought about the gun and how her parents would soon be asleep.

She thought about shooting them both.

She thought about shooting herself afterward.

She thought about shooting Dana first, because that would be kinder. What life was there after this? What could she give her daughter that would even begin to make up for this?

She pressed her face against the back of her daughter's neck, and slowly, silently, Beth let herself begin to cry.

CHAPTER FIFTY-NINE

Dana's mouth felt like it was filled with glue. That same glue had sealed her eyelids shut. It was stuffy as hell.

Because she'd pulled the blankets up over her head. And because there was somebody next to her.

She shoved the blankets down, and sunlight hit her in the face and startled her enough that she was able to yank her eyelids open.

The person spooned up behind her shifted. Mom. It was Mom.

"Hey, Dangerface!" Mom said softly and kissed her cheek. "How you feeling?"

Dana stirred her tongue around in her mouth. She tasted bad. Metallic. Dry. "Something's wrong with me. I think I'm sick…"

"No. That's not it. Try to sit up. I'll get you some water."

Dana tried. Her head was fogged, and her stomach regretted all that bad pizza and bad coffee.

Mom brought two little glasses of water and handed one to her. Dana downed it in a gulp. She shoved her hair back from her face and looked up at Mom for answers.

"Jeannie drugged you," Mom said.

"Wha...what?"

Mom handed her the second glass and took back the empty one. "She was afraid you were going to run, so she slipped you one of her pills."

Dana went white. "She didn't..."

She didn't bother to finish. Of course she did it. *Because she knew I was thinking about running. My fault. Again.*

She swallowed. "Can I get some more water?"

Mom nodded. She stepped back so Dana could stand up. The world tilted for one bad second but steadied, and she was able to walk. In the bathroom, Dana turned on the sink. She drank glass after glass of water and splashed more water on her face, trying to wash the glue and sand out of her eyes.

This shame had been haunting her since...since that other hotel. But now she was shaky and dried out, and it threatened to swamp every other feeling. Because she'd killed Dad, and now Mom was going to have to...Mom was going to have to...

It's my fault. I got her into this. She never would have let them get close, but I got stupid. She wouldn't be here if I wasn't in trouble...

Now she's going to...she's going to have to...feel like this. BE like this.

"It's not your fault, Dana."

Dana stared into the mirror. She hadn't closed the

bathroom door. Mom was standing on the threshold. Dana watched her mother's face in the mirror. She looked so sad Dana's heart twisted tight.

"Jeannie said you were going to ditch him," murmured Dana. "I thought you might, you know..." *Kill him.*

Mom looked away. Dana realized Mom had thought about it. She'd really considered killing her father.

Dana had a friend at school who was a cutter. She said it was a distraction, because the pain in her skin felt better than the pain in her head. Dana finally understood what she meant.

My fault. It's my fault she has to think like this. It's my fault we even have to be here.

But even as those thoughts threatened to drown her, Dana saw her mother's face shift. Ideas took shape behind her eyes, fitting together like puzzle pieces. Mom knew something. She felt something. She *understood* something.

"I used to watch the kids who got to go to school and had normal lives." Mom started rubbing Dana's back, slow circles on her shoulder. Dana wanted to turn and hug her, and she also wanted to scream at her to get away.

"All those kids who didn't have to hang out in the library all day and decide which librarian was a bitch so it'd be okay to steal out of her purse to get money for the snack machines. I was so jealous of them. I thought I didn't deserve the lives they had. I was bad. I stole and I lied, and I made my parents mad so they fought all the time. They told me our life was better, but I didn't love it like they did, and that had to be because I was bad. And sometimes I wanted to run away from them, and that made me worse.

Good girls love their parents. So, I didn't run away. I didn't tell anybody what was happening, because I was ashamed of myself.

"And Todd and Jeannie know all that, and they will use it against you, and they will use me against you, and your fear of the cops against you, and anything else they can wrap their minds around. Because their only hope of controlling me is controlling you. And they have to control me because I'm the one controlling the money.

"None of this is your fault, Dana. This was them from the beginning. They wanted to get to me, so they used you to do it. You and your father."

Dana heard what Mom was saying. Each word rang perfectly clear—it made sense. It was true. But it wasn't enough. It could not ever be enough.

"I killed him, Mom," she whispered. "I stabbed him, and I killed him."

"No." In the mirror, Dana saw her mother shake her head slowly. "You didn't. They did that."

"No. I had Chelsea's nail file. I was…it's all a mess, but I know we were fighting and we fell and…"

"Dana." Mom turned her around. She took Dana's face in both hands and tilted it up. Dana realized she was shaking all over.

"Dana, I have one question, okay? And you have to answer me absolutely honestly. Will you do that?"

Dana swallowed. She nodded, her cheeks brushing against Mom's hands. They were cold, her cheeks or Mom's hands. She wasn't sure which.

"Did you slit your father's throat?"

There were moments when the whole world froze, as if God pushed the Pause button. Dana felt it right now.

"After he got stabbed, did you do that, Dana?" Mom was asking. "Did you take that homemade knife and cut his throat?"

Blood, and Dad looking at her, and Dad pulling the knife out of himself, and...

And she was pulled backward and turned around, and her face was pressed into Jeannie's shoulder. She remembered her grandmother holding her so tight so she couldn't move.

So she couldn't see.

"No," breathed Dana. "No, I didn't."

"Because I saw him," said Mom. "After he died, I went in that room and I saw him, and I saw his throat. The blow to his chest was bad, but he might have survived. It was the throat wound that killed him."

I didn't kill him? I didn't?

"Dana. Did either Todd or Jeannie tell you directly that you'd committed murder?"

"They did. Both of them." *She held on to me so I couldn't see. And I couldn't get away.*

"They did that to keep you from running away, and then when that looked like it might stop working, they drugged you. That is what is happening here, Dana. That is what you have to hang on to."

I believed them and I let them, and you're here because of me. The poison bubbled up from the bottom of Dana's heart. "I'm sor—"

"Dana, stop," said Mom quickly, firmly. "You sink down

into shame you will think you don't deserve to get out of this, just like I used to."

"But…"

Mom laid her finger across Dana's lips to shush her. "Dangerface, listen to me. Some things changed last night. They might be about to start falling apart, and when they do, we are not going to have a lot of time. I need you to trust me. I think I can get us away, but I am going to need your help. So, I have to know for sure that you want to get out of here more than you want to try to save them from their own shit. You have to believe, Dana, that you are worth saving, and that I am too. "

Dana looked at her mother, and she felt the shame and the guilt crawling through her veins and her bones. She remembered being little, tiny Dana sitting on the curb with Mommy and wondering what she'd done to make the pink-hands man take her away. She must have done something. She must be bad. She must have deserved it.

That shame was real. All of it, and it was not ever going away.

Yeah, well, screw that.

"Mom?" whispered Dana. "Let's go home."

Mom smiled. A hot, dangerous joy shone in her eyes, and Dana felt her own eyes blaze in answer. The green one burned bright, and the brown one burned sharp. They hugged each other then, hard and mercilessly, like they were never going to stop.

"Well, now. What's going on in here?"

CHAPTER SIXTY

Beth stared, startled, at the mirror. Todd stood in the bathroom doorway wearing nothing but an undershirt and boxers, sleep tousled and disconcerted but trying to smile.

"I...uh...Mom was just letting me know what the situation is." Dana pulled back, stiff and scared, and Todd definitely noticed.

He knows something's up. He's going to expect a distraction.

Beth started gathering up the unused toiletries and little soaps that were still wrapped. "You know, Dad, we're going to have to think about money. The cash isn't going to last. And we might want to think twice about using the credit cards so much..."

"We got plenty to get us to Miami," he said. "It's only a couple days' drive from here. Once we're there, I'm sure you can figure out the pipeline. After all, need to keep our girl here in shoes, right?" He stopped. "So, just what was it you two were talking about when I came in here? You look like you were getting pretty upset."

"It was nothing," said Beth. She wasn't frightened. It was strange. They had failed to take hold of Dana's heart. They had tried their best, but it hadn't worked. It was as if Beth could not be truly afraid of anything else.

She was tense, though. Shit, she was practically vibrating. But as long as Dana was with her, there was a way out.

And I know what it is.

It was in Todd's blind spots. Including the fact that when he looked at Dana, all he saw was the weak link.

"Now, you've got something to learn here, Granddaughter." He bent down in front of her, hands braced against his thighs like he was talking to a two-year-old. "When I ask a question of one of my girls, I expect an answer. Do you understand that?"

Beth shifted the toiletries to the crook of her arm and put her free hand on Dana's shoulder.

"You better tell him, Dana," she said quietly but firmly. "Tell him what your grandmother said last night while we were gone. He needs to hear this."

Do you hear me? Do you understand? But Dana reached up and squeezed Beth's hand.

And all Beth could do was stand there and trust.

Dana licked her lips. Her face shifted. Beth knew that look. It was the one Dana got when another homework assignment hadn't gotten turned in, or a quiz had been totally blown off.

She was getting ready to lay it on thick.

"Um…when you and Mom were…out, Grandma told me…she told me Mom was going to get rid of you."

Todd frowned. He also straightened up. Beth took the

opportunity to steer Dana past him, out into the bedroom. She checked through the connecting doorway reflexively and saw Jeannie still curled up under the covers in the other bed.

Todd followed them. "What the fuck is that girl talking about, Star?"

Dana wasn't having any of that. Nobody answered for her. "Jeannie told me Mom was going to get you drunk and get rid of you, and that Mom and me and her were going to all take off together."

Beth sighed. "I tried to tell you, Dad."

Todd's fists curled up tight. Beth immediately slid between him and Dana. She lifted her chin. She remembered this too. Only he'd been so much taller then—a monster with a great, long shadow and yellow fangs. Then, it had been Jeannie behind her. Now, it was Dana, and that made all the difference.

"You set this up," he growled. "You told her what to say, just now, in there."

"Knowing how you'd beat the crap out of my daughter if you found out she lied? You really think I'd take that kind of chance?"

Because you know I'll do anything for her. You know I'd never put her in danger. That's what your whole plan hangs on.

He looked bewildered. He ran his hand back across his hair, an old gesture from when he was a younger man and had to push his hair out of his eyes. Memories were coalescing inside him, thoughts rearranging themselves into realizations.

Beth held her breath.

You're getting there. Almost there.

That was when Jeannie stirred and sat up in bed.

"What's going on?" she mumbled. "Why didn't anybody wake me up?"

All at once, Dana lit up. Beth saw in the mirror how her eyes blazed, and Beth's heart stopped.

Dana jerked around, ran into the other room, and threw her arms around her grandmother.

"I told him, Grandma!" she wailed. "I'm sorry! I couldn't help it! He heard me talking to Mom, and I had to tell him."

"Told him…" Jeannie's bewilderment and disbelief were every bit as strong as Todd's had been. She slowly lowered her hand to Dana's back, mostly because she didn't seem to know what else to do with it. "Told him what?"

"That thing you said, about what Mom was going to do." Dana lifted her face, confused. Beth felt her fist tighten. *Careful, Dangerface. Careful. Not too much.* "I had to!"

Todd stared at his granddaughter and his wife. Beth could practically hear the thoughts in his mind crumbling. He knew Beth would lie. He knew she could be dangerous. But when he looked at Dana, all he saw was a clone of the little girl Beth had once been. He saw Star.

Star was always frightened. Star had always been alone. She had always been trapped in a room with parents who would use her when they needed her. Her life had been about surviving them, not defying them.

He had no understanding that Dana might have had a different kind of life. He'd always made sure his women were too dependent, too ashamed, and far too frightened to move.

Except maybe not. Except maybe someone had lied to him. Someone jealous. Someone terrified he might actually leave. Someone who could not live without him. That he could believe. That he could understand.

Todd walked up to his wife. Jeannie scrambled back in the bed. Dana slid out the far side and backed away, but Todd ignored her.

"What's this about, Jeannie? What did you say to the girl?"

"Nothing, Todd! What would I say?"

Beth came up behind him, close enough to feel the fever warmth of his body and smell stale sweat and garlic.

"You better tell him, Mom," Beth said. "You know how much worse it gets if he catches you lying."

Jeannie scrambled out of bed. Dana jumped back out of her way. "What are you *doing*, Star?"

Jeannie came forward around the bed, intent on grabbing Beth, but Todd intercepted her.

"Jeannie…" He took hold of her arms. "Just tell me it's not true. Say it."

She kissed him, hard and sharp. "Of course it's not true!" She caressed his stubbled cheek. "Why would I even think anything so stupid?"

"Because you were afraid Dad was going to leave you," said Beth from by her father's shoulder. Here it was. This was where he would either believe or he wouldn't.

Maybe you were lying, Mom. Maybe you just wanted to get the band back together. But it was the wrong lie to tell.

"You know you can't make it without him," Beth said. "When have you ever even lived by yourself? Do you even have an actual driver's license? How would you even get your pill money?"

Jeannie jerked out of Todd's grip and circled around him to stand right in front of Beth. Beth did not retreat. Her heart squeezed down to nothing, fear and freedom crushing it into a hot, red pebble inside her.

She could not look at Dana, however much she wanted to. She had to focus on her mother. She had to sell it, to her father, to her mother, to herself.

"You were crazy desperate to get him back, but you knew you could never actually hurt him. So you had to scare him. You faked being sick. You put the idea into his head to get the money for treatment out of me."

There it was, the crystallized anger and the bitterness built up across years of having to constantly monitor one man's moods and pretend and shift and lie depending on his next whim. Jeannie had built her survival around being what Todd needed of her. It had given her power over him, and she wielded it with care sometimes, with abandon others. She reveled in that power, and he craved her dependency.

Each of them was what the other made. Each of them utterly reliant on their creation.

Each of them hating themselves for what they'd tied themselves to.

"Todd, this is bullshit," said Jeannie. "You know it is. She's just trying to get you mad enough to make a mistake, and then she can take herself and her girl away again."

"And go where?" Beth spread her hands. "You locked that door and threw away the key when you killed Doug, Mom, and now you're trapped in here with me."

"You need to stop lying, Grandma," said Dana. "Just say you're sorry, okay?"

"Shut up! All of you!" Todd screamed. He screamed. Not shouted, not ordered. Screamed until his voice broke. "Just...just shut up!"

His eyes had gone wide. He looked scared, like he was skirting panic.

What are you going to do now, Dad? You can't trust any of us. How are you going to keep it under control now?

And there was the question, the thing she'd almost forgotten.

Where's the gun?

Todd was still in his underwear, a sagging and pathetic old man. He did not have it on him.

Her father paced to the other side of the room, his hands flexing—open, shut, open, shut. He stood facing the window, and then he turned and swept his arm out, sending the bedside lamp and clock crashing to the floor.

"Now, this is what we're going to do." He was talking to the wall, and somehow that made it scarier. "We're going to pack up, and we're going to get in the car. And if I have trouble from any one of you, somebody is going to get shot, and I am not really going to care who it is!"

Jeannie moved to stand with him, choosing sides. "You heard your father, Star," she said.

Where's the gun?

Beth was trying to look in every direction at once. She spotted Todd's jacket hanging on the back of the desk chair. There? Still in that pocket?

Jeannie spotted her before Todd did.

"Oh, no you don't, Star," she said. Jeannie stepped backward. "Todd…"

That was when Dana charged.

Beth screamed and Jeannie screamed and Dana hit the floor in a heap with her grandmother.

"He's got a gun!" screamed Dana, trying frantically to grab Jeannie's wrists. "He's got a gun!"

Beth lunged for the chair and the jacket, but Todd got her first. He wrapped his wiry arms around her waist, dragging her backward, swinging them both around. She stomped on his foot—she was in stocking feet, but her heel was hard enough.

Dana screamed.

Beth had no strength left in her, but she tore herself out of her father's grip and lunged forward, skidding hard across the carpet, tearing skin. Hands clamped around her ankles, and the world spun.

And he was on top of her. Dana was screaming and screaming, and there were sirens in the distance, and the world flipped over, and there were hands on her face and her throat, scrabbling for some kind of hold, and she was fighting and she didn't know how. And there was a crunch and Todd shouted, and she was free and crab-crawling backward, and Dana was standing over him, the gun in her hand, pointing it, crying and swearing and shaking.

The sirens were getting closer.

"Kill him!" screamed Jeannie. "You have to kill him! He'll say you did it! He'll say you killed your father and your mother helped!"

"You bitch!" screamed Todd. "You fucking bitch!"

"Shut up!" shrieked Dana. "Shut up or I'll kill you!"

Todd shut up. Todd was not stupid, and Dana very clearly was all done with her grandparents.

"You used me!" she screamed at Jeannie. "You said you loved me! You said you wanted to be family. You said you needed us, but you used me!"

"Dana, I was afraid," Jeannie pleaded. "You saw what he did to me! I had no choice. He was going to kill you! And your mom, Dana! That's what he's like! You know! You saw!"

"You killed my father! My fucking, pathetic, stupid, useless father!"

She raised the gun. She groped for the safety.

"No, Dana," said Beth.

Beth had managed to get to her feet, right behind Dana. She laid her hands on her daughter's. "No, Dana," she breathed. "I've got this."

CHAPTER SIXTY-ONE

Dana's fingers went instantly loose beneath Beth's hands. Beth took the gun and stepped in front of her.

Kill them, said a calm, steady voice in the back of her mind. *Kill them both. Bang, bang. All gone.* Compared to the shotgun, the Glock would have barely any kick at all.

Dana would go to stay with Rafi and Angela. Beth would go to prison, or to her own grave, depending on whether or not her nerve held.

But it'd be done. What she should have done years ago, when she first found them. But she'd told herself there was no rush. That she could do it anytime.

Time's up.

The gun was heavy and warm, Beth's palm was slick with sweat, her arm was weak as water. The sirens were still going but not moving. The cops were here. How long would it take them to get to this room?

They'd see this. They'd shoot her.

Bang, bang.

"It doesn't matter what you think of me!" shouted Jeannie. "You know he's not going to stop coming after you! After your girl! He'll make me do it all again!"

"You better hope she kills me!" roared Dad. "Because I'm going to kill you if she doesn't! Kill the jealous bitch! Kill her! This was her idea!"

"You have to stop him, Beth!"

Beth again.

She should have called me Star. Star would do what she was told. She wouldn't know what else to do.

But Beth was another story. Beth understood the game.

"Mom?" whispered Dana.

They could have fought each other, could have done each other in years ago. But they hadn't. Despairing, furious, unable to understand how it had all gone so wrong, they lay there, looking for somebody else they could sucker into doing what they wanted. For the one who would save them from themselves.

That was supposed to be her job. That had always been her job.

Beth raised the gun a little higher. She thumbed the safety. She sighted along the barrel. She laid her finger across the trigger.

"Bang," she said.

And dropped the gun and kicked it across the floor so Dad could dive after it.

"Open the door!" she shouted.

Dana did, and Dana screamed, and the cops poured through.

CHAPTER SIXTY-TWO

Beth was knocked down and hauled out of the room and into the parking lot. It was a very big, very loud blur. She probably screamed. She wasn't sure. There was no way to keep track.

Eventually though, the shouting and confusion ebbed away, and she was able to hear someone asking, "Are you Beth Fraser? We've got your daughter. She's safe."

She didn't remember anything for a while after that. Not until she was climbing out of the police car in front of some squared-off concrete building, and Dana was pressing against her, gently this time. Beth held her and rocked her, and Dana began to cry.

After that, they were herded into a small room with a table and chairs. Beth sat down without letting go of her daughter. Maybe she was crying too. She didn't know or care.

After a while, the door opened again, and Detective

Patel came in and sat down beside her. Dana looked up and pulled away, wiping hard at her face and eyes.

The detective pulled cigarettes and a lighter out of her pocket, lit one, and blew smoke into the ceiling, probably in violation of all kinds of codes. Beth found she had no inclination to point this out.

"We have your parents in custody."

Dana blinked, but she stayed steady. Patel wasn't even looking at her. All her focus was on Beth.

"You're going to need to thank that girl, Chelsea Hamilton. She was a huge help, especially turning us onto that video so we had visuals we could start showing around. Of course, your dad helped too."

Beth looked at her, and Patel smiled. "People tend to remember 'a real charmer.'" She made the air quotes. "Would have had you yesterday, but there was some jurisdictional stuff. But none of that's your problem." She sighed and blew out another cloud of smoke. "So, you still exercising your right to remain silent, Ms. Fraser?"

Beth laced her fingers through her daughter's and felt the strength of Dana's grip in answer.

"I'm sorry. I'm sorry, Mom. I didn't...I just..."

"It'll be okay," Beth breathed. "Everything will be okay. I promise."

And this once, it was the truth.

Beth pulled Dana close, and she started talking.

EPILOGUE

Dana didn't recognize the girl in the mirror hanging on her closet door.

She was taller, her hair cut short and slicked back from her forehead. She had a unicorn tattoo on the side of her neck. She wore (really ridiculous) black-and-white-checked trousers and a bulky white chef's coat with the word INTERN embroidered in blue on the pocket under a logo of an ivy-covered cornucopia.

The eyes she recognized—the green one and the brown one. Bright and sharp.

It was summer again and already too hot outside. Finals had been pretty much a disaster. In fact, the whole last year had pretty much sucked. Mom had told Dana she didn't even have to go back to school, especially while she was out on bond and wearing the electronic monitor and everything was still all over the local news.

But Dana had wanted to show she wasn't afraid. Not

that she was in school much anyway. She spent more time in attorneys' offices and courtrooms and deposition rooms than she did in the classroom. Before she even took the witness stand, she'd had to tell her story a thousand different times to a thousand different lawyers and legal coaches to make sure she got it just right. Details dissolved into a sea of words and advice: *Don't look here. Don't clench your hands. Say it this way. And never, ever say that.*

Real life was no help. The few friends who decided she wasn't crazy didn't know what to do with her, or they wanted all the details, and when the details didn't match the story on the news or in their heads, it was like they started making shit up until it all sounded right to them.

It got so bad that some days Dana wasn't sure she really remembered what happened anymore. She just knew what speech she was supposed to give on what day. The rest was gone.

She tried to tell herself it had all been worth it. Even the part where she'd almost been sick right in the middle of the courtroom when Amanda Pace Martin got up on the stand and blamed Mom for everything, and then Susan got up right after her and lied for an hour straight about how Mom was stealing from Dad, and Dana'd had to be yanked out of there by one of the fifty-three lawyers because she started crying and she couldn't stop.

Because Jeannie and Todd might get off. They might come back.

They kept her out of court for the next two days. She missed Zoe Keyes on the stand, and Rafael and James Kinseki. But she did not miss the part where Thomas

James Jankowski and Deborah Ann Watts, aka Todd and Jeannie Bowen, were convicted of assault and murder and kidnapping and fraud and accessory to fraud and a whole bunch of other stuff. The judge, who was a mother and a grandmother, dropped ninety-eight years down on both of them. They were gone, and they were not coming back.

Except at night. In the middle of the night, they always came back. They brought Dad with them, and that was when Dana remembered everything and woke up screaming. Then, Mom would be there, and Chelsea.

That was one good thing. Chelsea was living with them now. She'd taken over the guest bedroom and redecorated it all in her secondhand Loli-Goth style. Mom had had a whole bunch of conversations with Mrs. Hamilton, and a few with Mr. Hamilton. She never did give Dana and Chelsea all the dirty details, but the upshot was Cody and his band were not arrested for dealing, and Chelsea didn't have to go home if she didn't want to.

Dana and Chelsea fought a lot more than when they'd been living separately, and Mom had a whole big conniption about Chelsea's Swedish death metal habit after she'd Googled a few of the bands. But it got better, usually after cupcakes. Or therapy.

That was another change. Dana and Chelsea and Mom were now on a first-name basis with half the talk therapists in the Chicagoland area, and a whole raft of psychiatrists. Dana had pills and she had appointments and no social life.

All those therapists warned her the anniversary would

be hard. It wasn't yet, but she could feel it, lurking behind her—waiting to open the door, waiting to slip something into her coffee or whisper a fresh lie in her ear.

Waiting for her to relax just a little and believe the wrong thing so it could cover her eyes and pull her away.

"Dana?" Mom was knocking on the door. "You done?"

Chelsea, who after nearly a whole freakin' year still had *no* boundaries, just shoved the door open and threw her arm around Dana's shoulders.

"Chef coat selfie!" She held up the phone and snapped their picture.

Dana glared at her and ducked out from under her arm, but she didn't really mind. Mom just stood in the doorway, pointing at her watch. Dana rolled her eyes.

"Ready to go?" Mom asked.

"Ready." Dana grabbed her purse off her dresser. Chelsea made a big show of brushing the wrinkles out of her sleeves until Dana made an even bigger show of getting ready to swat her upside the head.

Now Mom was rolling her eyes.

"Phone?" she asked.

Dana pulled her newest smartphone out of her back pocket and held it up.

"Mad money?"

She dug into her purse and brandished her wallet.

"Keys?"

She jingled the ring in her other pocket.

"Text time?"

"Whenever they let me off shift."

"Don't worry, Dana." Chelsea patted Mom's shoulder.

SARAH ZETTEL

"I'll take good care of her. I've got the whole day all planned out."

"God help me," Mom muttered. "My hearing may not survive this."

Dana's phone beeped and her app flashed. "Ride's here," she said. "Gotta go."

She planned to just breeze on out. No big thing. No looking back. No tears. She'd cried enough.

But she got to the door, and she opened it, and she turned around anyway, and Mom was right there.

"You are going to be okay, right? I mean, with Chelsea and everything…"

Mom met her gaze, and Dana knew she understood what was underneath that question. It wasn't really about Chelsea, or the internship, or the anniversary that was hanging so heavy over everything. It was just the same question she'd been asking every day since…it…happened.

And Mom smiled, and Mom hugged her and kissed her cheek.

"Everything's going to be all right, Dangerface," she said. "I promise."

This time, it was the truth.

ACKNOWLEDGMENTS

I've said it before, but it bears repeating. No book happens in a vacuum. This book, like all the others, is the result of a lot of work, care, and support from a lot of people. I'd like to thank my (very) hardworking editor and agent who stuck with me through all the rewrites, and my (very) patient writer's group, ditto. And as always, to my husband and son, who have always supported me throughout. None of this happens without all of you. Thank you.

ABOUT THE AUTHOR

Sarah Zettel is a bestselling, award-winning author. She has written thirty-five novels and multiple short stories over the past thirty years, in addition to cooking, hiking, embroidering, marrying a rocket scientist, and launching her rapidly growing son.